THE HAND

or,

Confession of an Executioner

YUZ ALESHKOVSKY

THE HAND

or,
Confession of an Executioner

Translated by Susan Brownsberger

PETER HALBAN
LONDON

FIRST PUBLISHED IN GREAT BRITAIN BY
PETER HALBAN PUBLISHERS LTD
42 South Molton Street
London W1Y 1HB
1989

British Library Cataloguing in Publication Data

Aleshkovsky, Yuz
The hand.
I. Title
891.73′44 [F]

ISBN 1-870015-28-2

This translation has been prepared from the author's revised, although as yet unpublished, version of the text that first appeared in Russian in 1980

Phototypeset by Computape (Pickering) Ltd, North Yorkshire
Printed in Great Britain by
WBC Ltd, Bristol

To my only love,
my wife

They argued that no man could have
been expected to talk all that
time, and other men to listen so
long. It was not, they said, very
credible.

Joseph Conrad

So, Citizen Gurov, in your own best interest, don't try to scam out of this. For one thing, it's no use. Your beauty of a dacha is surrounded. You'll give your testimony here. You'll crack wide open here. And right here on this table you'll lay out everything you've grabbed from the Soviet regime and the Soviet people, builders of Communism—may Communism rot in hell and you with it, Citizen Gurov. It's not our every Krupp or Rockefeller, by the way, who hits it so lucky—preliminary interrogation at home. But that's my style. I like to arrest you in your homes and hole up for a few days, so that you have plenty of time to let it sink in, what you're parting with for a while or even forever. So that when you cross the threshold you look back and I note, with satisfaction in my soul, that your eyes go dark and dead with unbearable anguish, your shabby heart breaks, your knees buckle, and at that instant you have just a single thought, which drills through your skull like a bullet and flies out into the void. What that thought may be I am not privileged to know. But I suspect that you'll either curse the day you were born or ask in sincere surprise what you did to deserve this torment of being wrenched from hearth and home, from loved ones and fancy TV . . . Or possibly I'm mistaken, and you won't feel anything more than a measly regret that you've brought along the wrong underwear, the wrong sweater . . . In my forty-odd years with the security police an enormous number of your kind has passed through my hands. I've lost count of you by now, though at first I held all my goniffs in mind, the way sport-fuckers keep score of the tens and hundreds of women they've pronged . . . I see you're restless to get to the point. Let's do that. Or maybe . . . let's don't.

I see a sudden gleam in your little eyes, Citizen Gurov. Well?

What's your offer? . . . A cool M? New roubles or old . . ? Handsome! Quite right! Life and freedom are easily worth a million. But how about, oh, fifty, sixty pretty carats to sweeten the deal? You'll spring for that too? Smart move!

I was jesting, however. And I make bold to assure you, Citizen Gurov, that I am an unsubornable executioner. For, in contrast to you, I consider life, freedom, and assorted trifles like peace of mind to be things beyond price.

You're right. We do have investigators and judges and prosecutors who can be bought. And forget the cool M with a few pretty carats, a Gründig stereo will do. I know such men personally, and I don't scorn them. The Soviet regime taught me long ago not to be surprised by corruption at all levels of social and governmental life. Where are Lenin's famous simplicity, modesty, and honour? Gone where the prick goes, as they say in prison camp.

Admit it, Citizen Gurov, not for the record but as a man of the world, as a friend: wouldn't you pay a nice price, just now, to have my spiel on tape? I suspect you would: a nice price. But, again as the camp jackals say, you're deuce-ace on that one. I've risen to the rank of colonel, Citizen Gurov, I'm in good standing in top circles, but I'm sick of playing cat and mouse with my enemies. Sick to death. I consider your case closed . . . Although I'll have an occasional little question for you . . . So make yourself comfortable. Don't worry about grub, piss call, or exercise. Summon up your patience and listen. *I'll* do the talking, at last, and you will hear what no man has ever heard before or ever will again. Did you understand me, Citizen Gurov? I repeat: *I* will give the testimony. And as we go along, we'll gradually clear up the dim and sullen something that is now niggling at your brain and your soul. Though I strongly doubt you have a soul. What do you think: do you have one . . ?

That's a cop-out, you're ducking the question. Let's get this straight in advance: you are not privileged to determine what's relevant to this Case and what's not. And my question has a direct bearing on it. Well, then? Do you, in your opinion, have a soul? All right. Fine with me. We'll leave the question open. Don't forget, the dacha is surrounded by my men—my own boys, my wolfhounds. And every one of them is such a wolfhound that if I say, for example, 'At 'em, Poxov!' and point my finger at Poxov's father, up go Poxov's hackles, and his jaws clack shut on his own dear daddy's goozle. By the way, what was your father . . ? A petty official. I see, I see. Has he been dead long . . ? Perished in the bombing . . . A peaceful death. A very peaceful and dignified death. Romantic, what's more, a death that I always find very hard to believe in, as an executioner . . .

Resourceful, Citizen Gurov, but stupid! We'll never finish *my* case if you keep spouting at me about prejudice, apriority, hypothesizing, lack of substantiation, provocative innuendoes, entrapment, frame-up, on and on. I know all about you! *Do you hear me?* I know *everything*! Asshole! Scumsucking bastard! Get this, I know all about you, everything, everything, *everything*, but you're working on my nerves, trying to prove to me, and even yourself, that you're not *you*! I have a professional hatred of lies—don't get my blood up, animal! Maybe you'd like to check into the Serbsky Institute for a consultation with KGB experts on the subject of split personality? *Deuce-ace*, fuckhead! . . . Excuse the outburst, Citizen Gurov, but really it's not proper, in a situation as unusual as ours, to suppose that I don't know all about you. Especially since, on the whole, the conversation is and will continue to be exclusively about me, and I'm not going to hide the littlest thought from you, not the teeniest little thought, during this great frisking of my soul. Just as I know all about you, you're going to know all about me. Everything!

To discharge the tension, so to speak, why don't I tell you a little anecdote. Or rather, not an anecdote but a true story. But a true story so improbable that the sleazy thing itself has suddenly realized it's legendary and has taken the monicker 'Anecdote', as a slippery way of prolonging its life for a time. And indeed, the very time, Citizen Gurov, our own anecdotal time, has been christened—not so much by our leaders as by their scuzzy flunkies, the poets and composers—a legendary time. With good reason . . .

To make a long story short: Budyonny's men bring in a defector. A White. Comrade Budyonny, sir, he says, in the twinkling of an eye I have grasped what's going on. The hopelessness of the White movement has dawned on me, I smelled the beauty of your Cavalry's ideas from three miles away, let me fight in your ranks. Fine. They gave him a new uniform, new boots, and a beautiful bay horse. The defector fought for a little while, but suddenly it seemed to him that once again, in the twinkling of an eye, he had grasped what was going on, and he beat a retreat to the Whites. Bravely he presented himself to Denikin. Your Excellency, he says, I made a mistake. Budyonny's a complete shit, he's surrounded by loathsome *hoi polloi*, you can't imagine a greater stench or a more total lie than the Soviet regime. Better death in our hopeless ranks, Your Excellency, than victory in the stinking retribution of plebeians deceived by maniacs. Grant me your magnanimous forgiveness. Ours is a time of troubles; you must agree, a soul may well seek after the true way.

Denikin wasn't about to debate the subject. He handed the two-time defector back to Budyonny. The defector started trying to make this stupid bearded cunt-louse understand that he wasn't a scoundrel but a seeker of truth. Finally, in a last attempt to save his skin, he blurts out something about split personality. Budyonny draws his sabre, tests the blade on his thumbnail for sharpness, and cracks the Red White's head open. Slashes him right to the ass, and from there on down he falls apart by himself.

'We Bolsheviks,' says Budyonny, 'solve the problem of split personality in our own way: by the sabre!'

There now, we've calmed down a bit, we've relaxed . . . I gather you're wondering why I use thieves' jargon and obscenities so often? At one time I did have an assignment working with criminals. As for the obscenities, I use them because dirty words, Russian mother-oaths, are my personal salvation in the foetid prison cell that is now the home of our mighty, free, great, etcetera, etcetera language. Poor sucker, it gets chased under the bunks by every thug in the cell: propagandists from the Central Committee, stinking newsmen, scabby literati, pulp-writers, censors, even our proud technocrats. They chase it into editorials, resolutions, interrogation reports, the lifeless speeches at meetings, congresses, rallies, and conferences, where it has gradually lost its dignity and health—it's a goner! They're beating it to death!

You're right. Perhaps, at heart, I do think of myself as a

thug. The observation does you credit. By the way, my colleagues and the big guns at the top call me the Hand. Take a look at my hand . . . I bet you never saw a larger one. When I interrogated my goniffs, Citizen Gurov, I didn't bash them with a paperweight, you know. I'd walk up to them like this . . . take ahold of their fucking kisser, sorry, their face . . . like this . . . brace the flat of my iron palm firmly against the chin, and grip the nose between my fingers . . . like this, Citizen Gurov . . . seal the lips, too, airtight . . . ream the eyes in till they see stars in the dark . . . shhh . . . quiet . . . it has to be quiet . . . and my fingertips bear-claw the skin from the back of your head, so that the creases on your brow fold up like an accordion and turn blue . . . like this . . . and you're choking for breath, not from the pain so much as a hypnotic horror . . . and now, take a look at yourself in the mirror . . . Take a look, don't be afraid. You heard me, meat-face: *look in the mirror*! You don't recognize yourself? Right. That's the whole point. I have restored you. I have adjusted your facial features to fit your inner essence, and no cosmetic surgeon can help you now. I have stripped you of your mask. Say thank you. I've done someone else's work. After all, this is usually a job for death. But death rarely succeeds in fitting the soul snug to the kisser before decomposition sets in . . .

Sit down. We'll brew up some chifir now, have a little bite to eat, and move along . . .

I see you had a lousy night, Citizen Gurov. That's my fault. This evening you'll get a sleeping pill. I'm surprised, by the way: my goniffs usually sleep like babes. And their dreams! After the hideous interrogations, the leap-frogging stresses, and believe me, I know how to induce stress, they dream the happiest, sweetest, most peaceful dreams. About their fathers, mothers, kids, mistresses. About resorts. About invitations to the Kremlin, where they'll be presented with decorations, gold stars, and honorary Mausers by Kalinin—brainless, spineless old goat!—or that stinking swine Shvernik . . .

Ah, you feel sick? You needn't eat your breakfast. That's your own private affair. Go hungry for a day or two. It can only do you good. You'll lose a little flab, work up an appetite. As for me, with your permission I'll gorp some more caviar and a shot of vodka. I never thought it would be so hard to get started talking—although I've waited a long time for this moment. A very long time. All my life, you might say. Sometimes, trying to picture it, I'd lose my nerve, I'd get scared, for I was playing a deadly dangerous game, and I understood that I might get nailed, bang to rights, at any moment. No, no, not trip up, not make a mistake—that couldn't happen to me, as you will soon be convinced, Citizen Gurov—just get nailed.

So I began hastening the arrival of this long-desired moment, in order to celebrate my sixtieth birthday in fitting style and not dream of anything any more . . . You're just my age, aren't you, Citizen Gurov? Just my age . . .

Half a century you've been riding the gravy train, haven't you? As the camp jackals say, you're too spoiled to eat a walrus prick—you didn't take even a crumb of bread with your borscht. Oh, I understand. Overweight. Clogged arteries. Constipation, day in and day out . . . But in the winter of 1929, you know, you came marching through our cosy, snowed-in village, our Odinka, you marched through our white peace and quiet wearing little felt boots and dog-fur leggings, a sheepskin coat with belts and straps, and a pointed Budyonny helmet specially made to fit your little head. You carried above you a red banner: 'Shame on the kulak! Bread for the Motherland!' You were twelve years old, Citizen Gurov . . . Don't interrupt. It's improper to interrupt when a man's giving testimony and wants to crack all the way to his prostate. You were twelve years old, and your Young Pioneer detachment, the 'Red Devils', came marching after you. You were singing the 'Warsaw Hymn', I think, or maybe even The Internationale—I don't remember exactly. Those goddamn songs! I have a persistent and chronic allergy to them. I used to gulp tranquillizers before all the plenums, conferences, and congresses, in order to get through the Party anthem. Of all the wretched songs in the world, that has to be the most diabolically cunning . . . Your detachment came marching after you, and we kids, our lips and noses melting little holes in the ice on the windowpanes, shouted to our fathers and mothers, 'The Red Devils are coming!'

Well, Citizen Gurov, still trying to scam out of it? You've decided to stonewall me? That wasn't you, period? At that moment you were a pupil at Bryansk Public School No. 131. You were in history class. You'd got an *A* for recounting the sadistic doings of eighteenth-century serfholders and spouting something about proletarian humanism, humanism of a new type. Is that so . . ? *You brazen cunt-louse!* You deny your Pioneer childhood, you slat-ribbed whore? I'll *kill* you, bastard! . . . Sorry . . . Sorry . . .

Next to follow, then, after the sons of the Revolution, would be your daddies: a 'Special Chekist Detachment'. In other words, a rabid detachment, a punitive detachment. Our village—not for nothing was it named Odinka, 'The Loner'—hadn't joined the kolkhoz. It had refused. A delegation had been sent to Stalin with a letter. In it the peasants stated their simple arguments, cried out for the salvation of the dying private farmer, and threatened to croak sooner than join the kolkhoz, since that would be worse than death. My poppa, God rest his soul, was bossing people around. He put the ideas into words, wrote them down, led the discussion, and headed the delegation. At the Central Committee the receptionist took their letter, then gave them a kick in the ass—ordered them to go on back and wait for an answer.

Meanwhile, our whole district had already been collectivized. Pop had predicted correctly. The good farmers, Russia's breadwinners, those who hadn't been scragged, of course, had been shipped off to Siberia, and their villages were left with the poor trash, homebrew bums, idiots, cripples, and old folks. But our Odinka declared to the leadership and its emissaries that no one better come poking his nose in here until an answer arrived from Stalin. We would hold the line. Let them send the First Cavalry with Budyonny himself—we didn't give a shit, we'd die all as one, with our last cartridge. That was the situation, Citizen Gurov, in case you've sort of forgotten, or tried to forget . . . Just calm down, now. Calm *down*! The Chekist detachment was led by one Brigade Commander Conceptiev. That's your name too: Conceptiev . . .

Oh? Trying to frame you, and crudely at that? Please look at this extract from the Registry of Marriages. I'll bet my epaulettes it's not jiggered. In 1939, you took your wife's name . . . Well, at last! At last, your jaw dropped and you blushed like a child. Your hitherto imperturbable adrenals started to function, and you had a little rush of juice to your shrewd and well-masked cerebrum! Sit still, my little cockatoo, birdie who sings and shits in flight, sit still and grind the old brains. They're a clotted mess, I know, but don't you dare have a stroke. That would be a dirty trick. I wouldn't survive. For I have no one to talk to—I repeat, with pleasure—no one else but you in the entire universe, including the Devil and the Lord God Himself. Got that, Citizen Conceptiev, a.k.a. Gurov? I'm off to the toilet . . .

Ah, you could use a slug of fine cognac? A twist of lemon to peck at, my little ruffled birdie? I must say, you have an excellent bar. First time I ever encountered a set-up like this. Bar, tape recorder, TV, stereo, push-button phone. The works! We could build a whole case on what we have right here. The case of Citizen Gurov's bar. I'm certain you bought it at some embassy . . . Agreed. I won't call you Conceptiev. The hell with it. I propose we drink to our shared objectively unhappy childhood and send Comrade Stalin a mental thank you for it . . . Fine cognac . . . A paradoxical phenomenon, you must agree: after you crack, you gradually lose the depressing sensation of a split personality.

But I wonder now, do you remember me . . ? I believe you, you don't. It's a thousand years since even I could recognize myself from one moment to the next. And I know why: I don't exist! I just don't, I'm not putting you on, I assure you. What you see here is dead meat, Mr. Crematorium, Comrade Colonel Morgue, the Hand! He functions physiologically as, and works as, an executioner. Party member since 1936. Monstrous! I'm saying this without emotion, but it's monstrous to remember and not recognize yourself! A goddamn fucking surprise, Citizen Gurov! . . . But I wasn't always like this. I wasn't always this corpse, cold as dry ice!

I pressed my hot nose against the frosty windowpane that day, and with this fingernail I scraped the peephole in the ice a little wider and watched you marching in front of your Red

Devils. You each had one big horn, not two little ones, growing on your Budyonny helmets. Remember how you began to talk to the peasants and spout propaganda by rote? Our poppas stood in front of the church—they shook their heads and tried to reckon how Mother Russia, out of the blue, had suddenly spawned all these snot-faced evil spirits. Was the end of the world upon us, perhaps? I remember it perfectly, but when I think of it I want to throw up. All your diabolical arguments in favour of collectivized hell. Jingles by that purulent kiss-ass Demyan 'The Poor' Bedny. Idiotic playlets. On and on . . .

'Hold it!' my poppa said then. 'We're waiting on an answer from Stalin. It's no use shitting us with Demyan Bedny. You're welcome to soup and kasha, but come nightfall you'd better be long gone! As for Demyan, you can tell him from us, he's a poisonous little turd and not even fit for manure.'

Our fathers kicked you out, as they had several times kicked out the city enthusiasts, who didn't know their ass from their elbow when it came to peasant labour.

And now at last, two days later, Brigade Commander Conceptiev arrived in our Odinka with his train of sleighs. The peasants couldn't see that the Chekists had either rifles or machine guns.

'Hello there, Bashov!' your daddy said cheerfully to Pop. 'I've brought your letter from Stalin. Here it is!'

He drew from under his cloak a giant envelope with five wax seals. The peasants cheered. Pop urged his own friends, Conceptiev, and the rest of the bloodsuckers, they were twenty in all, to come to our house. They shooed the women and children out. I alone managed to hole up in the bunk over the stove. And Poppa began to read Stalin's answer aloud.

Dear Comrades:

I have received your letter. Regrettably, I cannot concur with your 'peasant arguments', as I feel that bringing the idea of collectivization to reality is a historically necessary task. You have made your Odinka into a small islet of individual peasant hold-outs in a sea of collective farms. I do not think that you will prove capable of competing with our well-equipped modern kolkhozes or with men of the new type, who have made a decisive break with age-old *petit bourgeois* habits. Joining the kolkhoz is voluntary, of course, and we Bolsheviks attach enormous importance to the observance of this high moral principle. Time will show which of us is right.

J. Stalin

My father read this hocum, reflected, and told Brigade Commander Conceptiev that this was something else again, this was the right way to do things. Today's not the first day we've sown seed in this world, God grant it's not the last day we'll reap. If we live a little while, we'll see who's right and who has chosen a path that is crooked and wrong.

Your daddy expressed his desire that our peasants look closely at the changes taking place in the village, listen to the calm and peaceful voice of objective truth, and surrender their weapons. The Soviet regime, despite its infinite historical patience, would not tolerate a private farmer with a weapon in his hands. The weapons must be surrendered. All on a voluntary basis, of course.

Again our peasants reflected. From up on the stove-bunk I could see the villainous faces of these bandits who, in Pop's words, had taken the peasants' power into their hands. They were pacing up and down, but I couldn't hear them, and I realized with terror that the floorboards weren't squeaking under their feet, as if our hut had been invaded by a demonic force, weightless and incorporeal, yet clothed and shod. Their ugly kissers were pale; not a look, not a move betrayed their intended villainy. But this terrified me still more, and I was on the point of letting out a yell—with every fibre of my being, with all my broken boyish heart, I sensed a mortal calamity, final, irreparable—when Poppa stood up and said to the peasants:

'Friends, let us act according to conscience. A man doesn't plough with a sawn-off shotgun on his shoulder. The law's the law. We can't keep weapons. If we did fight, we'd be no match for the Soviet authorities. You can see that yourselves. We'd be no match, and besides, we'd be the death of our wives and little ones and old folks. So, as good Christians, let us trust Stalin. If he's right, we join the kolkhoz. If we're right, he has to break up his kolkhozery.'

'Well said, Bashov. A wise decision. It's a fact, men, you won't gain anything by force.'

Conceptiev said that: your daddy, Citizen Gurov. As he spoke, he licked his chops and sneaked a slug of vodka, for already his veins were running hot with anticipation of the bloody binge ahead . . . And you, Citizen Gurov, at that moment, were on your way back to Odinka with your Red Devils, to take part in the punishment. You had squealed to the Regional Committee, grassed on our wise and recalcitrant fathers, and were on your way back to Odinka. This time, instead of doggerel by shit-ass Demyan, you brought ramrods and whips . . .

Well, why not. I'll go along with that. Let's have another round, dilate our blood vessels. How about a Valium? Some nitro? Inderal? You take after your daddy: one minute your blood runs hot, next minute cold . . .

I don't suppose there's any reason, Citizen Gurov, to disbelieve your protestations that you were sincere in thinking of the kulaks as mortal enemies of the Soviet regime. You were kids, you couldn't have had any motive of personal gain. They'd stuffed you full of stinking lies, of course. At the age of twelve, moreover, you didn't know the first thing about village life. The village, they had convinced you, was tightening the noose of famine around the necks of proletarians and intellectuals, scholars and Red Army men, Pioneers and Komsomol boys. The fat, garbage-belly village was whetting its shiv to stab the Party in the back, and when every last drop of blood had spurted from the wound, power would be restored to the landowners and capitalists. I understand all that. And you don't need me, Citizen Gurov, to tell you about the power and the horror of total indoctrination. For years I couldn't understand it, just couldn't take it in, my soul couldn't fathom it: how had it happened that you boys and girls of twelve and thirteen felt neither pity nor sympathy nor nausea at the sight of blood, why this utter lack of reaction to another's pain? And conversely, why did your eyes burn, your cheeks flame, malice intoxicate you like jackass vodka, why were your lips, your still innocent lips, twisted in a voluptuous smile, with your nostrils quivering and your wolf-fangs bared, when you flogged us, when you jeered at us as we lay trampled, no longer feeling your blows, no longer raging at your globs of spit, for the unbearable horror of what your fathers had done was more boundless than pain and mortification . . . Only years later, after I'd seen something of you and your kind at interrogations, in prisons, during searches, arrests, and executions—only then did I finally catch on. In 1917 they had severed you from the umbilical cord of everlasting culture and morals. They had raised a 'man of the new type'—a little wild beast, half donkey, half jackal. 'If the enemy does not surrender, he must be destroyed.' 'Onward fly, our locomotive! Stop not until the commune!' 'He who was nothing shall be all!' And so on. You gobbled it up, and your leaders infected you with a syphilitic terror of reprisals and total destruction at the hands of capitalists, landowners, and kulaks. 'It's either them or us', the leaders convinced you, and when you pounced on 'enemies', especially unarmed ones, you acted without mercy or humanity. Scaly bastards . . .

We'd better have a smoke. One minute more and I'll pound you within an inch of your fucking life. My hand is itching, just itching . . . A smoke . . .

The peasants surrendered their weapons that day. Yes; unfortunately, they did. They might just as well have stood up for themselves and their women, slaughtered their executioners, and then, with a clear conscience, faced a legitimate firing squad . . . They surrendered their weapons. They sat at the same table with the Chekists in our hut, guzzling cabbage soup and homebrewed vodka. In the cosy fart-stink atmosphere of Stalinesque democracy, they were placidly blowing off about how they'd have this civilized competition with the kolkhoz, which all the thieves, drunks, and lazy bums had voluntarily joined. Then Conceptiev stood up to speak.

'Bashov,' he said, 'thanks for the hospitality. Now we'll reckon up with you. You've wasted enough of my time as it is. The letter I brought you isn't from Stalin, it's from me personally.'

Just then I heard shots in the village and understood that sure enough, the hour of reckoning had come for all of us. The Chekists whipped out their Mausers. They positioned themselves at the windows and doors. The sturdy peasants of our village, who had been through the German war and the civil war, lost their starch in nothing flat. Their shoulders sagged, they shook their heads, and my father said to them, 'Friends, we're outnumbered by these bandits. They've got us. But our blood will cost them dear, and our curse be upon them to the end of time. Shoot, bastards!'

The Chekists dropped eight men with their first salvo. My father alone remained.

'I was right,' he said. 'No man ought to live on the land and bring forth grain under this pack of beasts. I was right. Shoot, devil! I don't fear you, and I don't fear death! Lord, receive our souls!'

Poppa knelt before the icons and crossed himself, and your daddy, Citizen Gurov, replied, 'I've got plenty of time to finish you off, kulak scum. But first, listen to how beautiful life will be around here after you're gone. Have a taste of what you've passed up, take a look at the world I paint for you.'

He puffed out his chest, his voice shook, his wolf-eyes gleamed, and he poured it on, painting the arrival of total Communism in Russia ten or twelve years hence. Machines would take over all the labour of the peasants. The village would become equal with the city. The peasants themselves, fat and learned, wearing white shirts and black slacks, would sit indoors and press buttons, managing the farms, grain elevators, herds, ducks, geese, and fish by remote control. 'And you, Bashov, will be rotting in the earth—you who because of the malice of your character and reactionism of your soul did not wish to see the earth flower with kolkhozes. You'll rot, and you'll never know anything that beautiful! You won't see man freed of the weighty burden of property and the tribulations of kulak farming. You won't see it!'

'You won't either, lowdown beast!' Poppa said. 'And if you wish, I'll paint you a different picture.'

'Go right ahead. We're listening!' your daddy chortled, Citizen Gurov. And my poppa, before he died, predicted it all, with such amazing accuracy that later, every time one of his predictions came true, I felt horror and ecstasy: Ivan Abramych had seen it in a crystal ball!

You can smirk all you want, Citizen Gurov. Conceptiev and his henchmen smirked too, but it all proved true. The Soviet regime ravaged and exterminated the wise and knowledgeable farmer. They oppressed the poor trash and the remnants of the true peasantry as no one in history had ever before oppressed his slaves.

Anyway, there's no need for me to list my father's conjectures. He was clear on the main point: the logic of the disintegration of the peasant soul when bound in slavery, deprived of the right of ownership and private initiative, the right to work his own land in harmony with his animals . . . Ivan Abramych foretold it all. The fact that the peasants, like slaves, would be paid the barest minimum, just enough to keep them from croaking—i.e., he foretold the work-day system of payment. The fact that they would lose their passports and be forbidden to move, on pain of death. The demise of crafts, the impoverishment of the soil, the fact that the parasitic cities would gradually be weaned from meat, butter, and fish. Even the fact that sausage would practically be made from shit at your meat-packing plants, Citizen Gurov—that, too, Poppa foretold. He didn't forget about wheat, either. He was wrong on one thing, though. We use our gold to buy wheat from America, not Germany. That's immaterial. But didn't the Chekists cackle! They must have believed they had a deadly enemy and madman on their hands.

'And here's another picture for you,' Poppa said. 'You are demons. You'll strangle yourselves to death, and your satanic spawn will go begging. Lord, forgive them! The parasites, they know not what they do . . .'

To answer your question, Citizen Gurov: I didn't see who shot Poppa. Your father, some other lout—I didn't see. And I'm not about to lie. But I've always been sure, always, that he was the one. To whom else, do you think, would he have entrusted such an honour: drawing a bead on the leader of the Odinka reactionaries?

I didn't see who shot my father Ivan Abramych, and I didn't hear the gunfire, because I was in shock. My poor childish soul had collapsed. I even think our psyches have a safety switch that sometimes blacks us out in life's insane moments . . . I was in shock, and when I snapped out of it my side was roasting hot. Our beloved log cabin was on fire. The floor had caught first, the Chekists must have splashed kerosene around, fire was already licking at the icons, and I couldn't see Poppa in the flames . . . Just don't pretend you can't recall that conflagration, Citizen Gurov . . .

I bashed the window out with my head—though I don't remember doing it—and you, Citizen Gurov, pulled me out of the snowdrift! You! . . . What's the matter? Recognize me? Know me? Remember me . . ? Open your gullet, scumbag! Open up! It's too soon for you to croak! Swallow the cognac, bastard, and stop chattering your teeth, you'll bite through the crystal. Swallow! You're going to live a while yet, cockroach. Drink, I say! There, that's more like it . . . With your hand on your heart—now that I've saved it from a coronary—answer me this, Citizen Gurov: is it pleasant to return to life . . ? Ah. You don't want to live! But I didn't want to either, and if the Red Devils hadn't bound me hand and foot I would have dived back into the flames and burned to a cinder, along with my father Ivan Abramych . . . But you bound me and set me astride an ice-coated log, a giant tree trunk, along with other kids my age who had escaped the bullets . . .

Please use your brain for a moment, please think back to that day. So: all the grown-ups have been shot, every last one, even paralyzed Uncle Shoshin and the old blind woman Belyaikha. No witnesses to the bloody atrocity, except us kids. Nothing left of Odinka but black holes in the snow, steam and smoke rolling out of them. And not a soul in the whole wide world knows about it. In the West, great friends of the Soviet Union lick the sweet snot from their lips, deeply moved by the historic reconstruction of social relations that Stalin is accomplishing in the villages. The mob of poets, writers, artists, composers, and sculptors is already sinking its rat fangs into the golden vein of collectivization. No one, no one, knows that long before Guernica, before Lidice, before Katyn, the scorched huts of Odinka and tens and hundreds of Odinkas stand black against the snow. The dead peasant farmers, the murdered people, have been dumped in a pile, and the starving wolves, freely and with impunity, are gobbling their corpses in the thief-dark night . . . Forgive my lyricism. So: it's all over. Twenty-five below zero. The kids who have survived the carnage sit astride the ice-coated log, and you . . . Yes! Yes! Yes! you, Citizen Gurov, flog us as enemy degenerates, with whips, you and your little devils flog us and order us to sing:

> We will raze the world of coercion
> To its foundations, whereupon . . .

Turn on the television, please. Thank you. There you have it, The Internationale. I got carried away and I completely forgot that my KGB colleagues, as well as the entire Soviet nation and the vanguard of humanity, are celebrating the centenary of the birth of that great lover of mankind, friend to children, knight of the Revolution, the iron Felix Edmundovich Dzerzhinsky . . . Too bad we missed hearing my boss, Minister Andropov. But do listen to our former national anthem, which you rammed down our childish gullets. Listen a moment, refresh your memory, and then turn off the goddamn box. I don't care to attend the gala concert honouring the centennial of this cunning, supposedly inspired and sentimental, executioner.

Oh, yes indeed. An outstanding executioner he was. An executioner of the new type. But what a fiendish puss he had! A ringer for Asmodeus. Of course that's no accident, his striking resemblance to Satan . . . Poxov! Get some grub for us. Something nice and tasty . . .

It's no accident, Dzerzhinsky's resemblance to Asmodeus. No accident. I'm glad you agree with me, Citizen Gurov. Your humble servant the Hand, Executioner, has reflected at length on Good and Evil, taking a neutral position in respect to both. Neutral because the goal of my life is, and always has been, not the defence of the copper-hearted 'ideals' of an Evil that masquerades as Good, and not the service of true Good, but a thirst for vengeance, a pathological lust for vengeance, if you must know, vengeance, Citizen Gurov, vengeance, a thirst which to my misfortune, my damnation, can be slaked only for an instant, and right now I take your skull again . . . like this . . . shhh . . . easy . . . in my hand . . . and I seal your lips and nostrils shut, risking that you will suffocate at this instant, and with my thumb and little finger I ream your eyes into their sockets, and with the other three fingers I bear-claw your scalp! . . . For you, a terrifying twenty seconds of death. For me, a sweet instant of revenge . . .

This time you stood up better to the only physical torture I use. Which, by the way, you deserve. But even if you come to recognize that you deserve torture and punishment, recognize it to the fullest, to the point of voluntarily accepting death as the supreme chastisement for the inhuman cruelty you have perpetrated against me personally, I will not forgive you. In other words, I can never slake my thirst for revenge . . .

Never, and therefore I feel I'm a complete shit . . . Now if I could whack off a formula for my own life, a miraculous equation in which the violence done to me and my loved ones and to everything we held sacred would be cancelled out, at a specific point in time, by my acts of revenge for that violence—then I could lead a simple and beautiful existence, sitting by the fire in an easy chair, sorrowfully reminiscing about the bygone follies of my fatal Count of Monte Cristo complex. Alas, alas, Hand! Now that you're enmeshed in the satanic mechanism of revenge, you'll never find your way out. So go ahead, get your kicks, keep it up till you croak . . .

Oh, turn on the TV, would you, Citizen Gurov? Let's watch the news. Just as I thought. Vnukovo Airport. Politburo members, ministers, Central Committee department heads, lesser fuckamucks—the whole damn mob of them, walking out onto the airfield. Their hearts pound with excitement, the suspense is agonizing. For the third time today the top brass from the Kremlin, the Old Square, and the Lubyanka have negotiated the route from the Kremlin to Vnukovo in their elegant black armoured cars. Seeing people off, meeting them, seeing them off . . . Down the ramp comes smiling Leonid, our darling, beloved General Secretary, the indefatigable President Brezhnev! Down he comes, and already he's in the arms of the

Politburo! They swap long wet kisses, in front of all our many millions of people. See here, parasites, this is how you should love your Leader! It's only been a week, but we were out of our frigging skulls with loneliness. You're back, Leonid, back home with us, my dear! Joy, so much unfeigned joy! A steaming pile of it! Even Suslov has a crawly little worm of a smile on his grey, papier mâché corpse-face, even Kirilenko has smoothed out his iron furrows for an instant and limbered up the lips he clenched in 1937. In an ecstasy of reunion, the restrained tears of the Politburo have mingled with the stern but lavish tears of the General Secretary . . . Now the whole tribe poses for the television lens. They stand frozen, as in a banal vacation snapshot, and for the umpteenth time it occurs to me, Citizen Gurov, that these are the cobblestones of the proletariat, somehow oddly metamorphosed into men.

And here's a model stock farm. Cows. Calves. White streams flowing from pink teats. Open wide, gunsmiths of Tula, engineers of Saratov, pensioners of Voronezh! Drink natural unpowdered milk, steamy and life-giving, with the taste you have long forgotten. Drink! Wipe your lips! The correspondent leads us by the hand to the creamery. Hog down the butter, poor countryside—not French butter, not Finnish, not Danish, but our own. Native butter from Russian meadows. Milk . . . cream . . . yoghurt . . . butter! Wolf it down, poor countryside. Smear butter on the bread you buy from your mortal enemy, garbage-breath America. He was right, God rest his soul. The late Ivan Abramych was a thousand times right! The land and the peasant can't feed the urban *hoi polloi*, even if they bust a gut trying! Anything left over from the tables of the Central Committee, the regional and local committees, the military élite, the many millions of soldiers, Chekists, and police, the greasy fat Bohemians, scientists, academicians, hucksters, and other thieves—their leftovers, I repeat, are pilfered again by the jackals at depots and warehouses. What reaches the shops vanishes instantly into the greedy gullet of the crowd, like a teensy shrimp in the belly of a whale.

I consider it a major political blunder to show pig farms, creameries, calves, geese, poultry, and great fat flocks of sheep on television, for the Soviet people to see. These displays awaken a brutish appetite and an unhealthy mood in the poor countryside living on frozen fish and noodles with vegetable oil. It's disgusting, it's immoral, to tease the proletariat by showing them a suckling pig's ass! It's inhuman to stimulate the conditioned reflexes of Tambov, Penza, Omsk, Tagil, hundreds of Russian cities, with a story on the automation of sausage and frankfurter production. This must be especially clear to you, Citizen Gurov, as a top administrator in the meat and dairy industry. Drool, just drool, ye factory hands and engineers, truck drivers and construction workers, spinners and telephone operators, janitors and bulldozer jockeys, secretaries and teachers, lab assistants and book-keepers. Drool, gulp your noodles and potatoes, and go forth to build our bright future, Communism—in which the thugs who feed on you, the glorious commandants of your prison camp, have long been comfortably ensconced. Go forth to hard labour, plod through the day, and tonight we'll watch the news programme 'Time' together. The News. Up your mother's ass!

Don't jump, Citizen Gurov, don't throw a fit! Not *your* mother. Rest easy. You sent her to the grave yourself, thirty years ago . . .

Turn down the volume, please. Or turn the damn thing off. Where's my briefcase? Oh, here it is.

'Dearest Mama,' you write. 'Your letter reached me by chance, when I returned to Moscow after being gravely wounded. I could not read it without distress, because I am powerless to help you in any way. Food parcels are not being accepted. I myself am leaving in a few days for a job in the combat zone. All my available cash I donated to the defence fund. My allotment goes to Elya . . . As for finding out anything about Father, I haven't even tried. You will understand why. But I hear that they are sometimes allowed to atone for their crimes with blood. This is some hope. Chin up. It's a hard time for everyone. Try to get into a hospital. I saw the usual action. I've been awarded some medals and have risen to the rank of major. Love and kisses. Vasya.'

I trust we won't be calling in the handwriting experts, Citizen Gurov?

But I keep digressing, deviating from the main line. We should get out of the deep dark forest, my dear namesake

Vasya, back on the right path! We've wandered a little astray, wandered astray . . .

So. It's all over. Twenty-five below. A few kids who have survived the carnage sit astride the ice-coated log. And you, Citizen Gurov, flog us as enemy degenerates, with whips, you and your Red Devils force us, coerce us, to sing:

We will raze the world of coercion
To its foundations, whereupon
Our own world we will build, a new world,
He who was nothing shall be all.

I had jumped from the burning cabin in my underwear, by the way, and you made me sit astride the log just as I was, except that you took a sheepskin coat off a murdered peasant and tossed it over my shoulders. That was so I wouldn't croak, your mission being to re-educate the little kulak bastards, make them into builders of the new world.

Oh, well. I didn't quite die, and what's more I'm no mere builder. I'm one of those who hold the reins—the merciless iron reins—on the screwball nations of the Russian empire.

I didn't quite die, but, thanks to you personally, Citizen Gurov, I didn't become a man either—a man, a regular guy, a cocksman, cunt-chaser, husband, father. Thanks to you, I got frostbite on that damned log. You froze my balls, or my prostate, or the actual flesh of my prick—who cares about the diagnosis—and after that I never got a hard-on. *Never* . . . Thank you for the belated advice. I didn't consult the doctors, although eventually I became so powerful I could have dog-fucked the whole KGB Health Service. I could have put out the call to lads all over the world: Fetch the Hand a miracle drug from the other end of the earth, whip it up from dried crocodile liver, crushed humming-bird bills, and burnt polar bear whiskers, steep it with bile from a young panther and pollen from the Alpine edelweiss. But I didn't consult the doctors, didn't feel the urge.

The Party thought the sacred fire of hatred for enemies of

the people burned so hot in my breast that no other passion could coexist with it. This was the destiny of the few, the high drama of darlings of the Great Cause. Sometimes my fellow-executioners kidded me, and in a very raunchy, cruel way. But I never lost my temper, strange as that may seem, literally not once. I said lightly, 'Facts first, fuck later.' With the years, they pretty much left me alone, realizing that the Hand had better things to do.

As for the women, they never gave me a second glance. They simply didn't notice me—evidently owing to the total absence of any sexual electricity around me. Or if they did, they stared as if I were a monster.

I froze to the very core of my being in the year that I turned thirteen, and of course all my hormones got scrambled. That's how I grew up to be the big dumb ox sitting before you, Citizen Gurov. Admire me with fresh eyes, in light of the foregoing . . . Behold: the face horsey, the skin on it flaccid, the beard sparse and soft like under a girl's arm. The eyes behind the spectacles are ready to start from their sockets, their colour is faded, but the stare is still a machine gun! That I know for certain . . . Behold, admire your handiwork! See my shoulders? They're round, a woman's shoulders. They should have been like those of my father Ivan Abramych, but the hormones missed my biceps, and—see—if I just shrug one shoulder . . ? I have no waistline at all. It's a straight drop from my spine to my ass and down through my puffy thighs—also womanish, of course—to my size thirteen feet. Whopping big feet, but weak, for even here the hormones missed their target . . . missed their target. But I do have my hand. Its length is phenomenal: thirty centimetres. Its strength, without exaggeration, is mystical. I trust you don't doubt this? Good. Well, what do you say? He's a pretty good size now, isn't he, the poor little kid who was frozen solid and force-fed The Internationale till he puked?

I like it that you're relatively unflappable. If you'd heaved a sigh or displayed anything like sympathy on your ugly mug, I don't think I could have restrained myself. I'd have bashed you on the conk with this porcelain platter.

A man. A regular guy. Cocksman. Cunt-chaser. Husband. Father . . . One time in camp—back when I was putting into practice Lenin's dialectics about the self-destruction of the underworld—I was approached by a little gun moll. She might have been thirty. And beautiful, goddamn her. Even in quilted pants and a peajacket she looked like a lady. She approached me without fear, though I was walking through the compound with all the camp screws around me, and she said, without fear: 'Greetings, warden! Haul me in to see you, on a matter of top priority.'

I hauled her in. What matter is that? I wondered. I gave orders to bring in some grub and brew a pot of chifir. The moll's name was Zoya. We're sitting there slinging the lingo, scoffing the grub, getting high on chifir. I had to laugh, Zoya punched me such a woolly line of bull. Supposedly she got seduced by Beria before she even hit twelve. She gave me details, and a lot of them tallied. But that's not the point.

'Warden,' she says, 'I've scoffed your grub and drunk your chifir. This makes me a scab, a rat. I can't go back to the compound. But the reason I turned scab, and you can believe me or not, is that I tumbled for ugly old you. You've got something about you that's savage as a tiger, and my thief's heart is hammering. Undress me and fuck me like a man, and we'll forget, you and I, for one sweet short minute, this whole rotten space and time. Look how beautiful I am,' she says, 'a real woman—look how beautiful.'

My jaw dropped, I blinked, and suddenly, out of the lousy prison-camp rags, out of the men's yellow long johns with their pathetic little drawstring, out of the felt boots soled with tyre-tread, rises a white, rosy, shining, clean, innocent body. I stared at the naked woman for I don't know how long, in uninterrupted ecstasy, until I started to shake with pain, horror, fury, and sobs . . . Yes, yes! Sobs . . .

I hadn't cried when you burned my Odinka, but now, because I could not experience what even rats experience, even tarantulas, even fish in the pond, I candidly confess I blubbered. She came after me, invited me, begged me, caressed me, pitied me, and I burst into tears like a small child, for the first time in many terrible years and noisily sucked her breast . . . Her nipple was taut with the sweet fever of life. I remember the taste, I won't forget it till the day I die.

Zoya flinched and went rigid. I took fright, and an unknown something suddenly released her.

'Why are you so wanting, Vasya?' she said.

'I got frozen when I was a child,' I said. 'Frozen solid.'

I told her nothing more. She got dressed. She hid her loveliness in lousy prison-camp grey.

'You should get your high some other way. Why don't *you* put out?' she says. 'Now, the warden of Section 6, the cons fixed him up at the chocolate factory. He sleeps with two big lugs at once.'

'I'm sorry,' I replied, 'but I really don't want or desire anything at all.'

'But is that a life?' Zoya said.

'No,' I agreed, 'I'm hard put to call it a life. But it's all I was offered. Stay with me till morning,' I begged her, 'please stay . . .'

For the first and last time, Citizen Gurov, I slept beside a woman, young and beautiful. She wanted to fuck, and she raved around till she was kayoed by sleep, like me. I dreamed about Mama . . . In the morning, before line-up, Zoya left for the compound. Her felt boots left tyre-tread marks on the floor, I remember; I found it rather gruesome that lovely human feet should leave tracks like a Stalin Motors truck. The next night, in the compound, Zoya was shivved. A meet with a screw! By scoffing my homefries and lard, drinking my chifir, and supposedly fucking me, Zoya had become a ratting whore.

Okay, stand up, Citizen Gurov. Stand up, scum, when I order you to! . . . Up! . . . Aha, look at that! So my story gave you an erection? You're embarrassed, of course, and you claim that man's nature, or more precisely your own nature, has an amazing capacity to integrate lust, horror, shame, base curiosity, and other jackassery, all at the same time? Sit down, goat! In all honesty, you've gladdened my heart. So you've still got lots of life in you! So you'd be reluctant to part with it, and you will now reveal everything you've grabbed from your beloved Soviet regime. Poxov, come here! Listen closely. Out with it, Citizen Gurov: the locations of all your stashes! Every last one! You realize, I trust, that we are speaking in deadly earnest. There will be no haggling. Write it down, Poxov . . . Don't forget, Citizen Gurov: conceal just one little stone, just one pearl or antique ring, and I'll stick you in a state-of-the-art lie detector. And then . . . don't blame me, you scaly bastard—but

Poxov will restore both your memory and your eagerness to talk . . .

Your villa is posh. Terrific! A honey of a villa. I like it. Seriously. A man might well pass the remainder of his days in a villa like this. And not just pass the twenty years, while them away, but rot in bliss, maintaining the fire of life in his limbs with vintage cognac and jolly wenches . . . Let's take a walk, Citizen Gurov. It's a fucking bore to sit in one spot hour after hour, day after day. Besides, I've done enough talking. More than enough. I'd show far greater restraint if I were writing up an interrogation report. 'I, Citizen Bashov, alias the Hand . . . can testify on the substance of the case as follows.' Period. Having a talk is different. Especially a heart-to-heart talk—the first in my life, actually, and the last . . . No, I never did try for stylistic brilliance in my interrogation reports, I never fucked around with the extra epithet or flashy argument. Unlike many of my colleagues, when I wearied of the struggle with our foreign and domestic enemies I never daydreamed about switching to literature, entering the Writers' Union via the phone booth—a quick call from the Lubyanka—and raking in the dough for desecrating the great and mighty Russian language.

Many's the man we've given a champagne send-off to the quiet of a writer's desk. Wake me in the middle of the night, read me half a page at random, and I'll tell you like a shot whether it was written by a Chekist or just an ordinary quasi-literate piss-head. Pages by my ex-colleagues stink of juridical slumgullion, smoke-filled offices, holey elbows, haemorrhoidal asses, frayed nerves, and terror for their own skins. Quite a few of my fellow-executioners, you know, Citizen Gurov, have been drilled, dropped, blown away. The ones who got nailed, incidentally, were often the same Python Constrictoviches who had grown wild-eyed and insolent with inspiration; they were so uninhibited at interrogations, and concocted such monstrous phantasmagoric scenarios, that our chiefs, executioners with really very weak imaginations, clutched their heads in despair and made the effort to get rid of these 'poets' of their profession . . .

Yes, indeed! There was a time in the thirties, and again in the forties of our wonderful century, when the Lubyanka and other similar institutions in the major and minor cities of the Russian Empire might confidently have been termed Palaces of Literature. They were crawling with representatives of the various literary trends, who didn't even feud among themselves, for they all had the same goal: to create, with the aid of one or more unhappy prisoners, a literary work of a piofuckineering new genre: the Case. THE CASE! The investigator's idea developed toward this goal through various peripeteias, which we privately termed the scenario, and was supposed to end by gathering all the actors in the Case—the enemies of the people, and their accomplices—into one bouquet. The bouquet would be presented to the tribunal, and the tribunal, without even sniffing it, would send some of the flowers to the crematorium, others to the lethal cold of a prison camp. *Finis!* The Cases, these truly most elaborate works of Socialist Realism, were then forgotten, and the literary heroes—Soviet people, men of the new type—were sucked into the quagmire of oblivion.

But Stalin and the Politburo kept demanding new, more interesting Cases from us, kept demanding a more complete fusion of literature and life. The imaginary blood of fictitious characters was less to their taste than the warm, real blood of our prisoners—'loathsome villains who have lost all semblance of humanity in devising brutal assassination attempts on our leaders and their political ideas'. The trials, whether open or closed, were perceived by our leaders, and by spectators temporarily remaining at large, as mighty pageants where any deficiency in Shakespearean passion or depth of artistic thought was compensated for by the real-world setting of the opener, the real denials of guilt, the real pressure from the prosecutor, the forced confessions, and the details of the epic crime as reconstructed in soul-freezing dialogues between the judges and defendants. Then the culmination and finale.

You are quite right, Citizen Gurov, in observing that neither our leaders nor the spectators were present in the auditorium as mere bystanders, an audience empathizing with the action of the pageant as it unfolded before their eyes. No, they too were characters in it. Not unassisted by autosuggestion, hypnosis, and propaganda, they identified themselves with the Forces of Good, which, with the active support of our glorious Chekists, Knights of the Revolution, were overcoming the vile Forces of Evil. Crafty and perfidious Forces, vile enough to use the vilest of means! This was where we made our contribution, we anonymous playwrights and prose stylists. The prisoners themselves, on occasion, sincerely admired my own personal concoctions: the sly intrigues, the turns of plot, the miraculous technology of conspiracy and sabotage.

In short, the machinery of investigation and trial was so skilful in creating the illusion of mortal danger that honest Bolsheviks and Stalinists, completely engrossed in the spectacle, no longer noticed the illogic of the defendants' behaviour, the flagrant implausibility of the evidence, the gallows humour of Mr. Vyshinsky and his screws, the absurd self-slanders and schizoid 'last words'. They noticed nothing. Their throats rattled with the hoarse cry, 'Retribution! Death to the scum! To the wall with them, the prostitutes! Hands off our factories and kolkhozes!' And the blood flowed. Retribution was accomplished, it was real, it could be touched with the hand. But I personally noted the price that our lofty patrons, our Maecenases, our leaders, paid for this sensation of the full reality of the retribution, their own salvation, and the triumph of justice: they paid with the reality of the fear that permeated their souls . . .

You have a beautiful piece of land. Pines, cedars, firs . . . Hotbeds . . . Swimming pool. Sea's not enough, you old goat? The pool is faced with marble. Just as I thought; this marble was stolen from the construction site of the Literary Fund writers' colony. Pack of sneak-thief jackals . . . When the Party's feeding, you can't just gab and gape. You've got to eat, or some other dumb writer will get in ahead of you . . . We never had pricks like this in Mother Russia. Never.

These red footpaths of yours are nice too. Pomegranates . . . Peaches . . . Vegetable beds . . . Coriander . . . Mint . . . Aubergine . . . And on the walls of the villa, even a Renoir and some Dürer engravings. You're an operator, Citizen Gurov. A real operator. To go through such hell and high water, do so many wicked deeds, survive in one piece, stay in with the Party, build this palatial dump, provide a happy old age for yourself and your children and grandchildren—this takes know-how. You were wise, of course, to sign all the property over to your son-in-law. Very wise. His income is legal. They pay millions for his busts of Lenin, I know . . . But we're concerned with my case, not yours. Let's get back to my life, and the era of mass scribbling in the security system.

Summon to mind, if you will, the image of your daddy's closest assistant, Vlachkov . . . I'll help you. A big, beefy guy. Handsome. Genial manner. Always had a smile. Collar undone. With a song on his lips, he butchered the sturdy peasants of our province and drove them off the land. Loved to give speeches. He was Second Secretary of the Regional Committee by the time I got my hands on him. I had made a little list of the men in your daddy's detachment when I found myself in the security system. Vlachkov was the first to fall into these hands of mine . . .

I took Vlachkov myself. In those days it was easy to get a warrant for an arrest. An old buddy of mine cooked up the denunciation. It was simple as truth itself: Vlachkov had discharged a whole cartridge clip from his Mauser into a portrait of Stalin.

Vlachkov lived in a big house fully the equal of yours. For his building site, he had snaffled off a chunk of a Park of Culture.

I came alone to arrest him, without my men. I preferred it that way.

'Hello, Victor Petrovich,' I said.

'Hello, Comrade Bashov. This is a surprise. What brings you?'

'I've come straight from work,' I said. 'Sorry, but I have something disagreeable to discuss. It concerns you personally.'

By this time he was scared shitless, of course, but you wouldn't have noticed. On the contrary, as we walked through front rooms and hallways to his study, he kept up a stream of jokes, boasted about the carpeted interiors, and showed me his collection of antique weaponry, which had been confiscated from a harmless Dr. Glushkov. The doctor had been zapped for an 'attempt to organize terrorist acts against the Regional Committee, skilfully stimulating base bourgeois instincts by means of weaponry from the times of Minin and Pozharsky.'

In the study, Vlachkov's flunkies brought us vodka, caviar, sturgeon fillet, ham, marinated mushrooms and bush pumpkins—all equally good. I remember as if it were yesterday. And Smirnov vodka, genuine old Smirnov vodka from czarist times. We drank, though I damn near puked when we clinked glasses. My head reeled. I went crashing back, in memory, to the instant on our stove-bunk, and I gasped as Vlachkov sank bullet after bullet into my uncle. Bullet after bullet, while the murderer's eyes bulged from their sockets, for some reason, and turned white . . .

'Here's to good health!' I said.

'I'll drink to that. Tell me what's on your mind.'

'I have in my pocket,' I said, 'a denunciation against you. Not anonymous—signed. But I can't give you the name, you understand . . . Do you have a shooting gallery?'

'Yes. In the cellar. You know "If the morrow brings war, if we march with the dawn—"'

'Beautiful,' I said, and I read aloud the denunciation: He, Vlachkov, had his own shooting gallery, in which portraits of Stalin, and sometimes other members of the Politburo as well, were set up in place of targets. He whanged away all night, trying to hit the Leader in the forehead or even the eye. Sometimes he entertained whole groups here. They carried on sex orgies right in the gallery, to the sound of the shots—

'Bull!' said Vlachkov. 'Prize bull!'

'I think so too,' I replied. 'Pedigreed. That's why I came.'

I tore up the denunciation and threw it in the fireplace. Vlachkov shook my hand. We drank another round.

I had grasped that even though the denunciation was as simple as truth itself, it would be a pain to deal with. I'd have to present material evidence—bullet-riddled portraits of Stalin and his thugs—plus opinions from ballistics experts, and other garbage. That was no good. I had no right to risk it . . . no right . . .

'But the real reason I came,' I told Vlachkov, 'is this. Frankly speaking our work is being hampered by covert enemies and careerists. Some of them happen to hate you. They're spreading rumours that you were soft on the kulaks, back when you were Deputy Chief of a special detachment in the Shilkovsky District. Allegedly you were too lenient, you accepted bribes and appropriated valuables, with which you built yourself one very classy dump. The rumours,' I said, 'must be stopped. You're a clever man. You understand that in difficult times it's easier for the Party to lop off a superfluous head than to mess with infighting on the Regional Committee. That's why you have to take decisive action.'

I put it to him, and as I watched, Vlachkov crumpled a little. He lost his majestic contours and sagged like a sack full of shit. Through a teeny little puncture, he began to give off the stench of the arrogance of success and Bolshevik impunity, the stench of loudmouth bullying and tough-guy conceit. He was deflating! Accordingly, I pumped him up with stinking terror and watery bewilderment. Affecting to wish him well, I outlined the suicidal futility of hauling his sabre to the outhouse—proudly sticking his neck out to challenge the honour of his denouncers, who were expert mudslingers.

Vlachkov crumpled completely. You could have tied him at the neck, slung him over your shoulder, and lugged him to the cloakroom.

I'm not boring you, am I, Citizen Gurov?

Well, when I had pumped him good and full of watery fear, when he believed he had my support and sympathy, I advised Vlachkov to go for broke: write a letter to Stalin. I would send it direct, through our own official channels.

Vlachkov's head cleared in a flash. He charged over to the desk. All night he scribbled a letter to his Dear, Precious, and Beloved, while I sipped vodka and didn't get drunk. At the time, I confess, I was fascinated by the pursuit of this mad beast. I still hadn't brought him to bay. I must do nothing to betray myself. On this one, my first, I must perfect the behavioural technique for mercilessly hunting down my despoilers, who by now were well fattened at the Party tit. I had eleven men on my little list. The eleventh, Citizen Gurov, was your daddy.

Vlachkov finished his letter. 'Would you like to read it?' he asked, his face a swollen mess of tears and mixed emotions.

'I'd like to, if you trust me.'

'Who else can I trust?' he sobbed.

I took the letter. Reading it, I was all but destroyed. All but destroyed. I'm afraid to remember—those were terrible moments. I started to bawl, not aloud, of course, but my heart cried out, I trembled at these 'sparingly described facts, which demonstrate my wholehearted devotion to you, Joseph Vissarionovich, and to the cause of the Party'.

Where's my briefcase? Oh, here it is. I saved that letter. Read it, Citizen Gurov. Read it, and why don't we both get some sleep. Good night . . .

Poxov! . . . Good morning . . . All right . . . Thanks. That was quick. Ask them to make a tomato omelette for Gurov, please. Home fries in lard for me. And don't forget to put in some minced onion . . . Fix the coffee good and strong. Every day that goes by, or every night I should say, I get less and less shut-eye . . . Oh, by the way. Draw up a detailed description of all the valuables we've located. Do some digging on the origins of the larger rocks. We might be lucky enough to turn up a clue about the heirs to some of them. Any church items go on a separate list. Then bring them all in here. Let the lovely things breathe a little fresh air. They mustn't rot till the end of the world in the ground and concrete and furnace dampers. Gurov and I will admire them. Don't bring any coins or bullion or other yellow crap . . . That will be all.

Well, what did you think of the letter, Citizen Gurov? Did you notice that Vlachkov counted the formation of the Red Devil detachments as one of his greatest achievements? 'Young people of the new type, forged in the crucible of merciless hatred for the kulak, number-one enemy of the working class and the worker-peasant intelligentsia. Young people whose five senses I strove with all my might to win over to the service of class awareness, the fundamental emotion inherited by us from Lenin and refined by you personally, Joseph Vissarionovich.'

Notice that? Here he is, sitting right in front of me—the little Red Devil, grown fat-assed and old! This remarkable document, for which Satan Fiendovich Diabolov himself would give me a couple of kilos of emeralds, describes in some detail the operations to eliminate the kulak as a class. Vlachkov and you Red Devils believed that if a man didn't wish to join the kolkhoz, his last sack of grain was 'surplus'. For you believed that the proletarian was the only true labourer. The peasant was a parasite who plundered the land, drank the milk flowing of its own accord from the cows' teats, and stuffed his face with the meat of cattle slaughtered on lush meadows. A greedy-guts who had set himself the goal of starving the city and the proletariat to death.

You marched away and left any surviving souls to die of hunger . . .

But enough . . . It was no great trouble to get my hands on that letter. For a week or two, Vlachkov was quiet as a mouse. He didn't shoot in his gallery, didn't drink, didn't have sex orgies. From his own savings he bought instruments enough for a brass band, and presented them to the orphans at a home for children of enemies of the people. So the poor little kids were tootling 'If the morrow brings war', 'Our heart is an engine of flame', 'And we alone in all the world can truly laugh and love.'

Then one day I walked in on Vlachkov at his Regional Committee office. My boys waited outside for me, in the limo.

'Greetings,' I said. 'We need to have a little chat. It might be nice to do it at your house, over a shot of vodka and a few mushrooms.'

We drove to Vlachkov's. As we drove, I exerted the full force of my mind, which by that time was pretty sharp. How to bring down this wily old boar? Which side to tackle him from? He was damn near invulnerable. But I had to take him! It was high time—I had to, or I'd be too late. The sonofabitch would wait till Yezhov eased up on this purge, and then he'd be at it again, hacking up all the overt and secret enemies within reach. He could get to me, too . . .

Along the way we chatted about the fighting in Spain, the atrocities of the German Fascists, the horrors of concentration camp life for our comrades arrested in Berlin, the Stakhanovite movement, and so on. When we arrived, I discreetly ordered my boys to summon twenty more from headquarters and surround the house. No one was to be let in or out.

We sat there eating and drinking, still chatting away. But Vlachkov too was under terrible strain, I could tell, and as for me, I just couldn't seem to think how best to ice him. I didn't have a single scenario for him. He didn't fit—period. And suddenly, just like a novelist, I was struck with an inspiration. Behold, the image of a Case.

'Your pipe reminds me of someone,' I said.

Vlachkov turned white. Then and there, which I frankly hadn't expected, he cracked wide open: two weeks of accumulated fear had filled him to bursting.

'Yes,' he confessed, 'I once said jokingly, at a picnic in the Wildlife Preserve, that my pipe looked a lot like Dzerzhinsky's face.'

'I realize you had no ulterior motive,' I said, 'but you shouldn't have made that joke. Conceptiev took advantage of it. His denunciation reached Yezhov and was sent back to us with a sad memorandum: "Investigate, and punish the guilty."'

'I'll never confess to this for the record,' Vlachkov said. 'That would be tantamount to signing my own death warrant. All the witnesses to that facetious and harmless conversation, except for Conceptiev, have been shot as enemies of the people, which in point of fact they obviously were. But I've got something against Conceptiev too. If he's decided to save his own skin by ratting on me, I'll rat on him ten times over! Twenty! A hundred times! Bastard!'

This is it, I thought—this is my big break!

'But tell me,' I said, hinting broadly that he could try an unscrupulous defence, 'once when Conceptiev was potted, didn't he mention how he and Lenin had taken part in the first Volunteer Saturday? Think back. Didn't Conceptiev tell how he and several other Chekists, disguised as workers, had helped Lenin to carry a log? You remember. Not long ago, under interrogation, you know, an erstwhile enthusiast of Communist labour confessed that on orders from leftwing deviationists they had dropped the full weight of that log on Lenin's bad shoulder. This aggravated the brain disease that caused the Leader's death.'

'Why, the bastards! The worms! *They* certainly weren't asleep. I am prepared to corroborate the confession of the leftwing deviationist sleaze,' Vlachkov said. 'And I remember Conceptiev smirking and telling us in 1923, "Lenin won't last long." Write it down, Comrade Bashov!'

I spent the next twenty-four hours writing down Vlachkov's 'testimony' in what was to be the case against your daddy.

'Now, tell me frankly,' I said to Vlachkov, on the second day of our conversation. 'Do you really think that this Asmodeus-face you're filling with Holland tobacco bears any resemblance to the face of Dzerzhinsky—our Iron Felix?'

'Yes, I do,' he answered, 'but of course that's just between us.' He puffed at his pipe. 'The pipe is old workmanship, by the way. Therefore any knowing mockery of our Knight of the Revolution is out of the question. Absurd. I'll never admit to that chance remark. Help me get out of this sordid mess, Comrade Bashov, and I'll make you municipal chief of the NKVD. I give you my word as a Communist.'

'No,' I said. 'You were right to note the extraordinary and diabolical resemblance between Dzerzhinsky and Mephistopheles. You must confess this. Nothing will happen to you, because I'll characterize your analogy as the epitome of militant atheism. Yes! You saw Dzerzhinsky as a Red Devil, i.e., an activist in the fight against God. And it wasn't an accident, was it, that you gave the name Red Devils to teenagers of the new type? That being the case, it will be natural and logical to declare the informer Conceptiev a secret enemy of atheism, who does not acknowledge the theomachistic mission of our Leninist Cheka. Come to think of it, there's more of Asmodeus in Lenin's face than Dzerzhinsky's. And another thing—Stalin smokes a pipe. See what I'm driving at?'

In sum, I had Vlachkov thoroughly conned. He put on a sob act and signed my whole ten pages' worth of scribbles. And then, unable to fight down my loathing and hatred, I took his ugly smush in my hand, just as I took yours, Citizen Gurov, and reduced it to its essential aspect.

'Scum!' I shouted. 'Cockroach! Fifth column! Jackal of Trotskyism! *Nouveau riche!* You crap on Stalin at every step! Fascist! To your knees!'

You know all too well, Citizen Gurov, the emotional state of a prisoner whose kisser has fallen into my clutches. Vlachkov experienced the same.

He plopped down at my feet, nestled his cheek against my boot, and just plain wailed—he wasn't weeping, he was wailing: 'Save me, Bashov, save me! It's all yours! I'll give you everything! Save me, and I'll build socialism with the rank and file!'

'You lie, you pile of Zinovievite shit!' I said. 'Kamenevite blister! I've had my eye on you for a long time. You forced your way into the Party for your own personal enrichment! To you, Bukharinite pisspants, Socialism is merely the best way of fleecing the aristocracy, the working class, and the peasantry! You've hit the ultimate in cynicism: smoking a pipe that symbolizes the skulls of Comrades Lenin and Dzerzhinsky simultaneously. Worm! You seem to be hinting that our ideas are smoke. Smoke! Smoke! Confess: where have you stashed the pipe with Comrade Stalin's face? Stand up! I've got salt stains on my boots from your cruddy tears. *Up!*'

Not you, Citizen Gurov. Do sit down.

'Forward, march! To the shooting gallery!'

Vlachkov and I marched to the shooting gallery. Or rather, I marched, and he crawled behind me on all fours, wailing, 'Save me, Comrade Bashov, save me!'

We arrived in the gallery.

'Slimy Rykovite bum,' I said, 'take down the portraits of the Founding Fathers of Marxism-Leninism and stand them against the wall.'

He did it unquestioningly. The will of this huge and still-strong brute, I saw, had completely atrophied. Any instinct to resist was gone. Therefore I calmly handed him his military rifle and cartridges and commanded . . . not a sound escaped the gallery, I should tell you, or reached it from outside . . . and commanded: 'Aim at Marx and Engels, founders of scientific Communism. Fire!'

I looked and saw one little round hole appear in Marx's beard, another on Engels's forehead.

'Aim at the right eye of Lenin, leader of the world proletariat. Fire! Left eye. Fire! Dear and Beloved Comrade Stalin, brilliant successor to Lenin's cause, best friend to the children of enemies of the people. Fire! . . . Stand up!'

Vlachkov stands up.

'Comrade Bashov,' he says suddenly, like a very old man, 'I beg just one favour. Tell me, what . . . what's going on? It's beyond the grasp of the human mind!'

'You'll get your answer,' I said, 'but first sign this interrogation report. I'll fill it in myself, tomorrow. You just sign it, here and here.'

He signed. His hands were shaking. Putrid ratmeat, his hand didn't shake when he aimed at his precious Founding Fathers. Insect. Again I stretched his scalp down on to his forehead and reamed his eyes into their sockets. Then I had him taken to my place, the inner prison. Next morning I spread the rumour around town that Vlachkov had been caught red-handed, smoking tobacco from the skull of Lenin-Dzerzhinsky. He was in his shooting gallery, drunk, firing at all the leaders, training his eye and hand for future assassination attempts.

I did a masterful job drawing up his case. I reported it to Yezhov himself and asked permission to personally shoot this scum who had sneaked into the Regional Committee. He gave me *carte blanche*.

I went to Vlachkov's cell . . . You're not sick of listening . . ? I went in and I said, 'You wanted to know what was going on. It's retribution,' I said. 'Nothing more. I am the Count of Monte Cristo from the village of Odinka, Shilkovsky District. Remember how you and Conceptiev burned it? Remember how you shot unarmed kulaks in the head? Remember how you stacked the corpses in the field for the wolves to gnaw? Remember? I am the son,' I said, 'of Ivan Abramych, who carried a letter to Stalin and received an answer from Conceptiev. Remember? Well, now here's a letter for you. See? Stalin's handwriting. This time it's me passing sentence on you: "Shoot him, as a mad dog who has not rid himself of the giddiness of success. J. Stalin."'

I won't conceal it, Citizen Gurov—I stood in that cell just bursting, I was so high on my revenge. Feeling liberated from anguish and loathing, I stared with delight at this rat, who in his fear had lost all semblance of humanity. Yes, a rat! A rat! A rat! You, too—you're a rat! And so was your daddy! . . . Silence, Gurov, don't get my blood up!

'But that's not all,' I said. 'Besides retribution, there's also a restoration of democracy going on in Russia. The Bolshevik Party has been disbanded. The land has been given back to the peasants. The workers will participate in the distribution of profits. The intelligentsia has been guaranteed artistic freedom. The world awaits the dawn of a Russian renaissance. Stalin has been elected as the country's president and invited to a Big Four conference, where all-out war will be declared on the Red contagion! Are you getting the picture?'

This gibberish, without my realizing it, had inflicted a most terrible blow, which struck at the very fibre of Vlachkov's being. As it happened, we could hear, reaching the cell from the street, the merry cries of propaganda-drunk enthusiasts, whose tables 'always have room for one more' when the 'whole Soviet land awakes with the dawn', and who 'alone in all the world can truly laugh and love'.

'Hear that?' I said. 'The masses are cheering.'

And he believed me! He believed me, Citizen Gurov! He believed me, and that was the most horrible part of this story, this brief little episode in my long and bloody career.

Again he plopped down at my feet. He licked the city mud and puke from the vamps of my kid boots—excellent boots they were—and swore that he had long felt the vicious nature of Bolshevism and of what the Bolshevik leaders, in defiance of the laws of logic, economics, and the evidence of their own eyes, called Socialism. He had long felt this, and he had been horrified, more than once he'd been sick at heart over what was going on—the crumbling of the structure of human relations built up over the centuries, the forcible destruction of all bonds between men and their familial, material, and cultural values. He had been sick at heart, but he had ascribed his horror to a weakness of faith in the historical necessity of what was happening. An extra few thousand lives, suffering and woe beyond calculation—all this was chicken-shit, small change, in comparison with the wad that the Communists stood to win from the bank of history. He believed, you see, believed blindly, and despite 'a number of conclusive doubts' his sonofabitch faith had prevailed over the fearful howls of a reality being hacked up by 'enthusiasts', this dumbfuck reality that spat on the efforts of the 'enthusiasts', that kept trying and trying, with its weakening hands, to stuff back into its ripped-open belly its own spilled innards—the poor heart, the delicate liver, the unhappy guts, the damaged kidneys . . .

'So you must believe me, you must, Comrade—excuse me—Citizen Investigator, when I say that I had a presentiment, a *presentiment* of the event taking place outside the windows of my prison. Save me! I've had experience! I know whom to punish, I'll punish without mercy, and last of all I will punish myself. But before my well-deserved death I will clear at least part of the blame from my soul, which was treacherously deceived by the times.

'Do you suppose I *wanted* to execute hard-working, prosperous peasants?' this scoundrel and sadist asks me. 'Do you suppose I have no regret that my behaviour was not of the best in that episode at . . . excuse me, I forget the name of your village? Save me! Save me! Forgive me! And please, might I ask you two or three questions?'

'Go right ahead, insect,' I said.

'Does this mean that Stalin, all these years, has been implementing a brilliant strategy of his own? Does this mean that he's been undermining, from within, Marx's objectively unsound doctrine, which was developed by Lenin in one isolated country? Does this mean that the sacrifices made by our valiant nobility, intelligentsia, agrarians, generals, officers, and proletariat were not in vain?'

'Their sacrifices were in vain,' I said, shuddering to think that curs like the one lying at my feet held Russia in their grip, the way thugs hold a prison cell.

'Why in vain,' he said in surprise, 'if common sense has finally triumphed over our objectively self-destructive penchant for Bolshevism's harebrained schemes, which even I find organically alien?'

The strangest goddamn thing happened to me at that moment, Citizen Gurov. Believe it or not, my apt and pitiless jest about the Restoration had somehow scrambled my own grey matter. My hypophysis and hypothalamus got crossed. Momentarily out of my senses, I believed that this Russia, suddenly restored and purified of devilment, was the absolute reality—'given to me in sensation', as Party lecturers explain.

'Yes,' I told the snot-streaked and tear-sodden Vlachkov, 'they were all in vain—the sacrifices of the Civil War, the economic disasters, the famines, the dispossession of the kulaks. In vain. They needn't have happened. They needn't have. That's the trouble. They needn't have happened, if a dozen or so leaders, who infected people like you with their fury, who awakened in people like you a social envy and a slumbering lust to kill, who justified all of you and provided you as well with perfect mechanisms for self-justification—if, I repeat, a dozen or so leaders, seduced out of their motherfucking minds by the Idea, had been seized in good time by the healthy forces of society and isolated as murderers and madmen, then *no* vain sacrifices would have been made by the peoples of the Russian Empire. May their souls rest in peace! Rest in peace . . .'

'You're absolutely right! Oh, God, how right you are,' the reptile says. And my soul overflows with peace, a luminous sorrow overflows my forgotten soul, thank the Lord this is all behind me, one more stretch of the Road is paved with corpses but perhaps it's the last, Lord.

'You have brandished your sabres,' I said, 'and plunged your bayonets into people's ribs. You have overfulfilled the norm for the letting of blood—the healthy national blood, accumulated over long hard ages, peasant-red and noble-blue! Enough, Citizen Vlachkov!' I said. 'You've had enough of a grubfest these twenty years! You've scoffed caviar from the czars' china, nibbled at pheasants, toyed with white fish on gold trays. Enough! It's shameful,' I said, 'despicable, to pay for the gurgling of an envious stomach with blood and tears. It's shameful to deck your broads in ermines copped off noblewomen and merchants' wives. It's shameful to travel to the exclusive Lenin Sanatorium in a deluxe private sleeper alone with your gutter-slut. Stinking goat,' I said, 'no more summoning poor little girls to your country villa from the Krupskaya Ballet School you founded. No more of that, swine! All your property, your worthy offspring of the celebrated upstart-intellectual Vlachkov and the horny nihilist Vermina, has been confiscated: the priceless coin collections, the weapons, the free passes to the Central Committee dining-room, the private mansion, the two dachas, the pack of borzois, the jewellery, the motorcycles, the Packard sedan, the racehorse Marlena by Marx out of Engelsina, the Sèvres porcelain, the Persian carpets captured from Uzbek rebels, the platinum dental plates from Jewish bankers, the Patriarch Germagen's Panagia, your Impressionists, your Nonconformists, Princess Beloborodova's necklace, Milyukov's library, Carolus Linnaeus's microscope, Giordano Bruno's telescope, and the yacht *Masha P.* Your personal movie hall has been confiscated, your Guarneri violin, the death masks of Pushkin, Beethoven, and Nikolai Ostrovsky, the lotus seeds, the icons, the spinning wheels, the semi-precious stones from church utensils, the Rembrandt etchings, the candelabras, Count Vorontsov's *écritoire*, the tapestries, the English silver—your every last motherfucking thing, Citizen Gurov, and is this what you learned from Mr. Marx and his humble comrade Lenin?'

Sorry, Citizen Gurov, I'm so shot that I've confused you with Vlachkov, and some of his plundered valuables with yours. Sorry . . .

'But,' he protested, 'it could be said that I preserved all this—well, except the free passes to the Central Committee dining-room—for the people. Whereas mountains of treasures were burned and lost, and mountains of them were sold to foreign countries by Lenin and Stalin—yes, I can assert this! By Stalin! If he is now President of the Democratic Republic of Russia, he too must bear responsibility for participating in this monstrous experiment and concealing from prominent Party officials his strategic plan to restore capitalism. If they try me,' Vlachkov cried, 'then let them try the accursed Stalin too, and Kaganovich, and Molotov, and all, all, all of Budyonny's bandits! I swear, I'll help you uncover all our Party bosses' evil deeds, Citizen Investigator, I will!'

'Don't bother,' I said. 'We'll manage. Our industry is shit, our agriculture's on its last legs, but our security system's the best in the world. We'll manage, we'll sort it out—who's to get their snot wiped, and who's to get their butt poured full of lead and stoppered with a champagne cork and be forced to dance the kazatsky!'

In a kind of blackout, literally, I sketched for Vlachkov the administrative and economic structure of Mother Russia after she emerged from the horrors of the Marxist experiment.

'We will declare to the whole world that it's successfully concluded,' I said. 'That is,' I explained, 'twenty years of experimentation have fully proven that the supposed dictatorship of the proletariat is morally and economically unsound, and also that so-called Socialism regularly destroys the means of production and distorts the development of productive forces. We will declare yet another historical law: when a lawful regime is overturned—not without help from part of the population, led astray by a bunch of fanatics, adventurists, and thugs—there arises in its place a new regime, a Soviet regime, which serves as a mighty tool for the suppression and annihilation of all freedoms and indeed the whole nation, including that damnfool part of it which, being swacko on mule vodka, has handed over its own lawful authority—its imperfect, sometimes assbackward authority, foolish, weak, carefree, skylarking, but nevertheless lawful—to cruel, greedy, lascivious, lazy, Vlachkovite thugs!

'Do you understand,' I said, 'that you and your gang, all the way down to the District Instructor, are prison-camp trusties? Do you understand? Do you understand that you have marched the people out to hard labour, you've been standing over them, goading them, ordering them around, sapping their strength and energy, lashing them with whips when they didn't meet your notions of proper work tempos, stopping their protesting mouths with gingerbread, gags, disgrace, and bullets, distracting your crushed slaves from their own human and social interests by means of horror stories about saboteurs, Trotskyites, engineers, the military, Chamberlains, and the cloudless sky of Spain? Do you understand?'

'I do,' he says, 'and I welcome it.'

'Welcome what?'

'The Democratic Republic of Russia, headed by the great Stalin.'

'Stalin is now president,' I said, 'and therefore cannot be great. In due time, he too will take responsibility for having abused his official position.'

'That's right,' says Vlachkov, reviving and turning cocky. 'That's the democratic way! Everyone must take responsibility! I vote with both hands! But if you'll excuse my asking, what are we to do now with Comrades Marx and Engels? And with Lenin, after all?'

At this point, Citizen Gurov, I broke into crazy laughter, I laughed till I choked. I must have been releasing deep-rooted stresses, as they say now, and like an idiot I came within an ace of destroying myself. I forgot all caution—got fat and sloppy, in other words. Gaily laughing and stuttering, I began feeding Vlachkov a fantastic line of bullshit. Marx's portraits would show him with bare chin and shaven head, like a zek. Engels would have an All-Russian Society of False Scholars named after him. And a tentative decision had been made to move Lenin's body to Highgate Cemetery, next to Marx. This was being negotiated with the Mayor of London.

Vlachkov was smirking and tee-heeing too. 'But,' he says, 'what will we do with the mausoleum?'

'The mausoleum,' I answered, 'is now called Frozen Music No. 1. The Jazz Comedy boys are going to rehearse there—'

Just then my colleague Kruminysh bursts into the cell. He used to steal his case scenarios from Shakespeare. What does he see but an investigator and a death-row prisoner laughing their heads off. He gives us a suspicious stare and says what kind of a bacchanal is this, and had I by any chance gone bananas from overwork?

'No,' I said, instantly snapping out of it. 'Everything's under control. I merely resorted to a bit of psychological torture.'

'Finish him off quick,' Kruminysh grumbled. 'There's a royal table set. Everyone's waiting for you. What the hell are you doing?'

'Royal table? Royal table? How do you mean, royal table?' Vlachkov babbled, turning pale and backing away from me into the corner. He contracted with horror, and it was scary to watch that hulking body, before my very eyes, shrivel to nothingness as if it wanted to become a point rushing about in space, beyond range of a bullet. He shrank into the corner, that was as far as he could go. I marched on him, drawing my pistol and seating the cartridge in the chamber—this is it, pig, the last thing you'll hear in your vicious life: the clack of steel, the ring of my metal heeltaps on dead concrete.

'How do you mean, royal table? How do you mean, royal table?'

Vlachkov scuttled away from me into the latrine. Stinking swill sloshed over the edge . . . 'How do you mean, royal table?'

'Here's how I mean,' I said. 'The czar we shot in Ekaterinburg was a stand-in, with a stand-in family. The true Czar has been working in the Kremlin boiler room. But today he's riding into our city on a white horse. So the man in the street, having forgotten "God Save the Czar!" is yelling "We conquer space and time." For you, however, it's the end of both—you murdering, thieving cuntface.'

And that was when Vlachkov—calmly and with immense melancholy, sensing the inevitability of his expulsion from existence and therefore hurrying hysterically—once more asked me the question that I was later to hear over and over again, wrenched from lips loathsome and supremely pure, soulless and divine, resolute and pale with terror: 'But what . . . what's going on? It's beyond the grasp of the human mind!'

'My father Ivan Abramych,' I said into Vlachkov's ear, almost puking from the stench but afraid that someone would overhear, 'my beloved father Ivan Abramych couldn't grasp what was going on either. Drunk with the lust to kill, you cracked a grin and took aim at his forehead. You did! Now remember my father and his friends as they stood before you and Conceptiev and your whole gang. Remember, bastard. I give you one second, no, five seconds to live, but just to remember this! Think . . ! Remember . . ? Poppa died like a man and came before God pure. Whereas you—picture your blood a second from now, mixing with the shit and urine. But if you are fated to see, in that next world, souls yet unborn, tell them a word or two from me, about how they must behave on Earth, how solicitous they must be with their own life and others'. And warn them, earnestly warn the yet unborn souls, that never in their future life are they ever to sing that diabolical ditty The Internationale.'

I babbled something more, I don't remember exactly what, and suddenly came to my senses: I was babbling to a corpse. Damnation. I had fired a bullet into Vlachkov's mouth, apparently, somewhere between the words 'Remember?' and 'Poppa died . . .'

Do you know who put the brakes on your assignment to the States, about six years ago? I did. I repeat, modestly and quietly:

I did. If it weren't for me, of course, you'd have succeeded in carrying with you, or sending out with your son-in-law's foreign guests, Princess Beloborodova's necklace, let's say. Then you could've taken a powder and spent the rest of your days in Holland. Was that roughly the way you saw your future shaping up? Not to mention the twenty-eight-year-old Dutch girl, rosy and white as my Grandma Anfisa's buttermilk. You'd have spattered your filthy sperm on her and brought five little brats into the world with your putrid genes, which are totally superfluous and unneeded by the glorious Dutch nation.

The Mediterranean cruise, too—I was the one who kept you from going on that. And yes, you guessed it! The gala opening of the meat-packing plant in India—I couldn't possibly allow you that either. I shepherded you, my silly little calf, I watched you graze, and the only reason I didn't arrest you was that I hadn't attained the inner maturity for a last conversation with you. But more than once I broke out in a cold sweat at the thought that suddenly, through some strange means, because of some Soviet fuck-up or oversight—chance, ultimately—you would succeed in hightailing it over the border of your burgled fatherland. Next morning I'd be informed of this news, and my mouth would fall open in stupid amazement. I'd sit there like a total jerk, twitching my jaw muscles and furiously considering how best to trick you back . . . Hideous.

But you realize, don't you, that it's fully within my power to transport us both, with our pretty rocks, across Turkey to that same Holland. Let's sit back and have a cup of coffee, a nibble of toast. Pass me the cheese sticks. The cream, please. And a slice of sausage, if you would . . .

So, we're already there. Sitting in a café, our souls at peace—impossible to imagine a more comfortable path to our still-distant death. And the amiable Dutch don't even suspect what sort we are, these little old men, these characters out of Russian history, who have extricated themselves successfully from its bloody, leaden stream and are now drinking coffee before their very eyes. One of the men, his lubricious gaze following the taut young bottoms that are straining to break out of their jeans to freedom, asks the other man, whose huge paw, like a warm nest, tenderly shelters his little white cup of

Turkish coffee lest it get cold, God forbid—asks him, with the rumbling purr of carefree old age, the happiest of all possible conditions under the sun, 'Shall we play a little game of chess or checkers, Citizen Investigator?'

And this second man, who attracts the attention of passing Dutchmen by his bored, horsey face and lack-lustre eyes, answers quietly and sadly, which doesn't fit with his appearance at all and therefore amazes the very kindly waiter—this second man answers, bitterly and pensively, 'No, never. For the Czar and Czaritza will never sail their wooden galley back across the Lethe to Ekaterinburg, the wooden galley will never tie up at the wall, that very wall, where Time has not effaced the childish writing, "Papa + Mama = Love", the Czar and Czaritza will never, letting the princesses and prince pass ahead of them, walk back through the wall of death to a live existence, the little Czarevitch Alexei will never, at the breach in the wall, cast out the bullet that flew into his heart, the good Czar will never stoop to pick it up or say to him, "We're waiting for you, Alexei!"'

See here, swine!!! Did I or did I not ask you to pass me a slice of sausage? Bastard, yes or no? Then why the fuck are you sitting there stuffing your face and not passing me the sausage? Just trying to be rude . . ? I most assuredly am not playing psycho! I don't care to put up with rude table manners, you purulent prick! I see you're studying how to drive me berserk, little by little. It won't work! I'm sitting here as decorous and noble as if I'm in a London club, having a peaceful conversation with him about something, reminiscing, I ask him to pass me the sausage, and well, you see, at that moment he's too damn far from the sausage! Why, the bastard! Too far from the sausage! Just which sausage, Citizen Gurov, were you too far from? The mortadella, the bologna, the tongue, the salami, the cervelat, the Moscow, or the egg liverwurst? Answer me, fuckface, or I'll . . . Take that, you rat . . . you rat . . . you rat . . . I'll grind you up, I literally will, you sack stuffed with slimy tricks, lies, pus, diamonds, my green snot, The Internationale, your own mother, other people's woe, emeralds, medals, your own father, shit, a Party membership card, treachery, sack stuffed with my balls! Take that! Here's some cream in your kisser—wake up, dead dog! Stuffed sack! You're a sausage yourself! Yes! Yes! Yes! You're not a rat, you're a sausage! Sausage! Sausage! I'll grind you up, you blob of spit on the Turkoman carpet! *Sau-au-sage!* . . . Poxov! A doctor, quick! Hurry! And a glass of valerian for me. Clean up the broken dishes, and get that goddamned food out of here! I'm not hungry!

You marched out of Odinka in formation, singing. At twelve years of age you had looked your fill upon the death of your enemies, drunk your fill of their spilled blood, steeled your little hearts with the sight of other men's suffering. Your fathers had bestowed on their little whelps an opportunity to unleash and exercise the instinct for cruelty, which is alive in nearly everyone. You marched away, stinking greasetails, with banners on your bayonets, as it said in your song, while your scurvy fathers threw us into a sleigh, and our own little orphaned horses jogged off to the children's home . . . The children's home . . . That's a memory that makes the dank sensation of permafrost in my crotch even worse.

Don't interrupt me, though. And stop making idiotic declarations about how you were never a party to the despotic acts of degenerates, and pure ideas get distorted by maniacs. *Deuce-ace!* I've heard that one before: the idea was good, but the execution sucked . . . The idea *must* have carried in its genes all the revolting stuff that spilled out later, all of what you're trying to call 'degenerative phenomena', all the effects whose blood relationship to the causes that engendered them you resolutely deny . . . The execution sucked! 'Execution.' What a word you've found! In our lingo, Chekist lingo, execution is capital punishment! If that isn't Asmodeus himself speaking through your lips, Citizen Gurov, it's one of his propaganda phraseologists. 'Execution!' Oh, yes, Satan's idea was good. Just dandy! Never since the creation of the world has the Devil had a better idea than Communism. Never, the ringtail sonofabitch! But he muffed the execution, he really did, right here in Russia, even despite the fact that the Demons took power into their own hands.

The Devil must have had a moment when it seemed to him that the 'execution' was proceeding as expected. The Soul of the Individual and the Soul of the People were just about to shudder and go numb, forever and amen. The executioners seemed to have severed all the roots that linked Souls with true Existence. Familial roots—by pitting Brother against Brother, Father against Son, Son against Father. Spiritual roots—by destroying the Temple where the soul communed with the sense of Infinity and by committing outrages against the Temple's votaries. Cultural roots—by puking all over the heritage, the traditions, the House that had taken centuries to build, and at the same time declaring that the mission of art was to serve the people.

For one instant only, Satan rejoiced, and all of a sudden felt blue, for he's not such a cretin that he can't sense the ultimate futility of his own efforts, and the Creator's invincibility on Earth and in man. Even in the Soviet masses, these men of the new type, so completely crushed and sundered from all freedoms, Satan senses an obscure resistance to his snares and delusions. First one individual, then two, then three, a hundred, five thousand purify and liberate themselves. It horrifies and depresses Asmodeus that these Souls still exist, that they have held out all these years, often in the face of death, but untouched by hell's pollutions. And the severed familial, spiritual, and cultural roots put forth new shoots, sometimes in utter darkness, sticking out in all different directions like the pale little sprouts on potatoes underground. When they do emerge from underground into the light of day, they grow and gather strength. The question of social roots is trickier, Citizen Gurov. We'll discuss them separately . . .

But what do we observe, if we make a cursory inspection of the globe through the Devil's eyes? Much has been done, and is still being done, in this one-sixth of the planet. Though not so fast as he would like, Soviet Fascism is metastasizing successfully. The terrorizing thugs are still on their binge.

Civilization, which Satan has been nurturing for several dozen centuries now, always knocking it off the straight and narrow, the bastard, just as he does to his beloved handmaiden science, has at last begun to bear fruit for him. Darkened skies. Rivers puking shit and Moloch's undigested grub into the seas and oceans. An all-out undeclared war being waged on man by things, which occupy the Time and Space of his existence. Hundreds of millions of human souls already taken captive. The swirling, howling, eerie white blizzard of drug addiction . . . And Satan keeps perfecting weapons of mass destruction to use on Souls. 'Just you wait, fuckheads,' he must be thinking, this Supreme Con of all times and peoples, 'I'll exterminate your Souls, every last one of them. And I'll be goddamned if I expect any trouble with your Bodies. I've got everything ready for the "last decisive battle"—the annihilation of life on Earth. Human life first, then animal, bird, plant, fish, amoeba, and so on down! You can sit me on a shishkebab if I ease up before I squash the last virus on your wretched planet!'

But all the same, Citizen Gurov, nothing will come of it, *for Satan thirsts to destroy All, but the Creator wants to save Each.*

Don't bug your lamps at me. I haven't lost my marbles, but the ideas I've been putting out in this chaotic fashion are not my own. I recently had occasion to interrogate a certain dissident. A young man. Russian Orthodox. He'd quit the physics and maths department of the university. His religion had made him agitated about human rights.

He was interesting to talk to, that young man. The serpent—it was as though he'd read my own thoughts and observations. I warned him I'd put him away if he didn't cease his anti-Soviet activity.

'You can take your threats and shove them,' he said.

We parted friends. I barely restrained myself from shaking his hand.

He had a pure and steadfast Soul. Far cry from yours and mine . . . Don't forget my little question: do you actually have a soul, or don't you . . ?

I've been expecting this, expecting you'd ask me the same question some day . . . The answer is, I don't know. Think what you like. But we'll get sorted out at the Last Judgement. That's no transit camp; as the cons say, it's one place where a scab can never pass for a true thief . . . I'm an executioner. I'm a monster. I'm a flunky for a regime that I curse. I'm shit! Ivan Abramych, Father, forgive me!

Yes! I'm shit . . . not the Count of Monte Cristo, Citizen Gurov. Do you know where I happened to get my hands on that great book?

You guessed right—it was simple. Yes. At a home for boys—sons of kulaks and enemies of the people . . . The Anti-Fascism. I'm not joking, that's exactly what it was called. The 'Anti-Fascism Children's Home'. A filthy menagerie by day, despicable terrarium by night . . . Po-o-xov! Where the hell have you gone? Another cognac . . ! A menagerie . . . A terrarium . . . Poxov, where are you . . ? The Anti-Fascism!

It had everything. 'Tea for breakfast, songs for lunch, at night a jolly meeting . . .' They beat us more often than they fed us. The perverted 're-educators' supposed that bodily pain and constant humiliation (they hadn't forgotten the soul, either) were the only way to achieve full contact between these degenerates, these unaccountable survivors, and the world's first Soviet reality, where 'we alone in all the world can truly laugh and love'. But the Anti-Fascism Children's Home also had a corps of activists, made up of kids who had caught on to the fact that it was better to beat than be beaten. They walloped us too, on their own behalf and on behalf of the re-educators, walloped us for everything: the wrong gesture, the wrong smile, the wrong amount of zeal or work or appetite, the wrong moods, the wrong thoughts, the wrong past—on and on. If there was no pretext they made one up, fabricated it, and forced us to confess. When we did crack, of course, the lock-up seemed like paradise compared to the interrogation.

Mornings they lined us up in front of the portraits of Lenin and Stalin. Calisthenics, then one or two of Lenin's favourite songs, then the firewood, then a half-bowl of slum, clean-up, and political ed. Weak, broken, but wiser now, the little wild beasts wrote denunciations in class. A denunciation was considered a faint sign of moral rebirth in an enemy bastard. It got him a handout of white bread. You should have seen them, Citizen Gurov: the well-bred sons of engineers, doctors, left-wing deviationists, noblemen, clergymen, former landowners, manufacturers, men of letters, when they couldn't take any more hunger, brute violence, and humiliation, turned into little wolves . . . Not all of them, of course. Far from all. Many still had a glimmer of a soul in them and resisted collapse—some meekly, others furiously . . . Escapes, the noose, ground glass, self-mutilation, vinegar essence, scalded hands, hunger strikes, the Anti-Fascism Children's Home had it all. As did the prison camps later, though even worse . . . I think I'm getting smashed. Enough for today . . .

By night, a despicable terrarium . . . The activists ran through the dormitory with hard-ons. They wanted affection. In return for a sweet, for a chunk of lard, for bread—or for nothing, out of the fear that clutched at their throats—the poor, pale, bald little boys with dark circles under their eyes would expose their hapless bottoms to the young goats . . . Some later became perverts, some submitted, some hanged themselves, some wept quietly . . . Poxov! Poxov! I'll have . . . the teardrop of a child, shall we say . . . As you were! Sorry . . . I'll have . . . Karl Engels, Vladimir Stalin . . . Gorky Krr-rupskaya! Bring them here, I say! . . . They saw it, they saw it all . . . from their portraits . . . The mirror of the Russian Revolution, Tolstoy, he hung there too . . . Haul them in here, Poxov. *Forthwith!* I'll shove their . . . Perovskaya, haul her in . . . Zhelyabov too . . . I'll shove their noses in it . . . shove them, shove them all, shove their big old beards, moustaches, spectacles, wise brows, ugly smushes, shove them in the hapless bottoms of little boys . . . first semen of young goats . . . a teardrop, goddamn it . . . Enough . . . enough. Thank you, Citizen Gurov . . . This'll be my last glass . . .

I had a big bozo come butting in on me once, too. Bastard, he wrote verse in imitation of Mayakovsky. I grabbed him by the prick with this hand of mine, led him straight out of the dormitory, and clobbered him on the conk with my huge fist. I used to slaughter sheep that way in the village. I was strong for my age. He went down like a ton of bricks and lay there till morning. Luckily for me, I had bashed the memory out of him. The dirtbag forgot everything he knew, even 'The-darkling-storm-doth-hide-the-sky', The Internationale, the 'Daily and Nightly Routine for the Children's Home', and who wrote *Leftism: A Childhood Disease*.

Come, let's . . . go for a walk . . . a swim . . . right now . . .

and enjoy a happy moment . . . on your beach. Poxov! We're going for a swim; take measures. And no excesses, Citizen Gurov, no attempts to break for Turkey or anyplace. Hands behind your back! Prison discipline . . . Off to exercise! No talking! . . . Smoke? Don't you dare, cockroach. You can smoke with Trotsky at line-up! 'Arise, all ye that slave and hunger . . .' *Sing!*

Where's my briefcase? Oh, here it is. Read the statement you gave to the Party Committee at your Institute, Citizen Gurov, repudiating your father. Go ahead—I'm all sobered up, read it . . . Is your memory coming to life? Is your adenoidal infant conscience babbling goo-goo? You destroyed your daddy, you know, with this impassioned letter. How beautifully preserved it is! Not one maggot, not a whiff of odour, no cadaverous blotches, no decomposition, and the vein-blue squiggles of your penmanship are pulsing yet, pulsing with—smell it?—the inky, shitty blood of patricide.

At the time, you thought your daddy's fate was sealed. You saw the palatial Party apartments in your building emptying out, and the ranks of your classmates at Institute lectures growing correspondingly thinner: your comrades and their families were being swept up by Señor Arrestim Yezhov's purge. They had started it, under the Czar, and here was their own monstrous villainy coming back on them, a crooked sneer on its thuggish puss . . . And now you really hit the jackpot: saved yourself and cemented your career. Not, let us remark, without the aid of chance.

Yes . . . chance . . . chance, sweet chance . . ! I'm thinking there's not a thing in the whole wide world more bewitching and wonderful! Or perhaps it's not a thing at all, it's . . . a creature. Not carnal, not spiritual, but still, a creature! A creature so tiny that we can't begin to know the time when it will arrive or the point where it will touch down on the little green glade of Fate.

You, Citizen Gurov, are a scab. You didn't know for sure whether your daddy would be arrested or left untouched; his position, at the time, was more solid than most. But just in case, so to speak, you decided to take no chances, and besides, you sensed your father's panic. So you whipped off this little letter. You had things figured right, actually. After his arrest, a disavowal of your father wouldn't be worth diddlysquat. But before his arrest, this whorish trick would bring a high price. Very high indeed . . . So, when your mummy made a bitter joke of assembling a basket of underwear, tobacco, sausage, and bread for your daddy—many others were doing the same—you understood. The time had come!

It was charming the way you played right into my hands in your haste. Despite the stack of denunciations and ready-made case scenarios that I had concocted in the dead of night, I was having trouble undermining Conceptiev. Real trouble. Your daddy was firmly ensconsed in the Party easy chair. His belly was full to bursting with past accomplishments and snugly girded with an antique Georgian belt, a little gift from Stalin. Central Committee member, head of various societies, a father of the New Serfdom. Demagogue. Dogmatist. A leery old bobcat, cynical and mean.

My belated thanks, Citizen Gurov, dear sonny-boy of the new type! I thank you.

Events developed as follows, I believe. Daddy and Mummy, to divert themselves from their worries, took off to go hunting at the New Wildlife Preserve. Hounded by fear for your own skin, you gave us a buzz at headquarters. The leftwing deviationist scum have gathered at their hideout, you said. Heads up, comrades! The call was anonymous. Afterwards, you came forward at a general Party meeting and read out your vile repudiation. You emphasized, Citizen Gurov, that you were doing this at a time when the secret enemy was still at large.

'Pavlik Morozov lives, dear comrades! And he has grown up. He's a grown man, he's more vigilant than ever, he is armed with a doctrine before which no man hostile to Socialism, no matter who he may be, can ever stand his ground! Pavlik's name is—the Young Communist League!'

With nary a trace of bashfulness, you struck up The Internationale. You were adopted on the spot by a woman of forty-five, the stoolie and sadist Brutnikova, and now at last I've got my hands on a man who murdered his own father and mother. I thank you!

Well, how's your mood? Confident, or nauseated? Melancholy? Serene? Has anything stirred within your soul?

You don't care to talk about this? Well, fuck it. Let's eat. We'll get back to your daddy another time. After lunch we'll take up your mama . . . Tomorrow at twenty hundred hours you will place a call to Madame Gurova in Paris. Your daughter and her husband are there too? Good for them! You all know how to party. The Côte d'Azur. A plastic surgery clinic in Bordeaux. I could take your wife and pull tight the wrinkles on her fat smush with this hand of mine, faster and better than the charlatans over there . . . Poxov will give you some kind of script for the conversation . . . Did you have a fleeting notion to yell something into the receiver? No? I don't believe you. Don't try to raise a ruckus. It will do no good . . . Let your folks enjoy their peaceful, shameless respite from our Soviet paradise, in the capitalist hell. Their visas will be extended. The cultural exchange with France can only gain by this, and you and I will keep busy here a while longer. We'll watch the news programme 'Time', observe as the nation dashes towards its sixtieth anniversary. When's your birthday? It's over already? Too bad. Mine falls right smack on November seventh. We'll definitely celebrate. My treat . . .

Remember how you gave the order, before you left Odinka, to slaughter all our cats and dogs? Yes, yes, you personally! It was you, after all, who had command of the devils. Of course you gave the order. I certainly didn't, Bukharin didn't. First-class marskmen! Bang, bang! Bang! Me-ow-ow . . . Bow-wow-wow . . ! Ah. You don't remember that either, and for the first time in our whole conversation you summon witnesses to your defence. Kitty, kitty, kitty! A nice cat. But I don't care for Siamese. Trilby! Here, Trilby! I don't care for these either. I like moth-eaten old Toms and Tabbies, eternally yapping Bowsers, Chiefs, Rovers, and Blackies . . . You slaughtered them, slaughtered them all . . . Are you suggesting that this may have been done purely for 'humanitarian' reasons? Better death than homelessness, in your opinion, for a domestic animal? I see . . .

After that little letter and the Party meeting, I had no qualms about nailing your daddy. I paid him back for everything, in full. Or so I thought, at any rate. I didn't take your mama. She was a splendid, unhappy, faithful woman, innocent of her husband's crimes and dealings. She didn't disavow him, she brought him parcels, wrote letters to Stalin, and aged twenty years overnight because of your treachery, Citizen Gurov. I didn't touch her, but your daddy thought his wife was a whore. He heard drunken cries from scenes that I arranged at the Chekist bordellos. He received letters with curses and monstrous revelations, cooked up by my scribes, allegedly from his spouse: 'You never satisfied me, but for the Party's sake I let you nurse the illusion you were terrific. You're a lousy jerk! But your Investigator is a romanticist of our organs and feelings . . .'

Crude, of course. Stupid and untalented. But after all, I too was a punk kid of twenty, trembling and raving because of the Count of Monte Cristo complex grinding in my soul. I didn't care what I did to get your daddy. The main thing was—get him! And I went for him. The way I got him . . . But that's a subject for another day . . .

At night she'd be pacing under the windows at Headquarters, waiting for me. She would throw herself at my feet and beg me to let her share in her husband's fate, help him build Socialism under any circumstances, even penal servitude, for it wasn't the circumstances that mattered but practical conformity with our ideals . . . The Count of Monte Cristo of the NKVD did not succeed in saving your mother from exile. No. But from execution, yes. At an opportune moment, I thrust on the attention of a certain big gun a masterpiece by my flimflam artists: a dreadful, thoroughly despicable denunciation purporting to be from the ex-wife of Enemy of the People Conceptiev. That did the trick. Karaganda. Disease. Hunger. Hopelessness. In those years, by the way, this emotion blanketed the sky over our one-sixth of the planet like a cloud of locusts. Polar expeditions pushed through the locusts to the Pole, aeroplanes pushed through them to America, and that fucking fool

America, gaping in magnanimous delight, welcomed them with open arms and expressed a gentlemanly envy of this mysterious land, which hadn't had time to comb the lice out of its unruly forelocks or shed its bark sandals but was already conquering time and space by means of the 'engine of flame' that Stalin had installed in place of its heart.

Neither the World, nor young enthusiasts like you, nor the average man perennially left at large, nor Romain Gorky, nor Rolland Tolstoy, nor Bernard Shawlokhov noticed that these planes, spattered with the locust flesh of anguish, were flying on blood. Or that their wings were smeared silver with grey matter, which our glorious Chekists had obtained from the smashed skulls of innocent victims of Terror Edmundich Yezhov. I repeat: of innocent victims. I don't put your daddy in that class, Citizen Gurov. He and his kind got back from their pupils everything that they themselves had embedded in the codes of conduct and morality.

One-sixth of the planet was like a prison cell then, like the grounds of a prison camp, like the barracks where Stalin's scabs were desperately hacking up Lenin's thugs . . . Enough. We'll get back to Terror Ilyich another time . . .

Your chat with your wife will go roughly like this: 'Everything's the same as usual. I'm fine, although the humidity is getting me down some. Been reading a lot. Met an interesting fellow. We often get together and talk, and we've become friends. Our paths have crossed occasionally in the past, and at one time we even used to see each other. That was some years ago. When you all get home I'll introduce you to him . . . Bring back a nice vintage liqueur . . . How's Paris . . ? No, I'm not bored. I'm not sleeping too well. Dreaming about my father and mother. Bad dreams, like a child's . . . Talk to their sorcerers over there: why do people dream about their parents . . ? Seems I betrayed my father, and starved my mother to death . . . Hideous! . . . I can't help telling you— Damn the francs! Get this far in life, and I can't talk a couple of minutes overtime to Paris? Well. So I'm lying in a bathtub of champagne. It has rose petals floating in it. There's something erotic going on with an invisible nymph. And Mother is led past—by Forces of some sort, not men, not an armed guard, just Forces. She can't walk on her own. She's clinging to someone's incorporeal arms. Because of this, her gait seems infinitely heavy, and at the same time quite airy.

'"Vasya, my darling, make me a little sandwich," my mother begs. "I'm dying, Vasya, I'm slipping away!"

'And would you believe it, Elya, my arms are numb, really numb, from the champagne fizz, and besides, that slut of a nymph is in my way. That's the end . . . And my dreams about Father have been so horrible I'm popping Valium. Well, enough of this. Regards from my friend. A kiss from me. See you soon . . . Oh, yes, I forgot to mention! I keep dreaming a silly phrase, too: "What did the grandfather say to the grandmother in an intimate moment?" I strain every nerve to catch the answer, but I can't, and I wake up in a panic . . . Oh, don't worry. Stress during our sleep is extremely useful. It's as if our psyche's rehearsing for our next encounter with the delirium of existence—working out, building up strength. If it didn't, we'd go crazy at every turn! Lots of love!'

Are you clear on your phone conversation, Citizen Gurov? Hey! Don't you dare kick off, animal! You don't get to die this easy, not after your foul life! Poxov! The CPR team! No more dominoes and banging the nurses! Quick! Holy shit, his eyes are rolled up to the chandelier. Everybody! Or I'll wring your necks with this hand of mine! Gurov! Scum! What have I done to deserve such a punishment . . . to touch . . . my lips to your . . . icky mouth, you lily-livered toad, and breathe the breath of my own life . . . into the garbage pit of your guts . . . Whore! Breathe, or I'll put a bullet through my head! . . . *Poxov!*

You're wrong in thinking I was frightened yesterday. Not in the least, Citizen Gurov. That wasn't a heart attack; you had a strange fainting spell. A blackout. You, too, have things you can't endure, it turns out. I wasn't really frightened. If you croaked, you croaked—and so what if you never saw, out of the corner of your eye, the vindictive grin on Monte Cristo's flytrap . . . Tell me, instead, how are *you* feeling? Glad to be back in this world? Don't lie. I don't believe you . . . You're not really depressed. You're happy. You're sipping little gulps from each passing instant, and if I weren't looking you'd be glad to make them last a little longer. Have I guessed right? . . . Aha! Thank you for the confession.

I didn't sleep worth a damn last night. You know how I occupied myself . . ? I kept going through your pretty rocks, sifting them from one hand into the other. I lit the candles and pulled the candelabra close, the gleam of crystal washed my eyes clean, and I didn't even recognize them, looking at myself in the mirror. An amazing mirror, I must say. Obviously from the time of the French Revolution, no less . . . I slipped the rings on my fingers, adorned my sports shirt with the sapphire brooch. *Voilà!* A Count . . . I padded peacefully around on your carpets and felt only love, the purest of love, for these beautiful baubles, which were none the worse for having been sullied by involvement in a certain scurrilous, bloody affair with a shit like you.

But one pair of pearls I recognized, a pink and a black. Think of it—I recognized them! But I have absolutely no interest in the question of how they came to you from Vlachkov's trunk. We won't get into that . . .

We had been talking about your dear mother, I believe. Can you imagine the emotional hell she lived in till she died of starvation? Where's my briefcase? Oh, here it is. And here are two more letters from you. Two in seven years! You ask her not to write to you, inasmuch as you're working at a top-secret facility . . . The top-secret facility was actually a meat-packing plant. You were chief engineer. It was the start of your business career. Inventing additives for frankfurter and sausage stuffings. Choosing cadres to convert black-market goods and surplus products to cash. You correctly understood Stalin's motto, 'The cadres decide all.' The cadres are mafiosi. And you chose better than Stalin. In three decades, no one ever fingered you or sold you out, not even once . . . But you couldn't write to your dear mother about all that.

You were never at the front, either. During the war, since you'd paid for a draft-exemption card—Oh, don't throw a fit. Dr. Klonsky, who fixed you up with it for fifty big ones and a couple of Victrolas, is still alive. Here's the diary that he kept on the q.t. all those years, out of old intelligentsia habit. Read the revulsion with which he describes your visit and his consent to the transaction . . .

Anyway. All you had to do was make one phone call—to some crook in Karaganda, who was buying up precious baubles dirt cheap, on your orders, from evacuated aristocrats and heirs of Bolshevik profiteers—and your mummy would have been saved from disease and starvation. You starved your mother to death because you feared your kinship with her, which by now you had fucking buried without a trace. You feared the verdict of your mother's conscience, and other implications of her return from exile. Her papers—a whole packet of replies from the offices of Kalinin, Stalin, and Molotov, and the three letters from you—remained at the neighbours' apartment for many years. God rest her soul . . . She wasn't the only one writing letters and pardon appeals to her executioner. One highly placed thug assured me that in the regional capitals they baled those letters and loaded them into freight cars. Then they made up a special train. The train pulls into, let's say, Kazan Station. Kalinin meets it. Waves his hand. Hobbles along the platform with his cane. Then he takes a stick of chalk from his pocket and writes on the red plank walls of the boxcars, which are stuffed to the ceiling with howls, complaints, and tearful pleas, 'Denied . . . Denied . . . Denied . . .' The train goes rumbling back. And Kalinin hobbles along over to the Kremlin to dine with Stalin. Deaf-mute goat!

Now that you won't be having any more birthdays, Citizen Gurov, and your thoughts revert to your youth, do you feel your iniquity? Or do you think of it as the iniquity of that other man, the young Conceptiev-Gurov, savagely greedy for life and already used to the smell of the blood of strangers and family?

By the way, I am prepared to pay, and generously, for a sincere answer. Name your price . . . I must guarantee the safety and social well-being of your daughter? Have I understood you correctly? Don't you give a damn about your son-in-law? But that's none of my business . . . It's a deal. An executioner's word of honour is your best guarantee . . . You want three days' rest thrown in, to meditate and sort out your memories? Haggling, yet! Agreed. Go ahead and meditate. Goat!

How strange, Citizen Gurov, that you missed me over these three days.

I, too, had a bit of a rest. Did some swimming. Pottered in your garden. Took a better look at your possessions. After all, they're mine now. I'm fabulously rich. But what am I to do with these treasures? Play Monte Cristo? Hunt up the relatives of the poor sad wives and poor sad old men and women who bartered them at the wartime bazaars for your lard, sausage, lungs, heart, liver, and white margarine, Citizen Gurov? Hunt them up, magnanimously return the heirloom trinkets, and leave a note in the communal bathroom on the sly, saying that justice has triumphed? Shit! There's not a thing I can do with your—sorry—my treasures.

Kitty, kitty, kitty . . ! Hey, look at where old Siam-face curled up! I'm going to take my ever-loving Walther and plant a pea right between your eyes! Quit twisting your head, repulsive animal! Crowbait, how can I aim! Calm down, Citizen Gurov. The least little scare, and next thing I know you're dashing in front of the gun like Alexander Matrosov. Maybe you yourself would like to have a bullet through the head—be done with me, and your pointless life too? Then sit down and suck in your guts.

You'd do better to tell me about your moral development. Our agreement remains in force. Your daughter won't be bothered. She'll keep on as she has been, broadcasting to seething Latin America on issues in Communist education—for as long as the Latin countries will listen, of course, to this shitty lie about the very pure moral atmosphere of life in Soviet society. On top of everything else, it turns out your daughter's been stooling for us ever since school. A rat. A true rat. Your flesh, your teeth, your dead greyness of soul. She stools, the dirty whore . . . Silence! I repeat: *dirty whore*. She digs up traitors as fast as Stakhanov dug coal. She fingers anyone who tells a joke or spreads gossip or buys threads on the black market. And her colleagues will never raise a stink about the scrimey pig, because in our country the functioning of stoolies has now been integrated to perfection.

Once in a while we disavow lowlifes and curs, or perfectly decent folks, and it kills two birds with one stone. The lowlifes stay within bounds, unless they're on a slide into the shitpile.

But decent folks, when they discover that people think they're stoolies, get nervous. They moderate their liberal inclinations. In the end, some cease to trust themselves and really do begin to stool, in a small way. Others become highly nervous, highly neurotic, highly incautious, and do silly things purely to avoid being thought stoolies. They sign protest letters, disseminate samizdat, relay news from the foreign radio stations—and we've got them right under our thumb.

Anyway, your daughter will have no trouble . . . Rat! Dirty whore! And she's regarded as a liberal, yet! Not so long ago, to protect her cover, we kept the little bitch from going to France; we knocked her material for being insufficiently militant, and as a better smokescreen demoted her temporarily from Latin America to Australia, to fabricate articles on the moral make-up of Soviet youth, builders of Communism. That's what's going on . . . So. Tell me your story. I'm listening . . .

How simple it all seems, looking back! Cold calculation, born of a hysterical fear for your own skin. At such moments you perceived neither your father nor your mother as blood relatives. Blood relatives—hah! You didn't perceive them as people at all, individuals to whom both their bread and butter and the air of freedom were precious and biologically necessary. Such is the triumph of the absolute principles of Communist education, dreamed up by Satan and brought to realization by homunculi like you, Citizen Gurov.

Not all children, thank God, betrayed their parents, neighbours, friends, and close relatives. Not all. I realize that you were merely one among many. But still—you hold the record. Nailing both mummy and daddy! You must agree: even in a Eulenspiegelish era, that was counted a world record for villainy. Even the basest of souls wouldn't venture to challenge it . . .

So: fear, calculation, and the loathsome act itself, after which there was no turning back. Then the survival-adaptive mechanism by which the impulses of anxiety, pain, regret, compassion, and empathy for your father's and mother's situations were crowded out of your psyche. Oh, and time.

Time, which erases from memory both deeds and faces and the twitch of a dying man's feet in his last convulsions of shame . . . Yes—looking back, it all seems so simple.

Would you care to know to what chance event, exactly, you owe your perverse good luck in saving yourself, living long enough to turn grey, and becoming a millionaire? While I was hung up on your daddy, while they were shipping me first one place and then another to trap enemies of the people, I never got around to you. And when I did—it was in 1940, I think . . . I called up the Regional Committee one day and ordered them to deliver you direct to my office.

Your father's Special Assignment Detachment had already fallen to bullets, heart attacks, and madness. I had wasted my eleven enemies with my own hands. Before the end they experienced if not all the tortures of hell then at least the most piquant and dismal. And Gutman—the Gutman who, in addition to everything else, raped my sister and aunt—that Gutman had the opportunity, before he died, to feast his eyes as some filthy thugs, plucked from a prison-camp disciplinary barracks, banged his daughter, his wife, his cousins, and two aunts . . . I, stinking executioner, Senior Lieutenant Montecristov, was the one who treated him to this. I fed some really innocent women into the meat-grinder of retribution . . . I! For me, I repeat, there is no forgiveness . . . no salvation . . .

But I exulted, quietly exulted, praying that my mother, my father, my aunt, my sister would look down from the heavens and see this retribution. Exultantly I savoured the last drops of life, the ferment of lunacy and woe, in his bandit veins. I hammered at him constantly with memories of Odinka, and when he could take no more and began trying to bite his vein open—and he was a long time biting it, because he had grown weak—when he was howling, when by means of his gold fangs he was reaching the shores of his own life, his own little River Odinka, when possibly he was trying, with a corner of his consciousness, to find the instant, the step, that had led him to such inhuman nightmares—I did not hinder him, no, I did not. Gnaw yourself, rat. Gnaw. Sink your teeth in. A little longer and you'll be blinded by your own blood, blinded as you were blinded by lust in 1929 in the already burning barn, for my living aunt, my living sister. Gnaw yourself, rat . . .

Sixteen hours it took Gutman to reach his vein. I'm sure that these hours seemed an eternity to him. He was paid for everything, in full.

But strange as it may seem, the amount of justice in the world is not augmented by a man's attempts to counterbalance coercion and evil with the cruellest retribution—although there's something lively and graphic about the idea that retribution is edifying. Like a wise vulture atop a mountain of corpses. Evidently the image does restrain some people from evil and coercion. But we won't dwell on this ticklish subject, or else, deep in your soul, you'll resurrect the hope that after shepherding you for years I have arrested you only to conclude our conversation with an impetuous brotherly reconciliation.

Admit it: did the little bird of hope flash by, fan you for an instant with her sweet breeze? She did . . . Perhaps you also wanted to ask what I'm driving at, and what will be the limit of your hour of travail? You did . . . And by any chance did your body, aware of its utter soullessness and walled off from Being by the muck of its own deeds, want to use its last ounce of vital energy to duck out of the current of its meaningless existence? If so, then ask me to put a bullet through your head . . . Ah. You've had no such wish, as yet . . . Fine then, carry on. Live.

But I think I had a conversation in these very same terms in 1949, with a certain Pole . . . or Lithuanian . . . or Hungarian . . . anyway, somebody from a country occupied by us. The dog asked point blank, didn't I want to check out of the security system, out of this doleful hell, if only into a cool purgatory. And if I wanted to, but lacked the nerve to shove off, he'd be glad to put a bullet through my head, with the sole aim of helping a neighbour break loose from Satan's clutches. Then and there, he swore it on the life and freedom of his sons, he would put the second bullet through his own head . . .

That got to me.

'Why, you ringtail bastard!' I said. 'Aren't you, yourself, a malefactor before God—in whom you claim to believe—if you want to commit this most terrible double crime: kill me, and do away with yourself besides? Isn't this a sin?'

Now the German . . . or was he an Estonian . . . or a Jew . . . fell into a reverie. He thought for a long time. Off and on he cried, dissolved in tears like a child, blew his nose, smoked.

'Thank you, Citizen Lieutenant Colonel,' he says suddenly. 'Thank you. I will pray for you. Verily, man possesses infinite possibilities: even in suffering, he still lapses into terrible Pride and thinks to dispose of another's life and his own . . . Our life belongs, not to us, but to the Creator, although by His will we are so free that we both kill ourselves and lift our hand against our neighbour, in covetousness, unconcern, and madness.

'We hang, like fruit, upon the branches of the immortal tree. When the flowering is done and the fruit has set, we fill and ripen, anxiously we await the hour of our joyous maturity and a touch from the hand of Him who created us. We await our hour. But how absurd, in our view, would be a fruit of the tree—imagining it, for the moment, as endowed with the gift of self-consciousness and free will—how absurd would be a fruit that fell from the branch of the immortal tree by its own caprice, before its time, before its hour, a fruit that continued to participate in the round of life, but did not make glad the Master at the autumn fruiting!

'It cannot but happen that the wind will knock the fruits down from the Tree, that the hail will strike them, it cannot but happen that the birds will peck out their cores, a portion of the fruits cannot but be afflicted with rot, the shadow of robbery cannot but threaten the fruits, yet the Tree shall stand and the fruits be gathered, to the joy of Him who nurtured them and to the increase of Existence in the Universe.

'All else is less than life, Citizen Investigator. He who makes an attempt on life loses this gift and murders his own soul. You are an executioner. But you and thousands like you, though you destroy one man, though you destroy thousands, shall not put an end to life.'

'Oh yes indeed, Franz,' I said. 'That's a splendid spiel, you have a terrific line, Vlastimil, you make a good case, Mitya my boy, you sure can sling the lingo, Jonas! Here's the limit, and the answer, you say? But how would you know what lies beyond that limit? Too bad I can't wrest testimony on this point from the executed Conceptiev, Vlachkov, Gutman, Gurevich, Ismatullin, Latsis, Dumbian, or the others! Too bad!

What if it's the peace of eternal life that lies beyond this limit? In that case, they ought to be grateful—not to your God, who condemned them to their stupid daily grind in the bloody millstones of the Soviet regime, but to me, their executioner, who has rescued the former executioners from their dirty work.

'Get my point, August? Well, then what does lie beyond that limit? A void, or forever green fields and infinite harmony? Have you ever peeked over there, Bohumil? Are you maybe an authorized agent and custodian of Revelation, Vintsas? What's the answer, over there beyond that limit? Absolute clarity of the fact that the Spirit is immortal? When you stigmatize suicides, isn't it because they're pathfinders, so to speak, pioneers, the avant-garde of humanity? They step across the limit with mad bravery, and the only thing not within their power is to cry out exultantly from over there, to those left behind, "Hey, fellas, don't be chicken. This is just great. Come on over, why do scutwork for nothing?" I'm sure that when people get a guarantee of immortality, when they hear the personal testimony of these dare-devil, questing romantics who have departed to the next world, they'll be flocking to drown themselves, like lemmings. They'll be raining down out of windows like apples from a hard-shaken tree. They'll interrupt services on public transportation by lying down on the rails. They'll turn in their treasures for ropes, knives, poisons, and bullets. And we executioners will become millionaires, masters, saviours . . . We'll have tons of work, and it will be respected by the people. Premature death, Zbigniew, will become a reward. Anyone who tries to crash the gate into immortality we will forcibly return to life. Public servants who have abused their official position, corrupt rascals, influence-peddlers, and other bribe-takers in the World Death Organization who have given out passes to the crematoriums—these we will mercilessly condemn to life, sometimes to two and three lives. Four would be too cruel a punishment, and a violation of the Declaration of Human Rights. We will teach disgust for the Earth, the created world, the natural realms of Existence. We will instil love for my glorious satrap the Antichrist. And we will inculcate the attitude that alienated work is the main goal.

'For your God, Pavlo, any work is a means. A means of

preserving true and worthy forms of life. Whereas for us, labour is a goal, an affair of honour, valour, and heroism. In pursuit of this goal, the hoodwinked masses murder life, emasculate it. They turn themselves into efficient, soulless robots. With the increase in the number of dead souls, if only in a single individual country, the reserves of life on earth are correspondingly diminished. And when life begins nearing the limit—you can call that limit Communism, Jan, it's all the same to me—we will triumph. One more instant of eternity and *no one* shall be saved, for we will destroy *all*. So then what will we do? That, Florensky, is a nasty fucking crack, and the answer is, we won't have a thing to do. Period. Sign the interrogation record, bastard, or I'll brain you with my statue of Dzerzhinsky!'

What do you suppose this Stepan Ivanovich said to me?

'Out of my sight, Satan,' he said. 'I won't sign! Let's have a test of muscle! I have this to say to you, Executioner: here's the globe, and growing freely on it is life. In the words of the prophet, there is a time to live, and there is a time to die, and these times and seasons have been set in conformity with the laws of growth. They are revealed to the Husbandman but not to you, Asmodeus, try as you may to hinder Him from gathering the harvest, however much you hate Time or despoil the Field. No! And you try to hurry Man to depart this life, by depriving it of beauty, goodness, love, and dignity, by making it unbearable; but if you see that a Man has withstood you, that he cannot be broken by either pestilence or famine or woe, then, Executioner, you execute that Man, intimidating others.

'You, Citizen Investigator, will not succeed in comforting yourself,' declared František, 'by appealing to the Devil's premise that life is unbearable. Deuce-ace! You're a cynic, of course, and no fool. But there's a chill draught and a whiff of fear blowing through all your patter. You yourself are reluctant to kick off! Highly, oh, highly reluctant, I see, though sometimes the groove between your shoulder blades crawls with demons, and you're seized with disgust at what you have made of your life. You asked whether I had peaked beyond the limit. I don't suppose I have . . . Except for a fleeting glimpse, after your flunkies worked me over. May God grant you repentance, Citizen Investigator, and cleanse you of your horrible sins. Lord, forgive you and have mercy.'

'Stop, stop, Abram Solomonych,' I said. 'Don't be in a rush, please. And drop the idea that I'm merely an investigator. I am not. My dear Fyodor Mikhalych, I sit before you now as the Devil himself, in a leather armchair. Quit stonewalling, Friedrich. And don't think you've gone bonkers. You find yourself before me because you have successfully completed your transcension.

'If you desire proof—by all means! Here's a Walther pistol. Stand up, come closer. Take it in your hand and shoot me through the head, over the left eye, a shade above this little scar, and see what happens. The bullet will pass through—people have shot at me before—it will pass through, it will pierce Voroshilov's portrait and the Lubyanka wall, it will fly to the Kremlin, and when it falls, spent, it will quietly tinkle the Czar Bell. I, naturally, will remain seated here in the armchair, as before, finishing a phrase that I loathe with a passion: "on the substance of the case I can testify as follows". Well, come on! Courage. Take it. Tight grip, or else you'll get it in the eyes on the recoil. Aim. I'm going to settle back comfortably. All you have to do is squeeze the trigger smoothly. Or sharply, if you wish . . .

'Well, come on! Come *on*,' I yelled at him . . . Damn his soul, am I ever going to remember a last, first, and middle name for this character? 'Come on,' I yelled. 'Shoot!'

I didn't have even the tiniest fear of Death in me, just an odd little pricking thought in my ear: If there's no fear, there's no Death. Can you be afraid of something that's not there? 'Shoot, scoundrel,' I said. 'It's all very well for you; you believe in God. But what are your orders for me?'

Now this Lev Nikolaevich calmly lays the Walther on my desk. First he checks to see if there's a cartridge in the magazine—not trusting me, so to speak. He lays it down, and he says like a simple prison-camp gyp-artist, despite his obvious spirituality, aristocracy, education, and, I believe, priestly office: 'Go suck yourself, Citizen Warden.'

'What?' I said, disconcerted. 'Aren't you ashamed, talking like that?'

He said nothing. Stared out of the little barred window. Smiled.

'Gábor,' I said, 'it's not good to duck a serious question. Not good! Do you have the right to depart for Siberia and leave me here to go crazy, all by myself? Scum, who gave you the right to not even try and resolve a sinner's doubts? Why are you so haughty towards a lost sheep?'

'You're not a lost sheep,' this character replies. 'You're a cold-hearted gambler, chilled by life.'

'Fine and dandy, Alexei Alexandrovich,' I said, 'but for God's sake tell me, how would you advise a man to behave when he has been an eyewitness to monstrous atrocities committed against his nearest and dearest, committed with impunity, with relish, under the banner of a progressive idea? Which is more just: to kill oneself, or to avenge humiliation? What can rejoice a man knocked down from the Tree of Life by a degenerate with a stick? Where can the fallen fruit find comfort? In the fact that with time it will rot? That a bird will come and eat it? That your Lord God might pick up the fallen apple, take a bite, and say, "Why, fallen fruit can sometimes be extremely luscious"? Whom can this man blame? To whom can he present the final bill? Answer me!'

He sat there and said nothing. I paced back and forth.

'I suspect,' he replied finally, 'that you have lived through a lot. You have been in the kind of bloody mess I've never even dreamed of. I suspect that the story of your life is extraordinary, and impossibly tangled. But by posing the questions, by becoming aware of the extent of the powers of Darkness and Light within you, the extent of your ambition and revolt, guilt and responsibility, you have already set foot on the path of salvation and humility . . . I suspect many things, looking at your face and puzzling over your abnormal physique. I don't mean that as any fucking crack at you, Citizen Warden. You won't spill your guts, of course, this isn't a confessional, but I sense within you a terrible personal secret; the burden of it has altered the features of your face. Therefore I can't help you with practical advice. I will pray for you. Love those who hate you. And it wouldn't do you any harm to leave the security system. Make a break for it. Be a stevedore. Look what huge hands you have! A stevedore has it good. He tosses a few sacks and boxes around, and flies home light as a bird. But with the burden you have on your soul, you'll soon be a goner, crawling on your belly to the mournful infirmary.'

'You'll be leaving now,' I said, 'but it's still not clear to me: have you forgiven your enemy, have you come to love him who hates you? How do you feel, yourself?'

'This question,' says Pavlo . . . says Georgi Leontievich . . . says Christian . . . yes, it was Christian, I think, but never mind, never mind . . . 'this agonizing and possibly ultimate question, I am very deeply convinced, bears the stamp of a Higher Reality. But Reason, in a specific, highly complex situation, high-handedly and cunningly transfers it out of the sphere of the Soul, the sphere of voiceless feelings, into his magnificent computing centre.

'And human feelings, the human Soul, are so touchingly unwise in their truly naïve state that it's a cinch for Reason to perturb the human Soul with pragmatically obvious logical categories, foisting on her the answer that suits him and does honour to the impeccable operation of his computing centre. That answer isolates Soul from the Light of Truth . . . Do let me have a drop of vodka. Thank you . . . You asked me: do I forgive you, and have I come to love you, my executioner, as I depart into obscurity?

'Let's assume I find myself in the habitual everyday attitude towards the symbolic and semantic structure of this question. Yet again, Reason has proven—proven, the scoundrel!—that to forgive and love my enemy is out-and-out bullshit.

'But now, with a last effort of will, I blast open the cell in which Soul has been incarcerated by so-called common sense, I hurl my handcuffs to hell and gone, out to Dzerzhinsky Square, out through these bars, which my meek gaze alone has melted away. I spit on the regime of intimidation, and now . . . because I believe in the higher reality, I am transported to it! I feel neither pain nor resentment. But I do not say to you, "I love you, my enemy, I forgive you", for words cannot explode the accursed vicious circle drawn by Reason. Simply, I now find myself in a state of mind that stuns my whole being, a space of serenity and freedom where there is room for everything: for you and me and your domestic security system and the terrible past and the absurd present and the redemptive future and many, many things both good and bad. I sincerely invite you, Vasily Vasilievich, into Higher Reality! You are welcome! I bow low to you. Were it not for you, I might never have been visited by such a state of mind or such understanding. This doesn't mean I excuse or endorse the activity of executioners. Goodbye. I bequeath to you the Holy Scripture taken away from me when I was searched. Maybe it will help you relieve the torments of your prisoners? Tell Stalin he's a swine. Forgive me, Lord, for having so frequently strayed from the course of the Higher Life . . . Goodbye, Vasily Vasilievich!' . . .

We've taken another detour . . . a long one . . . Anyway, I was looking through a little album that depicted torture instruments of extreme antiquity—I had confiscated it from a certain theoretician of Socialist Humanism—and waiting for them to haul you into my office . . . I'm back on the subject of chance now.

Suddenly the phone rang. It was my buddy Vcherashkin, who was secretary of the Party's municipal committee at the time.

'Your man Vasily Conceptiev croaked,' he says.

'What do you mean, croaked?' I yelled.

'Very simple: a three-ton truck went through the ice, with an Agitation Brigade. I had dispatched it to a kolkhoz, to get the workers out of an undesirable mood. Between the suppliers and the State procurement officials, the kolkhoz is really getting screwed. The suppliers aren't delivering anything, and the procurement officials are hauling everything away. The poor kolkhoz workers are chewing shoe leather. Now my truck will lie there under the ice till spring. A damn shame. A shame about the two accordions, too. Sometimes two accordions will do the job of a company of Chekists. As for the corpses—well, eternal glory, as the saying goes . . .'

What an idiot I was! I should have gone out there, taken some Special Operations divers, and dragged up the corpse. I'd have known right away: it was your cousin, not you, who went down with the government truck.

I gnashed my teeth, bitterly gnashed my teeth, that Fate had zigzagged you past the Hand. There's your chance event—lucky for you, unlucky for your agitator cousin.

Chance . . . it's a very strange and horrifying thing, at times.

If anything had happened differently, it would have been curtains for you. Curtains, Vasily Vasilievich. And after all, several other men and two accordions perished with your cousin. Certainly the ones who perished had fates and guardian angels too . . . But wait! Maybe the whole point is that those who perished *didn't* have guardian angels.

Someone I knew used to say that a man who has destroyed his own soul is abandoned by his guardian angel, so naturally he's defenceless against hostile Forces and the fatal blows whose trajectories so densely penetrate the space of man's existence.

No—I can't accept a set-up like that. I just can't. A three-ton truck is on its way to distract some malcontent kolkhoz workers, and Fate loads it up with twenty-six guys abandoned by their guardian angels, plus two utterly innocent accordions, especially on purpose so that Citizen Gurov, this prick, this cruel weasel, this purulent turd who has sold out the whole damn world, can continue to plunder the State and foist off fuck-knows-what on the people instead of normal sausage and frankfurters? So that he can continue to live, breakfasting on Ragout of Papa's Ears à la Pioneer, lunching on Mother's-tear Soup garnished with diamond cufflinks, and dining at the Metropole with cuntheads from the Council of People's Commissars? Who can acquiesce in a set-up like that? There must have been at least one righteous man or ordinary sinner aboard that truck. If so—if utterly innocent Young Communists perished in order to deflect the attention of a senior security official from one V. Conceptiev, sentenced to death in absentia—this is cause for bewilderment, doubt as to whether our concepts of justice are identical with those of the Higher Forces, and total incomprehension of the mechanics of Fate. Or is Fate simply unable to reconcile herself to the interference of the domestic security system of the USSR in her own domestic affairs? 'No matter how villainous Conceptiev, a.k.a. Gurov,' she says, 'his hour has not struck. Let the swine live. I'll show you, you animals, you perverts! Behold: just to intimidate you, I'm going to destroy a truck, twenty-six men, and two accordions! And next time, think twice before you stick your spokes in my implacable wheel! *You* are to blame for the utterly innocent dead!'

My blood boils when I think of the situation during the war. Tens of millions perished, burned, rotted alive, in blood, pus, guts, bones, mud, and suffering—tens of millions, but Citizen Gurov, meanwhile, with the aid of his operators all over the Union, was bartering dollops of lard for jewellery and paintings. He starved his mother to death, he bred filth, lies, and debauchery, but the forces of Destiny guarded him, guarded him. How to understand this? Did the Devil personally keep watch over you, Citizen Gurov?

Strange. Strange . . . Must the blow of Fate that is deflected from you inevitably strike another? Do the guardian angels try to find time, as they deflect the blow from their wards, to inform their fellow agents of Providence that on such-and-such a date, at so many minutes and seconds, at such-and-such points in space, they should not omit to take the necessary security measures—so that the brick will fall to the pavement without accidentally hurting anyone . . . the departure date for the wedding trip in the new Buick will be postponed . . . the fungi with the ghastly resemblance to meadow mushrooms will not be fried . . . the stocks will not be bought . . . the girl will not go to the evening party . . . the boy won't drink the denatured alcohol . . . the accordionists will go not to the kolkhoz but to a wedding . . . the young lass in Gori won't put out for the shoemaker . . . no one will conceive the idea of collectivization . . . my father and mother won't be murdered . . . my village won't burn . . . So that the angels will take measures, and I won't sit on the giant frozen log, and we won't be staring at each other right now, Citizen Gurov! What do you say . . ? Here too, you think, the Evil One had a hand in things? No doubt. I'm only surprised that in my preoccupation with you, I completely lost sight of *him*.

It was he who saved you from the Hand! It was he, Satan! And whether he acted for good or ill is up to you to decide, Citizen Gurov. As for me, I'm going to go drink to Fate, which we can't understand anyway, and acquiescence, which is a gift given to few. Very likely you find it easier to acquiesce in Fate's behests than I do . . .

But time marches on. Already the chiefs of the various Communist Parties are flying into Moscow for November the seventh . . . Look at them swapping those long, slurpy kisses! Later, you and I will watch the coverage of the anniversary session of the Supreme Soviet. We'll watch the latest apotheosis of dissimulation—the weavers, miners, lathe operators, generals, writers, and the rest of the pack, unanimously voting 'in favour'. In the entire history of this phenomenal supreme organ of popular sovereignty, *no one* has ever voted 'opposed'. Why not?

I look at the deputies' faces, wise, learned, obtuse, talented, businesslike, fanatical, bold, illiterate, conceited, the faces of really quite different men, but all frozen in the same expression, and even if only for an instant, my sense of reality abandons me. At bottom, what's going on has no relationship at all to reality, and I feel: this is . . . this is . . . yes, the absurd. I crack my head, bedewed with the black sweat of my brief lunacy, against the invisible wall dividing real life at all levels of existence from the demonic kingdom of a theatrical bureaucracy that plays, with the frenzy and conviction of a paranoiac, at having meetings, congresses, conferences, gatherings, friendship months, special labour stints, anniversary sessions, Volunteer Saturdays, protest rallies, judicial elections, and demonstrations of national enthusiasm and unheard-of unity with our very own Party and government—and I ask in dismay: But what's going on, comrades? Won't you ever wake up? If you recognize that your play-acting is a horrible lie and that the boys at the top frankly think of you as pathetic puppets, why does no one vote 'opposed'? Not once! Ever!

Turn off the damn squawk box. After the session, by the way, the deputies each receive the latest-model portable colour TV. Not to mention the party-favours. Caviar, sausage, fish, muskrat caps, sheepskin coats. In sum, these little automatons are plied with gifts the way aborigines were, two hundred years ago. Activists get fed. Without them, the thugs have a tough time. Without them, it's a challenge to hold the prison cell, the barracks, the camp, the district, the region, the republic, the country. A challenge!

Let me tell you an entertaining yarn. It was told to me, in turn, by a rather talented young madman, during his interrogation . . .

Stalin slammed off. Using Stalin's own methods, Nikita massacred his former colleagues and allies. He put in his own boys wherever he could. He consolidated his position, settled in, and got cocky. Made a million dumb mistakes—and a fair number of businesslike decisions. He improved a few things, relaxed the reins in a few places, broadened the rights of department heads in a few respects. But he edged into pragmatism like a rheumatic getting into cold water. Like a maiden sidling into the palace pond, covering her lovely secrets with her little hands, discomfited by the sharp eyes of Marx-Engels-Lenin-Suslov and other dull, sclerotic old dogmatists peeping out from behind the bushes.

The Thaw (a difficult season for the security organs—it had been dangerous to walk down the street in uniform) came to an end. The liberals crawled back into their cracks and special niches. Their ranks thinned. Nikita, champion of right and abolisher of the Stalinist tyranny, had compromised himself in their eyes by purging the cultural institutions. Suppressing the anti-Chekist uprising in Hungary. Refusing to pay off old government bonds held by the people. Slackening and totally halting his criticism of Stalin's bloody satraps. Raising the price of butter and meat. Forcing corn—his one selfless and eternal first love—on the Russian peasant, who was accustomed to living with wheat and rye.

Yet although the time was over when the liberals had drunkenly mocked our glorious revolutionary past, the romance of class war, the splendidly staged dramas of our time—the political trials of Trotskyites and Bukharinites, and the counter-intelligence operations, stunning in the beauty and elegance of their execution, that had massacred the Jewish and Polish top brass on the eve of the Second World War—nevertheless, the wind of retribution was fanning feverish brows; warmth was returning to the faces of those who had done a quarter of a century in the camps, and their relatives; the eyes of those who had been rehabilitated, and who were included once more in the Party's work, lit up at the mention of Nikita's name. In return for his humanity, unheard-of in the leader of the Communists and this tyrannical superpower, Nikita was forgiven his foreign policy blunders, his incredible lapses in the field of economics, his bestowal of the rank of Hero of the Soviet Union on the Fascists Nasser and Amer, his foolish interference in the affairs of Yevtushenko, the steadily rising price and simultaneously deteriorating quality of vodka, his kingly gifts of airliners to leaders of African tribes—Nikita was forgiven all, in return for having proven that it was possible for the State, and especially society, to be governed by a man: drunk and sober, foolish and wise, tight-fisted and free-spending, uncultured and supportive of science, thoughtlessly rude and intuitively cordial, in sum, not an icebox crammed with the corpses of friends and enemies, but an ordinary man.

At this point, the story goes, liberal representatives of certain enlightened Communist parties in the West expressed their bewilderment to Nikita.

'Why is it,' they are supposed to have said, 'that not a single deputy, in the entire history of your parliament, has ever voted "opposed"? You've had a definite tendency to suppress the will of the deputies, evidently? Your organ of legislative authority, like the human brain, couldn't possibly, by all the laws of thermodynamics, cybernetics, and logic, have made decisions determining the basic life parameters of the State and society without serious critical discussion, which presupposes natural regulation of the always imperfect mechanism of government, possible correction of half-assed schemes, abandonment of notoriously ineffective ventures, and the defence of the rights and interests of citizens. The rank and file of our Communist parties, and we ourselves, are interested in the working principle of your brain trust. Whose will guide its activity? If your Supreme Soviets merely appear to be the brain trusts, while in actual fact someone else does the thinking for them, then what are they for? Why don't you come right out and tell the whole of festering capitalism that you have abandoned parliamentary chitchat and concentrated your authority in the hands of the fifteen Politburo members, who guarantee the populace the immutable infallibility of their thought process, the absolute correctness of their geopolitical concepts, freedom from economic breakdown, a steady growth in revenue, the defence of individual rights, and so on. Why in hell do you want a Supreme Soviet? The workers of Italy, Holland, England,

Spain, France, and San Marino would like to take power into their own hands, but they're alarmed at the prospect of sitting in their countries' parliaments with persons cut off from earthly affairs . . . cut off from the possibility of making decisions in conformance with a deputy's duty to his class-brothers, his brothers in labour, thought, and art . . . sentenced to voting only "in favour", in utter prostration of their will and strength!

'Come on, Nikita Sergeevich, it was you who flushed the bloody vampire out of the Mausoleum. Be consistent. Struggle against the methods Stalin used in leading the country. Give us an example of true people-power. We're strangling without it, we're red in the face, we can no longer hide from our Party members the horrifying truth about the reality of Soviet life. We cannot, simply cannot, go on proposing our apparently ideal model of man, Soviet Man, to replace the model of Divine Man offered by the reactionary Vatican. Divine Man, unfortunately, has proven no less tenacious of life than Soviet Man, no less moral and cultured, no less able to laugh and love his country as his bride, no less cognizant of his supreme responsibility to the human race, the environment, and his Comrade Creator, who allegedly organized the whole shebang. That's the straight poop, Nikita Sergeevich! We're splitting at the seams. Revisionism's pouring through all the cracks, like water into the hold of a sinking ship. The rats are all jumping from us to the socialists. Help us out, give us at least a couple of deputies who vote "opposed"! *Please!* Don't tell us you can't find even a couple, in a nation of two hundred million?'

At this point, they say, Nikita knocked back a tumbler of government vodka, pure as Joan of Arc's tears. He grunted, nibbled a sweet Nezhin cucumber, and reflected. After a moment he said, 'You'll find no such couple of deputies here, and we don't intend to hide the fact. Unlike you, we crapped on *petit-bourgeois* parliamentary tricks a long time ago. A couple of deputies—a working man, let's say, and a kolkhoz woman—who vote "opposed" in the highest organ of power . . . that's already mutiny, comrades. Mutiny! Chain reaction! Do that, and who knows? Like as not, all two hundred of our millions will be wanting to say *Nyet*! to the plans of the Party, the plans of the people.

'But look, we'll come up with maybe one fellow for you. Not right away. Something like this takes more than balls, as we say, Messieurs Comrades. What we need here is thorough preparation, like before a sputnik launch. Otherwise, the minute the blast hits we'll go flying in all different directions, we won't even have time to say *ciao*. Anyhow, we'll come up with one fellow. It's time. I can see it myself: it's time! We've got more brown-noses than you can shake a stick at, but not one critic selflessly in love with our ideals. Not one! Go on home. Reassure Western public opinion. We'll make a man. You'll have your Mr. Opposed—or as we say, your rebel traitor!'

The reassured leaders and representatives left. Nikita issued a strongly worded order to ransack the personal dossiers of all the deputies and find one with impeccable credentials: Russian nationality, working-class origin, educated, war vet, medals, community involvement, and all that. Must have sonorous and beautiful surname, on the pattern of 'Karenin' or 'Yepishev'. Check for alcoholism, skirt-chasing, mother-oaths, marital status, and international position.

Find him an understudy, of course. Better yet, a female understudy. But no singing the same tune, no sexual intercourse or collective boozing. Prepare the nominations. I personally, said Nikita, will choose the best man and his understudy.

Well, the advisers dug around in the deputies' dossiers, they racked their brains, they sweated, they shook with fear, and finally, out of the whole gang that had been apathetically elected by the people, they offered Nikita a couple of dozen crack deputies. Nikita sat down with his son-in-law Adzhubei at an antique oak table on his Crimean estate. They killed a bottle of Stolichnaya, with mushrooms and aubergine as accompaniment. They thought for a while, looked at photos of the deputies, and settled on Boronkov, Fyodor K., metallurgist from Nizhni Tagil, a robust and handsome peasant with a cheerful puss hardened by the heat of steel. As his understudy they chose the actress Applekina, People's Artist of the USSR. She was ninety, an old maid. Non-drinker, non-smoker, non-lesbian. Total loss of awareness of her own individuality, from her many years on stage in other people's shoes. In sum, just what the doctor ordered.

So, they began training the pair to cast their solemn vote, at the next session of the Supreme Soviet of the USSR, against approval of the activity of the Party and the government. They trained them separately, to avoid creating an organized 'Opposition of Two'.

Three days remained till the session. Nikita took measures to step up vigilance at all posts. He ordered it to be announced in the TV schedule that the report from St. George's Hall would be followed by the USSR-Czech hockey match, lest the people pour out onto the streets, God forbid, when they got an eyeful of the deputy who voted 'opposed'. Military units were brought up to the outskirts of major cities. Blue Beret divisions spent the night in aeroplanes, expecting to be dropped into the Union Republics, especially the Baltics, in the event of an outbreak of unforeseen disturbances in the midst of some population nursing a grudge . . .

The academicians took no responsibility for predicting how the people were likely to react to a display of heroic, unprecedented freethinking by one of the deputies. But KGB experts did not rule out an uprising by alcoholics, sporadic outbursts of sexual revolution, the desecration of Revolutionary shrines, the burning of a certain number of portraits of statesmen, an Armenian demand for a declaration of war on Turkey, Jewish pogroms, the leafletting of Pasternak's poetry in public places, proclamations of independence in Georgia and the Ukraine, the flight of kolkhoz workers to independent farms, the physical annihilation of consumer service workers, and holdups at banks and the special limited-access shops.

All in all, if the Czar or the Provisional Government had taken even a thousandth of these precautionary measures to combat opposition, the broad expanses of one-sixth of the planet would never have had even a whiff of the October Revolution . . .

The plan was that after the voting all deputies would depart simultaneously from St. George's. Fyodor Boronkov, utterly alone and distraught, was supposed to stare vacantly into the eye of the television camera until the announcer said, 'We invite you, dear comrade viewers, to watch the hockey match between . . .' At that point, as the directors conceived it, Fyodor would blur and gradually turn into a hockey stick, then into a puck and ice.

In sum, Citizen Gurov, on the day before the session was to open—when the deputies had already begun to assemble in Moscow and had been issued coupons to a free restaurant and the limited-access shops, and one muskrat cap each—our country was on the threshold of a new life, and its leaders on the verge of heart attack. Suslov was spitting blood and readying a plane for his escape to China. Nikita's desk, they say, was piled high with health reports on the top brass, the leaders of the republics, members of regional and district committees, and other lesser thugs. They were in terrible shape. Many had not left their offices in days, and the most powerful microphones were picking up a seemingly soundless question, which issued from the depth of the despondent officials' being: 'What next . . ? What next . . ?'

There was a rash of suicides among certain persons who had rich imaginations and their fingers in the pie. Gromyko, they say, was considering the noose. He sat in Smolensk Square and said nothing. But over and over again there resounded in Nikita's office the inner voice—amplified by a fantastic device that transformed his eloquent silence into sound waves—of the minister who to this day is dragging his portfolio up and down stairways and across continents, despite fantastic failures of foreign policy: 'But what next?'

At this point Boronkov's understudy, the actress Applekina, passed away because of the physical impossibility of continuing life on stage. She took to the grave the text of her last role.

Boronkov, meanwhile, was being kept in utmost isolation from the world. They showed him film footage shot by our agents at meetings of the various parliaments, knessets, folketings, congresses, stortings, dancings, and other forms of bourgeois pseudodemocracy. They coached him, naturally, on how he must behave before voting 'opposed'. Jerk his leg discontentedly. Shrug his shoulders. Crack a sarcastic grin. Shout an ironic 'Bravo!' Interrupt the speeches of right-wing leaders with the expression, 'It won't play in Pinsk, buster!' And also make various coarse remarks, under his breath, about leaders of the ruling party and the government, deride their ideals and whatever they held sacred. In all these subjects, Boronkov passed the test with flying colours.

When only a few hours remained till the opening of the historic session, the mighty superpower's first, only, and greatest oppositionist, the deputy to the Supreme Soviet of the USSR from the Nizhni Tagil electoral district, was delivered to the office of the all-powerful Nikita by a van with a sign on the side saying 'Drink tomato juice' . . .

'So this is who you are!' Nikita said. 'Well, then, Fyodor, what *is* next?'

'Next we vote "opposed", Nikita Sergeevich, in accordance with my orders and my personal responsibility. I've got a bunch of pent-up grievances myself, you know.'

'Well, but against *what* do you plan to exercise your mandate, which was given to you not by Eisenhower but by the people? Against what?'

F. K. Boronkov smiled boyishly. 'Everything,' he replied, honestly and frankly, and went on to explain. 'I've been grinding the old working-class brain about this. Why the hell waste myself on trifles, all those items, articles, and paragraphs? If I'm going to speak out in opposition for the first time, I've got to speak out against everything. Why the hell agonize, Nikita Sergeevich? Did I come a thousand kilometres just to fuck around? We protest to our leaders at Party meetings. If we can say "opposed" there, why go farting steam and collapse into a funk at the Supreme Soviet session, like the assholes in their fucking parliaments? Am I on the right track? I've been working up to this for a long time. But they always spooked us when they handed out the deerskin caps: Don't forget now, we're all "in favour".'

'So that's how things stand in the minds of the advanced working class, our tried and true torchbearers!' Nikita said. 'All right then, Fyodor, my boy, let's sit down and figure this out. Just what are you planning to vote against? After all, the whole world's watching you, thanks to the plague of journalists. Do you realize your historic responsibility?'

'I do! With all my heart, I do! I've already said goodbye to the wife and kids. I'm being launched into space like Gagarin, and, as they say, I'm a hundred per cent ready for any misfortune. I'll go all the way, I'll stand my ground, Nikita Sergeevich. You had it even worse, and things came out okay. We'll dummy it through somehow.'

'Good,' Nikita said. 'Will you vote, my boy, for confirmation of the State budget for the current year?'

'But why? Of course not! What the fuck do I want with that?' Boronkov confessed artlessly.

'Fyodor, my boy, explain why not,' Nikita demanded, 'if you know the score on powdered eggs and the international situation.'

'Too big an outlay for weapons, too little for auto manufacturing. We want to live even better than Ford's hirelings, go on fishing trips in cars. Another thing: we're not turning out enough rugs and TV sets. Our shoes are shit, and you can't buy a decent coat anywhere. I may be a metallurgist, but I want to build up light industry, not heavy. Heavy's already given every guy in the country two hernias apiece. Should I continue?'

'Carry on, carry on,' Nikita said, morosely but with great interest.

'I'd also like to transfer part of our capital investment from the atom to agriculture. Pretty soon there won't be any grub.'

'Next?'

'Next, I request that the budget indicate a precise figure for the funds we spend to fatten up the foreign Communist parties, when all they're doing is watching for their chance to make a quick getaway into the jungle, like wolves.'

'You've got a point there, Fyodor. But we're stuck so fast in the quagmire of the popular liberation movements, I don't know what to do myself. I'd be glad to crawl out of that shit. Suslov won't let me. Fool—he loves the stuff.'

At that, Boronkov belted down a tumber of vodka from the crystal decanter and became quite bold.

'I want the budget to show, without fail, that the people are to be paid money for their bonds. We gave loans to the Party and the government in good faith. Every payday we deprived the kiddies of a chunk, if I may say so. But you go whap! and all our bonds aren't worth a hill of fried shit. That's not good. It used to be that only thugs in prison treated folks that way. I'm opposed!'

'Perhaps, Fyodor, you're also opposed to the Aswan dam, which we're building for our Egyptian brothers?' Nikita asked.

'Opposed! They'll pull the chain on us anyway, and the money, our billions, will be down the drain. I'm opposed! I think Indonesia's going to pull the chain on us too, pretty soon, just like China did! Our build-up of China came out of our own hide, it turns out. Why, for the same money, we could have constructed a slew of schools, invented a new model of shoes, increased our herd, and launched ten frigging extra rockets into space! How come we were so stupidly short-sighted? Thank you for snapping out of it. But in my opinion, we ought to make our major capital investments not in the friends, so-called, of the Soviet Union, but in trade with our enemies. They could turn out to be friends forever. Our buddies, they're just waiting for a chance to slicker us, they'll really screw us, and then at some opportune political moment they'll pin the donkey-tail on us. Just between us girls, Nikita Sergeevich, who's more precious to you: your own people, or the Nassers, Lumumbas, and other Kim Il Sungs?'

'At the Supreme Soviet, in short, you don't plan to approve our class-oriented foreign policy, which aims, under Gromyko's leadership, to emancipate everyone from the power of capital and imperialism, and, while we're at it, grab back the millionaires' oil deposits, businesses, and trusts?'

'No! I'll vote "opposed"! Nothing will make me approve a foreign policy. We've got no fucking business in Africa or Asia. There's plenty to do at home. No point becoming imperialists ourselves. We in Nizhni Tagil are opposed! Unlike Gromyko, we see the big picture! Opposed! And besides, why emancipate them from capital in America, Sweden, Australia, Canada, Finland, and various other nations including Japan, if they're raking in five or ten times as much as I do? In order to lower their standard of living? What's the sense of that? I don't get it. I'm opposed. I'm rooting for my class-brother the proletarian, really rooting for him, and I don't wish him ill, but every payday I envy him. We can't help how we feel. Let's have a snack, Nikita Sergeevich. Nice vodka you've got! Spring water!'

The two statesmen downed a drink and a snack, and Boronkov went on, with animation: 'It wouldn't be a bad idea to take the businesses and minerals away from the Morgans and Duponts, of course. But there's a danger here: suppose it doesn't sit right with Rockefeller? Suppose he gets skittish and says fuck this? One kick of his hoof and it's war. I'm against war. I don't acknowledge any vital Soviet interest in foreign colonies, countries, or businesses. Your health, Nikita Sergeevich!'

'Amazing! Amazing!' Nikita said.

'Christ knows, we do what we can!' Fyodor said modestly.

'I see . . . So, you're voting against the budget and the strategic goals of our foreign policy. I see. But do you agree with our huge investments in the nuclear and space industries?'

'Opposed! Opposed! And opposed again!'

'Why?'

'I don't even know. If everyone's "in favour", I'm "opposed". The thing is, what's the big hurry on space? It's not going anywhere. I don't like the pace we've set for mastering it, because there are lots of things we need here on earth. Sometimes our faggot local docs can't tell appendicitis from the flu. They don't get taught much, and they're barely given enough time to treat you. There was this guy on my crew, Mironov, he kicked the bucket—they thought he had the quinsy and diarrhoea, but they missed his peritonitis. We've got to improve medical training. We're not porkers on a pig farm. And you're talking space!'

'What about corn?' Nikita inquired cautiously.

'I'm opposed. My son-in-law says that the peasants in some places curse it. This Queen Corn of yours is a joke, in more ways than one.'

'If you don't like corn, Fyodor, it follows that you're against the Party's resolutions on the future development of the theatre, cinema, artists, music, and literature?'

'Of course! And why not? Those resolutions just make films and novels worse. They add to the fear of people in the arts. And what fear does for art we see on TV and read in *Ogonyok*. And in the putrid books and crapped-up films and other so-called masterpieces of Socialist Realism. I'm opposed! I'm goddamned fucking tired of seeing one thing at the factory and on the streets, and reading another. What am I, crazy? It's only the madmen and yellow-bellied hacks whose concepts of Soviet life, so to speak, differ from actual reality, and vice versa. We're not idiots. We see all this, we understand, and if everything we read, watch, and hear is shit—well, there's nothing else left for us to do. Except maybe drink? And we do drink, now and then. I swear to God, that's more fun than grinding our teeth in deadly boredom at a lousy film . . . I'm opposed. Talent's not iron, I don't think. It shouldn't be cast in identical moulds. Let it flow along the ground the way it wants, till it gels. In the shop I like to look at the hardened overflows of metal, the different-shaped little puddles. But I can't stand the sight of cast ingots. Am I getting through?'

'You are, Fyodor my boy, you're getting through. And how! You're practically through my gut.' At this point Nikita switched off the amplifier, so that he wouldn't be bothered by the general chorus of 'What next?', in which were mingled the treble voices of the Poles, Czechs, Romanians, Hungarians, and all the other little brothers who use our tanks to conquer their people's biological incompatibility with what is commonly called Socialism. 'You're getting through, Fyodor. You don't agree about Pasternak either?'

'No! Here too, I'm opposed. You should have let us read this *Zhivagoo* first, and flung mud at him after. At least we'd've known if you had good reason or it was just more of your foolishness.'

'And cultivating the virgin lands?'

'That's not a bad thing. But you should calculate how much a pood of grain costs on virgin land if you're carting your machinery from the other end of the Union and back, and if half the grain rots, burns, or gets lost because of general fuck-ups and poor storage and because the city young people, who became farmers by fiat, have no feeling for the land, the ear, and the kernel. You needn't have crowed so much. As if mankind hadn't conquered virgin lands before us! The whole globe's been ploughed, but you don't hear any trumpeting about successes—even though the Western farmer, all by himself, turns out the work of twenty of our lunkheads! I abstain on this one.'

'How do you feel about Stalin . . ? Have another drink. Go

ahead, don't be scared.'

'I abstain on Stalin too. I can't go against you. But you've barely begun to cleanse the Kremlin of the cult. The job's less than half done, and actually they say it's being cut back. Why talk about half a job? That's like sticking it in, pulling right out, and waiting nine months for nothing. I mean, you've got to finish the job.'

'Cuba?' Nikita asked curtly, beginning to turn purple.

'Opposed! It's expensive as hell paying Fidel eight million a day, if not more. And dangerous. After all, America's no elk, she can sense someone creeping up on her. And Fidel, he's not much to our liking in Nizhni Tagil. He yells from the rostrum like our Party Committee secretary, and he's always clowning and camping. I'm for Cuba, but against overseas adventures. Eight million in new money! Fucking crazy. You raised meat and butter prices for *this*? I'm opposed. Besides, because of official optimism, the whole country's busy faking each other out.'

'And currency reform?'

'A fucking fraud! You know that yourself. And if you don't, drop by the farmers' market. How much did a bunch of parsley cost before reform? Ten kopecks. What's ten kopecks now? One kopeck. How much does parsley cost now? Twenty kopecks! How much are prices up by? Call the Minister of Finance. He'll tell you. He's a brain. I'm opposed!'

At this point, Nikita's secretary comes in. 'Nikita Sergeevich,' he says, 'Yuri Levitan is ready! He's had three eggnogs to clear his throat. He's dying to go on the air. We can hardly hold him back. The deputies are already in the foyer. They're buying shortage goods at the kiosks, drinking lemon fizz at the snack bars, the representatives of the working class are indulging in beer and sucking on scarce *vobla* fish. We await the historic vote.'

'Get out,' Nikita tells him. 'Order Levitan to forget the script of his news report. Have him go on all the radio stations and read some doggerel by that monkey Rozhdestvenko: "The Party is the strength of our class! The Party is the brains of our class! The Party is the glory of our class! The Party's no woman, it will never deceive me, tightly it cleaves to me!" Have him read it loud and clear! Let the whole world hear him, let all the liberal Communist parties tremble at our titanic inflexibility . . . As for you, Fyodor, I ask you: How could you say "opposed"? How? I just can't get this through my head. I've seen a lot, but never anything like this! Horrible! *Hor-rible!*'

'But after all, you . . . yourself . . . a briefing, they called it,' Fyodor stammered, losing the logical thread of existence.

'What do you mean, me? What do you mean, myself? What do you mean, a briefing, you fucking rebel traitor? Up your blast furnace! Okay, they taught you, okay, they briefed you, they could even order you to vote "opposed", they teach us all kinds of bad things in life, don't they? Stalin taught me to be a total bloodsucker, but I didn't become Stalin. I re-ha-bil-i-ta-ted! I published *Ivan Denisovich.* I didn't send Pasternak to the wall. I stepped over myself, you might say. I stepped over the gutless old Stalinist farts, stepped over the KGB, the MVD, Suslov, Ibarruri, Mao, Molotov, and that revolting bloody lug Kaganovich, the Cain of our time, who killed his brother Abel Moshevich. And I stepped over the Iron Curtain. But you? How could you?'

'They were preparing me for . . . a historic step, they called it . . . they taught me . . . Tests, too . . . What I was saying became a part of me. This "opposed" got to be sort of like family—like you and the Party and the government . . .' As he spoke, Fyodor began to grow sullenly sober and angry.

'That's not what I mean. I know they taught you. I personally fathered this scheme. I'm asking you, you sonofabitch, how could you *yourself* go opposition—organically, so to speak? You *yourself.* That's what I can't get through my skull! How could you yourself?! Let's say the Central Trade Union Council ordered you to betray your own father and starve your mother to death. What would you do, start playing the villain? Yes? And you wouldn't have led the troops into Hungary?'

'I wouldn't for the world have led the troops in! Love cannot be compelled!' Fyodor said.

'What next? What next? What next?' Nikita began pounding his fists and stamping his feet.

'First I'll vote, and then we'll see,' Fyodor said carelessly.

'No, Fyodor,' Nikita is supposed to have said. 'Kulak White Guard modernist kikeface, you will not go and vote. You will abstain. We will simply inform the comrades privately, "He abstained." One can't be opposed right off. Liberalization is an endlessly lengthy process, like the path to absolute truth. There's no hurry. Stay put. Here's the key to the bar. Drink anything you want, listen to some music . . . Then you'll go home. We'll defend our fundamentals. For the life of me, I just can't understand it: how did you agree, organically, to be opposed? Shut up, sonofabitch, and say thank you we aren't liquidating you on the spot, like we did Beria!'

Fyodor, they say, was left to finish his drinking in the office. As for Nikita, his closest colleagues never forgave him for giving them such a shock that they crapped in their pants. How it all ended, Citizen Gurov, you know very well . . .

I'm tired. Insanely tired. I'm going to rest. I'll lie a while in a nice shady spot on the beach. I'll weed the tomatoes, pinch them back, prop the apple trees. Have you ever read *The Count of Monte Cristo*? Then do read it. My favourite book has been obtained especially for you, from the library at the writers' colony. I had to laugh—I was over there the other day rummaging through our classics, and worthy authors in general, and then I stopped by the mess hall and looked sadly around at the drones, horseflies, bedbugs, bats, lizards, turtles, crayfish, jackals, hyenas, pussycats, caponized cocks, the chameleons prized by the authorities because their skin steadfastly maintains its red colour; I looked at the spiders, pigs, storm petrels who forecast eternal calm, the sables who had devoured their own kind, the oxen who plough and harrow in fertile national fields, the vixens, the moles, the blindfolded tame falcons, the vultures who perch on the clean-picked bones of the classics, proud as eagles on the cliffs; I looked at the mountain eagles who eat from the hands of their jailers and executioners, the low-brow gorillas who have learned in captivity to make up words to very vulgar songs, the parrots who in return for seeds and nuts will say, 'Solzhenitsyn's a fool! Sakharov's an enemy!'

I looked at the nightingales, lovely nightingales, melancholy and voiceless, the beautiful dogs of all breeds, bereft of their scent and hereditary characteristics, suffering from their tedious work and general manginess, the former pacers, harnessed to large carriages and mincing along the fuckholed Russian highroads, the donkeys, poor little donkeys, the camels who hadn't drunk for months, the baby lambs ready to become shishkebabs in the Devil's kitchen—I looked, and I saw distinctly that the writers' colonies were merely a privileged type of prison-camp barracks. The diet, clothes, and job assignments of the inmates were merely a bit better, cleaner, and easier than those of prisoners doing hard labour. Even this barracks has its trusties, who can take furloughs. They live it up for a while on the outside, in England, for example, and return. It's nice on the outside; but camp, though not better, is homier. After all, they were born on the bunks and grew up there.

I realize that, Citizen Gurov. Among the inmates of these creativity barracks there do exist so-called decent writers, playwrights, and poets. I'm not going to argue about the several figures you mention. Don't make me out to be an idiot. I only meant to say that when I looked sadly around at the diners in the camp mess, I was suddenly pierced by a passionate thirst for freedom—though I'd never tasted the stuff in my life, never tasted it, and had been sure that if such was my fate I could fully resign myself to not having it, the way I'm resigned to not having coconuts and . . . not being able to roll in the haystack with a girl as robust and tangy as an apple . . . But what organ is this in a human being, in a man like me, who's been messed up by God knows what, if all of a sudden a thirst awakens within me for freedom, though its form be unknown to me, its flesh untasted, and its colour fathomlessly dark!

I mull it over, and I can't understand. Is it possible that, like wild beasts born in menageries, we are not cognizant of the significance of the steel bars, the barrier between us and freedom? But suddenly, with every fibre of our being, we sense that it's abnormal to be separated from pure existence by this eerie thing, which we have ceased to perceive but which drives us mad at the moment when our soul and imagination are struck with the thirst for freedom . . .

Was that my own voice just now? Quick, tell me! You didn't notice anything? Strange . . . That idea about freedom makes sense, but I think I was speaking in the voice of . . . I don't remember who . . . he was innocent of the Devil's work, that I'm sure of . . . he got the minimum . . . I can't remember his name, or his face either . . . Well. Read *The Count of Monte Cristo* . . .

Good morning! How's the book . . ? You can't force yourself to read something you dislike . . . Indeed . . . You 'adore' other kinds of literature . . . On travel and animals . . . I see. We executioners sometimes know how to make a diagnosis, Citizen Gurov: you avoid moral problems when stated in deathless, gripping form. Am I on the mark . . ? And how do you like detectives? Did you hear me . . ? And how about murders? I'm thinking of violence committed by you personally. Poison, cold steel, firearms, strangulation . . . What do I take you for? That's a hard question . . . Well, but how about it?

Your hands have never been soiled with another's blood. You haven't shot or poisoned or strangled anyone. I agree . . . But if you'll pardon my curiosity, why haven't you said a word about cold steel? Did you brain someone, or stick him in the ribs . . ? You did no such thing . . . But here I won't agree so easily. Your foster mother, Collectiva Lvovna Brutnikova, born 1894, age forty-five at the moment of her death in 1939: what did she die of? A brain haemorrhage . . . You saved the death certificate . . . Let's assume it hasn't been jiggered.

Recall the meeting where you read your statement repudiating your father. At that emotional moment, the Bolshevik Collectiva Lvovna Brutnikova assumed sponsorship of you and declared herself your Party mother. She was forty-three at the time. A two-fisted broad, and beautiful. She shaved her moustache, since if she didn't it grew out as bushy as Budyonny's. A comrade-in-arms of Plekhanov, then Trotsky, then Lenin. Stalin didn't let her near him, but he used her services. Collectiva Lvovna sold an incalculable number of her Party buddies into death and exile . . .

Have you recalled that meeting? Afterwards, did Collectiva take her little son by the hand and lead you home to her place? She did . . . Feed you? Give you a drink? Put you to bed? Lullaby and goodnight, and now hug me tight? Is that how it went, in rough outline? Not quite. Perhaps you didn't live with Collectiva, sexy bandit of the Revolution . . ? You did . . . I know nothing about sex, you understand, Citizen Gurov, but I can imagine how warm and sweet it must have been for the forty-three-year-old Collectiva, burning like the eternal flame of the unknown soldier, to lay you down—a tall, ruddy, healthy stud—in her little bed, to pounce on you, pricking your lips with her stubble, and hump you all night, as if you were a fair young maid. And I can imagine your revulsion, welling up during intermissions, then vanishing in a volcanic fuck, at which—to quote a lover of hers, still alive, I looked him up—Collectiva was no slouch. That's a Party momma for you. Did she tell you tales, in bed, about the romance of conspiracy, about being interrogated by the Czar's gendarmes, about living in exile, about that glorious October, about serving in the Crimean Cheka, where she, personally, stubbed out home-rolled cigarettes on the sex organs of White Guard boys and old men, and about the legendary dispossession of the kulaks? You don't remember the pillow talk . . . All right . . . Then what did Collectiva die of, on November 7, 1939? A brain haemorrhage, and I can go fuck myself . . . All right. We'll drop this conversation for a while . . .

Let's go back to the time I got seven days in the cooler, the black box, the hole, for cracking the skull of the horny activist with my fist. Several other guys were in the hole with me. We played a wild game of finger-flick, using a deck of homemade cards. As luck would have it, I kept losing. My head was already buzzing from being flicked. But when *I* hit *my* streak, I thought, just one of my finger-flicks will be more than any of you fuckers can take! I bided my time. I was gradually becoming enraged, but I didn't get the chance to recoup my losses. Some shark pulled a fast one—made the pass, or packed the deal. First Grinberg told the shark that if that fuckhead Kerensky (the shark's father had served as Kerensky's aide-de-camp) hadn't betrayed Kornilov, the ass-peddler Bolsheviks would have been dropped in their tracks. Russia would have become a normal bourgeois democracy where people breathed freely and ate and drank a gutful. They wouldn't be out of their heads with civil war, red terrors, famines, industrialization policies, and the giddiness of our successes.

A fourteen-year-old prince gave Sasha Grinberg his full support. Kerensky, he said, had screwed his own mother. For which Lenin had praised him.

'Shut up, you little shit,' Kolya intervened. His father had been a leader of the so-called Industrial Party. 'If it weren't for your high-society mob—whoring around the Crimea and abroad, heedless of the nobility's duty to the fatherland and the people—we wouldn't be playing cards in this stinking hole. We'd be at the university. Bastards!'

'Great bunch you are!' said the kid brother of a Workers' Opposition member, jumping into the argument. 'Especially you Menshevik pricks! You were always kissing it up to Lenin, so now just take eight in the mouth!'

The Menshevik prick immediately cut loose at Sasha, declaring that it was all the fault of the Jews, not the genuine Marxists. Sasha tried to vindicate himself by saying that his dad was the one who had taught the leftwing deviationist bitch Kaplan to shoot, and he now cursed Marxism as such.

Next a Constitutional Democrat entered the fray, and then the brother of a disgraced poet, the nephew of Trotsky's personal chauffeur, the son of a Kronstadt mutineer, two starving kids from along the Volga, the stepson of a bordello madam, a street urchin, and some merchants' sons.

At this point Pasha Vcherashkin stood up for Sasha. Pasha's father had been Supply Chief at the Kremlin; he had been caught stealing and was now in the Lubyanka. Sasha and Pasha were friends, despite the differing political platforms of their imprisoned fathers.

A wild and bloody free-for-all began. I sat and watched. Look for someone to blame, I thought. Crush each other, you bums, just as your daddies and mummies did. But we poor peasants had to pay for it all, even worse than you. Some of you lost your chains, others found them, but we lost both land and loved ones.

'Hey,' I yelled, 'break it up!' The kids were fighting like animals, driven crazy by their accursed life.

I began pulling them apart. Bop,. bop, bop on their heads

with my fist. I didn't hit hard. Just enough to make their heads swim. As soon as I connected, down they went. I cooled them all out. And Pasha Vcherashkin I saved from certain death. The prince had already raised the shit barrel over Pasha's head, but I restrained him in time.

Chance . . . Chance, Citizen Gurov, chance! If the prince had conked Pasha Vcherashkin with the shit barrel, we wouldn't be sitting here in your villa. You'd be opening a meat-packing plant in Angola or Ethiopia, obviously. And as for me . . . But it's folly to seek the variant of another existence . . . folly . . .

I pulled the scuffling kids apart and threw the cards in the shit barrel. No more ruckusing, I said. But the inmates of the Home wouldn't stop yapping off. They were always after each other—the descendants of Bolsheviks, Constitutional Democrats, aristocrats, Lumpens, NEP-men, bohemians, Mensheviks, leftwing deviationists, *petit-bourgeois* liberals, Bundists, God-seekers, bankers, priests, kulaks, really all the riffraff of Russia, which had been skilfully divided, and was now ruled, by Satan.

As for me, after my forcible peacemaking mission I was called in by Director Sapov. He said, 'You don't want to learn, you unregenerate kulak. All you do is glower. So get out of my sight—be warden of the hole. Break the proud, torment the meek, keep an eye on kooks, and report anything out of the ordinary.'

And I came to love my prison within my prison. Attached to the hole was a secluded nook where I had a cot, a little box for my spoon, mug, and bowl, and one of Lenin's lightbulbs. Word of my great strength had already spread through the Home, and the kids under punishment behaved quietly in the hole. The prince, Sasha Grinberg, and Pasha Vcherashkin became, in my conception, the janitors, stokers, wardens, gruel-dispensers, orderlies, laundresses—in a word, my right-hand men. I kept them around, undoubtedly because something told me that they would somehow be linked, either all of them or one of them, with my destiny, my big break.

Fraternizing with my helpers, I sensed something very important, which determined my subsequent tactics and behavioural strategy. I sensed in them, as I did in myself, a bestial, staunch, inextinguishable hatred for Bolshevism, Communism, Leninism, Marxism, I don't care what it's called, Citizen Gurov, the Force, the Force, the Force—it was off on a wild binge through Russia and had dreams of swallowing up the world, it had annihilated our homes and our kin, it had thrown us into the Anti-Fascist Children's Home for a meaningless life.

We pups, we punks, before all the other kids our age and before a lot of the old farts, had guessed right: underneath the sheep's clothing, underneath the flittering of philanthropic Party slogans, underneath the sweet promises, underneath the invitation to the housewarming at the World Commune was the wolf-toothed grin of diabolical Forces! We understood how easily this false and perfidious Force, after calling upon the mob to institute new human relationships for the sake of the triumph of Communist morality, could introduce mad chaos into the common dwelling of humanity, how easily it could sweep away the household goods that the soul had gathered with difficulty, through dark ages and bright, to be increased in the future by children and grandchildren.

With our puppy-dog eyes, not yet clogged by the rainbow puke of Soviet illusions, we saw how our well-to-do country had become hungry and ill-clad. Under the banner of building a new life, chaos had penetrated trade, daily living, the economy, justice, culture, and art.

Chaos rode to its job at the State Planning Commission in a Lincoln. If anything anywhere was being built, repaired, grown, or produced, this was not thanks to the concern shown by the diabolical Force for the fate of the country and the people, but in defiance of it. *Defiance*. From under the hellish tar that had been poured on the field of our life little stalks of Nature, which the Devil hates, were working their way up. The nature of work, the nature of family, the nature of joy, the nature of order.

Despite the demonic orgy of agitation and propaganda that enmeshed soul and reason, we punks sensed what was hidden behind the slogans and fine words: a deathly abyss or a latrine full of shit. The words hid from us a monstrous tyranny, bloody carnage, the collapse of the five-year plans, the bankruptcy of the routine propaganda campaigns, the abuse of power, all-out thievery, moral degeneracy, the mockery of faith.

The Forces, in their high-handed attack on what was human, used the Word, they used Language, and at the same time tried to destroy its essence.

The Forces remade the world on this one-sixth of the planet, having seduced the gullible mob with the advantages of remaking the world over explaining it.

The Forces understood, they understood perfectly, that explaining the world was fraught with potential for beneficially remaking that same world. Remaking it for the better—which would be undesirable, mortally dangerous to Satan's main goal: the introduction of ungovernable chaos into the world order.

Here the Forces played on Reason's instinct for haste, his passionate, childlike curiosity to hurry up, quick, find out what those little springs and wheels are in the mechanism of societal life . . .

'What are these doohickies, these little mysteries that our asshole philosophers are always explaining? They're no damn good, if people die the way they've always died and Putilov's got his whores swimming in champagne! Why the fuck explain! Remake this whorish world, or bust!' the mob howled. Both they and their leaders, horribly aware of the ever-present time limit on a man's existence, were impatient to hurry up, quick, gallop over corpses and values, conquer Space and Time, ride full tilt past Fate, and, wiping the blood from their brows, ride into the golden age of the World Commune.

I'll be through in a minute, Citizen Gurov. This is yet another thought that's not my own . . . not quite my own . . .

The soul of a word, like that of a man, is easy to kill. The use of dead words is the method behind the phrasemongering of the Bolsheviks, or any other demagogues; the Fascists, for example. 'The people are master of their land.' 'Glory to the Communist Party of the Soviet Union!' 'Long live our dearly beloved government!' 'The USSR is the land of mature socialism.' 'The USSR is the land of advanced democracy.' 'Soviet trade unions are the school of Communism.' 'Our justice is the most democratic in the world.' 'Art belongs to the people.' 'We will arrive at the triumph of Communist labour!' 'Resolved: That hereafter we shall combat further misappropriation of socialist property.' 'The people and the Party are united.' 'Up with the flag of Socialist Competition!'

What, we ask, is behind these words? A lie, if not a void. A void, if not a lie. The words gradually cease to be perceived as words. Their content is scooped out of them by the thieving ladles of highly paid propagandists. The dead word loses its connection with political, economic, and cultural reality. It forms a new reality, a dead reality existing solely in the skulls of our leaders and those western idiots, great friends of the Soviet Union, who know our life from advertisements and extravagant displays at exhibitions . . .

In the hole, then, even though I was just a punk kid, I grasped that if there exist, no matter what their names, Forces that fly around on brooms above our unfortunate souls, there must also exist other Forces, which struggle, which resist, which are within us, which do not conspire merely out of a fear of being sold out to the Cheka, but, no matter what their names, are in a secret conspiracy to do everything they can to overcome diabolism.

In my nook in the hole I devoured book after book, book after book, by day and by evening and by night. I devoured vulgar Soviet stuff and the classics, doggerel and detective novels. I wanted to read, passionately and uninterruptedly, the way Sasha and the other kids wanted to masturbate. So I did read. And because of the chance to read, I came to love my prison. It had order. I halted disturbances with one flick on the forehead or blow to the crown . . . It was Sasha who brought me the books. His imprisoned papa, the leftwing deviationist, had had time to stash a load of books from his own library at the home of a paediatrician friend. Sasha would run into town on the sly and lug books back to the hole. And one day he brought *The Count of Monte Cristo*.

Instantly, the thirst for vengeance overwhelmed me. I came to hate all the things that had led, by very complicated paths of course, to the horrors that I personally had observed, that I had suffered through, that made me leap out of my cot with a wild cry in the night and run blindly till I smashed into the first wall. The thump or the pain would bring me to my senses.

I came to hate Utopians, Marxes, Engelses, Lenins, revolutionaries, socialists, Dantons, Robespierres, Chernyshevskys, and other demons. I came to hate the promises of alleged friends of the people, who assured the nervous and sceptical that it was possible to create a new order on earth. I wasn't thinking philosophically, of course, or even politically. This was all stewing and baking in my heart. But even then, my feeble little mind could not help correlating the glaring reality of the Soviet hell, or the hell of the French Revolution, with its ideological and moral sources. The Dzerzhinskys . . . Menzhinskys . . . Uritskys . . . Budyonnys . . . Pavlik Morozovs . . . Blüchers . . . Tukhachevskys . . . Yaroslavskys . . . Ostrovskys . . . Krupskayas . . . I had nowhere to hide from these ugly demon-faces.

And after my horrors, which recurred almost nightly, I would imagine that my nook in the hole was the Count's island cave. I was the Count, trying on the coat of my Chekist uniform before setting off with a rapid-firing cannon and a detachment of trusty friends on a vengeful crusade against Stalin, Fourier, Kamenev, Saint-Simon, Trotsky, Voroshilov, Zinoviev, Karl Marx, Pyotr Verkhovensky, Yagoda, Campanella, Bukharin, and the rest of the gang . . . I daydreamed; in my dreams I wrought retribution; and I did so, purely for reasons of camouflage, in the Chekist uniform that I hated.

I imagined myself entering the office of one of the fathers of the Red Terror, Zinoviev for example, and saying to him, 'Zinoviev! You're a shit!'

'Er . . . how's that, Comrade? A shit?'

He bugs his lamps at me, and I bop his beezer with a finger-flick. 'I'm no comrade to you, cocksucker!' I say. Then another flick, a third . . . Next day I stand by the newspaper kiosk, just as grey-faced, unremarkable, and scared to death as the other low-level functionaries. I buy *Pravda* and read a report on the sudden demise, from a triple brain haemorrhage that injured his cranium, of a true Bolshevik and Leninist, our dear comrade, the Utopian Zinoviev . . . fallen on his writing desk . . . up to his last moment . . . in our hearts . . . the enemies of the World Commune tremble . . . and all as one we fight and die for this . . .

You were claiming, just now, that while we freaks, bluebloods, and disenfranchised exploiters were rendering our verdict on revolutions, mass enthusiasm, great accomplishments, the wreck of the icebreaker *Chelyuskin*, and other birdshit that had little bearing on real life, you and those like you were living a life of self-denial, collecting kopecks and scrap metal for the International Revolutionary Aid Fund, laying out public gardens and ponds where the churches had been, taking generally no less than three months of the year to prepare for parades stupendous in their vulgarity and tastelessness, and sitting your ass off at meetings and rallies in honour of the Romain Rollands, Dimitrovs, Thälmans, and other heroes of our time. You were the romanticists, you claim, and we were the slag of history. No! That was all just for show, a backdrop to your true life, Citizen Gurov!

From your daddy and his pals you learned even the manners and hair styles of the ruling class. You watched as your daddy, almost before washing his hands of peasant blood, went rabid with a suddenly awakened plunderlust. He carted home the junk he confiscated from arrestees. He wangled his own personal Ford. He built a big classy house and threw up a fence around it. In the Central Committee he raised the issue of the intolerability of treating Party workers at public polyclinics, the necessity of creating a Party network for the supply of food and other goods, the desirability of promoting the children of tried and true comrades to high executive posts.

That is, he legalized an idea which until then had languished in hiding: the formation of castes, which would be a bastion guaranteeing to Conceptiev himself, as well as his children and grandchildren, many years of access to a feed-trough full of social privileges.

The personal asceticism of the leaders, which had so impressed the mob as it charged concertedly into the hellfire of revolution—after power had been seized, and then usurped by Stalin, this asceticism, though it was universally hyped in the

Party press, actually became, in both the capital and the provinces, the hurly-burly of thugs scrambling to the feed-troughs, dividing up the skin of the slain bear, snatching their piece of the fabulous multi-storey pie.

That's what you were learning, Citizen Gurov! And later, unable to reconcile yourself to the way the younger thugs were outflanking you, grabbing for the throats of old wolves such as your daddy, you decided to pay the terrible price of treachery, in return for a chance to keep your hand in as the pie was ripped apart. You would bide your time and then bake a new one, your own—the very one we're padding about in now . . .

Well, so we were living in the hole, reading books, talking, getting educated unawares, playing cards, and growing up. No one bothered us, they didn't invite us to rallies. They thought of us as curs, congenital jailers, dirt-mouths who would soon be automatically transferred to a corrective labour camp, where in due time we would croak, stamped as moral degenerates and vestiges of the old world . . . The most tranquil period of my life was spent in the hole . . .

Pasha Vcherashkin, after getting clearance from me, would prowl the city for days on end, trying to locate the buddies with whom his father had taken Tsaritsyn, crossed the Sivash, and thrown Wrangel into the Black Sea. Pasha searched as if possessed.

'You'll see,' he would say. 'I'll find somebody with clout. I'll save my Poppa. The others make off with freight-car loads, but all he ever pinched was a sack of sugar and two hams.'

He was collecting snipes one time, near the Bolshoi Theatre. I had sent him there. It was *Swan Lake* night at the Bolshoi. The latecomers—People's Committee members, Central Committee secretaries, Tukhachevskys, Tolstoys, diplomats, ambassadors, hookers, scholars, and so on—usually dropped their half-smoked cigarettes and cigars right at the door. Pasha would stash them in his kit bag. We'd blend the tobacoo, divvy it up, and have ourselves a smoke while we read interesting books. A nice, mellow high.

Well, suddenly some joker grabs Pasha by the scruff. A man with medals and big straps all over. He grabs Pasha and says, 'What do you think you're doing, you little bastard, when we're urging our great wings, I mean birds, in their flight to the devil knows where? When we're starting to dig the, ah, Metro, they call it, and conquer space and time? What are you, berserk?!'

Pasha looks, and he recognizes this joker with all the medals. Recognizes him!

'Uncle Kolya! It's me, Pasha! Vcherashkin's son! Help! Evil forces have ruined my father! Trotsky undermined him!'

'What's this? Where's the force that could ruin my friend, I owe my, harrumph, my life . . . sonofabitch, Pasha, tell me, who taught you to smoke in our heroic age?'

The big man's dame was already turning up her nose at Pasha, though very likely she herself, the slattern, had learned to wash her hind end only the day before yesterday, at a lecture.

'Nikolai, we're late,' she says through her nose. 'The Rykovs and Rosenholtses will take our whole box again. Let's go, Nikolai!'

'Silence, pig!' yelled the man—Uncle Kolya—and as Pasha tells it, his ears turned white. His eyes narrowed and grew bloodshot. A blue vein on his forehead started ticking crazily: tick-tick-tick.

'*Fuck* your dying swans, and your bluebirds too! My friend, the militant and commanding Vanya Vcherashkin, has fallen into the clutches of finks! Silence! Go home! Box? I'll show you a box!' the man yells to the dame. 'Forward, to your manger, ma-arch! . . . Pasha, come see Stalin! I'm not going to leave things this way!'

His dame up and dusted from the Bolshoi. Pasha was more dead than alive. Uncle Kolya led him straight to Stalin's box.

'This, Joseph,' he said, 'is the son of a friend of mine, someone you respected—Vcherashkin. The Trotskyites have incarcerated Vcherashkin. They trumped up a case in order to wipe our cadres from the face of Red Square. Tell your story, Pasha!' Uncle Kolya commanded. And he gave orders to have the swans wait fifteen minutes on their lake. Nothing would happen, they wouldn't fucking die in those few minutes.

In petrified silence, the whole Bolshoi Theatre waited for the end of Pasha's conversation with Stalin. Pasha told how his father had been transferred from military duty to manage the stockroom in the Kremlin. How Kamenev's and Zinoviev's wives and the other women kept bulling their way in, to get coffee, tea, salmon, caviar, veal, capons. How hard it had been for his father to please everybody. Trotsky, especially, had crabbed at his father, once when he was constipated and there weren't any prunes in the stockroom because they'd been eaten up by Bukharin's sister-in-law and Kuibyshev. So Trotsky had crabbed at him and begun to wait for his chance. Another time the caviar for May Day had struck him as insufficiently red and fresh. Vcherashkin had told Trotsky that if he thought the caviar was spoiled he could throw it into the aquarium. Wait and see if it hatched small fry—then he could yak about whether the caviar was fresh or rotten. 'Some people in the Kremlin are so goddamned spoiled they wouldn't eat a walrus prick,' he had said. 'In the stockroom, we see it all.'

Trotsky crabbed worse than ever. 'Vcherashkin,' he says, 'you stuff all the best lambs into Stalin's gut! You're selling out the world revolution for shishkebab!'

Stalin listened closely to Pasha and kept filling his pipe with tobacco. His secretary wrote things down. As for Uncle Kolya, he was blowing his nose and mopping white tears with his red bandanna.

In the end, Trotsky personally caught Pasha's father. The latter had loaded up a truck with odds and ends for the New Year, so as to have something to snack on when he raised a glass with his regimental comrades. Right by the Spassky Tower, Trotsky detained the truck, although there were receipts for it, permission from Kalinin, and other vouchers.

'I see, I see,' Stalin said quietly. 'Constipation . . . Lambs . . . My gut . . . The shishkebab of world revolution . . . This is a call to Louis Bonaparte's 18th Humidor.'

Pasha used to swear that those were Stalin's very words: '18th Humidor.'

'Free Vcherashkin, tonight! Reinstate him in his job!' Stalin ordered. 'Go, Pasha. Quit smoking. You'll make a good Party worker!'

Uncle Kolya brandished his sabre, the conductor raised his baton, and the ballet began . . .

You and your kind, Citizen Gurov, were 'born to make fairy tales come true'. And in fact, from the first hours of the Soviet regime, fairy tales began happening at every turn—scary tales, and also tales with happy endings. Russia, all of Russia, seemed then, to people who had happily and unexpectedly escaped prison and death, or vice versa, who had suddenly lost property, their accustomed peace of mind, their loves ones, relatives, liberty, and life—all of Russia seemed then, and indeed it is little changed, an eerie kingdom of Chance.

A mind-boggling and soul-chilling orgy of witches and demons had begun . . . Millions of people, outraged, deprived, bereaved, or robbed, set out mentally—or actually, on Shanks's mare, like the bonny brave lads of fairy tales—to wage war against the wicked magician Kashchei, who with his all-powerful stooges had ensconced himself in the Kremlin . . .

Best beloved! Your father is in our evil new prison-house. The key to it is in a swan's egg. The swan's egg is in a prince's tights. The prince is a ballet dancer at the Bolshoi Theatre, and the theatre is in Moscow. Moscow is the capital of one-sixth of the planet. That is where Stalin lives. He loves the ballet. Go to the theatre. Collect cigarette butts. You will see a Dragon with medals all over his chest, and a foolish Dragoness. Boldly run up to them and ask for your wish. Gaze without fear into the eyes of the Chief Serpent, but do not look at the lake. There the swans of our hopes are dying . . . That was Pasha's fairy tale.

How many people went wandering in search of the hidden egg in which lay the key to the trunk of good fortune! Through terrible dead corridors teeming with rat clerks they roamed the hell of Soviet bureaucracy. Some went mad with despair. Some had soul and reason blunted. Others perished absurdly, eaten alive by rats and spiders. Still others, plastered with wood lice, howling with horror and disgust, miraculously broke free—after abandoning all hope of achieving anything or saving anyone—to the fresh air!

But oftentimes what might seem to be the most unresolvable stories, the most tangled webs of fate, the most desperate situations, were instantly, as if by the wave of a magic wand, resolved, untangled, and settled. Someone in the prosecutor's office would succumb to incantations, someone on the

Regional Committee would be scared of Spirits, someone in the Council of People's Commissars would cast a spell over the rats, someone would make the guard at the Central Committee drunk on a love potion. Then the carved oaken gates opened, and Little Ivan the Fool, without shyness, entered the great work-palace of Secretary-Prince-Sergei, bowed from the waist, and challenged him to a duel of honour. For a whole hour he fought, he did not return home empty-handed, he brought bricks for the cow shed, for the cow shed where the cows would winter and give their good milk for little children, and the cows wouldn't freeze to death, poor dears . . .

That's how it was, Citizen Gurov! Of fairy tales like this, and others a little scarier, I know more than Pushkin's peasant nanny. If I had grandchildren I could tell them a story or two, indeed I could!

You too, for you lived with Baba Yaga Bony-legs, the wicked bitch Collectiva Lvovna, your Party momma . . .

And then I found *myself* in Pasha's fairy tale!

His father had been doing time on the Solovets Islands. A plane was dispatched from the military airport. Pasha's father was brought to Moscow. He got back his job at the Kremlin stockroom, his medals, apartment, and dacha.

One day Pasha returned to the Children's Home in an open Lincoln convertible. He and his father walked into the director's office. For ten minutes all you could hear in the Children's Home was the director being socked in the smush and kicked. Then the activists tossed the director into a van, and he disappeared forever, no one knows where. The prince, Sasha Grinberg, and I went riding off in the Lincoln to a huge dacha in Barvikha, near Moscow. Uncle Ivan Vcherashkin told us, 'Live here and study. I will be a father to you. Tomorrow we'll fix you all up with new birth certificates. Now, begin your new life. What do you want to be?'

The prince wanted to become an actor. Sasha, blushing and stammering, said that his dream was to study sexual relations in science and in life, because in his view they held an important secret for people.

'I want to be a Chekist,' I blurted. 'I want to crush enemies of the people! I'll crush them till the day I croak!'

'Me too—a Chekist!' Pasha cried.

That first night after the Children's Home, I dreamed strange and terrible dreams.

I sally forth to single combat with a many-headed dragon. Behind him, along the asphalt, stretches a trail wet with slate-black slime. And all the dragon's heads are ugly kissers familiar from portraits. I chop off one, and another appears. I whisk off three at once, but three more spring up, they grow back on the loathsome bloody stumps of the three necks. I chop and chop and chop . . . But they keep growing back. I'm ready to drop. I've lost heart, the fight has gone out of me. Now the late Ivan Abramych gets off a tram, via the rear platform. He breaks free from the grip of the ticket-collectors, who rampaged like demons in those years, and he says, 'Leave them, Vasya! Leave the heads. To hell with them. Better to save your soul, so that we can meet again. Save your soul, Vasya! The dragon will rot by himself! We must be reunited, Vasya!'

In my terrible anger that he had disturbed me with doubt, I shoved my father Ivan Abramych in the chest and said, 'I am the Count of Monte Cristo! I will avenge you!'

Ivan Abramych wept bitterly into his hands, and the ticket-collectors led him away from the platform along the dragon's wet trail, along the slate-black slime, into eternal separation from me, into the pitch darkness of a side street . . .

What? Am I boring you, Citizen Gurov? Such a terrible thing life is, you say—monstrous, and staggeringly inexplicable? Have a shot of your excellent cognac and you'll feel better right off. Right off, things will be clearer . . .

Then I was immediately gripped by another dream. This was odd, because my dreams had been extremely rare at the Children's Home. They had been impassive, their meaning and images clouded by doleful, pitch-dark weather, woven of cold little threads of graveyard drizzle . . .

I stand excited, strong, a middle-aged man already, beside that same ill-starred log. I am holding a two-handled saw, and there's a crowd around me. I summon from the crowd, to have a test of muscle with me, first Marx, then Krupskaya, then Mussolini, then Mikoyan, then Hitler, then your daddy. But all of them, after sawing a while at the giant log, which is frozen solid as death, solid as iron, give up and walk off to one side, wiping their brows. And suddenly it's you jumping out to the saw—a kid in a Budyonny helmet. We saw the log into four blocks, as easily as if it were a rotten little aspen. Effortlessly, to the applause of the crowd of celebrities, we begin to split the blocks. First into smaller logs—with big swings, from the shoulder, axe-heel to the block—and then, kneeling, into chips. But now the crowd, the giant log, and the chips are no longer there beside me. I'm alone. Completely alone, and I can't think where I am, or why I am, or even who I am. Who am I? And I have a hard-on, like the boys at the Children's Home, it's sort of a good-sized stick. But all I feel is its total uselessness to me. It's in my way. Without pain, blood, or regret I snap it off, I rip it off and throw it away, into the River Odinka, and an eddy sets it whirling like a random twig . . .

It was nice, of course, goofing off at Vcherashkin's dacha in Barvikha, but I honestly confess I'd liked it better in the hole. Such an awful lot of highly placed crumbums I had to rub elbows with. But I'd read *The Count of Monte Cristo* ten times over, and I knew: if I wanted to gut the Force that had wiped from the face of the earth my village and my loved ones—and not only mine, but those of millions like me—then I must clamp down on myself. I must brush my fangs with Onward tooth powder, I must clip my nails with ladylike little scissors, I must smear burdock oil on the hairs that rose up in fury on the nape of my neck. I must, above all, learn to see, to hear, to understand, to compare, to control my will and my face even better than Stanislavsky and Nemirovich-Danchenko. I must become steel-hard, like Stalin.

Ivan Vcherashkin firmly impressed on me that I should forget everything that had happened. Forget it—not a peep, not a poot, no gritting my teeth. Period. Ivan Vcherashkin himself had found me in Rostov, in the toilet at the railway station. I had been peeing on the floor and bawling. My mother had died of typhus right in the station, which fact Vcherashkin had learned from the mob of passengers. As for my father, a Bolshevik recidivist who had robbed the Czar's banks, he had been executed by Denikin personally. Such was my past, and Vcherashkin had adopted me, being a socialist humanist.

All that kind of phraseology, too, he taught to Pasha and me, explaining that it was a kind of slang. In today's gangs you couldn't get anywhere without it.

Pasha and I went to a small school outside the town, a private college, so to speak, for children and relatives of top officials. We weren't much for studying, though. We did the work, but that was all.

I forgot to tell you about Sasha Grinberg. It probably wasn't easy, but Vcherashkin spent two weeks courting four guys with rhomboid bars on their collars—and Budyonny himself, I believe—ferrying them back and forth to the dacha. They had a smoky, drunken blast, and in the end Vcherashkin did obtain the release of Sasha's father . . .

One day we were walking in the woods. We were gathering mushrooms. I have a wonderful nose for them, even now. I'm a country boy, after all! We were walking in the woods, Ivan Vcherashkin, Pasha, the prince, and I—Sasha had left us to live with his dad after he was freed—when suddenly, in a little fir grove, I saw a man in a white military tunic. He had a basket in his hands. He was standing with his back to us, smoking a cigarette and lifting the fir branches with a stick.

Pasha, out of habit, went up to him and said, rather insolently, 'Leave me the butt, will you, mister?'

The mister turned around. Stalin!!! I gasped with horror. Pasha stood in stunned silence. Ivan Vcherashkin and the prince were still walking along, somewhere farther down.

'Have a smoke, Pasha,' Stalin said in an undertone, taking a pack of cigarettes from his pocket. 'Have a smoke. But you're a scoundrel—you didn't quit after all. You're supposed to become a Party worker. Where's your father?'

'Pa-a! Pa-a!' Pasha yelled. But he quickly lit up and took about ten deep, greedy puffs in a row. It knocked him for a loop. He threw the cigarette away and told Stalin that this was the last, Joseph Vissarionovich!

Now Pasha's father came up.

'Hello, dear Joseph, my saviour!' he said.

'Don't thank me for that. Don't offend me,' Stalin said. 'Tell me, instead, why the mushrooms don't come to me, Ivan. Even the Russula, shittiest of the shitty, ugly as Krupskaya, doesn't want to hop into my basket!'

'You're a highlander, Joseph! Eagles are more used to shooting down their rabbits from a height. And besides, men like you aren't accustomed to bow low.'

'A good, scientific explanation,' Stalin said. 'I don't even see any flattery in it. I really don't like to bow. But now who's this, with the full basket?'

'This is Vasya! He's lucky with mushrooms! He's gathered forty-seven boletuses!'

Now Ivan Vcherashkin rapidly told Stalin about how my father had robbed banks with him three times—Stalin must remember him—but the Whites had executed that remarkable hold-up artist. My mother had died of typhus. After Ivan was liberated, thanks to Joseph, he had sprung Pasha and me from the deadly Children's Home founded by Krupskaya—may her eyes pop. How long would the Trotskyites mock our youth and maim them with sodomy?

'Don't be in a rush, Ivan, don't be in a rush. Fair and softly gets you there for Yuletide,' Stalin said.

Just then, Citizen Gurov, just then, not barking, not wheezing, a gigantic Alsatian shot out like an arrow from somewhere behind the birches, her jaws frothing with foam. Her mad eyes were glazed, their whites bloody. She shot out and raced straight for Stalin, with her muscles swollen into resilient lumps, her teeth bared, her muzzle gathered into furious wrinkles—we stood nailed to the spot, hypnotized by the dog's incredible, rage-distorted beauty. She sprang up into the air, already certain that in a second her fangs would clack shut on the throat of the moustachioed man in the white tunic, with the cigarette in his mouth.

In his surprise and fascination, Stalin didn't even stir. I was standing nearest to him. I didn't think or take aim—when the dog sprang, I landed her a hammer-blow to the spine with my fist. She fell at Stalin's feet, stunned. Just a fleck of foam plopped on his white tunic. Before the dog came to, I grabbed her by the hind feet, spun the elongated hulk around me a couple of times, and with all my strength smashed her skull against the trunk of an old birch. Her brains spattered on Stalin's boots.

'I invite you all to a modest repast,' Stalin said, imperturbably and in an undertone, as before. But as he lit his cigarette, he hid his pale face in his hands.

I sat down on a low stump, because my knees were shaking. I dropped my basket. The mushrooms spilled.

'Vasya, show me your fist,' Stalin said. I showed him my fist, which had begun to smart from the blow. 'Yes! That's a hand! Breaking the back of a mad dog—that's a true Chekist hand!'

Stalin stooped down, collected my mushrooms into the basket, and repeated his invitation.

'I feel sick, gentlemen. I'm going home,' the prince said.

Pasha and I followed along behind the Leader and his gangster buddy.

The repast at Stalin's dacha was delicious and festive. He himself raised a toast to christen me the Hand, and hardly anyone since, especially not a colleague, has ever called me by any other name . . . Twice—at the recollection, I'm sure, of the Alsatian racing out of the birch grove with teeth bared in fury—Stalin turned pale, and the pockmarks darkened on his nose, his cheeks, his forehead, becoming more noticeable and disgusting. He drowned the recollection in a gulp of wine, nodded amiably to me, and, in amazement, lightly stroked his Adam's apple, which only by a miracle had not been bitten in two.

As we said goodbye, Stalin told me that he would come for me tomorrow morning at ten, to repay his debt. A heady sensation!

'Well, Hand, you've got trumps!' Ivan Vcherashkin said at home. 'You're in favour! Hang on! Play this for all it's worth, and don't forget your friends!'

'I won't forget the good deeds,' I said. 'As for the evil deeds, I won't let certain other people forget those.'

I fell asleep with my blanket wrapped around me like Monte Cristo's cloak. I remembered the faces, every last one: yours, your daddy's, and those of his buddies in the detachment. There would be no limit to my revenge—no limit! Undone by all these events, I sobbed myself to sleep, as they wrote in oldtime novels . . .

I went swimming in a light rain this morning and realized you could have lasted another twenty years or so, here at the villa. Really. Sea, iodine, fruit and vegetables, marvellous air. . .

The other day I got several photos out of your album. Where's my briefcase? Oh, here it is . . . Take a look . . . Don't turn purple, now. Watch your blood pressure. You used to keep it under control, even when summoned to the Central Committee . . . Despite all, there was something sickeningly attractive about Collectiva's mug. A face with that slimy era recorded in its features. Purity, you might think, and openness, but in point of fact the most transparent immorality, untroubled by pangs of conscience. The general line of her hip . . . Her breast, which instead of a nipple boasted a badge for marksmanship. On her brow the passionate thought, 'Proletarians of the world, unite with me!' And her moustache—what a moustache! Kerchief. Leather jacket. Every inch the gun moll. Personally—if I'd been a functional man, of course—smirk all you like, but personally, I wouldn't have climbed on Collectiva. Not for money or a hunk of smoked sausage, as they say in camp. I'd sooner kill her, the bitch! Lie down beside her, touch her, kiss her, start to climb on . . . No! I'd sooner kill the stinking slut!

Here's a glass . . . By all means, go ahead. I won't have any . . . I'd rather kill her, the animal! Didn't that thought cross your mind? But how ghastly to realize, in addition to everything else, that Collectiva saw herself at this moment as a young, untouched virgin, who was just about to find revealed to her, for the first time in her life, something she had read about in Maupassant, something that was coming on like a thunderstorm, something that was crushing and releasing her and already piercing her like lightning from head to toe, thundering in her temples and delivering itself of drops of rain . . . rain . . . rain . . . You open your eyes; she sees in you her own youth, and you see in her a seedy whoredom, alienness, death . . .

In the mornings, Mama Collectiva gave you coffee, made sandwiches, and saw you to the institute . . . But now Electra—so named in honour of Lenin's lightbulbs—returned, after her father's death, to the home of her dissolute mother, Collectiva. Electra, Elya, daughter of your hated mistress . . .

Elya arrived—hold it, Citizen Gurov! Ah. You merely wanted to take a stroll in the hall. Go ahead. On the way out, take a look at one more photo. You and Collectiva and Electra, under a cypress in Yalta. It's perfectly clear that you've fallen for the daughter, head over heels. You're careful to conceal it, but it jumps out at me! No, I don't suppose you do see it. But I would guess, though I can't say for sure, that right then under the cypress was when you sensed that you goddamn had to rid your nights of this howling, scratching hellcat.

You're ashamed. Collectiva must understand this. No, you desire her as before. Your passion is nicely mixed with respect and gratitude, but even so, even so, it's better for you to sleep apart. Physically, you too are very distressed by the situation, but the bed mustn't squeak right under Elya's nose! Oh, don't talk nonsense. I do want you, I do! And when Elya goes off to school or the skating rink, we'll have our way. You're my first woman. You taught me everything. But let's sleep apart . . .

What? What did you say? At long last you feel you're a villain? Now that's more like it!

But notice, Citizen Gurov, notice! You became aware of your own villainy, for the first time in all our long and sometimes terrible conversation, not through your father's shock at the news of your rat-fink caper; not through your mother's suffering and death; not through the many outrageous acts of your life; but through your revulsion at being raped by your Party momma, Collectiva Lvovna!

You've forgiven yourself everything. But you'll never forgive the fact that, even though you were dying from the vomity filth of her alien body, you slept beside it, you took it—without warmth, without passion, without indifference, which would have been a blessing—you took it, hating both it and yourself . . .

Look at one more photo. Collectiva Lvovna's last . . . Red Square. November 7th, 1939. Collectiva is gay, slightly drunk; a parade is her element. You march arm in arm with Collectiva and Electra. But notice the involuntary tenderness in the way you clasp Elya's arm to you, notice how lifelessly your hand droops on the pocket of your mistress-momma's leather jacket. And your face looks pasted together from two halves. The half towards Electra is alive, aroused, full of smiles. The other half, which Collectiva unconsciously tries not to look at, is squeamish, irritable, dead. Hatred has tightened the skin on your cheekbone, narrowed your eye, flattened your lynx ear against your skull. Above you are the banners: 'The cadres decide all!' 'Long live the all-conquering doctrine of Marxism-Leninism!' 'Stalin is today's Lenin!' 'Make way for proletarian humanism!' 'We welcome Soviet-German friendship!'

Innocent Elya's pretty little mouth opens in a sly smile. Half turning to you, she sings,

We love our country as our bride!

You can't help singing along. You round your lips:

Pro-o-tect her as our loving mo-o-ther!

And Collectiva, looking at the mausoleum grandstand, continues:

For the young we everywhere make way!
The old we everywhere respect!

Look a little lower, more to the left. Here, if you please, is yet another chance circumstance: the fellow in the twill coat with the nickel-silver buttons and mouton collar. A ridiculous figure. His arms are long. His face is distorted by nausea and a fanatical passion for revenge. But his colleagues take this expression for weariness: the Hand has been up all night interrogating, but look, he's come out, even so, for the parade and demonstration. My service cap fitted me badly that day, and my box-calf boots pinched . . . pinched . . .

Do you recognize me, Citizen Gurov? Do you recognize your victim, also your executioner? The Hand is not singing 'Broad Is My Native Land'. He is staring at the Lobnoe Mesto, the white stone executioner's block that looms beside St. Basil's Cathedral. In contrast to the cathedral, the executioner's block is simple. A circle of white stones, sturdily laid in gummy blood.

I stand on it, wearing, as is proper, a red shirt. With my huge hand I caress my huge axe. I pull my forelock down over my eyes, to be a little more terrible and mysterious. An executioner has much the same allure as a beautiful whore, who also causes men to lose their heads. Around me is a whole sea of heads, and above them white banners with black letters: 'Gentlemen! It turns out the doctrine of Marx is not all-powerful!' 'The peasants say thank you for the land!' 'Slave-wage labour be damned!' 'Long live liberty, restored to the people!' 'Glory to God!'

I stroke my huge axe with my huge hand. One by one they are led to the Lobnoe Mesto. They wear military tunics, soldiers' blouses, peasant shirts, suit coats. Quite obviously, each is a gangster of the new type, who does not shudder at the memory of spilled blood, the pollution of his soul, his base and evil deeds, or the verdict of men. Pitiful, sullenly pouting, quaking in mindless fear, they see no light in either past or present or future.

Here is Kaganovich. Not without help, he lays his head on my block. I raise my axe. Souls shudder, and I sense that the crowd would roar with delight and purification if the execution were stayed and Imperial clemency shown to the disgusting, malicious, worthless villains.

Fuck it! The crowd may pity, but the executioner will not forgive! I will not forgive! Ha-ah! . . . *There's nothing on Kaganovich's head to grab in order to show the crowd: the railway robber is bald.*

Molotov is led up. 'Regards from Ribbentrop!' I say. 'Do you know,' I whisper, 'what kind of buddy you have in Berlin?' Ha-ah! *This one's bald too.*

I lay Voroshilov and Budyonny side by side. 'Now I'll really show the crowd my stuff,' I say. 'As military leaders you're worthless. You're such shit that it's better to cut your heads off than let you send hundreds of thousands of soldiers to their graves in the event of war.' Ha-ah!

And now at last here's Himself, walking leisurely up to the block, puffing at his pipe.

'Thank you, Vasya,' he says. 'Thank you. You saved me. I gave you your start, placed the Chekist sword in your hand, and now I myself shall perish by that sword of woe. Thank you. Make shishkebab out of Stalin!'

'That's about the size of it, Joseph Vissarionovich,' I answer. 'It's your own fault. The time has come to erase you. If I don't, it's appalling to think what you'll do to Russia by your friendship with the Führer. World War II will make the Civil War look like a piece of cake, and collectivization a picnic. How much can you bleed the country? There's a war breathing down on you, a war more terrible than the nation has ever known, with pestilence, famine, the coming of the Beast—but you, behind your tobacco smoke, don't you even smell the deadly misfortune? Your health, dear and beloved Joseph Vissarionovich, our friend and teacher! Ciao!' Ha-ah!

Do you recognize him in the snapshot, Citizen Gurov, the fellow wearing twill and nickel-silver, with the gold sword emblazoned on his sleeve? It's me. Me! And at this moment you and Elya and Collectiva walk right past me, past my white stone block, past the Lobnoe Mesto. Collectiva waves her little hand at Stalin, not looking in your direction, she sings 'Protect her as our loving mother', and this is her last snapshot. In three days' time Collectiva Lvovna will be gone.

Where's my briefcase? Oh, here it is. And here's Madame's death certificate. Cerebral haemorrhage . . . instantaneous onset . . . blah-blah-blah . . . signature. You weren't on friendly terms with the physician, of course? You hadn't secured his support in advance? You hadn't weighed the murder plan with care? The idea of marrying Electra hadn't even occurred to you, prior to the death of Collectiva Lvovna? And finally, the black and pink pearls, like many other things, came to your young family by direct inheritance from the confiscated property of people arrested, exiled, or executed?

Fill the glasses. Let's drink to the memory of Collectiva Lvovna. A bit of lemon, if I may . . . Thank you. As for God resting her soul, I don't know about that. I think Madame is in the other place—where you and I are also expected.

So all I get from you is no! The third pearl, the white one—you didn't present it, on a black velvet cushion, to the doctor who gave you the death certificate? No. All right. If the answer's no, it's no.

Come on, let's go bake in the sun, you old crocodile of the Nile! My voracious anaconda! Tiger shark! Rat!

But Dr. Vigelsky, who signed Collectiva Lvovna's death certificate, drowned in an ice-hole on January 1, 1940. Drunk, supposedly . . . I can't help thinking you were a party to his death. But we won't concern ourselves with that issue. Vigelsky was a bad doctor and an unsophisticated man. He got what was coming to him. He should have known whom he was dealing with, what he was getting into . . .

As before, you don't care to come clean? Fine. By the way: your wife, daughter, and son-in-law, on orders from me, will not receive their visa extensions. Any day now they'll be saying goodbye to *la belle France* and departing for their homeland. I need them here! What for? Come clean and I'll tell you . . . If you don't want to—let's move on . . .

Stalin really did come for me that day, at exactly ten o'clock in a black Lincoln. His guards followed behind. As I saw at once, they had split up the surrounding area into sectors and were reconnoitring them in a hyperalert manner with their supposedly all-seeing eyes. When a sudden gust of wind swept the low shrubs growing by the fence, the guards were thrown into an indescribable panic. The second car lurched forward and took up a position between the shrubs and the Lincoln, in case there were Japanese intelligence agents lying in wait in the shrubbery. Japanese intelligence was a big favourite with our Leader that year.

We sped up the Minsk Highway. Flying ahead of us, standing on its hind legs on the radiator cap, was a metal dog, shining in the sun. Stalin couldn't take his eyes off it. He felt calmed by our speed and by the fact that the dog was not flying at him, like the dog yesterday in the forest, but away from him. Over the highway towards Moscow, towards the Kremlin it flew, its breast cutting the air, its graceful paws beating . . . Stalin kept silent, and I did too. I was thinking, Does my late father Ivan Abramych see me now, or doesn't he? If he does, what does he think of all this? What would he want to say about it? Should I maybe pulp Stalin with one blow? Ivan Abramych didn't answer. No, I thought, don't pulp Stalin. You can't kill all the leaders. We've got shit like him by the bucketful. There'd be ten Stalins after his place, gnawing each other's throats. I'd better settle accounts with Conceptiev's detachment first, then with Conceptiev himself, then with sonny-boy. *Then* I'll go to work on the rest of the vermin . . .

'What are you thinking, Hand?'

'I'm thinking I should go into the security system, Joseph Vissarionovich. I should study up and get in. That's where I belong now—although I wouldn't refuse a place in your service.'

'Or work for the Party, perhaps? We need cadres the way shishkebabs need skewers. Think it over, Hand.'

'No, I'll be more useful in security,' I answered, and I displayed my enormous hand to Stalin. 'Pasha can work for the Party.'

'Perhaps you're right, Hand. But tell me, why are you so eager to get into the Cheka? Whom do you hate?'

'I don't know that I hate anyone personally,' I said. 'But all around me I feel this . . . well, this force. It needs to have its brains bashed out against a tree, like a mad dog! Excuse me if I've said something wrong,' I said, clutching. But as it turned out, I had scored a bull's eye.

'On the contrary! You're exactly right, Hand! I too feel this force. It hinders people from living. I've been over-lenient with it, but its days are numbered!'

So there I . . . Just what are you sulking about now, Citizen Gurov? I don't know where your cat Trofim and your dog Trilby have disappeared to . . . I repeat: I don't know! I'm not following them around like the Japrat stalking our man Zorge! Is that clear? Do you think you'd have Trofim and Trilby for company in a cell in the Lubyanka? In there, you couldn't unburden your soul to even a cunt-louse, you miserable bastard! 'Trofim and Trilby, where are they?' Oh, blackmailing you, am I, and by the most despicable methods! Well, and why shouldn't I blackmail garbage like you? Poxov! Poxov! Where have the cat and dog disappeared to? I didn't give orders to guard them, but you *were* told not to let so much as a fly get in or out of here! Find them! Deliver them to me, dead or alive! Proceed immediately! . . .

I used to ride home from the Kremlin with Stalin. I was considered his bodyguard for special missions. Stalin loved the end of the day; it promised temporary deliverance from fears and hatred. The dog that flew off the Lincoln in a favourable direction soothed his poor nerves and confirmed his faith in good luck . . .

One day he said to me: 'Hand, the inquest has established that the Alsatian you liquidated really was a mad dog. What makes me suspicious is something else. The dog's master, a Trotskyite named Illarion Matveevich Kurl, who owns a neighbouring dacha, has disappeared without a trace. He once vexed me greatly. He gave me a slap in the face in front of Lenin; even Stalin is not secure. A political enemy. Cruel as ten Neros put together. An unmitigated Marxist dogmatist. True, he successfully liquidated the rabid Leningrad aristocracy, and he did help me in '29. Get busy on him. I want to see what you're good for. We destroyed the Czar's law and order. We tossed the canons of classical justice on the garbage heap of history. For that reason, our investigative organs and judicial system are far from perfect. And for the same reason, Hand, be free in your actions. I'm indebted to you, but I don't forgive mistakes. Get going!'

You can understand, Citizen Gurov, how I flamed with desire then, how my blood and flesh, imprisoned for ages, surged to life! My first order of business was to inspect the dacha that Kurl had boarded up and abandoned. Like you, he had been swiping wood panelling and trim, leather couches from baronial drawing-rooms, paintings, bronzes, porcelains, and other junk . . . All as one for this you fight, as one for this you die, bastards! Kurl had obviously fled. He'd had an intuition: the jig was up. Most likely he'd melted into the masses or skipped to Turkey. I inspected the dacha. I had no training as a detective. Just passion, a mad passion for the hunt. And an interest in seeing how executioners reacted to their own pain, humiliation, and inevitable death. Alas, I found nothing that would even suggest a direction for my search. I decided I would have to declare an official investigation. I stood dully in the yard: as a detective, I stank, and I was scared stiff to cross Stalin's path. Suddenly—bzzzzz, my veins started humming in resonance with Chance. Of course I hadn't noticed her at that precise instant, but for no reason at all she had led me to the dog kennel. Or rather, it wasn't a kennel but a doghouse, which somehow recalled the Mausoleum. A little wooden pyramid, sort of. The corners had been planed and some carved mouldings tacked on, lest there be too gross a resemblance to our well-known architectural masterpiece. But the kennel's intended parody was obvious. The fugitive Trotskyite had probably felt the same way about both of his enemies, the dead one and the living. A chain, and a collar with a decorative plate engraved ALPHA. The collar had not been worn through, the dog had not slipped it; someone had removed it. I crouched down and looked at the huge, simply huge, bones that Alpha had gnawed on. Whole sheep pelvises, not even chopped up. Pigs' legs complete with hooves. That's one big fucking oven, I thought, if they can put the whole hog in it . . . There was no such oven in the dacha. No coals or spit to be seen on the grounds. But the odd thing was, the hooves and the edges of the bones were burnt black, burnt to a crisp, burnt to a cinder. Oh-ho, Vasya, I thought, check out your hunch! After all, it was your ass that got frostbitten on the cursed log, not your head.

At first I wanted to take along three men from the Special Section, to which I had been assigned in accordance with a phone call from Stalin. Then I thought better of it. I got a pair of 'tough lucks', just in case, and a car.

'To the crematorium,' I told the chauffeur. 'Get going.'

'Yes, sir—the crematorium!'

Night. Rain. Melancholy. But if I was wrong? Melancholy and rain. We pulled up. I knocked on the iron gate. No one. I vaulted over the gate from the top of the limo. I looked in the watchman's hut. The watchman, oddly enough, was dead. Not yet cold. He may even have died at my knock on the gate. There was a bottle on the table. The glass he had dropped was on the floor, in a puddle of vodka. The watchman hadn't had time for his pick-me-up. Stroke—a lucky death . . .

Well, dead is dead. I ordered the chauffeur to open the gate and pull up to the crematorium itself, preferably quietly. Rain. The repulsive grey building was closed. I looked for a back entrance and found it. A staircase led to the cellar. The voices of persons of the male and female sex were audible, as they write in interrogation reports. Laughter that sounded lewd even at a distance . . . I was in civvies, though Stalin had immediately made me a lieutenant. To this day I hate the uniform bitterly . . . About ten people in there, I thought. I'll dispatch them with the two Mausers and my pair of big fists. I drew one 'tough luck' from its holster . . . I stood at the door for a moment. They were having a riotous feast in there. Toasts, nasty goddamned jokes, talk of world revolution. Infamous bastards, I thought. Whores and wine aren't enough for you! You still need a world bordello! I took the second 'tough luck' from its holster, squatted on my haunches, and looked through the keyhole. Huh! So much for class war! In the middle of a weird enclosure stood a table . . . Let me emphasize, it was just an enclosure, with no regular outlines. It had a low, smoke-blackened ceiling. One wall was convex, semicircular. A second wall, sickeningly concave, formed an obtuse angle with the floor. Some sort of black niche was visible near the ceiling. The third wall, as I realized, was actually the gate of the crematorium itself. Partly Dutch tile, scorched and cracked from the heat, and partly steel: sliding doors with peepholes, ammeters, voltmeters, thermometers, buttons, lights, and two imposing Siemens knife switches. Absurdly out of register, by chance or necessity, the space of the enclosure was disgusting and unfit for habitation. In the middle, although the middle of such a space is very difficult to determine, stood a long, low, rectangular table, like the coffee tables we have now. On the table, on an iron stretcher with wheels, lay a roast pig . . . Not a suckling pig. Full-grown. I don't see why you needed that clarification, Citizen Gurov. The pig lay—

Oh, on your personal order? The meat-packing plant had issued it to your drinking buddy Kurl . . . And again, only chance prevented you from being at that party, with a girl? Stupendous! . . . You failed to send your wife Electra to the Bolshoi Theatre, and lo and behold, once again, our meeting was postponed for decades!

And it wasn't just a pig, but a young hog. In point of fact, a barrow . . . I'm astonished! A young roast barrow lay on the table, looking like a high official who has been lolling around tanning at Sochi and dozed himself into sunstroke. Salad greens. Cucumbers, tomatoes, mushrooms, bottles. Last of all I turned my attention to the revellers. There were only four of them, which was also strange. But they were chattering, screeching, laughing, yelling, making enough noise for eight or ten. They were sitting on little red hassocks, completely naked, except for one handsomely built man with a tasselled Turkish fez adorning his dark head. I had made no mistake, then. This was Kurl: Trotskyite, romanticist of world revolution, sadist, bigtime thief and executioner.

From the keyhole, stuffy heat and a roast smell assailed my nostrils. The enclosure, by the way, had no windows. Quietly I pushed the door. It was open. I walked in. They didn't notice me. I walked closer to the table, just as Kurl took an antique cutlass and started to slice the head off the hog.

'Too bad this isn't Stalin!' he said.

'*Hands up!*' I barked. The wretches were accustomed to act as they pleased with impunity, but before they could even think they threw their hands up to dry on the clothesline, as the jackal thugs say. The antique cutlass remained resting in the nape of the hog's neck. A full goblet froze motionless in the second naked stud's uplifted hand, and red wine spilled over the brim, down his hand and elbow into his hairy armpit. The trembling of the whores made their pink and scarlet nails flicker. Their breasts sharpened, their nipples paled . . . I remember it all as if it were yesterday . . .

I commanded the whores to get dressed forthwith. I took away their passports and ordered them into the limo to wait for my return. Make it snappy, Shock Workers of debauchery, I told them. They cleared out.

'What's the trouble, Comrade?' Kurl asked, coming to his senses.

'Against the wall!' I said. 'Quick! Up!'

They both stood up, face to the concave wall. I put one 'tough luck' in its holster. With my free hand I clawed up Kurl's face and scalp, the way I did yours. It was the first time I had tested this trick, which kills the body's spirit, life, and will. Kurl went limp and gulped at his snot. I took the second stud's kisser in my hand . . . turned him around . . . and the blood rushed to my head. One of Conceptiev's brave lads! No mistaking him, the worm! His face, when he took leisurely aim at the peasants, had been just the same as now. Just the same!

The years had erased from this face the sinister voluptuousness and sullen, cruel efficiency, but I had restored its true expression, and I recognized it! Already knowing exactly how I would proceed, I smashed my fist down on his sweaty bald crown. Out cold. Kurl didn't move a muscle when his drinking buddy fell. I smashed my fist down on him too. Out cold. I put the 'tough luck' back in my belt and opened the doors to the crematorium oven. It was dark inside and smelled of roast pork. The oven had already cooled. I threw the pig and the other food off the iron stretcher, put Conceptiev's laddie and Kurl on it, and sent it down the sloping rails, straight into the oven. I shut the doors. I opened the peephole and waited for the bastards to wake up. I gulped a tumbler of vodka: I was so excited, every fibre of my being had begun to quiver with the inhuman pleasure of wreaking vengeance for the first time.

Watch, Ivan Abramych, watch from the other world! You too, my poor mother, Maria Sergeevna! Watch!

I wasn't about to eat anything. This pig was from no Russian oven . . . All right, I'll call it a barrow. You're a pain and a pedant, Citizen Gurov! . . . I chewed on a piece of parsley and glanced through the peephole. The piglets had begun to stir!

'Kurl,' I shouted, 'Kurl! Crawl to the peephole!'

He crawls over. His slobber is squishing in his mouth, he's letting out thick little yelps of horror.

'Comrade,' he mumbles, 'comrade, save me . . . Everything . . . I'll . . . give you everything . . . everything . . . comrade!'

The other one comes crawling too. Like a wild animal he knocks Kurl away from the peephole. He can't say anything, he's just wailing: 'Ee-ee-ee-ee . . .'

'Kurl,' I said into the peephole, 'before you gunned down hundreds of souls, before you had your fun with the Petersburg nobles and innocent peasants, if you'd been warned it would end this way, would you have murdered, tormented, and robbed?'

'No! No! No! I swear it—no! Comrade, save me! I . . . I . . . I was doing the will of the Party. Save me!'

'And you, joker,' I said to the other one. 'Do you remember the village of Odinka and your commander, Conceptiev?'

'Ee-ee-ee,' his teeth chattered. 'I'll never d-do it agoon, goo it gagoo-goo-goo . . . do it agoon . . .'

'Right! You'll never do it again,' I said. 'This is an order from Trotsky! He came to power when Stalin was killed in Barvikha by a mad dog. The rank of Brigade Commander has been conferred on the dog. She has been awarded the Medal of Honour.'

At that, they snapped wide awake.

'*Bastard!*' Kurl bawled.

The second stud flung himself on Kurl, butting his head against Kurl's face and shouting with fury, 'I told you! I told you! Stalin's a louse! Trotsky's a whore! You're all lice! Lice! Lice!'

Their shouts blended together. I turned on the first knife switch, then the second, turned the handle of the rheostat all the way to the right, and began watching the instruments and the thermometer. As the oven grew warm and then red-hot, they must have been dancing, writhing, howling, thrashing, and sizzling in the hellish fire. I didn't look in. One of Lenin's lightbulbs started blinking red on the panel. I realized it was all over. I turned off the switches and peered through the peephole. There was nobody in the oven. Nothing but shapeless heaps of dark grey ash, lying on the stretcher and the oven tiles.

I raked the ashes out with a long-handled shovel, poured them into a champagne bottle, and collected the belongings of the cremated men. Leaving the hog to lie on the floor in utter solitude, I departed from the ghastly cellar, where the concave wall depressed me horribly and the convex wall drove me just plain crazy.

The whores were exiled to Kazakhstan that very night. The director of the crematorium was fired and made a stretcher-bearer in the Red Crescent.

'Joseph Vissarionovich!' I reported. 'Your order has been carried out. Kurl no longer exists in nature!'

'How's that? Where is he, if not in nature?'

'Here!' I displayed the champagne bottle to Stalin and poured a few still-warm ashes into his hand. 'From the viewpoint of materialism, this is Illarion Matveevich Kurl.'

'You have exceeded my expectations, Hand . . . How strange. Kurl was, and Kurl is not . . . Just a handful of ashes . . . A small pile of dust . . . I think the Soviet people should be informed that I have discovered a fourth state of matter, after the gasiform, liquid, and solid: an ashiform state. I've always felt there was something missing between the solid and the gasiform states. What did you tell Kurl?'

'That I was reducing him to ashes on orders from you.'

Clutching his belly, Stalin burst into gay, pure, childish laughter.

'Go, Hand. As for me, I'll work on Chapter Four of my history of the Bolshevik Party. I want people to feel nauseated when they read the ideas of Marx and Lenin! Thank you! Continue your on-the-job training! Scatter his dust to the wind, in keeping with tradition.'

Towards morning I fell asleep, and again I dreamed of my father Ivan Abramych.

He begged me, on a black square in a dead city, to abandon vengeance, not to damn my soul, in order to give it a chance of being reunited with them all. And again I shoved my father in the chest, so hard that he staggered back, and I told him, 'My vengeance for the slain, for all of you, knows no limit, nor ever will!' Bitterly my father Ivan Abramych wept, and my mother comforted him . . .

Did you have a good night? Lousy? Well, nobody ordered you to think instead of sleeping . . .

Not long ago, solely in the line of duty, I had occasion to summon a certain odd young man for a conversation. His ideas came to mind just now. He feels that the talk about human rights is sometimes altogether too abstract. He feels that the salient point is often obscured by the liberals' demands for artistic freedom, freedom of speech, freedom for street demonstrations, and so on. The essential human right, he feels, is the right to live in the natural atmosphere of Being and breathe Freedom. In the atmosphere of Being, Freedom is as unnoticeable as air; it's the true and indispensable condition of every person's existence and independence—not the bottled ersatz air that the 'opponents of *détente* in representative forums force our leaders to issue to the citizens of the USSR.

'Does this mean, parasite,' I said, 'that you go even further than those who want to write whatever comes into their heads, draw whatever the inner eye sees, and emigrate to any place they feel like? Further than those,' I said, 'who long to be judged fairly, as in England or Denmark, who long for the government to report to the people on foreign policy and discuss strategic goals, who long for it to abolish criminal liability for trying to hold an individual opinion on the activity of all Soviet social, cultural, and commercial institutions? Is that so? You want Gromyko to account for every kopeck spent in Somalia, Egypt, Ethiopia, Chile, and Cuba? My,' I said, 'haven't you got big ideas! I expect you want the state's functions in consumer goods, the food industry, and other public services to be handed over to private parties cognizant of their responsibility for the people's living conditions, stomachs, clothes, and health? And,' I said, 'you want to conduct a national referendum, don't you, for the purpose of ascertaining whether or not, in the opinion of the citizens, socialism exists in this country? And then wouldn't you go even further? Wouldn't you try to learn what the different generations think about Communism? Do they have even a smidgen of faith that it can be built?

'Are you confident, perhaps,' I asked, 'that Russia is a million times richer than Kuwait and Sweden, and if it weren't for the Soviet regime and its brainless, lazy, adventuristic, dog-in-the-manger State Capitalism, we'd have wrought forty economic miracles by now? Answer!'

'Yes! I *am* confident, and I do wish for everything you've listed in your sensible but intentionally provocative speech!' said this odd young man, puffing with enjoyment on a cigar that a stoolie from the Cinematographers' Union had forgotten in my office.

'I realize,' he said, 'that you can't go right out and make radical changes in the structure of our state or its economic and social life, any more than you could in the USA or Japan. That's why I sent a letter to the Politburo, with my return address, demanding that they begin to co-operate forthwith in the matter of creating a natural atmosphere of Being in our land, in accordance with the freely expressed will of our citizens. "I will not prescribe methods for you in this matter," I wrote. "You have an institute for the study of the economy of the USA, as well as hundreds of organizations working on other diddlyshit matters. So commission them to take up this problem." You know the rest, Citizen Investigator. I received a reply from the Central Committee. It was full of baloney about my being an agent of Zionism and the CIA. I'm a hundred per cent Russian, and for the most part my sympathies lie with peoples striving for self-determination: Lithuanians, Ukrainians, Armenians, Jews, Russians themselves, Hungarians, Poles, Tibetans, and many others.

'I'm sending another letter, addressed to all Politburo members, Central Committeee candidate-members and secretaries—the names barely fitted on the envelope. Here's what I say I want, specifically. To start with, we must eliminate from our great, mighty, and beautiful Russian language, as well as from other no less beautiful languages, the hundreds of *Word Graves* in which lie buried the *Original Meanings*, which are long since rotted and eaten by worms. Communism. Socialism. Soviet regime. Socialist competition. Elections to the Supreme Soviet. People's court. Soviet trade unions. Radiant future. Unity of the Party and the people. Glory to labour. Glory to the Communist Party of the Soviet Union. Socialist Realism. The most progressive art. Proletarian internationalism . . . Our country has hundreds of graves like these. After liquidating the word-graves, let's begin by finding our sense of reality. Next, we must give a decent burial to our No. 1 deceased, Lenin. As a former friend of mine has said, there can be no order in a land where even one dead man is left unburied. It's grotesque, and not very pragmatic to forbid belief in the living God while forcibly inculcating a love for the dead scarecrow that you, my dear comrades, have placed on exhibit in a marble cellar, exposed to the weird stares of a snookered mob instinctively seeking someone to worship. For the desire to worship is an ineradicable passion of the soul—and the Forces of Evil play upon this desire.

'Then I wax lyrical in describing to the members of the Politburo the outlook for our development when the atmosphere of Natural Being begins to revive among and around us, and so on, all the way to Judgement Day. We will cast off our concerns about the ban on freedom of speech, freedom of the press, artistic freedom, and emigration to other countries. The bad writer won't get published, and the good one may not get read. After all, that's how it used to be.

'"But I insist," I wrote, "that the struggle for the rights of man be co-ordinated with a struggle for the rights of the men who occupy the highest posts in our government, Party, army, and security system. We must begin this struggle forthwith, and on a world scale. What do our leaders spend their lives on, when they serve an imposed idea? Why must they sacrifice the joys of a personal existence for the sake of a reign of dead dogmas? Why must they suffer, enmeshed in the postulates of a doddering Doctrine? Why? Let ordinary men of good will exclaim, all together: Free our leaders from the false Communist Idea!"'

How do you like this odd young man, Citizen Gurov? You don't—but he amuses you?

Staving off a worse blow, I ordered that this nice young man be held in the KGB psych hospital for a couple of months. Now he thinks his global thoughts at the Lyre Café, I expect, over a shot of low-grade vodka.

But, actually, why was I telling you all this? Ah! Now do you understand that one can respond to an idea just as if it were a woman? Do you understand that Stalin responded to the Idea with hatred and loathing, just as you responded to Collectiva? He would have been glad to take the step you took, but he couldn't: never mind a reformation, revisionism of any stripe would have been fatal to him. Shuddering in helpless fury, hating his cursed Idea, he slighted and discredited her wherever he could. He took revenge on her hot-blooded lovers, young and old, for all his humiliations, his fear, and his life imprisonment. He dreamed of sending them all to damnation, every last one. But the Terror, however total it seemed, was too feeble to do this. You may think this is a cockeyed notion, but I am personally convinced that the war presented itself to Stalin as an ideal ally in the cause of annihilating Lenin's old cohorts, the intellectual Bolshevik élite, and perhaps the Idea herself.

Yes! He dreamed passionately of playing at war and for that reason, that reason alone, did not heed sensible warnings from his hypnotized advisers, dispatches from talented spies, or reports that presented alarming pictures of the actual situation. The war must become an objective worth applying his strength to . . . Let the Führer's tanks plough and flatten half of Russia . . . Let millions perish—he had plenty more beyond the Urals . . . Let the Gestapo zap the surviving Bolshevik fanatics and the jealous priests of the Idea. Let it happen! When the German tanks and soldiers had done their purgative work, he would say, 'Death to the Fascist invaders!' And men would rush to the attack, with his name on their lips. They would liberate the occupied territories, and we'd think up something to do there. We'd start to build something new. 'And mayhap on his sad decline love with farewell smile would shine . . .' He needed a war in order to rouse up a country depressed by domestic upheavals, in order to make people forget the millions of their relatives who were dying in the north, in Kolyma, in Kazakhstan, in Siberia—or behind barbed wire, two or three kilometres from the doors of their own homes.

He alone understood that he wouldn't last long in a country living in a virtual state of siege. Court trial for tardiness or absenteeism. Collective farmers passportless, banned from leaving the kolkhozes to seek work in the cities. Army officers not confident of security. Chekists waiting their turn to be gunned down. The peoples of Lithuania, Latvia, Estonia, and other countries just yearning to free themselves from the Soviet yoke. The republics, the myriad thieves, the toughs, the Bohemians, corruption, rickety technology, and much else. Day or night, he had no peace from all this, he no longer knew whom to rely on, and naturally the idea of war seemed to promise salvation. During a war, even he would become another, different Stalin. Stalin the supreme commander. Stalin, Europe's liberator from Fascism—that blood brother to the hated Idea, disgusting brother-in-law to the Leader.

War! The only answer! It would occupy minds and hands, it would rally those who had been alienated in the confrontations, it would write off all the monstrous sins, it would kindle a feeling for the motherland in hearts that had cursed her, give unity to their efforts, and sanctify, with hatred of the enemy, the bonehead mistakes and unnecessary sacrifices. War!

Of course, Citizen Gurov, for lack of genius and sometimes also imagination, Stalin had pictured the start of the war and its course quite differently. Ten times a day, in October of '41, sucking at his cigarette-holder and walking sedately to keep from betraying his funk, he withdrew to the can. There he suffered through the most critical, truly dangerous moment of his life, not knowing how his very risky game would end for him and experiencing ordinary human agitation, which imparts an awareness, not entirely pleasant but authentic, of one's personal existence. He felt that he had ceased to be held prisoner of war by the Idea. Never had her fate so depended on *his* behaviour and decisions as before that winter's Battle of Moscow . . .

Poxov! Is that you? Come in! Well, now! Trofim and Trilby have been caught. We're invited to have a look at them, Citizen Gurov! . . .

I can understand the shock of a man whose best, gentle, and most favourite friends don't recognize him. But believe me, 'my veterinarians' gave them no shots. Especially none that woud destroy their habitual bonds with their master and his comfortable home. I swear I had nothing to do with this . . . It was not I, unfortunately, who devised this torture for you. Not I . . . They were caught at the Sukhumi Ape Farm, after being discovered there with the help of our secret agents. Both Trofim and Trilby were eating from the same trough as the gibbons and sleeping under a tree that had been chewed bare all the way down to the ground. The apes accepted them benevolently, studied them, and hunted their fleas. They joked and played, rather roughly but not cruelly. The keepers thought the scientists had flipped their frigging lids this time, conducting a new experiment on the problems of coexistence of different animal species within the framework of Soviet-Ethiopian scientific collaboration.

But why your captured pets are giving you the cold shoulder and don't recognize you, I wouldn't know. They don't recognize the house, either, or their favourite comfy perches and sleeping places. Everything here has suddenly become strange to them. We've locked them up. Go and socialize, clarify your mutual relations. I'll think a while. This is food for thought . . .

Trofim scratched you, and Trilby bit you? Congratulations! Give up, for the moment, on your desire to make sense out of this event. I see what the trouble is. The cat and dog are fleeing from you. The innocent creatures have scented your villainous soul, your black misfortune, and the terrible emptiness of your abode. Look at yourself through their eyes. An old wretch rushing around like a rat in a maze, in search of an exit. Your pets don't recognize your eyes, features, figure, gait, posture, or tone of voice. You're scarier to them than a stranger, because they can't comprehend the change that's come over you or what caused it. Probably you're radiating horribly unpleasant waves of some sort, or smells, if that suits you better; probably you're giving off vibes without either of us realizing it, probably Trofim and Trilby couldn't stand my yelling, the mysterious transformation in your personality, the whole atmosphere of the house these days. Probably they assimilated the horrible facts somehow, began to panic, and finally fled. Then they hung around one place or another till they made it to the farm, where the ape society struck them as almost human.

Evidently they mistook a huge male for you, because they jumped up at him and licked his paws, yelping and purring affectionately. They put up a desperate resistance when the keepers forcibly tore them away from the gibbon, who was trying to figure out what was going on in the pen entrusted to his care. Even now they're whimpering, refusing food, and pining for the primordial communism of the ape herd. They want to save themselves, as I understand it, although they themselves don't know from what. Quite possibly they've stopped accepting you, for some reason, as a member of the human race.

Do you happen to remember whether you experienced anything similar before you repudiated your father?

Can it be that you didn't calculate at all, didn't reckon, didn't figure, didn't finagle, just simply saved yourself, like a panicky animal with a premonition of trouble?

You say that may be exactly what happened. But I don't believe it was. You don't operate in a mode of self-exposure, like the dazed villains who sometimes paint themselves even blacker than necessary in order to feel their guilt more keenly. Your mode is self-justification, Citizen Gurov . . .

I know that the day you received your Party membership card, not without Collectiva's help, was the most marvellous day of your life. Correctly and accurately, you thought of the Party card as your ticket to the feed troughs that held all these things—the villa, the paintings, the jewels, and a long life knee-deep in cognac and ass-deep in whores. That's an old story and doesn't interest me.

But you said that day, not aloud of course, and to no one in particular: 'Bastards, I'll show you! You shat on the ideals we imbibed with the milk of the mad cow. You forced me to murder my father and mother. You're no Communists, you're profiteers, cunt-chasers, drunks, sadists, nobodies, informers, traitors, and cowards! I know you! And if that's the score, I'm going to get what's mine! I was nothing, but now I am all, and I'll go after what's mine, like a wolf. A wolf, comrades! I'll snap at everything I can, till my fangs clack shut for the last time on a tempting morsel. You wanted to take everything away from me? Look out! With my Communist Party card in my pocket, I'll spit in your faces and become a capitalist! I'll revenge myself on you! I'll be revenging myself every minute, for I'll be using each one for my own fun and profit! My own! My own! And you, sleazy bitch, you, my saviour and rapist—you're the first in line! You! Your last moments will be horrible, you moustachioed crowbait, pimples on your thighs, lie down then, lie down, dipso, spread your loathsome fat legs, don't go kissing me, finish this off, get your pleasure, you'll never get it again, never, never, never again, *come*, prostitute, last chance, *come*, snake, I hate, hate, *ha-a-ate you*, undercover spy-face!'

I'm not fantasizing, Citizen Gurov. Today, let's say, you receive your Party card. Tonight, a boozy celebration. The next day—according to the death certificate signed by Dr. Vigelsky, chief of the special Security System polyclinic—Collectiva Lvovna Brutnikova dies of a cerebral haemorrhage. You had one big break on the timing: Electra was visiting her paternal grandfather. Correct . . ? Correct.

Psychologically, it had to happen, everything I've improvised. Had to! So what if it wasn't in just these terms, so what!

Your mood, your thoughts, your preparedness, your realization that today was too soon but the day after tomorrow would be too late—I can vouch for all of it. Don't you look silly, affecting to study the Matisse sketch? Does it all come back to you? Are you stunned by the subtlety of my scrupulous reconstruction? What? I'm no detective, I'm shit? You can tell I'm in a good humour and not about to clobber you for your rudeness. No, I'm not shit. I've accomplished a nice piece of work, and I'm pleased with myself. Yes, indeed . . . Don't crack if you don't want to, sonofabitch. The day will come when you'll crack all the way to your ass, and from there on down you'll fall apart by yourself . . .

So. Feeling wronged by the Idea, hating her as much as you hated Collectiva, or perhaps even more because you couldn't erase her, you formulated a distinct set of tasks and goals for yourself. You couldn't annihilate the Idea that had raped you and your Fate: if Stalin couldn't, how could you! So you started shitting on the Idea with dirty tricks both large and small. Having murdered one of her shining exemplars, you laughed and rejoiced as purely and gaily as a little boy. You had emancipated yourself! You planted a loud kiss on Freedom's fresh, hot, ruddy living cheek, and promptly married Electra . . .

In brief, the ideal Soviet reality can't be created even if Satan busts a gut trying. His ideals and lesser ideals have long since been eaten away, by both worthy and ugly forms of life. You are one of the millions of little beetles who have chewed through the frozen log of the Devil's Idea . . .

Oh, you make me sick and tired with your incompetent questions about the Devil. Why do I sometimes call him Asmodeus, sometimes the Fiend, sometimes Satan? Those are his aliases. Thugs, the underground, and the Demon love all kinds of pseudonyms and aliases. You too have changed your name a couple of times. Conceptiev, a.k.a. Brutnikov, a.k.a. Gurov.

Repeat that! I didn't understand . . . What party does Asmodeus himself belong to? Our conversations haven't driven you clucking crazy, by any chance? I don't suppose he belongs to any party. The swine would have to keep in mind that his mission is to destroy all, but the Creator wants to save each.

And now you're wondering ironically, does God want to save you personally? He does! He does! Till your last scoundrelly breath and heartbeat, He will not stop wanting to save you.

Yes. Right this minute, Citizen Gurov, right now . . . 12:17 Moscow time . . . God wants to save you. Oh no, don't worry, *I* don't want to, not I. He wants to save you . . . Did you personally, by your own hand, murder Collectiva Lvovna Brutnikova? Come on. Crack!

What a bastard you are, what a blackguard and a liar! Crack, or I'll run smack out of patience! I'm not the Lord God, after all! Did you murder her? No . . . hard as a diamond. To hell with you. Scum! I'm going for a walk in the garden. I can't stand the sight of you right now, I need to get away from your voice . . . Trilby, Trilby! Trofim! Kitty, kitty! Let's go for a walk!

Yes! Don't drop your flytrap. Your beasts and I have been getting along pretty well for some time now . . . And don't call them, don't whine. They won't come . . . A drink? I've forbidden Poxov to give you anything. You may not relieve your despair with alcohol. Sufferings should be pure . . . Shove it!

What now? Bawling like a crocodile, right on the crystal platter? What brought this on?

Oh, stop it! Don't forget, tears will make the crystal turn yellow and crack.

Here, tell me this: the black and pink pearls came into Electra's possession by inheritance, did they . . ? Hmm. But I have precise information that you presented her with the pearls on your wedding day.

If you don't want a personal confrontation with your good wife Electra, who is about to arrive—confess. I'm waiting! Swine, you should have told me long ago! So you gave her a phoney story about how they were the only family heirloom you'd saved from confiscation. . . Your grandafther had presented them to your grandmother the day Alexander II abolished serfdom. You wouldn't happen to remember what Grandfather said to her in that intimate moment, would you?

I'm not joking. Here in this briefcase, along with a pencil stub, along with the purest of confessions and the testimony of a most lofty spirit and beautiful mind, along with your repudiation, dossier, documents, and denunciations, I have a grandson's denunciation of his grandfather and grandmother.

The grandson was born into a normal family. The father, mother, grandfather, and grandmother were from a long line of doctors. Good doctors. They treated the sick, saved lives, set bones, relieved suffering, delivered babies, closed the eyes of the dead. The mother died of consumption, but really, I think, from the anguish and grief that struck her in 1917 and tormented her until 1920. The father was put in prison in 1935. Or rather, he wasn't put in—one day he wasn't let out. He was the prison doctor. A good doctor, I repeat. He dropped by the office of the warden of our largest prison, spat in his face, punched him, then became hysterical and crippled him, as a gesture of protest against the slaughter and torture of prisoners.

The grandson was left with his grandparents in the big apartment in the Arbat. He poked a little hole in the wall and eavesdropped regularly on what his grandfather was telling his grandmother in intimate moments. 'Intimate moment'—that's the grandson's expression, frequently encountered in his denunciation.

Well, then. Speaking softly, which inflamed the grandson and egged him on, grandfather would tell grandmother, to the best of his knowledge, strength, and purity of soul, the meaning of the witches' Sabbath going on around them, which the old folks perceived as being practically the end of the world. I have sometimes used his ideas in my conversations with you . . . grandfather called a spade a spade. The devil's work was diabolism, Stalin was a shit, a cur, and a nothing, his comrades-in-arms were worms, pubic lice, appendixes stuffed with thumbtacks, murderers, shysters, and churls. Grandfather was a conservative and a believer. He did not know how to measure the greatness of an era by the number of innocent victims offered on the altar of an idea. He could not reconcile himself to obvious vileness, to a moral collapse masquerading as enthusiasm.

The grandson was seventeen. Neatly he wrote down his grandfather's frequent speeches in a notebook. Never failing to number them, he would begin, 'In intimate moment No. 17, I heard Grandfather make the following statements regarding trials of enemies of the people . . .' 'During intimate moment No. 29, Grandmother agreed that the Soviet-German pact meant the start of a terrible new war. Grandfather suggested that they begin to stock up on matches, salt, butter, groats, tea, sugar and spirits.' 'Intimate moment No. 39. Critique of works by Soviet writers. They excoriated Alexei Tolstoy as a Count, a prostitute, and a brown-nose. They differed with respect to his talent. Grandmother agreed that poetry and prose had strangled on eulogies to Comrade Stalin. Grandfather recited something about the three little pigs, but I didn't get the point.'

I counted about two hundred such intimate moments in this all-purpose notebook. The grandson spied on his grandfather and grandmother for a year and a half, eavesdropped, took notes, and numbered them. This notebook will die with me some day. I'll take it to my grave. Mankind has much to be ashamed of, but I can't insult human nature, the human soul, by letting people see these lined pages. It would be cruel. What I have read to you are the few pages innocent in style and content. Words do not exist to characterize the rest. The emotion that grips your soul when you read them is inexpressible. It's beyond understanding. But it's worse than death, humiliation, disgust, pain, shame, despair, it's worse than nonexistence.

When I read the notebook for the first time, on orders from the People's Commissar, I foolishly burst out laughing. I didn't believe my own eyes. I read it again. God knows, by that time I had seen a lot. Deaths, tortures, executions, blood, tears, monstrous denunciations of loved ones—I had seen everything. But as I read it a second time, I felt myself turn pale, my arms fell to my sides, my knees buckled, my eyes went dark. I felt rising to my heart, against my will, a fear more terrible than any encountered in the most pathologically loathsome nightmares, and flying from my mouth with a groan the breath of last life . . . And if my parents' fate, my fate, millions of horrible fates bore, in spite of everything, some relation to Life and Death, that notebook bore no relation to either. Man could not have written it! Of all the things I had ever known, read, seen, or suffered, this, it seemed to me, was the most outrageous. And when I had read the notebook to the end, finishing it only because I hoped, unconsciously, to find at least the shallowest semblance of humanity there on the last page, in the last line, in the full stop—instead of which there turned out to be three exclamation marks—I slid from my chair and lay on the floor for half an hour . . . not puking, probably only because I was too weak.

I could not avoid setting a case in motion against the grandfather and grandmother. But I did everything possible to prevent them finding out about the grandson's notebook. Taking a risk, I advised them to sign under Article 58, Paragraph 10—agitation and propaganda. I concocted some sort of gibberish, threw in a couple of anecdotes about Budyonny, and the old folks signed gratefully. They received only five years apiece, and ended up on a quiet 'farm' near Omsk. During the war they were freed . . .

I called in the grandson. Nothing peculiar in his appearance. I sent him over for psychiatric evaluation. Absolutely normal. I took his application.

'But how can we accept you for a job in the security system,' I said, 'if you're betraying your grandfather and grandmother?'

'I'm not betraying them, I'm exposing them. One betrays one's friends. But these were enemies who hadn't been finished off. I couldn't stay on the sidelines.'

'At intimate moment number one?'

'Yes! These are the very moments when people reveal themselves utterly to one another. I could make a pretty good speciality of procuring materials at intimate moments in the life of an enemy.'

'Would you explain what an intimate moment is?'

'It's a moment when two close confidants candidly expose to each other their thoughts on our era, Stalin, Fascism, and the building of the new life,' the grandson replied, in the tone of an A-student. 'Moreover, I don't acknowledge a blood relationship.'

'But do you know,' I said, 'that in one of the intimate moments you haven't numbered, your grandfather and grandmother conceived your father?'

'Yes. Of course I know.'

'We won't take you into the security system. You're a potential traitor. Or do you love us better than your grandfather and grandmother?'

'I do, I swear it! Ever since I was ten years old I've dreamed of working in the security system!'

'I don't believe you! Right now we've got a crowd of lowlifes and enemies who dream of sneaking into our ranks. You're under arrest!'

I handed over the grandson to a colleague, and finally he confessed that he was trying to infiltrate the security system in order to gather intelligence later for Franco. Ten years. He croaked in a prison camp, after rapidly sinking as low as he could go.

Strange! Looking at him, talking to him, for some reason I experienced no horror or loathing. I didn't feel sick. Too bad. Wish I'd puked right in his ordinary expressionless eyes . . . Here it is, that all-purpose notebook . . .

It's time we remembered your daddy.

I was sitting one day in the little room next to Stalin's office. Through the peephole, I was watching what went on in there. I kept everyone who came near Stalin in the sights of my quick-firing Smith & Wesson. I smiled at the innuendoes in the Leader's remarks: 'A dog must die a dog's death.' 'The moon does not heed the barking of dogs . . .'

Stalin pressed a button, came out from behind the desk, and cordially greeted his next visitor: your daddy . . . I won't describe my state, which was close to shock.

They gabbed a minute, and then Conceptiev invited Stalin to a hunt, promising to show him one of Russia's last purebred borzoi packs in action. Stalin started waving his arms. Dear me, the very idea! He was a busy man. Couldn't stand dogs. The hour would come when he'd devote himself heart and soul to a magnificent hunt! Falcons, traps, red flags! Conceptiev would be invited. But as for dogs, the only one he liked these days was the metal one on the radiator of his Lincoln.

Things looked bad for my cause, Citizen Gurov. To prevent any mistake, Stalin called me in and explained all about Conceptiev. A right guy, he said. A real wolfhound. A dreadful murderer, but devoted to him personally, to Stalin, with every ounce of his gut. Look, listen, and remember, Hand. Before long we'll have an excellent hunt . . .

Things looked bad for my cause! Conceptiev was well in with Stalin. Well in. More than once I've regretted that I didn't waste them both that day . . . Your observation is correct. In one instant, I could have become an historical figure. But I didn't. Unlike you, I don't give a damn about popularity down through the ages. I was absolutely confident that Stalin would be finished, he'd go straight to hell and damnation, as soon as he had slaughtered the Idea's most furious, most fanatical, most diabolical campaigners. He'd be left in a void, and it would finish him. Gradually the void would be filled by life . . . I was a fool . . .

Pasha too, Pasha Vcherashkin, he was Secretary of the Regional Committee then, he came running into my office on the 30th July, 1941, didn't say a word, just grabbed me by the lapels and slammed my head against the wall. Slam, slam, slam.

'Bastard!' he yells. 'Animal! Why did you save him? Why? Why?'

Pasha was in hysterics.

I said, 'You must be crazy! Let's get out of here, you damn fool!'

We walked around Red Square, leaned against the white stone of the Lobnoe Mesto, stared at the marvellous cathedral. Tears of fury and pain flowed down Pasha's cheeks, his hands shook, his teeth chattered, and he said thickly:

'Bastard! Bastard! What has he done, Vasya! Why did you save him? Why did you save *me*? Here we stand, and out there, this minute, thousands are dying at one blow, ripped to pieces by bombs and mines, riddled with bullets, twisted by shrapnel! What has he done, Vasya! And then the fucker says to us, "My brothers and sisters!" Goddamn dirty bastard! What did we do to deserve him, what? I'm going to the front. I can't take it here, I'll croak! I'll move a division against Moscow, beat the living shit out of Stalin, and use the entire nation to smash Hitler! Whole armies of soldiers are being taken prisoner, Vasya! And the rest go to the attack yelling, "For the motherland, for Stalin!" They're dying for him! For the dirty bastard who's guilty of the slaughter. Vasya, everyone's off their head! Let's go and get drunk . . . I can't take this! Look over there—they're evacuating the eternally alive corpse to a quiet place. There's nothing they value more! They're evacuating Lenin's mouldering stuffed body, and out there billions have been left behind, our labour, our harvest, our cattle . . . The little kids, Vasya, and the women . . . Oh my God!'

I was practically in tears myself, but to calm my buddy I said, 'Come on, Pasha, or I'll put you on exhibit in a museum as *The Weeping Bolshevik*.'

'I'm no Bolshevik! Fuck Bolshevism! I'm a Russian!' Pasha yelled. 'I'm a gentleman! A gentleman! Secretary of the Regional Committee! Landowner! State capitalist! Master! Governor! Fuck Socialism and the goddamn radiant future of all mankind! I feel bad for the people, and the nation's wealth! Fuck your Idea! Give me a break!'

'We're all agreed,' I remarked. 'Fuck the Idea. But that doesn't get it off our backs.'

I could see the man was going mad. The whites of his eyes had turned yellow. I took and forcibly dragged him from the Square, scaring off two nosey dicks with my Party I.D. card.

So I've had more than one occasion for deep regret, Citizen Gurov. More than one . . .

Crying again? What is it this time? Perhaps you're regretting you didn't fight in the war? No? You'll never forgive your cat and dog their vile treachery, for the simple reason that they aren't people? You feel that people may have an excuse for sneaky tricks; people are dirtier, and consequently their sneakiness is more forgivable. But we don't have to forgive animals. It's impossible to forgive them: they're pure . . . Not one of the most conventional ideas . . . Quit blubbering! You heard me: *quit blubbering!* . . .

Instead, why don't you imagine your daddy in the 'intimate moment' when he read your letter of repudiation and the transcripts of your testimony on the content of his conversations with friends and colleagues. You had thrown in a few extra little lies, you know, just in case . . .

Imagine your daddy, and me watching the expression and colour of his face, watching his eyes gradually widen, watching his face, the cursed face of my enemy, become so distraught, crumpled, and pitiful that I had no need to claw it up with this hand. But you, after all, are neither cat nor dog, you're his son . . . His son . . . His son . . . That blow afforded me great pleasure. I had wanted to slip in a few cruel digs about the fundamentals of Soviet pedagogy, to toy with the wounded beast, tease him. But the beast suddenly took himself in hand. He spat on your name, threw the filthy papers on the table, and said: 'I always knew he was a slimy shit. I feel sorry for his mother. Will you witness my signature on an official curse?'

'I can't do that,' I said. 'Your son is a national hero now. *Young Communist News* is coming out with his portrait tomorrow. They want him to write a children's book about how he spied on his enemy father from the age of seven. Ten whole years!'

I had hit home.

Again your father's face turned green and numb with hatred and malice towards you, Citizen Gurov. He did not forgive you, since you were a man, not a cat or a dog.

I brought the *Young Communist* to him in solitary. A half-page portrait of you, an article, and a commentary by some big expert on the education of young people . . . Our printing house would even mock up that émigré rag, *The Spark*, with whatever bullshit we needed for an investigation. They ran off versions of *Young Communist*, *Pravda*, and *Pioneer* every day.

That was when I observed one of the ugliest and most striking phenomena of Soviet reality: its boundless trust in the press. And, consequently, its utter defencelessness in the face of the total lie . . . Where's my briefcase? Oh, here it is . . . But let's save this for the morning. Poxov! Get them to show *The Godfather* to us tonight . . .

If I were you, Citizen Gurov, I'd keep quiet about the horrible mafia and its network of organized crime. Keep quiet. That's what the Soviet regime is—perfectly organized crime. And right now I don't want to discuss it. I want to read out loud for you, and for myself, the testimony of Frol Vlasych. Veterinarian. Age fifty-one. Jailed because his wife denounced him. Where's my briefcase? Oh, here it is. And here's her denunciation. We'll read a couple of passages from it.

'I lived with the above-named Goosev—who refused to exchange his religious name and patronymic for the progressive Vladlenst Marxengich—for one and a half five-year plans but, early in the first plan, I was already thinking about divorce ahead of the target, because Goosev sabotaged the quality of our collective marriage. He always smelled of his animals, but he refused to go to the bathhouse even on the eve of November 7th or the anniversary of Lenin's death. Goosev mockingly wanted to join the Party just to get "purged". In reply to my civic reproaches Goosev invariably, in front of witnesses . . .' Here the little bitch lists the names of the witnesses . . . father, mother, janitor . . . 'invaribly told me . . . so as not to repeat his terrible words I shall resort to concise expressions . . . told me to kiss the terminal point of digested food, calling it first one thing, then another, and also referred me to his male organ, which in principle does not enlarge at the present time because of our ideological disagreements . . . In the era of our record-breaking sex life, Goosev, by his own account, ate breakfast and supper with his animals and from the same bowl. He developed the idea that people had no moral right to perform experiments on animals. He called Academician Pavlov a vile swine and felt that experiments should be carried out not with dogs but with Stalin, Molotov, Kaganovich, Yezhov, and the rest of the pack. Goosev refuses to recognize them even as animals, let alone men. Once, after eating a fried egg with brisket, he sighed deeply and asserted that "these half-hyenas, half-skunks, quarter-vultures" had been sent down to us by balloon from some other howling, stinking planet and hadn't been inoculated in time . . . He kept trying to prove that Young

Communist workers were the offspring of parents suffering from typhus, cholera, or brain trauma, or else had been conceived after their father or mother had been poisoned by moonshine and Leninist ideas. But that's only the beginning, comrades! Foaming at the mouth, Goosev would explain that the Devil sits within us, making breakfast, lunch, and supper of our conscience, shame, will, and other *petit-bourgeois* feelings which cannot conveniently be enumerated in this confidential letter.'

Here are excerpts from the written testimony of prisoner Frol Vlasych Goosev, protector of people and animals. I sat in my office rereading *The Count of Monte Cristo*; he ensconced himself comfortably at my desk, smoking occasionally and sipping strong tea, and scribbled his testimony with fearless inspiration. Every so often he got up from the desk, stretched his legs, stared out of the window at black, nocturnal Lubyanka Square, and once more took up his pen.

I, Frol Vlasych Goosev, accused of having exploited my official position as veterinarian of the First or Air Force Precinct, Stalin District, City of Moscow, to argue in divers public places the indubitable existence within every Soviet person (and within the inhabitants of other countries retaining their legal governments, respect for traditional cultural institutions, and moral codes) both of God and equally of the Devil, who is called in common parlance Satan, the Fiend, Asmodeus, Unclean Spirit, Father of Lies, Bugaboo, Old Blazes, Split-foot, and other aliases and is the personification of Evil, *fully confess my guilt and on the substance of the case can testify as follows.*

On the 25th October (Old Style) 1917, being on an official mission and suddenly hearing a canon shot, which subsequently proved to be a shot from the cruiser Aurora, *I understood that* The Devil Is Human Reason Bereft of God. *When stopped by a patrol of officers because of my standing dumbfounded on the Anichkov Bridge with a smile of supreme illumination on my lips and light shining on my brow, to the question, 'Dolt! Why are you turned to stone at such a ruinous time?' I replied without delay, feeling Joy, a supreme spiritual uplift, and at the same time horror, faintness, and gloom:*

'As the Kingdom of God is within us, so also within us is the Devil's hellfire, Gentlemen Officers. And the Devil is our reason, bereft of God.'

'You're absolutely right!' said one of the officers, courteously and sadly seconding me, for which I am personally grateful to him to this day and request that I be called to account under Article 58 of the RSFSR Criminal Code for participation in an officers' plot. The second officer, quite expectably, was rude. He asked:

'Where were you before, you shithead philosopher, you fucking Hegel?'

The officers did not wait for my reply but drew their pistols and hastily ran off, shouting, down the Nevsky . . .

Trudging slowly along the Moika Embankment, I was distinctly aware of myself as a precious vessel and the abode of two astonishing substances: the Godlike, immortal, and infinite substance of Soul (in variant readings, the Spirit; whose readings I do not recall) and the no less wonderful and Divine but unfortunately, or fortunately, corruptible, not eternal—the personal, so to speak—substance of Reason.

Once again stopping spellbound, I raised my astonishingly light head and began to cry free, bright tears. I was standing by the house in which Alexander Pushkin died of a mortal wound to the peritoneum. The obvious fact that I was not here by chance shook me to my foundations. Light poured from the windows of Alexander Sergeevich's apartment. Past me, back and forth, dashed carriages and coaches, pulling up at the entrance. Alighting from under the bearskins and white woollen rugs were ladies of indescribable beauty and persons of the male sex whose first and last names I categorically refuse to commit to this official document. Caught up while they were still in the street by music the composer of which I would prefer not to name, they fluttered into the beckoning entrance and disappeared from my view. And suddenly the figure of the poet, familiar since childhood and, if I may say so, dear to my heart, drew near to one of the windows. Without visible expression on his face he watched the twilight of his beloved city, as if paying no heed to the sounds carrying from the direction of the Neva, the shots and cries of the madding crowds.

'This duel is hideous!' So saying, the poet surrendered himself into the arms of his beautiful wife, who had come to him. A mazurka swept them away, and the light in the windows died. My overbrimming state of emotion was such that I immediatley poured out my heart to the coachman of a most luxurious carriage, the identifying features of which I did not commit to memory. I exclaimed:

'My friend! Verily there is not, nor ever was nor will be, any

example in Russian history of a more perfect and harmonious existence in one universal genius than the Couple forever betrothed by the Creator at creation—Soul and Reason.'

'Clear out, old soak! I expect the missus is waiting!' the coachman replied good-naturedly. He seemed to me a kindred soul, and his most naïve incomprehension of my meaning struck me as delightful. Another point is that I was not drunk. I was Frol Vlasych Goosev. A mob that came from out of nowhere drew me away behind it. It was drunken, black, and merry, like a boorish funeral feast.

'Who has died, gentlemen?' I of course asked. A cackle of like-minded laughter went up.

'Pushkin!' exulted a pseudohandsome young lummox, who subsequently proved to be the prominent antipoet Vladimir Mayakovsky. They left me clinging helplessly to the parapet of the embankment. The autumnal river breathed the dark cold of grief into my soul. It sobbed mournfully when spent lead, shot skyward by the saluting guns of the crowd, fell into the bitter water. Gusts of wind at once destroyed the ripples that spread on the water, wavelets covered them over and raced away.

I do not remember, Citizen Investigator, how long I stood like that. I recovered from my trance when an absolutely faceless, nimble little man in a pince-nez, who was of no obvious age, introduced himself to me as Outraged Reason and demanded that I remove from my back the overcoat I wore as a clerk of the veterinary department. I promptly did so, experiencing not the slightest sense of loss. This indifference, I suppose, resulted from the certainty instilled in me by a number of great Russian thinkers that my overcoat too must sooner or later be removed by a Terrible Force.

Taking pencil and paper from the coat pocket of my uniform, I complained softly and bitterly and wrote for the first time ever, on a page that was damp in a trice, the first and last name of the robber: Outraged Reason. I was chilled to my foundations, whereupon I crumpled the page and threw it into the water. The wind snatched it up. My eyes followed it to see when it would sink into oblivion. I addressed my letter to Akaky Akakievich Bashmachkin. The text of my letter is closed to investigation until Judgement Day.

Whereupon I crouched on the pavement, as can be corroborated by the witness Ilyushkin, torn to pieces in 1923 during his attempt to prevent the defilement and destruction of the Lord's Temple by the crowd. I crouched on the pavement. Rank miasmas of the swamp oozed through the stony flesh of the city risen up against God. I felt sick. Storming the sky in my poor overcoat, Outraged Reason was hoarsely shouting a song—'Always prepared to win or die'—from the top of the Alexander Pillar.

A fresh gust of rain-filled wind plucked the faceless, nimble little man from the pillar, and except for my outstretched arms he would surely have been smashed to smithereens. But he proved to be unnaturally light. His only weight, in fact, was from the overcoat, pince-nez, scarf, turtleneck sweater, trousers, and his poor old boots and scuffed rubber galoshes. The little man's flesh was a sort of weightless down.

I carried him in my arms to a neighbouring tavern. The merriment of the people drinking there was darkened by clouds of tobacco smoke hung with sorrow. I sat down opposite the faceless little man and looked around . . . The creatures dancing, singing, and drinking at the grubby little tables were as much like my robber as peas in a pod. But they had been stirred to outrage in different ways, just as their helpmate Souls were dead in different ways. I could not make out what all these creatures were singing, eating, drinking, and dancing, much as I would have liked to. The waiter came over to us, a sprightly fellow who gave his name at yesterday's confrontation as Molot Voroshilych Kaganovich Budyonny.

'Bring me something ideal,' Outraged Reason requested. I, however, expressed an interest in tea and boubliks with wild strawberry jam. The waiter gave me notice that from this moment on there would never again be either boubliks or wild strawberry jam in the taverns and saloons of the vast Russian Empire.

I was shaking from the cold and the anguish I felt. The tepid and colourless tea neither warmed me nor slaked my thirst.

'Well, but sir,' I asked my vis-à-vis, *who was cutting up some sort of food on his totally empty plate, 'where is your helpmate, where is your wife? Why are you alone?'*

'I deserted her!' And Outraged Reason, with an airy smile, related to me the story of his emancipation. 'The decision to desert my Soul had long been ripening in my mind. But as the saying goes, yesterday was too early, and tomorrow's too late. Make sense?'

I nodded, and stopped my ears so as not to hear the bellow of drunken Reasons: 'Let us win emancipation by the strength of our own hand!' My vis-à-vis *went on: 'I won't hide the fact: at some point in time I began to be horribly irritated by Soul's Immortality.*

Incidentally, I don't remember my childhood. Seems I never had one at all. Yes, sir! Irritated! . . . *The question arises why I, if I may say so, am all-powerful, I peep into the secrets of matter as if into my own home, I'm always on the go, in a whirl, on the hustle, on the grift, if you'll notice I study the serpents of the sea, I've got a rose of the vale in my herbarium, I know the weight of the Earth, wake me up at night and I'll tell you the righthanded corkscrew rule, I can see a gene without my glasses, you seem to be missing the ninth chromosome, old fellow. As for the speed of light, intersecting parallels, and my lab assistant Roentgen, I won't bother to mention them. I cherish a dream of whacking off a general field theory, finding quarks, establishing a new order in the microcosm, and skipping into the macrocosm. My fingers itch to get at a black hole—oh, most curious, yes, most magnetic, that black little hole! And I've long been no stranger to art. To have spawned so many "isms"—this, old fellow, is something your Benvenuto Van Gauguin Rublyovs never dreamed of . . .*

'In short: I, Reason, have run myself ragged, day and night I cudgel my brains, and yet, they're not immortal like my darling Soul, they are, if you'll allow me to remark, sir, corruptible! Unlike some people—we won't point any fingers—they are not privileged to peek beyond mortal bounds. They get no peace, my brains, from the second law of thermodynamics, things are turning cold right before our eyes, we must save them, but Soul, if you'll excuse me, doesn't give *a fuck! All she ever does is sit on her hands, she curls up like a pussycat and seizes the moment in this common Body of ours, which leaves much to be desired with respect to its construction, potential, margin of safety, vulnerability, the outrageous principle of bioincompatibility, and defencelessness versus the play of random forces of nature. I long to get the Body corrected, and I've raised this problem with the bioengineers. In what I've said there isn't a grain of falsehood or exaggeration of my merits, my dear Mr.—'*

'Frol Vlasych Goosev, protector of people and animals,' I said, introducing myself. 'I love Pushkin too, strong tea and boubliks, and wild strawberry jam.'

'Yes, sir, Frol Vlasych! Soul is infinitely lazy because of her guaranteed immortality, and for that very reason she's as egoistical as the royal "we"! Oh my, yes, great egoists are "we"! After all, say we, we have many days, many millions of years. Why are you always on the go, Reason? Seize the moment, like me . . . Hear that? I'm supposed to seize some miserable moment, squander myself on

trifles, when there's a ton of work to do, when everything's imperfect, literally everything I've invented, except the wheel. There's nothing more you can do to the wheel. An imperfect thing exasperates me, but I can't stand perfection either; I figure if your mind's at rest, it's narrow. Seize the moment, indeed!

'In a word, one day the difference in our age and attitude to the three faces of time made itself felt. I said, It's all very well for you to go on about the Kingdom of God, trying to drag me into it, but if I'm really Godlike I want to build the Kingdom of God on Earth. My dear Soul, I said, take a look at what's going on in the world! Labour and capital in an unholy mess, exploitation, wars, diseases! Haemorrhoids! *How could He possibly have closed his eyes to haemorrhoids when He issued man? At this point she burst out crying. Tears. Why, please tell me, did He invent tears to clean the eyeball of dust and rubbish, when Soul's the main one who uses them, and not as intended, but for purposes far removed from the flushing of the pupils and whites? And that's the way with everything! It's not* rational*!*

'And vice versa, Frol Vlasych, take the member of our body. Why does Soul consider, in the case of tears, that weeping and wailing over some dead dog differentiates us as being better than the animals, whereas our member, which craves diverse pleasures, which has made quite some trouble in art, life, politics, and finance—our living, restless, tireless, venturesome, daredevil member—is supposed to be exactly like a mole's or a tiger's, functioning exclusively according to schedule, as an organ of procreation? Why? How's that for dialectics? First weep to differentiate yourself from the swine, then be continent in desire like the dinosaur. No wonder they died out, sticking to schedule. Sexual revolution or bust! Make sense? But never mind all this.

'We're descended from the monkey, I'm convinced, but the point is, Soul has no ideas. How, I shouted one day, can you do without ideas? Soul started to cry again. I just like to live, says she, I don't need ideas at all. But do you have goals? I asked sternly. Or don't you need goals either? No, says she, I don't—life itself is the idea and the goal. That's going too far, Frol Vlasych! Our joint idea and goal, so to speak, has got to be more than I personally can take. Soul's everlasting jealousy of my handmaid Science has become unreasonable and obsessive. Sermons at every turn. Moralizing. Change my way of life . . . Another glass of tea?'

'Thank you, this isn't tea,' I replied courteously, and with my

spoon I sadly stirred the leaden liquid that had dripped into my glass from the storm cloud of cataclysm.

'It's all very well for you, I told her, to preach love for thy neighbour, the world, the dear little flowers and nanny goats—you're immortal! but I'm corruptible! Corruptible! This body of ours that we've lived in for nigh on thirty-four years—lo and behold, it dies, and then what? What? You, after all, and don't tell me you don't dream about this, you *will pass into another body, right then and there. But me? Where will I go? Blue blazes? Thanks a lot! One has to get all he can out of life! And I will! I'm not alone! There's millions of us outraged by the order of things! Our own world we will build, a new world, he who was nothing shall be all!*

'I had a feeling Soul would break down under the insult, she'd walk out now. But no. All she did was agonize and weep! Drive me to sadism! So who, I yelled, did you live with before me? What did you tell him, that man, in your other life? Did you spook him, too, with your God? You won't spook me! Your God doesn't exist at all! And if He does, then why does He make you suffer by keeping His secrets under lock and key? Why haemorrhoids for the body and suffering for you? Why the rich and the poor, the merry and the unlucky? Why men of talent and tram ticket-collectors? Why film stars and Dunka the Hunchback? What the frig do we want with antinomies, I ask you, Soul? Do you perhaps need *tragedies? Well,* I *do* not! *If your God won't take away the tragedy of existence, I'll do it myself! Me, on my own! In the long run, not only can I raze the world of coercion, I can move the planet right off its axis! Today we don't have a fulcrum—tomorrow we will. We'll invent one . . . draw one . . . boil with anger . . .*

'To make a long story short: a dreadful quarrel. No more tears, I grant you, but obstinacy on her part, a mulishness and lack of logic, and charges of my having a shitty character. Reason, says she, you're behaving suicidally. Never mind Science, now you've taken up with Pride. And yet, we could have lived in perfect harmony, as we did in childhood, or as wise people do. We could have. But you, says she, are unfaithful! Your idea is dearer to you than I am, dearer than our difficult, unique Life, dearer than the world that you want to remake. If you're tired of explaining things—take a holiday. You'll only remake the world for the worse. Let's go to the sea.

'Yes, I told her—I'm not boring you, Frol Vlasych?'

'Please, do go on. I'm very interested to hear,' I replied.

'Yes, I told her, I can remake the world—not for the worse, not by the strength of my *own hand, the point is, we're in this together with my great idea of the dictatorship of the proletariat, which will be so mighty and universal that the state will die of its own accord under the weight of it, like a snake under a log. And don't you try to stop us! I was referring to myself, my handmaid Science, and Pride. Pride—she's an amazing little hussy! She's got this trick of setting you on fire and then not even letting you have satisfaction. She'll hold you in voluptuous tension for a month at a time . . . We're in the Party now, I said, under the Great Idea. The Party is the only thing that will not betray us. And I've had it with your wretched little class-transcending thoughts about "Thou shalt not kill," "Thou shalt not steal," "Honour thy daddy and mummy." Why* not *kill a millionaire, why* not *grab the millions he made on our blood and toil? Make sense? In a way, it's extremely strange not to kill and not to steal. Why do you forgive such boorishness in them, yet summon me to humility, trade unionism, gradualism, and respect for the values we share with the Morgans, DuPonts, Ryabushinskys? What do we share, I said, if everything I own is inferior? (With that question I knocked the ground from under Soul's feet.) Diamonds? Estates? Minerals? Cooks? Formal balls? Showgirls? Resorts? Palaces? Mills and factories, maybe? You bitch, I argued, you* want *to see me seedy. I don't even have an overcoat! That's what I'm reduced to! I've got nothing to wear, I can't go out on the street with my class-brothers and hand all power to the Soviets.*

'Believe me, Frol Vlasych, in a quarrel we exploit our immortality, we're by no means averse to nasty counter-arguments. Oh my, no! Here's where we're especially venomous, cynical, and out of control! Here's where we show our true face!

'You, she tells me with a downright murderous calm, rather than drink your talent away, go out and earn yourself that overcoat, and some new boots too. By the way, Frol Vlasych, what size feet do you have?'

'Having disliked numbers since childhood, I buy my shoes by guesswork,' I replied sincerely. 'Imagine, I've never been wrong once, and besides, one doesn't often have to buy shoes. Why do it often?'

'How very strange. You don't take my shoe size, but I seem to take yours. Is that possible? Or is it another reactionary antinomy?'

'It's possible!' I answered, laughing open-heartedly, as could be

corroborated by Darya Petrovna Annushkina, who was subsequently robbed and raped by bandits on leaving the pawnshop where she had taken her wedding ring on account of her children's hunger.

'Hm,' said Outraged Reason, sizing me up with a glance, and went on, 'You enjoy it, I told her, when people point the finger at my inferiority! That's why you exploit your immortality to go on about values I hold in common with Rockefeller! Madam, that is arch-cynicism! And it's why you order me to scorn the "satanic" Soviets!

'Oh my, yes! Now we break down! Now we resort to our nastiest tricks, the better to keep certain people under our pretty little thumb! Whatever gave me the idea she was immortal? Whence, says she (we're a great fan of the haughty shift to formality!) your neurotic confidence in earnest guarantees? I, sir, have no guarantees—I have faith, I am happy that I have faith, and I should like to share with you both my faith and my happiness in offering up prayer to the Creator's feet . . .

'But it's sad, do you see, infinitely sad (we love to claim that all our feelings are infinite, no less!), when by all my actions I'm destroying her, my Soul, destroying both myself and her because I've rebelled, betrayed my divine function, and started to serve the false idea of emancipating the working class. From what, says she, do you wish to emancipate it, sir? How many times do I have to explain—from the power of capital and the exploitation of man by man. We'll divide the surplus value and get rich, until Communism arrives, when there'll be no money at all, and the need to toil will have become every bit as basic as the desire for a drink and a snack. Notice, Frol Vlasych, how terrifying and difficult it is for Reason and Soul to live jointly in the one Body, if Ideas and Goals are fundamentally alien to Soul! Not once, literally not once, has she ever had the desire for a drink: We have no need of this . . . we're drunk on life . . . ours is a permanent ecstasy! Disgusting *egoism, sir! Every time I want a drink I have to talk Soul into it. But she doesn't get drunk. She's deprived, sir, of that nice high! It's as alien to her, she says, as pain is to me.*

'I explained what I wanted to emancipate the working class from, in order to remake the world on rational principles.

'Oh my, yes! Now we mount our favourite hobbyhorse! You will, says she, emancipate the working man, engineer, and technician from the power of Putilov, but they'll be saddled with a force still more terrible and unscrupulous—faceless state capital, which in its turn will be managed by crackpots, tin gods, autocrats of all ranks, and suicides

like yourself, who hymn the labour of others and curse their own. Bethink yourself! Behold: I grow lifeless before your very eyes.

'In situations like this, I boil. Literally on the verge of vaporizing, I countered insolently, Madam, this is blackmail!

'Naturally, we had conniptions: You're a Reason who has lost God! You're the Devil! Bethink yourself! Each instant you have an opportunity for repentance, forgiveness, and resurrection. Surely you don't find it more painful to be deprived of a nice high than to lose God?

'Today, the 25th October 1917, I finally blew my lid. I stamped my foot. Never again, I said, will I set it in this house. Live here with your God. We'll survive somehow.'

At that moment, which struck me, Citizen Investigator, as historic, fantastical, and bereft of any foundation of logic, morality, or love for one's fellow man, into the tavern ran a little gentleman who smacked of the Fiend, Asmodeus, Satan, the Devil, and Bugaboo. Stretching forth his yellow palm over the smoke and the boiling of outraged Reasons, he exclaimed: 'Such a Party exists!' And he vanished like lightning, just as he had appeared in the beginning.

'Now that's the way to seize the moment!' my vis-à-vis said delightedly. 'Allow me to bid you, not godspeed, but farewell, Frol Vlasych. World affairs, sir!'

'But just a minute!' I said anxiously. 'How about your Soul? What happened to her?'

'That's no concern of mine. For the time being we're both historically compelled to abide in the one body. I am convinced that the hour is near when Reason shall triumph even over the challenge of dividing the floor space of the body. The little problem we're solving right now is just a bit tougher. The main thing is, keep boiling! Although listening to wretched kitchen-talk about how I've been the ruin of Soul, how there are heaps of marvellous marriages around, and in geniuses A, B, C, D, and E they get along famously with each other, Souls and Reasons do, they love life and perfect the world-order . . . is a supreme archnuisance. If you'd be so kind your boots and galoshes!'

'You yourself deigned to note that I don't take your size,' I said sensibly, to which Outraged Reason objected, no less sensibly:

'You don't take my shoe size, but I do take yours, oh yes I do. We have our own way of cracking these little antinomies. The Kants slaved over them, but we do it our way—toss me the second galosh, *please—the real way, the reasonable way . . . a little extra room won't do any harm. All the best, Mr.—'*

'Frol Vlasych Goosev, protector of people and animals,' I supplied once again, feeling not the slightest resentment, only grief and pity.

'Boldly into battle now we march for Soviet power, all as one for this we fight, as one for this we die,' the assembled company sang suddenly in unison and, to a man, all were dragged from the tavern by a mighty pull, along with the smoke and steam, as if there were cyclones and hostile whirlwinds at work outside.

To your direct question, Citizen Investigator, whether I was sympathetic to the revolution and the uprisen masses, I answer thus, having first familiarized myself with the article of the Criminal Code which stipulates the penalty for false testimony: This is the first I have heard of the revolution. I did not notice the uprisen masses. I saw a crowd of madmen who knew not what they did. I felt sympathy for them, foreseeing the vicious consequences of rebellion. I buried in the earth of the Summer Garden two cats, a dog, a crow, and a sparrow, slain by stray bullets and the cobblestones of the proletariat. On the substance of the case I can testify in more detail as follows:

I ended my nocturnal Odyssey barefoot and coatless, but prevailed over the cold of my feet. Past me, back and forth, dashed dead souls and faceless rebels boiling with anger. Once again, without noticing how, I found myself by the house on the Moika. To my surprise, its windows shone, and light poured into the street, together with music. The music was bright, like wise discourse. Once again the figure of the poet Pushkin, who had not died at all, drew near to one of the windows, and once again, glancing at the black twilight rent now by shots, now by flashes of light, he said sorrowfully: 'This duel is madness!'

I was transfixed by the happiness of fellowship with a man who understood and felt at least something of what was taking place. And I walked on, away from the city, condoling with those who had lost property and loved ones. I said, remembering the music that poured from the shining windows:

'Humble your cry and do not curse God! Is it not foolish to cry out, "O God, if Thou art, why dost Thou allow madness and destruction, why dost Thou sanctify the triumph of evil, the horror of wars, and the suffering of innocents?" It is foolish, gentlemen, foolish! Do not cry out! This is not God who does Evil, this is the Devil! And the Devil is our Reason, bereft of God. He is within us. But, when he uses for

ill the gift of Freedom, despises the wise covenant, becomes drunk with wilfulness, and deserts his Soul, Reason does evil, both in the history of the race and in his solitary human fate. Does God teach us enmity and indifference? No! Does He teach brother to rise up against brother, friend to betray friend, and all as one to fight and die for This? *No! A Reason who has lost God is stricken with terror; in his Devilish madness he rushes towards death, which is still more terrifying to him, and he finds it. But a Reason who gazes fearlessly into the mystery of the face of Death is grateful for the smallest moment of life, and he has that moment, thereby bestowing upon himself and us a joyful spirituality. Do not cry out, ye wronged and innocent! Take stock of him who stirs you up and calls upon you to burn the covenant in your heart! He has brought you instead of the covenant the Councils, his Soviets. He is the Devil! Fear his Soviets! A Soviet is an imposed idea!'*

Just at this moment a crow slain in flight by a stray bullet fell at my bare feet.

'O Lord,' I said, 'I thank Thee for the horror and joy of life, for light and darkness, for the song and death of birds, for heat and chill. I thank Thee that Reason and Soul abide within my body in a peace not outraged by reproaches, in harmony and childish wonder. O Lord, send to me, as to a bird, a chance death in flight! Save us all from the Soviets, that is, from the power of imposed ideas!'

In addition to the above I testify: As she died, the crow spoke the word 'Caw-w'. It seems to me, as a veterinarian, that there was something she did not finish saying. Exactly what, I cannot tell.

Signed: Frol Vlasych Goosev, dying of denunciations but still the living protector of animals and of false witnesses in his case. I have forgiven them . . .

Let's move on . . . Your daddy was solidly enthroned. Couldn't be undermined. And now—you called. You talked a lot of poppycock, but I took a chance and tried to follow up on certain points. Remember how obliging you were during the search? You crawled under the beds, pawed through the clothes, trotted out the sorry pamphlets by Trotsky and Bukharin, and finally fetched your daddy's little treasure chest from its hiding place behind the wall. In the treasure chest was yet another chest. In that chest was a miniature carved box. In the box was a tiny egg. Not an ordinary egg. Golden. And in the egg, to my surprise, horror, and delight, was Stalin's letter, the one your daddy had written with his own hand and read to the peasants of Odinka. That lenient little letter had disarmed the peasants. Conceptiev had gone a-hunting for them, and he had proved right in reckoning on this decoy.

I tucked the letter in my pocket and then took a good hard look at you . . . I checked my emotions. Everything in good time, I thought. I was a fool. But that kind of folly is sometimes an unconscious acquiescence in what must be, as willed by God and fate.

I thanked you formally on behalf of the security system. You replied that if you had several enemy fathers, you wouldn't think twice about unmasking them all.

Well, I got a paddy wagon and a small detachment, about twenty men, and I set off on the hunt like an oldtime avenger—off to the deep woods, to the wildlife preserve where Party bosses, warriors, People's Commissars, and the rest of the mob led their feudal way of life. Stealthily we surrounded the two-storey wooden castle. Not a yap out of the dogs. I gave orders to fire without warning at anyone who tried to flee. Shoot them on the wing when they started jumping out of the windows. But only if the worst came to the worst. I didn't wish them such an easy end . . . The borzois in the kennel were sleeping like the dead.

I'll skip the details of the arrest. There was nothing of interest. Before the muzzles of our 'tough lucks', all these men who were so brave with unarmed victims became instant wimps. Scared shitless. The only one to put up a fight was your daddy, but I gave him a karate chop to the neck, and he collapsed, in nothing flat. The prisoners' wives and bimbos I ordered locked up with the dogs till we clarified their role in the villainous plot against Lenin and Stalin . . . Yes, yes! Already the case scenario was beginning to take shape in my head.

The prisoners were counted. The hunting guns and knives were carried out of the castle.

'Allow me to telephone Stalin!' Conceptiev said. 'We're old Party friends.'

'You're such a snake and a traitor that he doesn't want to talk to you until you make a full confession. You have been arrested on his personal order,' I lied.

'All right. Then I beg of you, help me resolve this misunderstanding. It's ridiculous, a man of my reputation being suspected of the devil knows what!'

'A reputation,' I said, purposely sounding like a horse's ass, 'is not a dogma but a guide to action. If the devil knows what you might be suspected of, we'll summon him as a witness in your case.'

Within a couple of days, under my direction, the castle was converted to a comfortable cooler. Bars on the windows. Bolts on the doors. In each one a peephole, judas hole, for observation. Very strict discipline. No smoking, no lounging on divans and sofas in the daytime, no reading, no radio, no communication with the outside world, no visits or parcels.

Our printing house immediately began turning out Moscow newspapers with personal data on the arrestees and all sorts of fantastic blooey about their double-dealing: their links with foreign intelligence, the Trotskyite opposition, and domestic reactionaries. We had a couple of novelists and a certain now-deceased mammoth of journalism, the vile David Zaslavsky, who all did a glorious job on it. They found a gruesome fascination in the work, and I also convinced them that their discovery of new literary and journalistic genres would certainly be followed by medals, honour, and national fame.

I myself was so fascinated, however, that I let you out of my sight. Idiot! I didn't even know anything about your liaison with Collectiva. Quietly and peaceably you became Brutnikov. Then you murdered your adoptive momma and mistress and became Gurov. When I finally got around to you, it was too late. My plans had been foiled by a truck, twenty-six men, and two accordions. Foiled! But all right. What is, is . . .

Your daddy had been hunting in the national forests with his most trusted buddies, the remnant of his special Chekist detachment. A tremendous break! They all cracked wide open the minute they read your testimony: that they had condemned, at table and over the telephone, the senseless arrests of Vlachkov, Gutman, and their other close colleagues, and considered these arrests to be absurd acts of sabotage discrediting Leninist law and morality and leading ultimately to a dictatorship of the security system. But such primitive confessions weren't enough for me. I needed a baby lamb shishkebab!

After properly demoralizing the five prisoners, after hounding, jeering, blackmailing them, setting them at each other's throats, putting their faces in order with my huge hand, I had a Machiavellian conversation with each one separately.

'I may have stepped out of bounds,' I said. 'But you yourself are a former Chekist, and you know it's a highly nerve-racking job. Please excuse me. I realize you're not guilty of anything, objectively. But things have gone too far. Stalin doesn't wish to listen to you personally until you make a full confession on all counts. He has asked me to tell you that he's not an investigator.

'There is, however, a remedy,' I said. 'The charges brought against you are provocative and ridiculous. The more ridiculous the charges, the more absurd they are, the more improbable your confession will necessarily seem to Stalin. He will have to doubt the reality of the case, the circumstances of it, and the moral probity of the informers and false witnesses. The remedy is dialectics. Your salvation is to confess to something that could not, objectively, have happened. Think about it. We'll continue our conversation tomorrow. We must demolish the two main charges dialectically. The rest will wither away of themselves.

'The first charge: a diversionary action against the health of Vladimir Ilyich Lenin (who was then recuperating from being wounded by the leftwing deviationist Kaplan), at the first All-Russian Volunteer Saturday, by means of a huge log artificially frozen at Kaganovich Cold Storage Plant No. 1. This grave but idiotic accusation,' I said, 'is corroborated by the testimony of false witnesses: Kaganovich, plant manager Stepanian, Krupskaya, and three Young Communists who were working that day on the clean-up of the Kremlin grounds. Also by a medical report on the deterioriation in Lenin's health after the Volunteer Saturday. Do you recognize yourself in this photograph?'

'Horsefeathers!' Conceptiev said. 'That's not me, and not us.'

'True,' I said. 'But if you identify yourself and the others as the men carrying the log with Lenin, the lack of resemblance will be obvious. It will drive the first wedge into the charge against you. Do you begin to get the dialectical idea—proving your innocence through a full confession of guilt? You have no other path. My purpose is to demolish the accusation, and to show Stalin the true face of Kaganovich, Molotov, and Mikoyan, who are building their careers on your dead bodies and ruined fates. If you balk, I'll have to apply illicit techniques to help you rehabilitate yourself. What do you say?'

'If Lenin could only see what's going on! If Stalin could only see that he has placed his trust in lowlifes and crooks!' Conceptiev said. 'Murderers of the Revolution!'

'I repeat: what do you say?'

'What's the second charge?'

'The second,' I said, 'is so absurd and comical that we'll work on it after we finish with the first. Notice, Conceptiev, that if Stalin had meant us to annihilate you physically, we would have done so without formality—without this unnecessary criminological excursus, shall we say, this excursion into the past. Does that make sense?'

'Yes. But what if neither I nor the others confess to these monstrous slanders and fabricated phantasmagorias?'

'I shall be forced to inform Comrade Stalin personally that you insisted on your innocence. Obviously he will order that the investigation be concluded by a progressive method. You'll be erased the way Vlachkov and Gutman were erased, and the marshals, and Party figures more prominent than you. Moreover, I exclude the possibility that you will hold your ground steadfastly and adamantly. Gurevich is already begging me to let him sign any kind of poppycock, the sooner to expose that poppycock for what it is.'

'Gurevich is a swine! Damned kike! Which one is he supposed to be, in this mythical photograph?'

'Here's Gurevich,' I said.

'But that guy's Russian!'

'Indeed; a factual alibi for Gurevich. Do you see the difficult conditions under which we must conduct our investigation, the goal of which is the triumph of Socialist Legality?'

'Motherfucking dialectics! They're getting even with me!' Conceptiev said. 'Well, and which of these mugs is me?'

'That's you,' I said. 'And that's supposed to be Goryaev. Latsis. Akhmedov. Kvasnitsky.'

All right. I'll think about it. Have the others consented?'

'They're raring to go. But your situation is more complicated than theirs. I have no right to say why, for the moment. Hand in hand, point by point, we'll demolish all the charges. But not all at once,' I said. 'We'll demolish them little by little, step by step, ever so quietly—Lenin's way.'

'Thank you, Vasily Vasilievich. I'm sure that men like you are the true Chekists and Leninists. We'll smash this degenerate counter-revolutionary plot against the Revolution and Leninism. I consent. I'm no good at taking a long time to think.'

'Excellent. You have permission to smoke. How will you treat your son after you're rehabilitated and freed? Officially he's a hero, but actually he's a cur and a monster.'

'I don't want to think about it for the time being,' your daddy said, gritting his teeth.

'Right. Now do you understand the dialectical purpose of our country's latest Stalinist terror? It will reveal who's who. Admittedly, not without difficulty. But as the saying goes, if you chop wood, the chips must fly.'

'A farsighted view. Quite right. It's just that I don't like being a chip.'

'Nevertheless, you must agree, you can't always be just the woodchopper. You have to be a chip, too, for a while. By the way, your Party card will be returned to you today. You are not considered to be a prisoner but an assistant investigator in your own top-priority case.'

Would you believe it, Citizen Gurov, the old wolf couldn't contain himself. His shoulders shook, his furrowed brows smoothed, he dropped his face in his hands and started to sob. His Party card was the umbilical cord tying him to the Party, to its body and spirit, in which his own body and spirit had been dissolved. Forcible detachment from the Party was perceived, not only by your daddy but by thousands of Party corpses, as detachment from life itself, equivalent to death, and sometimes more terrible than physical death. Many actually did prefer death to renouncing the Communist faith. For a chance to remain in the Party ranks, they paid any price—lies, villainy, slander, utmost abasement—and ultimately lost their humanity. They became robotic Party corpses.

Well, how about it? I'm not a bad psychologist and improviser, am I? Not bad, but I couldn't have broken you that fast. You wouldn't have believed a single word I said. I'm not a hundred per cent sure, of course, that I'll ice you in the end—but ninety-nine point nine is close enough. Close enough . . .

Demoralized, snot-faced, their brains churning crazily with hope, despair, and my dialectics, which demolished their psyche, will, and capacity for logical thought, the five Special-Detachment Chekists signed everything I put in front of them. I was amazed at the way they entered into their roles and the prankish convolutions of the filmscript, participating in my investigative experiments with sincere inspiration. They unanimously identified the historic log, whose full weight (by prior agreement, reached at the secret apartment of the British ambassador) they had tried to lay on Lenin's hurt shoulder. The log had been hauled from a Pitsunda box grove especially for this purpose. The choice of boxwood was no accident. The apparently puny little tree trunk, which a set designer from the Meyerhold Theatre had camouflaged to look like fir, weighed more than pig iron. X-ray films convinced my prisoners that there had been terrible changes in Lenin's humeri, clavicle, and parts of his spine after the deliberately protracted carrying of the log from the Palace of Facets to the Czar Cannon.

Not without curiosity and aversion, I watched the five villains adapt to my hoked-up Socialist-Realist reality. As our investigative experiment proceeded, they made businesslike suggestions to each other, refined them, argued, and then, with despicable hypocrisy, addressed our wonderfully made-up Lenin:

'Please, Vladimir Ilyich! Step back, step back! It's too heavy for you! We'll manage it somehow by ourselves, Comrade Lenin!'

The actor played his part brilliantly. He had Lenin's speech defect down pat. He cast narrow-eyed glances at his comrades, letting them know, by his weary but resolute air, that this was an historic moment and that he, Lenin, would somehow rise to it, because he didn't give a damn about the pain in his shoulder or the oh's and ah's of his archnuisance doctors and wife. Especially since his comrades, the cameramen and photographers, were ready to record the birth of a new form of labour, labour that was consciously unremunerated, Soviet, Socialist, Communist.

I derived enormous pleasure from shooting the episodes of the 'investigation'. The motors of the dolly roared, the cameraman rolled along the track, the floodlights blinded us, assistants scurried about, the clapper clapped with the title of the film: *Lenin and the Log*. And over the painted paving stones, against a backdrop of painted landscapes of the Kremlin, shuffled the five saboteurs, Lenin's murderers, led by Lenin himself, with the log of iron wood on their shoulders. That log—it took me back to the cursed frozen log on which you, Citizen Gurov, had put to death my nature!

At that moment I ceased to enjoy the spectacle and went into a rage. They kept on lugging the boxwood log around. Bent double by the weight, their breath laboured, they looked at me with sad, doomed horse-eyes. Lenin wheezed, groaned, and made fun of his colleagues in a constricted voice. But I asked them to do take after take, sparing neither film nor electricity. I was the director, and at that point, for me, the cinema was truly 'the most important of the arts'.

In the end, the materials were edited by a leading documentary filmmaker. We dubbed in the testimony, which I personally had written during a sleepless night. Dunaevsky composed a marvellously expressive score, which the sound technicians synchronized with Lenin's hoarse breathing, the groans of his flesh being tortured by Communist labour, the ponderous steps along the paving stones, and the exclamations of 'One, two, three—heave! Again—*heave*!'

I could consider one case finished. But it wasn't enough. Reporting to Stalin with just one such case was risky. Very risky. I had to give the Leader a shock that would leave him in no doubt about Conceptiev's treachery.

I won't tell you about interrogating Gurevich, Akhmedov, Latsis, Goryaev, and Kvasnitsky. I didn't have to fuss with them for long. They realized that once they said 'A,' they had to say 'Bee-Cee-Dee-Ee,' this being, as I explained to them, the basic operating principle of the En Kay Vee Dee. To increase the persuasiveness of the argument that they were devoted to Stalin, I ordered them all to compile a list of their personal services to the Soviet regime, including the punitive operations and counter-revolutionary liquidation actions they had carried out.

The lists are in my briefcase. I won't let you read them. All the atrocities, the senseless destruction of cultural monuments, the annihilation of priests, nobles, kulaks, and prominent merchants—you, of course, would excuse them because of their lofty goal and celebrated historical necessity . . . No, there's no point in your reading these documents . . .

'Well, Comrade Conceptiev,' I said one day, 'we're making good progress. I have informed Joseph Vissarionovich that we will soon be presenting him with proof of your innocence. But we've got a problem! When they searched your apartment, they discovered a letter you had written in Stalin's name. The signature is so skilfully forged that it gave my graphologists trouble. What were the circumstances that compelled you to use the Leader's name?'

In reply, I heard what I very well knew. Conceptiev did not lie, did not gloss over the facts, did not refuse to accept blame for lynching the peasants and forging the letter. Time had shown that he was right to take extreme measures. The struggle with the old ways was not a game of footsie with a whore.

'I will try to convince Comrade Stalin,' I said, 'that your intentions were good and your actions necessary in that complex political situation. But the letter could work against you. Here's a denunciation that frankly calls you a *provocateur*. By brutally murdering the peasants and annihilating their villages, you meant to turn people away from collectivization. Does that make sense?'

'Yes. But it's the easiest thing in the world to distort the meaning of a deed. Anyone who believes me, who wants to believe me, will see my actions in the correct light! Who wrote that denunciation? What whorish bastard would say such a thing?'

'The handwriting must be familiar to you. Look.'

'Elizaveta?' your daddy shouted. 'I don't believe it! It can't be! I demand to see her.'

'Here's your wife's statement. Read it. She asks the investigation to spare her any meetings with you, since she finds you deeply disgusting. Read it. There are details of your life so intimate that a third person could not have known them.'

We had to resuscitate Conceptiev then. It wasn't his heart that gave out; he proved to have a heart of stone. The stoppage was in your daddy's brain. The poor human brain is often hard put to grasp what's going on, though directly or indirectly it bears the blame for all of life's inscrutable turnabouts, in which former executioners find themselves being executed by their own victims.

We resuscitated Conceptiev.

'Calm yourself,' I said. 'Funny you should have hysterics over a broad, when you so coolly shot your enemy in the head with your trusty pistol. I won't show your letter to Stalin. I'll conceal it for the time being. It would spoil things. Fuck them up beyond retrieval. Anyway, it's time for us to finish with you. I've got a pile of cases on my desk, going nowhere. All sorts of spies, saboteurs, and Trotskyites. But here I am, dicking around with you, a true Bolshevik, against whom enemy forces have aimed a blow! Collect yourself! Why, you're the man called Heart of Stone!'

'Thank you, Vasily Vasilievich!'

. . . Even today, it irks me to hear that patronymic. Ivan Vcherashkin had fixed me up with it on my new birth certificate. Forgive me, Father—Ivan Abramych . . .

'You're welcome,' I said. 'But we shouldn't be surprised by the behaviour of your son and wife. You and Stalin and I educated them to love the Idea. Such love is reckless; that's correct in a transitional period. Informers had only to cast a shadow on you, and both your son and your wife were ready to lay down their lives—not for you, but for the Idea and the Party. Bravo! But tomorrow we'll begin vindicating you in the next case.'

Wily I was, a serpent. I toyed with the five villains like a wolf cub with a chick. Their never-ending nightmare had brought them to the verge of collapse. Occasionally, not being used to this, my heart constricted with pity. But I reread the lists of services that each man had compiled with his own hand, and again I was engulfed by furious hatred. Easy there, Count, take it easy, I told myself . . .

The next charge I brought against Conceptiev was so absurd that when he familiarized himself with it he laughed merrily. The denunciation, fabricated by me, reported that Conceptiev and his assistants, calling themselves Praetorians, had worked out the details of a plot against Stalin and were preparing to implement it at a hunt in the Central Committee's wildlife preserve.

'Joseph Vissarionovich has corroborated that you invited him to go on a hunt with borzois.'

'The idea of a plot is so absurd I can't take it seriously enough to refute it!' Conceptiev said.

'Right,' I said. 'We'll use that very quality to refute it—its absurdity. The denunciation says that on New Year's Eve the five of you had a few drinks and decided to execute Stalin in Red Square, at the Lobnoe Mesto.'

'Beautiful!' Conceptiev shouted. 'We all have alibis! On New Year's Eve we were all in different regions. Gurevich was liquidating the ringleaders of the strike in Karaganda. Akhmedov was in Kazan, arresting a university professor who had once given Lenin a *D* in philosophy. Latsis was in Tashkent, delivering a lecture on "The Art of War: From Hannibal to Stalin". Goryaev and Kvasnitsky testified in the case against Zinoviev and Kamenev until four in the morning. And I . . . With this very hand I blew the brains out of the director of a trust, for nondelivery of spare parts to a top-secret factory. Beautiful!'

'Yes,' I said, 'you were lucky about New Year's Eve. We'll have to arrange yet another absurd filming. For the height of absurdity, we'll have to stage a scene of you executing Comrade Stalin at the Lobnoe Mesto. In conjunction with your documented alibis, the film will make an irresistible impression on him. He's suspected for a long time that the enemy has perfidiously begun to use the security system in a bloody struggle against the Party's best cadres, the true sons of the people.'

'Blackguards! Fascists! Sadists! I'll crush their Adam's apples with my own hands. I'd hate to waste the bullets on them!'

'Comrade Yezhov has called upon us to economize on lead and brass, but not at the expense of sparing our enemies' lives,' I said. 'My investigative concept is clear to you, then?'

'Must we really stage the execution? It's an awfully indecent spectacle . . .'

'We must. Stalin doesn't place much trust in written testimony, and he loves horror films. I advise you not to take any chances. The more plausible you look in the role of executioner, the easier it will be, in conjunction with your alibi, for you to rehabilitate yourself successfully in Stalin's eyes' . . .

Why have you suddenly interrupted me to express an interest in the fate of the prince, Citizen Gurov? You yourself don't understand the odd association . . .

I won't tell you anything about the prince. The fate of my friends is none of your business . . . Then again, my mood is a changeable thing. Before the war, the prince succeeded in escaping to France. From there he made his way to the States. A professor, an expert on Soviet affairs. I once saw his photo at the Minister's. The Minister thought of the prince as a clever, though noble, enemy. So he dreamed of getting rid of him. But he himself got nailed before he could arrange a car crash for the prince . . .

By the way, you wouldn't be feeling an awakened interest in your own future, would you? After all, your future is known to me, down to the smallest detail. Allow me to think for a second. Which would cause you more distress and torment: knowing or not knowing? Not knowing is more terrible, you assure me without hesitation. That makes sense. But we'll go a different route. What if the known should horrify you more than your premonitions?

Poxov! Get the doctor in here. Have her prepare Citizen Gurov to receive some information. I won't risk doing this without a light anaesthetic . . .

Here's what will happen to you in a couple of days from now, after I finish telling my loathsome tale and you confess to the brutal murder of Collectiva Lvovna Brutnikova . . . Yes, you'll crack. You can't hide . . . Give me your wrist. Quick!

Your pulse is like a cosmonaut's before the G-Force . . . Here's what will happen to you in a couple of days: I will order the family jewels to be returned to their rightful owners and heirs, wherever they may be. We counts have the power to do this. All your antiques and paintings will be hauled away and sold. The money they bring in I will deliver, under some convenient pretext, to people who have sat in prison for ten years and more, thanks to you. Many are still alive. In my briefcase I have a list of everyone you've ratted on.

Would you care to refresh your memory on some of the names? You'll do without? All right. Trofim and Trilby will be handed over to the circus. I know an animal trainer, a sweet woman, not cruel. Electra, your wife, will be . . . Psychotherapy really is a good thing: your pulse is normal . . . Your wife will be informed that you were her mother's murderer and, of course, her lover. Interested? Get up off your knees! Don't plead with me, scum! Don't let me hear your teeth chattering! Up! Everything will happen just as I say! Get that through your head! And that's not all.

Your daughter will be disavowed. Her son by her first marriage, your grandson Fedya, whose existence you haven't once mentioned, and consequently I have every reason to suppose that there's no creature on earth dearer or more precious to you—your grandson Fedya, a fine young man if my sources don't lie, will find out all about you, all about his mother, every last thing. Every last thing, in full detail! Have I made myself clear?

That's my punishment! And you'll all look into each other's eyes. You'll stare for a long time, and there won't be any first aid for you. No, toad, don't beg me to let you die amid the most gruesome tortures in exchange for the favour of leaving your wife and grandson in ignorance. You are denied mercy!

Then they'll leave, after signing a nondisclosure statement, and I'll shoot you like a dog. First in the groin. Then the stomach. Then the head. The villa will have to be burned. Before the fire is set the bullets will be extracted from you. Firemen are a picky bunch. I'll also destroy part of the paper money. The rest I'll distribute to my wolfhounds. That's all. But this won't happen before I finish telling my loathsome tale. You know the ending . . .

Deuce-ace! I haven't been fucking around for four decades in the prison of my life just to do *that*. In short, expect no mercy. Get *up!* . . .

Odd. We prepared you to hear in detail a final sentence, not subject to appeal, and you're fresh as a daisy. Oh, you crawled around the floor, let out a few howls, damn near chewed up my slippers. But it's over! You've combed your hair, blown your nose. Yes. Fresh as a daisy. Good for you! Keep it up. Executioners are impressed by this kind of behaviour . . . Or are you, in fact, upset, almost climbing the walls, but trying to put your psyche in a salutary mood? Trying to divert yourself? You remind me somewhat of the portion of mankind who live as fecklessly as if there were no chance they'll be blown sky-high at any second, with or without time to cast one last glance at the throng of unneeded things, the false goals and ideas, that have possessed their minds and souls, and the single true, simple goal, *Life*, which has gushed irretrievably from the common heart of mankind, to the horror and guilt of his failing Reason, already powerless to change anything.

What a memory I have. Where's my briefcase? Look at this fragment from a letter to the general assembly of the Academy of Sciences of the USSR, by a certain scholar who almost ended up in the KGB psych hospital . . . I've been quoting it word for word . . .

You don't offend me, Citizen Gurov, with your capricious and infantile declaration that you're sick of listening to me sing in other men's voices, and that these voices have turned my brain to mush . . . Let them rise from the dead. I've heard many voices. Even now I hear them . . .

Well . . . Go ahead and divert yourself, Citizen Gurov. Does death, for types like you, perhaps become more and more madly unreal, just as it's rushing headlong at you? Bastard, then why won't you crack? Why won't you confess to the murder of your adoptive momma and mistress? Why? You're provoking me! Do you want to take your secret to the grave? *Deuce-ace!* . . .

'Hand, let's go to the underground kingdom,' Stalin said to me once. 'The time has come.'

In the night we descended the marble staircase to the coffin of the leader of the world proletariat. I felt slightly sick: the marble walls were imbued with exhalations from the day's mob of corpse-idolaters—excited, idle, curious, fanatical, and half-witted.

'*They* think I come here to pray, whereas I descend these stairs to be quiet and think. *They* think Stalin pisses for joy if they call him the Lenin of today, whereas Stalin, unfortunately, is nothing but the Dzhugashvili of yesterday, and that's nothing to piss about, but rather to weep. Thank you, Lenin! Many thanks! Your dying wish was that we should kick Stalin out, like a dog, from the post of General Secretary. We vow to you over and over, this is yet another of your commandments that we shall honourably fail to fulfil!'

When Stalin, in the dead silence, raised his index finger and said, '*They* think,' I felt suffocated. It seemed to me that both Stalin and I had been buried alive in the marble cellar. We had been chosen, by an unclean power, to guard the corpse of a yellow little man in a military tunic with breast pockets, who lacked the final criterion of any connection with life—the ability to decompose as befits humankind, in the marvellous damp earth so lovingly created by God, or at least to become a handful of ashes. And we must guard his dead sleep for who knows how long, perhaps infinitely long, till Czarevich Ivan makes himself known by a silvery peal of horseshoes on the black stones of Red Square, till he runs down the marble stairs and throws the crystal lid off the coffin, till he rouses the dead man and tells him, smiling, 'Get up, mister! Your bed is all ready, get up and come sleep in your warm, downy bed!' And Czarevich Ivan will pick up the yellow little man in his arms, as one picks up children who have fallen asleep from sweet exhaustion when visiting, and carry him in his arms to where it has behooved all to repose since the beginning of time. He will pray on his knees for Mother Damp-Earth to receive at last something, at least one little cell, left of the unfortunate man, God's servant Vladimir Ulyanov . . .

The day after Stalin's nocturnal visit to the mausoleum, *It* began, but on a scale that I frankly had neither anticipated nor desired. The scope and character of the Terror gripping one-sixth of the planet could not possibly be rationalized. Common sense paled, convulsed, and fainted away. The agonizing attempts of thousands of people not guilty of Chekist brutalities or affiliation with the Party and the Marxist idea, the agonizing attempts of thousands of people to make sense of the horrors taking place before their eyes, ended in madness, arrests, broken and irreversibly traumatized hearts, a craving to escape at any cost, atrophy of the soul, curses upon the Lord God, a tragic consciousness of guilt and complicity with the doers of evil, a murderous suppression of the voice of conscience, betrayals stupefying in their cynicism, baseness, and suddenness . . .

In those days the Devil was just buzzing with pleasure, like a dry telegraph pole. Again he was reaping a harvest. Again his scythe made merry from the Black Sea to the pacified ocean. As for the fact that the best sons of his Idea were perishing in the slaughter—her most devoted interpreters, her priests and zealous guards, the same ones who from the start of the century up to 1937 had been using knives and whip-handles to drive the diabolical Idea into the minds and souls of the peoples inhabiting the expanses of the Russian Empire, the chosen site for the Devil's greatest Experiment—well, he couldn't do a frigging thing about it. If you chop wood, the chips must fly.

Or perhaps it was even for the better that distinguished Leninists should go flying as the forest of the people was felled by staunch Stalinists. Lately, certain Leninists had been dissatisfied with the Idea's behaviour. They were beginning to be worm-eaten by Revisionism, their intellect was casting aside all restraint, sometimes their conscience would awaken. They would open their delight-clogged eyes, and size up Soviet reality. Then their soul would pine for the reality from which they seemed to have been forever parted by Satan.

Let them fall. New ones would sprout on the fertilized fields. And these would fear more than death any attempt, even the slightest, to undermine Satan's own precious Idea. They would understand that if they crawled out from under the Idea's skirt into the daylight they would instantly—as complete nonentities who had lost the habit of human ways and lacked the simplest human occupations—be deprived of both their social unconcern, their moral irresponsibility, their portraits posted on every corner, their Crimean palaces, the machinery of glorification, their throng of servants, their diamond medals, their hunting grounds, and the brainy robot advisers who did their thinking for them and composed their speeches and *Selected Works*. Outside this system, guarded by the whole available force of the police and army, they would look like gutted sheep. Everywhere but in a tub of predigested thought they were fish out of water. Periodic terror was a basic component of the Great Experiment. Let them fall, the faithful allies, young and old. Let them fall! New ones would sprout.

After the Terror, as after a thunderstorm, after famine and pestilence, after earthquake and flood, they would be intimidated to the point of lacking any sign of the Soul's Divine Life. Base fear, not conscience, would become the instinct of their existence. The time would be ripe for the Devil to replace God's reality with his own, where people singing a ditty about building the Kingdom of God on earth would play fiendish little tricks capable of instantly annihilating His creation, His earth, His life.

But now comes my drama, Citizen Gurov, now comes the history of my fiendish self-deception, my stupendous delusion. Only after the war did I find, while doing a search, the work that opened my eyes to the Devil's tactics and strategy. In 1937, I believed in the existence of a tacit deal, involving millions of people, who consciously or instinctively resisted acknowledging the right of Satan's Force to rule over their minds and souls, uproot the tree of life from the everlasting field, and introduce chaos into the habitual world order. As I wrought my personal retribution on the executioners of the Civil War, the public prosecutors of the New Economic Policy era, the punitive detachments and ideologues of collectivization, and especially the ugly monsters of the Party apparatus, I attempted to chastise selectively, by virtue of my unique position at court. I personally did not arrest the innocent.

I won't say how many prominent wolves and cannibals I did in. Or how many times, while driving them insane with my hoaxes or pulling the trigger, I mentally addressed my late father Ivan Abramych. For you, Father! For you, my Mother! For all the innocent dead!

I raced around Moscow, the republics, and the regions in secret police cars, I slashed right and left, I interrogated, arrested, searched, avenged, and never failed to let them know—keeping myself covered, naturally—that all the absurd and obviously counter-revolutionary phenomena driving them insane were a *vengeance*! A natural vengeance, cruel and deserved, inevitable both for them and for their common cause.

Before their last minute of life, I sadistically and ingeniously demolished my victims' faith in Party and doctrine; I am witness that those who remained steadfast to the end were gross degenerates. The rest suddenly gained the ability to measure the true way of life against the mechanism of its destruction by the Idea, and they were horror-struck by the utter simplicity of the Devil's dialectics.

Whenever, and this happened often, any of them asked, with suffering in his voice, whether the Citizen Investigator wasn't ashamed to foist on the prisoner a fantastic case-scenario about a criminal attempt by a group of persons intimate with Bukharin to kidnap the League of Nations, with the goal of later blackmailing the Zurich gnomes and provoking England to attack the Soviet Union, the Citizen Investigator would calmly and vengefully return the question: 'And aren't you ashamed, you and your gangland colleagues, to foist a nonsensical life-scenario on the peasant, who believed your tall tales about land distribution, placed his power in your hands, and has now, from the place long settled by his ancestors, been exiled to Siberia with a brand on his forehead? Aren't you ashamed?'

For the sake of experiment and a certain secret idea of mine, I tried everything I could think of to destroy the sense of faith in Christians, Muslims, Jews, Buddhists, disciples of Cosmic Reason, priests of Eternal Harmony, and even fans of the transmigration of souls from communal to private apartments. Yes, I had that kind too. Of all my goniffs, they were the only ones who at least renounced their faith that the desired transmigration would take place during their lifetime. The others renounced nothing, doubted nothing, and did not lose the life-giving sense of faith, the sense that transmitted to their souls the tragic and instructive significance of what was happening. In response to all my crafty though not unfounded arguments regarding the strange behaviour of a Creator who spares not the innocent in the slaughter and who permits horrors repugnant to soul and reason, the faithful calmly objected that the Creator absolutely knows no evil, but that man's Reason itself, having lost God, is routinely stirred to outrage by all the world's Evil . . .

But here I will quote a fragment from the camp diary of a certain little old man, stubborn as a donkey, life-loving as a child with good genes, wise as I don't know who, and gay as a bird.

Where's my briefcase? Oh, here it is . . . This is what the grandfather said to the grandmother in an intimate moment. Not what I want . . . Here we are!

My dear zeks! I am sitting on the bunk, as all of you are too, waiting to be transferred we know not whither, and I thank God that I chanced to bend down yesterday and see a Hammer brand pencil. I had my notebook, and now, within your sight, I hasten to write something. For I have the sin—not a vainglorious sin, but one arising from the debility of my gift of reason—of not thinking aloud, or to myself, but writing a little. You can't write very much aloud, God forgive me for saying so, and besides, how much that's miraculous can you utter with your foul tongue, accustomed as it is to mother-oaths?

Well, and what kind of fate will Hammer have, I wonder, with a non-accidental name like that? After all, buying up our national treasures, dirt cheap. How much he has already bought on the sly only he and the sellers know. It's not right to take advantage of the people's misfortune. Not right. I curse those who get rich on the people's misfortune, and I have no thought of forgiveness—I take this sin upon my soul! But lo and behold, I found the little Hammer pencil. And you have made me happy, my pencil, little pencil! I can scrawl on the white wall of the barracks, 'Stalin is a shit! The Bolsheviks are devils!' But I will conserve you, save you for a subject I wish to contemplate, in a story to be titled 'Whither and Why? Or, Lament for a Little Pencil.'

Here we sit, orphaned and humiliated, grey, pathetic, empty-bellied, on the wood of our bunks. We wait to be transferred. Whither? Why? Once we walked free, along the free roads of the created earth. Across mountains and rivers, beyond seas and oceans we walked. Fair winds didst Thou send us, to our joy. Whirlwinds lashed our faces to test the stubbornness of our strength. Understanding urged us on. Some put down roots into the ground; others, caring not a hoot for the wisdom of halting, rolled on across the field.

But now, Lord, they throw us into cattlecars, slicing up the stream of us like sausage, whose taste our tongues have forgotten. Five zeks to a slice, they throw us from one hideous pit of open space to another, from that one to a third. How long, O Lord? How long? And is all this done by Thy will? The prison barracks turn away our vacant eyes from Thy Visage, for in today's life the innocent cannot understand the sign of a wrong so monstrously great. By now I am hoarse from telling them: Do not harden your hearts! He has given us of old the wings of Freedom. Is it not our own iniquity that we have flown to the wrong place, although we did not mean to fly here? Did not the prophets sing to us, warning of whoredom and lies at the stages of our long journey, did they not sing to us in their wrath: Fly, little birds, fly—though we know not where your shit will hit!

And here we are—in cages! Here we are—in snares!

The iniquity is ours, brothers, ours, and do not say it is not. It is ours! Thrice ours! Do not complain against God, as against a bread-cutter, that your bread rations are different, one man's has a makeweight, another's has sawdust, Sidorov's has no crust, Feldman's is uncooked. Do not complain that you were cheated of your share today! For if you were not, who would be? Your father? Your mother? Brother? Friend? Sister? Wife? Son? Neighbour? Would you transfer your cross to another's back?

Brothers, for those as yet unborn let us put into the money box each what he can, each what he does not begrudge. But if we do begrudge it, then especially let us put it in; for no gift richer, more unexpected, more joyful than ours will there be in the money box for him who opens it at an unknown time. But what do we have, on the wood of our bunks? Shit pie? Lice? Scabs? It seems there can be no creatures more destitute than we. And yet, is that so, brothers! Behold, an Invisible Someone walks through the barracks with a cap. Let us give him our hopes and our pure regrets, our yearning for our relatives and homefires, our love for them; let's not be stingy, let's give a tiny piece of Freedom, though you have little enough of that, I know; let us give our repentance that it never entered our minds until this second (when still at liberty we were locked up in ourselves, confident that life would end abruptly with us) to share with our descendants the things that would make them more free, more just, more gay and more fearless.

Identify with life, both past and future, and you will smile like a child, because a childish thought will flash through your heart: Hell's bells! We're the ones who fucked ourselves up! Isn't that enough fuck-ups? And you'll feel gay! As if the sun had come out from behind the storm clouds, you'll be squinting into the dazzling possibility of having time, at this instant, to live a just and grateful life.

So don't you weep, Trosha my lad, that you are only twenty and still unkissed, still haven't slept with a wife. Don't weep! You are young, but practically a lieutenant-general in terms of the honour that has been given you: at your young age you have earned the bitter bread of experience, which I am wolfing at seventy-two, toothless, familyless, condemned to a twenty-five-year hitch plus five no rights, five no cash, five no home, I expect my stomach ulcer will perforate any minute. Do not think, brothers, that there is life only at liberty. We are campfires half-extinguished on the wood of our bunks, but let us not douse the tiny flame of the coals with tears of despair and bitterness, let us conserve life, brothers, and sustain its burning ardour!

Lord! Lord! My pencil is almost gone, and soon we'll be put on the train, but my tongue has gabbed too much and the lead is worn down, and I still don't know whither or why . . . But what else, I wonder in a feverish tumult, what else to write, when the pencil is almost gone? Lord, receive the repentance of my soul, which has sometimes been absurd. I forgive Hammer. You granted me this sign, and I repent that without its help I had not come so far as to renounce bitterness. Send joy to him who dropped the pencil! What else, what else? Lord! On the train, give us herring that's not going bad, and water, water, water, and a cool breath in the heat, and a bit of firewood in the deep frost . . . My pencil is almost gone! Why didn't I spare it? Did I use it for the best? Why didn't I economize? Why the frig did I put in commas, full stops, question marks, curly capitals, why? And did I say the right thing with the pencil you sent to me from on high? Did I? Next time, Lord, next time, give me but the strength and the implement, and I will write a little better. My pencil is going . . . dwindling . . . dwindling . . . all dwindled away . . . Tha . . .

That aborted 'Thank you', Citizen Gurov, ends the stubborn old geezer's notes. I had chatted with him quite a lot at interrogations, learned much that was interesting, and followed his fate. After his death I obtained all his simple zek gear from the camp commandant. Old Vladimir Aristidovich Voinov died of a ruptured heart, before his pencil ran out . . . Where's my briefcase? Oh, here it is. And here's that very pencil. Look at it, Citizen Gurov; you may take it in hand. Write something with it, if you like . . . No . . . You have nothing to write with this pencil, this tiny little stub. Nothing . . .

Back when we were at the Children's Home, and then again later in Moscow, Pasha and I used to ask how it happened that the Experiment now under way was so calmly observed, and even rapturously applauded, by so many people in the West. Why did their Reason triumph? Why did the Bolsheviks' 'scientific discoveries' enrapture not only Communists and Social Democrats, but also scientists and writers and artists and average men and liberals and other idle observers? And what 'scientific discoveries'? The Red Terror? But terrors have been experienced more than once, historically, by France, Germany, England, Spain, Italy, Belgium, Asia, and the East! Collectivization? The marches organized by activists and passed off as spontaneous demonstrations of loyalty and love for the government? The poignant corpse-idolatry, which was also, by the way, imposed on the masses, perverting and disfiguring their instinct to worship a Higher Force and inspiring them to love the murderers who marked time on the mausoleum grandstand? The bold experimental attempt to convert a fellowship of free individuals into a faceless multitude? Or the annihilation of the essence of art by Socialist Realism? Or the 'institution' of concentration camps for the hundreds of thousands who did not consent to participate in the Experiment? Idly observing the course of the Experiment from afar, they believed, not the data and the heart-rending eyewitness accounts, but Romain Shaw, Lion Rolland, and Aragon

Barbusse, for whom Stalin put on 'shows' in the Crimea, model clubs and kindergartens and idyllic meadows littered with bottles of Georgian wine and roast suckling pigs. Other idle spectators, crowding in front of our laboratory cages, did believe the data on the life and spiritual tortures of the nation's many millions, but they continued to observe, applauding the exciting and sometimes breathtaking spectacles.

Wherein lies the answer to the psychological mystery of this heartless and unfeeling attitude? Wherein lies the appeal of the spectacle of another's suffering, another's death? In the fact that they are another's! In man . . .

Yes, Citizen Gurov, I'm at it again, profiting by someone else's thoughts. Yes, I'm stuffed to the gills with them! Yes, I'm devoid of any independent thought process! But I do have a few independent attitudes, thanks to my acquaintanceship with excellent and distinguished prisoners, though not with bastards and villains like you. Silence! I said *shove it*!

Frol Vlasych Goosev used to say that Man, with his ineradicable drive to grasp the nature of pain and death, unfortunately reacts to the pain and death of his neighbour in different ways. There is the brave feat of aid because one cannot bear to sympathize without acting. There is the rescue of another at the price of one's own health or life. There is very sincere compassion. There is the panicked flight from images of cripples moaning and doomed, and there is the torment of a soul utterly powerless to help the suffering, save the condemned, relieve the pain of martyrs. There are the numerous solitary explorers of their own pain, I forget what they're called, as well as both subtle and crude explorers of others' pain—sadists. Frol Vlasych Goosev cheerfully labelled surgery as sadism in the service of humanity . . . But there are people who contemplate with passionate curiosity and interest the grey troop of convicts drearily trudging to the construction site . . . the chimpanzee rampaging because his favourite female has had sex with some other lucky ape . . . the last convulsive spasms of the Adonis who has ended up under a trolleybus. At the moment of contemplation, only the brain is functioning in these people; as the material substrate of Reason, it does not feel, but soullessly processes data on another's pain, humiliation, suffering, and death. And the contemplator, most often unconsciously, is so glad of this opportunity to form an idea of what could have happened to him but has befallen someone else, so glad and happy to be alive and well and free, that the illusion of having saved himself must henceforth be maintained and made habitual. Efforts to demolish it through appeals from 'conservatives' for sympathy and insight, through warnings that soullessness is suicidal and his own death is imminent, are perceived by the contemplator as an attempt on his *Views*. By this word he involuntarily reveals the narcissism of his contemplativeness. He mistakes a suffering live soul, tormented live flesh, for his own reflection in the mirror, and often does everything in his power to avoid changing places with the reflection. As time passes, such behaviour deadens the soul and becomes cynically criminal.

Frol Vlasych did not insist on the absolute correctness of his analysis. But he maintained that so-called progressive men of goodwill take a passionate 'interest' in the tragic, absurd history of the USSR and the incredibly hard fate of its peoples battered by deprivations, wars, prison camps, and lawlessness, precisely because these great friends of the Soviet Union, as they are officially and tritely termed by the prostitute press, don't wish to see themselves in our place. Unconsciously they have made it a habit, and Frol Vlasych often stressed the unconsciousness of their attitude, to observe the Great Experiment, to think of us as eternal guinea-pig pioneers, but not to entertain any idea of starting an experiment, especially not of participating in one themselves, let's say in Norway or the principality of Lichtenstein . . .

We've really spent quite a while on this Terror. Tomorrow's the holiday. My birthday. Guardian angel, angel mine, aren't you afraid?

Something makes me think it was he, the wind of his wings over my soul, that brought on my melancholy. By then I had killed off Conceptiev's whole detachment with my own hands. I knew that you had supposedly vanished under the ice. Yet I continued to fulfil my official duties, annihilating the diabolical idea and its demons. My life was melancholy. Hideously melancholy. A bitch of a life. Good thing it's behind me . . .

I rarely went to my apartment. The apartment seemed dead to me. I hated everything in it. Except for the books—I would have felt bad to abandon them.

Standing on the threshold, I would slowly scan the vestibule with its cumbersome, empty, unneeded coatrack. It was made of mahogany. In winter my service cap hung there, in summer the damned Budyonny helmet with the horn on its crown, or, later, a cap with ear flaps. More than once I wanted to hang myself on that alien coatrack. Once I already had the necktie around my neck but couldn't find any soap. I was enraged. I went running around to five or six stores on my street. Not even one of them had soap. I walked in on a manager.

'Why isn't there any soap for sale, you sonofabitch?' I asked. 'Have we had a rash of suicides, or what? Answer!'

'Take mine,' he offered. 'Red Moscow. I just started it today.'

I spat and started home. I'll grease it with lard, I thought. Do you suppose there was any lard at the grocery store? When I got back to the apartment I went straight to my room without glancing at the coatrack. When I saw my books I forgot everything. I had lots of books. A priceless library. History. Philosophy. The classics. All of Dumas.

Yes, an excellent library. Better than yours, even though less expensive . . . You feel bad about your books, I imagine? After all, you had willed them to Fedya . . . I always fell asleep with a book in my hands—and with the fear that I would dream again about my father.

For two years, in my dreams, I lived an entire life with my father, my mother, and my brothers, in the village, doing nothing but work, winter, spring, summer, and autumn. I grew tall, grazed the cows, raced around on the horses, celebrated Christmas, Easter, Whit Sunday, ate cabbage soup with mushrooms, potatoes with lard, gathered raspberries in the berry patch and hugged the girls there too, sweated in our bathhouse, and pulled crayfish from under sunken logs in the cool willow shade. Then it came time to bury my father and mother. They died together, in my dream, on the Feast of the Protection . . . We laid them to rest, my wife Dasha and I and the little ones. My little ones . . . then teenagers, then fathers. And now they and our grandchildren were already burying

Dasha and me. She and I lay side by side, gaily intoxicated from the life now past . . . teardrops of resin on the fresh coffin boards . . . the earth waiting damp beside us . . . the birches and rowan trees murmuring above us, and our deep blue last sky afire with red berry clusters . . . the birds flying . . . Our sons and their women and the grandchildren, like us, were gay and radiant. They envied us. We'll meet by-and-by, they said . . . Goodbye, Dasha . . . Goodbye, Vasya, my darling. Goodbye, dear ones . . . Forgive us . . . Now the coffin lid shut out God's world. Suddenly all was dark, and our native earth was falling on us silent as thistledown, falling and falling . . .

Ever since the night I dreamed that my father begged me to abandon vengeance and forgive, so that we might be reunited in good time, might meet again and never be parted, I had not dreamed of him until I myself was buried in my dream. After that, I had only to fall asleep, and either his voice or my father in person would beg me, 'Leave them, Vasya, leave them! They'll be judged or forgiven, without your help! Leave them! Else we'll not meet again, Vasya . . . Leave them!'

And my father would be led away into pitch darkness, now by ticket-collectors, now by generals, now by Conceptiev and Vlachkov and Gurevich, now by the Red Devils—led away from the black square, over which crawled the slimy, slate-black mark of the dragon's tail . . .

But this, I thought, was Satan urging me, through my father, to let my mind wander from retribution. I rejected the notion of forgiveness, and my heart held no doubt . . . I saw myself as a warrior in the host advancing against the dragon. With might and main I chopped at one head, the next, the tenth, the hundredth.

The Count of Monte Cristo did not leave his office for days at a time. Interrogations and executions. Executions and interrogations. Interrogations—executions. Interrogations—tortures. Gradually I tired of hoaxes like the one I had pulled on Vlachkov, when I announced the restoration of the monarchy in Russia; they ceased to slake my thirst for revenge.

Suddenly it dawned on me that by the will of the Devil I was not in a new round of life, as I had expected, but the same old to-and-fro of death. The ones who survived the Terror were the more cynical, malicious, and soulless Party members, although not a few of these fell, too. By and large, the ones who perished were the switchmen, couplers, guards, conductors, station masters, dispatchers, the men in charge of depots and rails. But the fact that they were perishing did not change the train schedules. The timetable for the locomotive's progress to its eternal stop, the commune, was revised. The date of its arrival at this terminal was advanced considerably. The terminal was just down the track. The engineer, as the writers liked to say, was shading his eyes to make out its features as they came into view.

Suddenly it dawned on me that I was not struggling with the Devil—I was serving him. And the greater I thought my achievements in the struggle, the greater the service I was doing him. The snake! Of course, if this had dawned on me with full force, I would have hanged myself after all . . .

But I couldn't have put a bullet through my head, Citizen Gurov, though I don't quite know why. Even we villains can't help having a vague, if not a clear, preference as to the manner of our departure from life, our burial and resurrection. Aren't we men, after all? Or are we . . . We've ceased . . . ceased to be men . . . we don't have a Christian life, we'll have neither a Christian end . . . nor . . . But no use whining! Though the life remaining to you, Citizen Gurov, is about the size of that pencil stub in my briefcase. Have you forgotten? The pencil that belonged to a little old man, gay and free as a bird. Here it is. Look at it . . . That's odd; you're calmer now than you were several days ago, when you didn't yet see Death's features coming into view! Or are you, perhaps, not calmer but more lifeless? . . .

So it had faintly dawned on me that I myself was a Fiend and a swine. My doubts, torments, and fear arose not from a sober understanding and analysis of the situation but from processing the cases of such men as Frol Vlasych Goosev, protector of people and animals.

I was losing the sensation of life, like a little boy losing money from his holey pocket. When I woke up, sometimes in my apartment, sometimes in my office, I would stare goggle-eyed at the walls: where was I? It would take me a while, but dully and reluctantly the realization would penetrate that I was in the land of the living and had to summon a prisoner for interrogation in ten minutes.

I would go to the employees' toilet and observe, as if from a distance, the sleepy character at the urinal. His rumpled breeches, his soldier's blouse with the collar unbuttoned. Now he finished urinating. Rinsed his ugly puss. Combed his mop of hair . . . Strange gestures. A strange, inscrutable necessity—to urinate, to wash, and now also to have tea and sandwiches and stare at the black-and-white jumble called *Pravda*, then pick up the phone and give the order to bring in Frol Vlasych Goosev—governed the strange character's actions.

This was not life, if his unwillingness to part with his dream was stronger than life . . .

'This is not life! This is not life!' I shouted it out one day, howled it as I woke, and the department chief, happening to hear my shout in the corridor, responded by peering into my office.

'Why isn't it life?' he said.

'Because,' I replied, snapping to consciousness, 'there's no fucking ink in the inkwells, and the bursar won't order any fountain pens!'

The chief picked up the phone and said, 'Ivan Ivanych, my friend! Hello! Valetskis speaking. Listen, dear fellow, we're going to have to shoot you . . . Loyalty to ideas you have. Ink you don't. Without ink we can't cope. Ink's the lifeblood of our job. Please, now, don't bleed us white!'

He left, but I felt like a corpse. I kept falling asleep again at my desk. I started, opened my peepers, tried to think: Where was I . . . Who was I . . .

One day, when it seemed that I would die in exactly one instant if I woke up for good, and my throat was thick with the melancholy of my approaching chores, Frol Vlasych Goosev was suddenly escorted into my office. Life returned to me at once—not so much my own life, but real life, with no need of slow, difficult realization. Yawning and hitching up its trousers, it walked over to my desk and said: 'Good morning, Citizen Investigator.'

Frol Vlasych sat down and looked out of the window. His

glance kept skipping up and down, as drop after drop fell from the cornice. He was smiling. His thin dark wrinkled face wore an expression of utter unconcern and, at the same time, intense engagement. The face of a man engaged in true work, strange as that may seem. The toothless mouth half open. Nostrils quivering . . . He narrowed his eyes as if he had greedily seized a springtime sunbeam and didn't want to let it go—as if, there behind his pale, tired eyelids, he was rolling the warm, sweet little ray around, like a baby mouthing a sweet . . .

Yes! A breath of babyhood, happy and untroubled, was wafting to me from Frol Vlasych. My confusion forgotten, I soaked up the thing that he was joyfully and generously sharing with me—life . . .

By the way, he had one of those faces which at first glance not only give no impression of openness, zest for life, or freedom from care, but, on the contrary, suggest that their owner is a cruel man, reserved, neurasthenic, and eternally dissatisfied. I grinned, thinking of the face as the 'mirror of the soul'.

'Won't you ruin your eyes,' I said, 'watching the drops?'

'Why, no! Not at all! Don't worry!' he said. His attention had wandered from the drops, however. He was scrutinizing the portraits. His smiling but thoughtful eyes shifted from Lenin to Stalin, from Stalin to Marx, from Marx back to Lenin, and from Lenin to Dzerzhinsky. I was in the habit of ignoring these faces, but I would get miserably irritated when it seemed that my skin, the back of my neck, felt them staring.

'Well?' I asked darkly, taking care to conceal the pleasure I was deriving from the sight of this man. 'Shall we sit and smile?'

'Of course. Actually, what else is there to do?'

'Give testimony! Where were you on February 28, 1935?'

'Oh, no! If you need a testimony, you give it yourself. And I'll sign it, out of a personal liking for you. But I may not sign, either, if I get a bee in my bonnet. I'm a free man, strange as that may seem.'

My eyes were heavy, sweetly heavy with sleep, from the sound of his voice and his gay, infinitely calm way of speaking, which filled me with a terrible, greedy envy. I felt like a kid who had guzzled too much pork-and-cabbage soup. Full from supper, half asleep, I was climbing onto the bench over the stove . . . Too weak to climb . . . Asleep . . . About to tumble off the bench with a crash . . . Falling asleep . . .

'Take pen and paper,' I said, yawning, 'and write something on the substance of the case. I'll curl up on the sofa. I'm tired.'

'Splendid! I'll try not to disturb you. What time shall I wake you?'

'I'll wake up by myself . . .'

I fraternized with Frol Vlasych in this way for three months or so. I would rest for a couple of hours, gathering strength and life, while he happily churned out his comments, yarns, and treatises. They're all in my briefcase . . .

Something's making you fidget, Citizen Gurov. Yes. Your dear relatives are approaching the borders of the Motherland. The hour of your meeting is near . . . Very near. Oh, the punishment I'm fixing for you! You'll lick your fingers! Go to the toilet, go ahead. But no tricks . . . *Deuce-ace!* . . . Don't ask questions, just go. I see you're in a hurry . . . I have an unerring instinct for the moment when my subject is dying to go to the toilet, in order to change the trump suit in the interrogation, interrupt the rhythm of it, break free for an instant from the torrent that is dragging him to his end—and draw breath like a man, in the toilet . . . Go!

Well? Feel better? Ah, you're wondering how it is that I can combine a professional sadism with respect for all sorts of 'holy men' and 'fools in Christ', for 'religion' and 'church ethics'? And how it is that I don't feel my own 'baseness', my 'pitilessness that exceeds all bounds of reasonable revenge'? And what will I achieve by torturing you, humiliating and executing you?

'Reasonable revenge.' An appealing theme . . . But don't you see, I have arrogated the rights of the Supreme Judge? Don't you see that I have criminally arrogated to myself the right to judge and chastise, counting as sufficient reason thereto my own eternal wound and the torment and death of my relatives? You don't see. On the contrary. Demonstrating your magnanimity, which conceals a recognition of your own guilt, you encourage my right to revenge—but only within bounds of the reasonable. Aren't you the tricky shit! Reasonable revenge. Revolting. You'd like to rationalize the process of revenge, in order to make it more bearable. You've grown cocky enough to demand that the act of revenge be reduced to the idea of revenge. Just as pain is but the perception of pain, you assure me, revenge may well be but the perception of revenge.

The whole point of revenge is that when reason forcibly restores justice, or so it seems to him, when he renders measure for measure, plucks out an eye for an eye and a tooth for a tooth, he wants to feel, do you hear, to *feel* himself appeased, to feel, at last, the dying away of his lust for revenge, revenge, revenge. He doesn't want to have a perception of revenge. It doesn't sate him. He wants incontrovertible evidence that he was right not to acquiesce in villainy or deception . . . But his thirst is not slaked, for the black water of revenge has been salty from time immemorial . . .

There can be no evidence of the rightness of revenge. What we take to be evidence is illusory and provokes us to fresh acts of revenge. Revenge is always reasonable . . .

For the sake of revenge I have wasted my whole life, and I would have put an end to it if Frol Vlasych Goosev hadn't shared his life with me. But don't you pounce on me for talking about God with sympathy and the Devil with hatred, while I serve the latter personally and moreover violate not only Socialist Legality but also the natural law of man . . . At this rate you'll make a splendid dissident, Citizen Gurov, you'll even top your grandson Fedya!

Actually, why am I running on in such a muddled way about revenge and pain? Where's my briefcase? Let me read you something from the testimony of the benefactor who gave me the water of life . . .

I, Frol Vlasych Goosev, being accused by Citizen Investigator Vasily Vasilievich Bashov (who knows not what he does, and whose date and place of birth are unknown to me) of having left the Yermak Restaurant on the 28th of February 1935 at two o'clock, I don't remember how many minutes past, and entered the Kingdom of God which is within me, fully confess my guilt and on the substance of the case can testify as follows:

The substance of the case was nearing spring. Buds swelled on the lantern branches, ready to open. Stone houses, coated with the frost of a thaw, scratched themselves against the cats' backs, shook off the pigeons' pink feet, and shot upwards into a sky more than usually fathomless.

Pavletsky Station Square basked under the warm bodies of women who had arrived in the great village. Afraid to plunge into the stone forest, the women crowded around the horse-cab stand. Steam rose from the asphalt here, as it returned to life under the horse dung. The sparrows, after freezing all winter, were getting drunk on the hot food.

Lustfully but genially, the tram invited the women over. The women started towards it with the sweet lassitude of excitement and fear. The tram wanted them fiercely. The women let that one go by and boarded a No. 35, so named in honour of the year that had sired it.

Having tagged along after them, goodness knows why, I promptly returned to the coachmen, for they were all perched on their seats in the pose of N.V. Gogol on his posthumous pedestal, but disguised in different clothes and made up with various noses, eyes, hairstyles, beards, moustaches, and faces in general. There could be no mistake.

But in reply to my greeting—'Nikolai Vasilievich! How's the wife and kidneys?'—the first coachman swore filthily, a response prompted of course by objective causes, as for example: the degradation of morals, a consequent lack of fitting passengers, the price of oats, and the unregulable birthrate of all manner of inanimate trams. Cultured and mild, as intended by my parents and Motherland, I boarded the open carriage and exclaimed, obeying one of my many inner voices, equipotential in their orders and injunctions impacting unanticipated acts on my part . . . Forgive me, Lord, for the unexpected onslaught of the present active participle and past passive participle.

'To the locomotive, if you'd be so kind, for a drive together let us go,' I exclaimed, with more inversions than are permitted a sober man.

'Which one?' the coachman asked. He leaped up and instantly ceased to resemble N.V. Gogol.

'Brought . . . which to Moscow . . . funeral train . . . with body . . . Lenin's,' I replied, trying to stop the inversions by holding my breath.

'Cash in advance!'

'Means . . . all . . . by!' I said readily.

The horse flew along, as I remember it now, at an aeroplane trot. Here we were already, not far from the object of my journey.

'Hark!' I exclaimed, sensing that a miracle would be revealed to me

at once. 'Stop, coachman! Stop, my sister horse! You are living symbols of my protection!'

I was left alone with the locomotive, which loomed black in the thin, bright spring haze. It had been buffed to a high lustre by its nanny, the people. Even in the haze its raven flanks shone, its breast shone, the copper in its eyes sparkled, the copper of its little stripes and rounds sparkled, the oiled spokes of the black steel wheels were a gleaming red, the tender was coal black, and the black cylinder of the chimney perched immaculately on goodness knows what.

'You look like a toy of the Devil's childhood years,' I told the locomotive. Seizing hold of the shining handrails, I jumped on the running board of the ladder and sailed into the engineer's cab with practised ease, as if I did it at every change of shift.

In I sailed, and mentally bade farewell to everything that remained outside the window, everything that was already beginning to revolve around me in a small round of life. I released the brakes, closed the siphon, as they say, opened the ash pit, poured on the steam, I think, to the cylinders of the slide valves, and flipped a U-turn—only by a miracle failing to knock over a beer stand, scaring away the moustached porters with little white bibs on their chests, and all the while making an agonized effort to guess: was I on the rails or off?

Oh, how nice it was among all the little needles, stopcocks, glasses, pipes, levers, and wheels! How sweet to sneeze at the sourness of smoke in my nostrils, to crunch a crumb of coal between my teeth like a grain of sea sand!

I was having a modest snack, as it were, with my first gulp of space: quivering at the delicious, unearthly sensation of history moving backwards, I stuck my head out of the window so that the wind would spark tears in my eyes and not let them fall from my cheeks, so that it would carry away from my lips, to the rumbling accompaniment of the wheels, the words of an absurd little ditty: Backward fly, my locomotive! Make stops! Halt at each for hours, please. I'll cherries buy in paper sacks, made from Pravda *and* Izvestia. *And at the kiosk I shall drink a soda-pop, a soda-pop . . . I love, I so-o-o-o love any stop. Except the commune. Heigh-ho, fireman, come stoke up the coal in the furnace.*

'Hark!' I exclaimed anew, recognizing in the fireman, when he came out of the tender, an old acquaintance of mine. 'Isn't this a miracle, my friend?'

Answering not a word, the fireman threw coal into the fire box, and his smudgy face flamed with an unfriendly flame. It was he—Outraged Reason.

On this return trip he was taciturn, far different from on the trip out, and a deadly weariness made him rest at every stop. But since each of our stops was infinitely long, he had some wonderful rests.

'Where is your Soul, weary fireman?' I asked.

'She left me,' Reason answered, too verbosely, stirred to outrage solely on the momentum so beloved by our locomotive since earliest childhood.

'Where did she go?'

'Where indeed.' Reason stared at the flame of the fire. Goodness only knows why his face didn't char. He was sitting on a block of wood very close to the fire box, where the grate bars were melting, whiter than white.

At this stop I bought from a woman who embraced a clay jug resembling her figure, as I now recall, some oven-cooked milk with a crisp browned skin and little balls of churned butter. Her soft, fluffy, good, round bread might have been baked thousands of years ago. With a dignity inoffensive to another person, I bowed to the old woman, who was older than the bread. We sat down on the track.

As the giraffe water tower watched from on high, we ate bread and milk, sharing our food and our views on life with the railway birds. Reason informed me that he lived all by his lonesome these days, in his now-hateful body, which he was very *reluctant to go home to from his various meetings and disputations. His Soul had departed unseen, not even leaving him a note with a word of sorrow or insult.*

'Oh my, yes!' Reason said. 'That's like us! That's our style: make it nice and painful, scratch it nice and raw. Good thing I don't feel pain. I just get tired. In the long run, though, the perception of pain's no picnic either. But why should she think of that! We *are accustomed to think only of ourselves! It seems to* us *that pain is the exclusive property of the soul, not reason. And how would she know that? Oh, she has no wish, as she tells it, to know anything at all, owing to her indisputable wisdom. You've overdone the widsom bit, my lady! Even I have been known to suffer from loneliness and abandonment, and not from the perception of these conditions. This I'm compelled to confess. Yes, sir!*

'But on the other hand—look at the view from our locomotive! You won't deny our achievements, will you? Look! The foundations for new social relations have essentially been laid. We have built our own

world, a new world, and planes on duty in the sky continuously renew the motto that stretches from horizon to horizon but whose author has not yet had the honour to be born: "Communism is history that has gone into eternal retirement." Tremendous!

'In response, Frol Vlasych, to your objection that man's whole personality structure and so-called traditional values would be completely destroyed en route, *prior to arrival at the commune, I will reply as follows: Diamonds, my dear Frol Vlasych, are now created artificially! And we'll learn to grow the crystal lattices of diverse precious stones. In place of our souls we'll set sapphires, emeralds, chrysolites. Pearls white, black, and pink. Alexandrites. We'll set them in our bodies, and never on this earth, we'll exclaim, have there been blossom clusters more iridescent!*

'Every *man, every man in this land, will be truly precious, and the bright memory of what is unavoidably lost will light our streets, squares, avenues, naked forests, and empty zoos. When you make your gloomy prophecies, by the way, don't forget the unprecedented flowering of bioengineering in pre-Communism—don't forget that!'*

I understood that Reason had been distracted from moving backwards. He had forgotten himself at the station and was flying forwards, forwards. Cautiously I brought him out of this condition by alluding to the inevitability of our return to the locomotive. We started off. Clackety-clack-clack. Choo-choo-choo-choo . . .

We made a long stop at Gorky. The porters unloaded the coffin. A wide-eyed woman placed it on a child's sledge, donned her mittens, took the rope in her hands, and dragged sledge and coffin behind her over the snow, along a path trodden down by the townspeople, to a country churchyard. From there we heard the scrape of shovels on the frozen ground, and the blows of a crowbar . . .

We walked on. How wonderful to return to what seemed long forgotten! Who won't you meet at the stations and where the train is flagged to stop, on the sidings, in the waiting rooms of the railways! Dear faces, dear phenomena, dear things!

'Well, how goes it back here?'

'Well, how goes it out there?'

'We're doing fine!'

'A bird in the hand is worth two in the bush!'

'Climb aboard, why don't you!'

'Oh, no thank you, my dears! We've been lucky here too!'

'Goodbye!'

'Godspeed!'

Choo-choo-choo-choo . . . clackety-clack-clack . . .

The farther back we went and the longer our stops, the more nervous and tired my fireman became. He wasn't seething with anger like the water in the locomotive's boiler, he wasn't quivering with outrage like the instrument needles, but he was melancholy. Like anyone else who is stubborn, capricious, and guilty of quarrelling with himself, he did not seek the very shortest path to reconciliation after taking the first difficult step towards it. Rather, he yammered at the switchman, who had such a bad hangover that he nearly fell under the wheels; at the sleepy peasant women by the crossings, who signalled to us with the half-closed eyes of yellow lanterns; at the passengers, whose bottles, cans, photographs, shit, paper, cucumber rind, documents, cigarette butts, cotton wadding, Utopian books, chicken bones, goose bones, lamb bones, spectacle cases, and medals befouled the embankments, the track itself, and the black snows along the way.

'Everything's shit!' my fireman said now and then. For a long time he stared fixedly at the flame, forgetting to feed the cooling belly of the fire box. When it had quite cooled, we rode blissfully and briefly on the momentum beloved by our locomotive, and finally came to a halt.

Still Reason sat, watching as the blue, red, and orange flecks of light dwindled into nonexistence among the cinders, and the cinders themselves cooled before our very eyes. Now the ghastly cold of the death of movement breathed in our faces from the fire box, and behold, within it, pushing aside the dead cinders with its narrow green shoulders, up shot the little stem—engendered by the locomotive's last warmth—of an eternal train-stop. Now it bloomed, and its petals were an elusive colour that held all the colours of the world. Sweetly, sadly, and delicately, our nostrils were set quivering by the flower's first scent, as mysterious in origin as its first colour. Bees pressed close and then hovered, but the flower did not bow under the buzzing creatures, and the space of the fire box magnified a hundredfold the gentle, live scent of bee life.

'Oh my, yes!' Reason exclaimed, evidently continuing a conversation begun mentally about Soul. 'That's our style—criticize, condemn, and run away, at the very moment I most need support. She didn't love me! A loving Soul will die before she betrays, perish before she forsakes! But we are a fan of fine words! Are we capable of backing them with deeds? No!' A bitter irony distorted the thin lips. One minute his face took shape before my eyes, the next minute it blurred.

'Reason, you're stupid!' I laughed. Unexpectedly, he smiled too. He giggled as if a magic power, at that instant, had allowed him to look at himself from a distance. Something unquestionably childish flashed across his reviving, but still capricious and disagreeable, face.

'Yes, Reason, you're stupid,' I repeated. Trying to be milder and more charitable, I explained: 'Ratiocination has to be rationed. You were given your ration of reason in the times that preceded time, when the world hadn't begun to be depleted in wisdom and clarity, for Soul held sway and guided life. Your ration of reason—get it?'

Rather than stirring him to outrage, as I had feared, my words so startled Reason that he nearly fell off the locomotive. Clutching his belly, he kept guffawing and repeating: 'My ration of reason . . . Oh my! Oh my!'

'Yes!' I continued. 'Ratiocination has to be rationed, and the good thing about you, in your day, was that you didn't try to think about what was boundless and unknown to you. You did not doubt the existence or true development of the Creator's design. His infinite wisdom. The clear light of lofty harmony had not left your childish countenance.

'You were reasonable enough to blame yourself, and not the Creator, for the death of the fire on your hearth, for the wound received from the snow leopard, for the field trampled by monkeys, for illness, flood, lightning, failure, strings of failures. As a reward for your acquiescence in the measure of things and phenomena, there came to you without delay a happy unconcern and the possibility of triumph over circumstances.

'You expended the gift of freedom cautiously and did not know, when given a choice, that there was a path leading out of the kingdom that was within you into the desert that was all around. You did not set yourself against the world. You did not lose your temper. And you had no need to build the Kingdom of God on earth, for one simple reason: it was within you.'

'Oh, fucking shit! Oh, fucking shit!' Reason said hollowly and sorrowfully, like an alcoholic half awake. He buried his face in his hands and groaned, rocking from side to side.

'Do you remember what happened next?' I asked.

'I think I started to drink,' he replied.

'Yes. You expended the gift of freedom cautiously at first, you spent it on your essential needs, until you began to envy Adulthood, supposing it to be an opportunity for complete wilfulness—until you

took to drink, imagining yourself capable of being an infinitely wise, All-seeing, and All-knowing Builder, like Him, *like the Creator.'*

'She sensed that I'd gone wrong somehow,' Reason said, boiling over with anger again. 'But we're so meek and long-suffering, could we rush to my rescue? Oh my, no! We just whimpered a little and hid our eyes. We preferred to suffer in silence, and not interfere actively, so to speak, when who knew what the hell the stakes were! I condemn such non-interference!'

'It was impossible to drag you away from the gaming table. I am a witness. Imagining yourself to be a Builder, you proclaimed your Denial *of a loving explanation of the world and were full of your own ideas for remaking it. At once you found quite a bit to remake, of course. The claims you presented to the world grew and multiplied. You lost the capacity to be wise, not knowing what wisdom was, although Soul, who had nourished you with wisdom, did not sit on her hands, as you claim. She suffered terribly—that is, she did all she could, all that was in her power, to save you from your suicidal rebellion and your swelled head.*

'You accused the Creator of maliciously creating the world's multitude of ulcers, and immediately you thought you were filled with the world's pain. Truly this was not pain but the perception of pain—monstrously inflated, moreover, by a rich imagination.

'And now you drank away your last ten gold roubles of freedom. In your morning-after horrors, you imagined that this was unjust, and that consequently you had a perfect right to sneak into the Creator's treasuries, which were bursting with all kinds of Good Things and Understanding. At that moment—'

'Yes . . . yes,' Reason agreed. 'Oh, unhappy playboy!'

'At that moment you were stirred to outrage, you boiled over with anger, and it occurred to you that if you robbed His treasuries you could get to know the mechanics of chance and the world's very complex interconnections. Accordingly, as you delved into the nature of phenomena, you would be able to restore justice, tame the elements, and harmonize social and communal life. You did not tame the elements; you engendered new ones, against which you are not defenceless if you behave reasonably towards them. Having knocked freedom out of the foundation of social and communal life—'

'Oh my!' Reason's groan was long and penitential.

I deemed it permissible not to continue my thought. A man languishing in a morning-after fuddle needs quietude.

'Maybe I'd feel easier . . . if . . . if . . . we smashed up world imperialism a little?' Reason asked himself. At that instant he resembled an alcoholic who has decided to quit but whose mind keeps returning to the salvific glass.

'Not worth it. You'll do better to prevail over the abstinent state with some nice oven-cooked milk and a bit of bread,' I said.

'I was never so soused in my life . . . There's a lot I don't remember. A bald fellow with a huge forehead . . . Five-year plans or something . . . Stalin and his moustache . . . The Cheka . . . and bloody slogans before my eyes . . . my noggin's splitting . . .

'I made a mess of things, a real mess,' Reason said, rubbing his temples with his hands. 'But the Idea—she wasn't bad! A peach of an Idea! Took your breath away! She's something to remember. Or rather, hard to forget. Hard to forget . . . She was jealous, and I gave her good cause. In a word: the Idea turned a lot of men's heads, and then—goodbye! And good riddance. My Soul, even though she deserted me, my darling Soul is younger and nicer. But goodbye to her too! Should we belt one after all, Frol Vlasych? If we can't belt imperialism, then at least belt one for thermonuclear fusion? My blood vessels are constricted something awful. Let's get drunk! I'm unbearably lonely. And it reeks so of flowers here I can't think straight, my mind's playing tricks on me. What do we want with a swarm of bees here on the locomotive? And where, may I ask, is the honey? I loved it . . . in childhood . . . But what if she's . . . er . . . passed away, so to speak . . . died . . . Although how can we die! After all, we're immortal! And we don't give a damn about someone who self-destructs in world upheavals and the futile birth pangs of revolutions.

*'But that's just it—*we *are immortal! That's the whole point of my very unbearable tragedy. I'm wasting away, being ground into mincemeat, frayed into a pathetic little tag-end of rope before her very eyes: the seconds, minutes, hours, days, years are trickling out of me, implacably advancing the rude arrival of death's skeleton, and I'm supposed to "bite it", I'm supposed to "keep my pants on"! But why shut up? Why be patient? So that* we *will remain in a state of bliss and serenity, so that we won't have even a breath of tragedy in* our *egoistical little nest! No, no, no, a thousand times no! I don't accept that proposition! There's none of our hard-earned bread on your sumptuous menu!*

'Why are you, madam, said I, allotted all possible reserves of time, that is, why are you given infinite harmony for today, when all I get

is a few limp, droopy five-year plans? Even that would be all right, if I could spend those years in a swimming pool with sky-blue water like Rockefeller or Krupp, chasing goldfish in the company of supremely accessible perfections of the fair sex!

'All right. If that's how it has to be. We should have a nuptial compact, so to speak. You had yourself a high old time before me, my darling Soul, and you will again, goodness knows in what hostile bodies. Allow me at least some modest pleasure in my short life, at least a new overcoat and some greasy cabbage soup! Allow me at least to learn the secret of the structure of matter and the cause of the suppuration of life in the primary broth! Let me make use of my brilliant opportunities. Maybe at last I'll find the way out of this foetid labyrinth, where you and I from time immemorial have lacked harmonious conditions for the family life to which our one body is doomed. Make sense?

'So do you know, Frol Vlasych, what we chirped in reply to these thoroughly just complaints . . ? You're jealous, says she! It's hard for you to believe I haven't wronged you. I love you. Despite my awareness of immortality, I remember no one in the past, and I would wish no one but you in the future. What bothers you most is those bodies! You shouldn't drink so much. But I'm ready to do all I can for you!

'Then die with me! I declared in reply, logically and passionately. With one wave of your hand, resolve the unbearable drama of my fate! Die, light of my life, plague of my life—die at the same hour that I do! At least promise you won't abandon me! Deceive me if you must, but comfort me, I implored—often with tears, with groans drunken or sober . . .

'Always the same reaction: a proud, categorical refusal to answer, a theatrical demonstration of meekness—a defiant *meekness, let me stress—as well as a hint at the infinite, no less, depth of her despair and suffering. Is that so, I would say, is that so! Who cares! Even in the cold of loneliness I'll get on the move, I'll hustle the old grey matter. I'm not so alone! There's Parties of us! There's more of us than you, and we'll bring order to the thuggish business of this life! Our own world we will build, a new world!*

'But however much you swagger, however deep your mind delves, though you spit as far as the very quarks, even press your yearning face to Saturn's frosty rings—you shall have, as Pushkin said, nor happiness, nor peace, nor liberty! And at certain aggravating moments

I'm ready to throw in the towel, I'm ready to let go and trust all to my intended. Come to think of it, why should I care more than anyone else? I don't give a damn about the allegedly popular liberation movements! They just piddle away the days of your life, and the results are punk. Heartache. Chaos. Mountains of corpses. A fresh set of problems, already utterly beyond solution. A workload you couldn't unscramble in seven lifetimes.

'A lot of my colleagues, though, the utter nonentities who laid big bets in the Devil's game, have got no complaints. They tossed the rich folks out of the palaces and swimming pools and plumped themselves right down in the embrace of the amoebas or whatever, the naiads—in whatever they had on, in their sword-belts, puttees, Budyonny helmets—belching sourly like the eternally scabby louts they are. Stooges. Goodbye, degenerate scum, said I! Never again will I set foot in your brutish paradise. I am a reason still pure in many respects, even though outraged by the whole deal of Existence . . .

'The ensuing stormy reconciliation with my Soul took place in fantastically marvellous seclusion. We were enjoying ourselves, holding hands like little kids. The birds flew around twittering just like us. The vegetable and animal worlds exulted, driving us wild with their constituent gamma rays of colour and sound, ready for chance incarnation in something independent and wonderful . . . Frig it, I said, in my rather coarse, macho fashion. You win, Soul! Since you claim everything's going to be fine, then believe yourself, and relieve me of this worry. You win.

'For a while, I seemed to be living the life of a grand bourgeois *from the new breed of Soviet swindlers, one who has escaped exposure. With that good head on his shoulders, he has dived into timeless peace, into the embrace of the depraved naiads or whatever, the amoebas, that live in the swimming pools with the sky-blue water . . . Peace . . . Wisely I content myself with little, for I have escaped the worst. I love you, Life, as the saying goes, and I hope the feeling's mutual. But what . . . what's this, all of a sudden? After a mood of most perfect calm, the vulgar words of a most vulgar song suddenly wrench pain from the astonished heart, tears from the eyes! Is there a man in this world who would not shudder at the scene that followed, bursting upon my imagination from out of the blue?*

'The seasons allotted to me personally have come to an end, somehow without my noticing. I have died at my destined hour. I lie in the coffin. My brow, as usual in such cases, is cold, my nose sharp,

my eyes sunken. I get a distinct feeling that the pathoanatomists have defiled my defenceless body. Half my skull has been cut away; curiosity-seekers were interested in Reason. But my cranial cavity, if you'll pardon the expression, is as though the grey matter never existed. Empty. Good thing that as a reasonable man I'd left orders, in a timely will, not to stuff this cavity with just any old garbage the blackguard at the morgue happened to have handy. Only white cotton wadding, sprinkled with Sea Breeze cologne.

'Late autumn, take note. Sullenly ruffled birds on the bare black branches of the lime trees. Puddles frozen solid. Brass music, chilling the lips of the graveyard freelancers, thumps the benumbed distances . . . An ash-grey bus waits for me below. In it sits a big fat driver with an insolent, socially fortunate face. I'm his last one today. He hauls me away to my damp grave, or rather to the entrance of my tomb, takes a rake-off from my relatives, and heads home. To watch soccer. And figure skating—damn its vulgar immortality.

'My white paws are folded on my good black suit jacket. Cold chrysanthemums and cloth roses tickle my left ear and my right. The unbearably sweet, deathlike reek of fir, as if glad for man's withering, unites those who have arrived to say goodbye and the one they have temporarily succeeded in outliving . . . Beautiful, isn't this? A regular funeral march.

'Here are the rusty, lacy graveyard gates, survivors of the October Catastrophe. A metal handcart, crookedly and shoddily welded by some old souse and painted an absolutely hellish colour, takes my dead weight upon itself and lets out little screaks as if alive. This, more than anything else, distresses my Soul as she flies along, some distance away, in a transparent aspen grove, flies along like a black, weightless little scrap, a gauzy, funereal little cloud . . . My, my . . . Rain and snow. Slush. Heartache . . . My, my . . . But I'm lying there, and she's flying! My Soul is flying! That's what hurts . . . She flies around, and Beethoven and Chopin and that cardboard gypster Alexandrov flood the area and the coffin and me with music, which in my view is superfluous. The music also supports Soul in her sorrowful and sincere—this time I won't say a word—ascension from the corpse she has abandoned. Yes! The Corpse!

'In the grave, meanwhile, blue, lilac, and violet from drink, toil, and earthly cold, the gravediggers, prodded by their foreman, break up the hard clay to the last spade's depth.

'Tell me, what kind of a cynic, high-handed scrounge, soulless

executioner, and blackmailer of the deceased's unhappy relatives, who have lost the capacity to resist this purely Soviet graveyard boorishness—what kind of a scurf do you have to be, in order for you alone, out of all those gravediggers apparently in no way inferior to you, to get chosen as foreman on such a fantastic job!

'That, strangely enough, is what I imagine myself thinking at the damp grave's edge. That's as far as my outrage has got me . . . But this everyday brutality, in the last analysis, is not the point of my torments. So now they'll let me down, on the filthy ropes . . . down there. Then they'll bury me. Then they'll all be bussed away to a funeral feast for me, my funeral feast, they'll be bussed away to warmth, to a circle of bottles and food, to the sad, the most pleasant of dinner-table animations. And this animation arises from the fact that I am lying there in the darkness of the grave, awaiting the further instructions of organic life, while she, my animate Soul, is with you, among you. And however great her grief (is it grief?), she will still abide on earth, in her widowed state, on both the third day and the ninth and the fortieth. Well, and then, forever emancipated from my unbearableness, she'll set off to play the bride in other times and realms, in hopes of finding another Reason—a henpecked, non-outraged dishrag.

'No! I reject this! I will not reconcile myself to this unjust deal: some people dependent on death, others functioning forever in cycles of existence! I don't give a damn that I'm immortal, too, in my own way, as you put it. I aspire to be immortal not in my own way but in theirs! Yes, sir! And don't talk to me about continuity, cultural progress, contribution to the treasure house, and so on. Cash in advance! Time on the barrelhead! Or else I'll win emancipation by the strength of my own hand!

'And you, madam, I said, if you have true feeling, will please be good enough to come with me . . . on a bitter autumn day . . . to the grave, so that we won't be parted. It's not just on the third day, the ninth, and the fortieth that I need your indulgent presence. Make sense?'

'Fireman, you have a difficult and shitty character. Do you know what character is?' I asked.

Reason did not know.

'It's the form and quality of your relationship to Soul. When your bond with her is strong, when you trust her wise exhortations, then you find it easy, in this world, to reconcile yourself, forgive, endure *failures or not even notice their everlasting presence at all; easy to heal yourself, correlate the eternal with the temporal and corruptible, rejoice though at little, love the moment, not hurry, not be wrathful, not judge, not avoid reality, and not do a lot of other things. But you have only to stir yourself up by inventing grounds for outrage, and right away your attitude is spoiled. Your stubbornness, capriciousness, reproaches, squeamishness, inflated pride, insatiability, and envy come out, and you fall more and more under the sway of a single passion: the game!'*

'*Now there you've got something!*' Reason agreed.

'*You passionately believe that the game situation artificially created by your imagination, like the situation in which you have landed by chance or which was imposed on you, can serve as a model for all of life. Having fallen away from life and her inscrutable laws, you both nourish and devour your own self in the effort to learn by your own strength the laws and mechanics of chance in the game, to master them, to build the Kingdom of God on earth with their help, and in this way to disgrace the Creator, who, as it seems to you, created unbearable conditions for human existence.*'

'*All in all, that's roughly how things stand,*' Reason said.

'*Why "roughly"?*' *I asked, not at all from any pretension to definitiveness in my opinions.*

'*Because frankly, what I'm keen on is the game itself, not the purpose of the game. Who cares what it's called or what the stakes are?* Chemin-de-fer, *blackjack, chess, poker . . . A rouble more, a rouble less . . . Look at the writer most hostile to me, Dostoevsky: gambled his heart out. Chance . . . there's a lot of folks who get no peace from that little bitch. Even poetry's an eternal chase after her capricious tail, don't you think?*'

'*Poetry is Pushkin flying after her on Pegasus, not you acting outraged in the Council of People's Commissars because in theory it's already time for everybody to poop, but in practice we haven't even eaten yet. Your theory, whose validity is hypothetical, is letting you down, and already today you are horrified by the fee for testing its validity.*

'*I refer to your participation in the game "Communism is the radiant future of all mankind". That is the extreme case when you consider it permissible to choose the tactic of limitless sacrifice, throwing colossal resources and millions of human pawns into the battle. The incorrectness of your gambit is excused (this you impress on both yourself and the pawns, to the applause of foreign fans who crave exciting spectacles) by the same old goal—a showy ending to the big game, the world history experiment, the building of Communism. But goodness knows how to build it in one individual country, when mankind's global interrelationships and interdependencies are increasingly apparent in all spheres of life. Probably only Khabibulin, the toilet attendant at the Yermak Restaurant, knows the secret move that would lead you to a win. Khabibulin maintains that until people quit soiling themselves, at least in the toilets, they don't have a hope of seeing Communism, let alone cleanliness and order.'*

'He's right! With just one country, you do get crappy results. Now, if they'd let me hold a simultaneous world exhibition match on all the boards, I'd like to see where you and I'd be having this chat, Frol Vlasych!' Reason exclaimed, boiling with anger.

'Hold your shit, fireman,' I said. 'You'd do better to think about Soul. Is life without her really a life?'

'Think what *about her? Maybe I don't even care to know where the lady is! Oh my, no!* We, *after all, don't know what loneliness is! But I do! I have no idea where or with whom, but I'm sure she's somewhere with somebody!'*

'Enough of your guff, fireman!' I said severely. 'Soul has not forsaken you. Do you think it's you laughing when you laugh? No! It's both of you laughing—you and she! But don't try to force a guffaw. Go and rinse off under the water tower, drink some water as a pick-me-up, and right away you'll find things funny. Maybe bitter, but funny. Go! She's already leading you by the hand!'

But for my native restraint, I would have been racked with sobs: the pure light of trust had instantly washed away the facelessness from my fireman's whole character. His face was the face of a youth full of life, seeking occasions for laughter and surprise.

Lightly he spun the valve wheel of the water tower, which started laughing aloud as if it had been tickled, and a living waterfall fell on him. Enveloped in the being of the water, as if in a sunlit cocoon, there trembled another living being, washing the corrosive black of the coal dust from its little coals of eyes. And now, within the very man who had once astonished me by his absence of life, Soul was rejoicing and splashing as she felt the life-giving weight of man's flesh pouring on to her like water. The laughter of the water blended with his laughter, and now he had become naked, for his superfluous clothes had been washed from him and swept away with the stream.

'Engineer, you've returned me to life!' he whom I could no longer call Reason shouted gaily, sticking his head out of the waterfall. 'I thank you from the bottom of my soul!'

'Don't thank me, just live,' I said, and hesitated in surprise: he reminded me so much of myself. I seemed to be looking into the mirrorlike water of a well. Verily: the alive resembles the alive . . . But ripples spread suddenly over the water . . .

In addition to what has been said, I request that a reprimand be given to the railway police and the porter Yezhov, who have violated my image of the railway station, parted me from my locomotive, and in its stead sent a tumbrel to get me at my place of work . . . I was not a sympathizer, for I understood the falsity of their raptures. I was not a fellow traveller. The five-year plans I consider to be the Devil's progressive method of packing up instants to destroy the workers' livingtime. The Party I conceive of as a train made up of cars of different classes. I do not care to rush along, not stopping and not knowing whither, in either the lounge car or the public cattle truck.

Signed: Forewarned about liability for giving false testimony, Frol Vlasych Goosev, protector of people and animals, living with Soul in lawful and happy wedlock and being completely of sound mind . . .

Melancholy . . . I'm dismally melancholy, Citizen Gurov . . . But I do feel a wicked hilarity when I remember how I reported to Stalin's dacha with the metal box. That box held the films we had made, the episodes of Conceptiev's case. I had titled them 'Red Saturday' and 'Lobnoe Mesto'. Several political figures, not from Stalin's immediate entourage, were with him in the cinema at the dacha. They were falling all over each other to propose fantastic incentives for labour collectives and record-breaking workers. Marble, bronze, and gold busts in the factory shops . . . Casts of the hands of manual labourers . . . X-rays of the skulls of mental labourers . . .

The speakers misinterpreted the interest with which Stalin peered into their faces. He was trying to determine what, exactly, in these faces might be the sign that they were sentenced to death. It was obvious to me that all, literally all of them, were five minutes away from being corpses.

I said nothing, and Stalin kept breaking into soft, fiendishly eerie laughter. Not even laughter—the sounds merely symbolized his vulturine screech of triumph. Triumph! Stalin held in his hands the threads of several fates. He felt himself to be the master of chance, for it seemed to him that he alone, at that moment, knew precisely the extent of his victims' misfortune, as well as the extent of his own ability to save them from a seemingly inevitable death. He was savouring his triumph—it was not his first, but triumph and laughter did not sate him, just as vengeance did not sate me.

Infected by the Leader's gaiety, which was more flattering to their self-esteem than mere praise, the speakers laughed too and applauded Stalin. Sincerely, he applauded them. And I, for the nth time, rocked with laughter at the grisly image of men's ignorance and error about Stalin's attitude towards them, and at the image of Stalin himself, who was enjoying the impression made by his mask of fatherly concern and friendly encouragement. Through the eyes and mouth of that mask glinted the black muzzles of my revolvers.

After laughing and applauding a moment, Stalin said, 'We have one master—Socialism. Let us serve it with the devotion and loyalty of a dog, comrades.'

When everyone had gone, he continued, with loathing, 'They wear me out. We kill them and kill them, but there's no end to them. One can only suppose they find time to multiply before they die . . . What have you got, Hand? Let's hear about it. I've made a bet with myself: will you ever make a mistake, or won't you? That isn't to say I desire your death. Chances are, you'll never again make a mistake. And if your work is infallible now, it can only mean that you made your mistake before . . . Do you understand? Before. I'm not asking what it was. So don't be shy, let's hear what you've got—or whom. I doubt you'll make a mistake . . . Who is it?'

'Conceptiev,' I said.

'Proof!' Stalin said harshly, as if aiming at a point on my forehead and cocking the trigger.

I drew from my briefcase the letter with Stalin's forged signature, and the explanation that Conceptiev himself had written. I tried extra hard to be objective, in order to deflect any suspicion of partiality.

'How often did Conceptiev use my name?' Stalin asked, after reading the documents.

'Just the once, he claims.'

'That's odd. Very odd, that he concealed from me a fact I could have taken as a political joke. Odd . . . But what does he have to show for it?'

'It's clear, by now, that Conceptiev's goal was to consolidate opposition forces in an alliance with criminals of every shade, in order to usurp power,' I said.

'An alliance with criminals—that's an idea I slipped to Lenin, back in 1916. It was a splendid idea. Only idiots believe that the people took power into their own hands in Russia! It was the criminals who took power, and the bandits!'

'Conceptiev lost out,' I interjected, seeing my chance. 'He actually dreamed of overthrowing Lenin, you know.'

'None of your Chekist fairy tales, Hand. You have to know when to stop,' Stalin growled.

'I shall endeavour to convince you by means of confessions documented on film,' I said, without timidity.

Stalin sat down in an armchair. He could not hide his puerile excitement at the prospect of a lively show. I switched on the projector. Flickering in the upper left-hand corner of the wall-sized picture was Marx's portrait; in the upper right, Lenin's. The camera work in 'Red Saturday' was marvellous.

I gave a running commentary on the episode, and Stalin believed it: Overtaxed by the heavy log, Lenin takes to his bed for good. Conceptiev, in alliance with Trotsky, arrests General Secretary Stalin. They isolate him, if they don't liquidate him immediately. They convoke an extraordinary congress. With no trouble at all, they din into the delegates' thick heads the idea that Stalin is to blame for having Lenin appear at Russia's first Volunteer Saturday.

When the tired, sweaty face of the Leader of the World Proletariat was shown in close-up, Stalin squealed with laughter and slapped his hands on his knees.

'Chaplin! Chaplin!' he said, wiping his eyes with a handkerchief.

A shoulder . . . On the shoulder, a log of iron wood . . . The weight of the log drags the shoulder down . . . Conceptiev winks at Gurevich and Akhmetov. Lenin is miserable, but he poses for history. Sweat rolls down his face. He mops at his drenched skull with his familiar cloth cap. Here's a shot of Trotsky's hateful puss . . . Another shot of it . . .

'Blackguards! Degenerates! Traitors! Villains! Muckmouths! Intellectual prostitutes! Mmmgh—the bastards! Oh, Conceptiev! Oh, you shitty bastard! So all these years he's been kissing me up! What didn't he have? Dacha, palace in the Crimea, packs of borzois, hunting lands, trotters, cars, women, medals!'

But Stalin spoke that last sentence after we viewed the 'Lobnoe Mesto' episode. I had pretended, when 'Red Saturday' was over, to be hesitant about suggesting that Stalin view the next confession film.

'Begin!' he commanded. 'Stalin's nerves are up to it!'

'To make an example of the Leader by physically liquidating him before the very eyes of the people—that is our ultimate goal!' Conceptiev said from the screen, whereupon each of the defendants specified details of the conspiracy.

'Mad dogs!' Stalin screamed, and he hurled his pipe at the screen. I picked it up.

Then came shots of a May Day demonstration, taken from a newsreel. The cheering people, holding little children in their arms, were looking towards . . . the Lobnoe Mesto. On it stood Conceptiev, axe in hand. He smiled and bowed to the people. Now the chief accomplices of this Brutus approached the block, dragging a doll wonderfully made up to look like Stalin. Tunic, moustache, service cap, trousers tucked into his boots . . . A sea of heads. In the faces, the anticipation of something horrible, and a readiness for ecstasy . . . These were frames I had excerpted from a documentary about a 'Free Sacco and Vanzetti!' rally. A sea of heads, and above them, trumpeting from the loudspeakers, the irritating goddamn voice of Yuri Levitan:

'Being an agent of the Gestapo, Dzhugashvili liquidated the finest flower of Leninist philosophical thought. He and his assistants, with the aid of the Wehrmacht, intended to partition the territory of our glorious Motherland into so-called sovereign states such as Armenia, Georgia, Yakutia, and Palestine. He discredited the doctrine of Marx and Lenin. Forcibly introduced collectivization . . . Murdered the loyal Leninist Alliluyeva . . . Created an All-Union network of concentration camps, after consulting on this matter with various dictators . . . Immorality in his private life . . . Criminal cohabitation with the bloody dwarf Yezhov . . . Inordinate self-glorification . . . Collaboration with a handful of bird-brained lickspittles such as Kaganovich, Molotov, and Voroshilov . . . Preparation for an invasion by Hitler's troops . . . Embourgeoisement of the bohemians, technocrats, and scientific flimflam artists . . . Sentenced to death, in keeping with ancient Russian custom . . . to be quartered, at the Lobnoe Mesto!'

'That's probably enough,' I said, switching off the projector.

'Carry on, Hand. Dzhugashvili is not averse to gawking at Stalin's death. But they're such mad dogs! That bastard Levitan! Today he says, "Long live Stalin, our dear and infinitely beloved father, friend, and teacher, the great helmsman of our time!"—and tomorrow he reads my sentence! I'm right to hate the mob, right to humiliate them by making them worship me! They're all dogs! All bastards! . . . Roll it, Hand!'

Conceptiev hacked the arms off the Stalin doll first, then the legs, and finally the head. He held it up, and rags and red sawdust spilled out. The crowd bawled 'Hurrah!' and sang their song about how they alone in all the world could truly laugh and love.

'That's all,' I said. 'The prisoners were not subjected to any torture or pressure. After selling each other out, they tried to reveal as much as possible, in the hope of clemency. They request a personal meeting with you.'

'What for?' Stalin asked, after pacing the hall in silence for ten minutes.

'They're planning to plead for their lives.'

'Things have gone too far. I've always been too considerate of others. It's time to worry about my own personal safety. Execute all of them, yourself. No trial. No formalities. Slaughter them like dogs, Hand. Mad dogs. You'll receive the Order of Lenin for your investigative film . . . To accuse me of cohabitation with Yezhov! Scum! In which role, I'd like to know? Active or passive? Slaughter them like dogs, Hand! Understood?'

'Yes, sir!' I said. 'Shall I give them any message?'

The scene of his own execution had caused Stalin to lose his head completely. He wrote this note: 'Conceptiev! You are lower than Iago. But Stalin shall conquer death, as our pilots conquer space and time. Dog! Dog! Dog!'

'That's my message,' Stalin said. 'Let him read it before he dies. Me, an "agent of the Gestapo"! Oh, the scoundrels! Go. Thank you. This time, too, you have made no mistake' . . .

Tomorrow, Citizen Gurov, we'll have ourselves a party. After all, yours truly is going to be sixty! Trust Ivan Vcherashkin to put this glorious date on my jiggered birth certificate. He loved jokes like this . . .

After the war, Pasha and I went fishing . . . This time you guessed right: we went to the River Odinka. My first and last trip there. Where our village had been, not even the coals remained. The wells and everything else were covered with turf. Nothing left—not a stick, not a stone. But the giant log still lay, just as always, on the bank of the Odinka. It hadn't rotted, hadn't decayed, hadn't burned, hadn't been washed away by the rain and snow. Pasha and I spread a white tablecloth on it. We got out a bottle, an Easter cake, sweet cheese, decorated eggs, and chicken.

I remember I was hysterically cheerful, talking away, spouting nonsense. I knew that if I once started thinking about myself, about my relatives and our whole fate, I wouldn't be able to put it all out of my mind, and I might go off the deep end. I didn't want to live. I'd had it to the teeth with executions. And my father had stopped visiting me in my dreams; evidently he had cursed me and lost hope of our reunion. I had no urge to spill all this to Pasha, though. Not from fear he'd sell me out. I just didn't have the urge. But I didn't want to go off the deep end, either—as if I almost knew that sooner or later I was bound to meet up with you.

We ate, drank, and exchanged the Easter kiss.

'Yes, Hand,' Pasha said, 'it's clear by now. This Force, this damned asshole Idea, turns out to be stronger than we are. We could have put it to bed with a shovel, if we hadn't had the war. He saw that. He saw it, the moustached little bastard! He knew about the troops massing on the borders—in effect, he knew about the war itself. Everyone thinks that up to the last second he was hoping Hitler would think better of it, let off a little steam but not start a war. No, that's exactly what the scumbag feared: any pre-emptive move might actually have scared the Führer off, and then who knows how that period of history would have ended for Stalin . . . God rest the souls of all who perished because of this moustached cunt-louse!

'We can't overthrow the Idea now, Hand. Can't do it. Half of Russia's in ruins, but even so, we've got to live. Build and live. And I personally couldn't make it, in my sphere, without these half-assed mottoes. That hurts. And would you believe it, sometimes I panic. I'm ranting from the rostrum about onwards to Communism, and I see that there's a void behind my words, a bottomless void, nothing. All the same, I rant and quote, hammer away. I don't believe a word of it, but what could I say differently at that moment, I wonder? And you know who I envy, there on the rostrum? A Ford, or the governor of Texas. How come they don't traipse around to rallies two, three times a day? They don't issue appeals for increased efficiency and improved quality. They don't kiss lathe operators and milling-machine operators for overfulfilling the Plan. They don't weep for joy when they're informed of the millionth metre of calico woven by an heroic collective, and they don't run to Roosevelt and Truman with this flabbergasting news. They don't run, they don't lead rallies, they don't drag anyone to Communism—but they bring up coal, they pump oil, they've swamped the whole world with cars, and they've got plenty to eat, even though Truman doesn't go kissing milkmaids or awarding the Order of the American Banner of Labour to a farmer . . . It makes me want to puke, Hand, all this ballyhooing and toasting. My peasant serfs, robbed of the shirts off their backs—every night I dream about them . . . Hand, you don't suppose we'll just croak in the middle of this lie, clutching our truncheons and horsewhips, tossing gingerbread medals to the people on red-letter days. What do you think, Hand?'

I no longer had the strength to hold out. My lips started to quiver. Burying my face in my hands, I fell upon the giant log, on the spot where you had made me sit. The bottle toppled off, the Easter eggs went rolling across the soft first grass, down the bank into the little river, and I wailed at the top of my lungs, like a child. I couldn't believe that when I had eased my soul and dried my tears, I would glance around and see neither the village, nor the calves in the pasture, nor the first brood of goslings, nor my father in the vegetable garden, nor my mother with her yoke of buckets, on her way to fetch water. I couldn't believe that I would see nothing, and that I was I, a lonely, homeless, crippled creature who had dispatched to the next world several dozen people—victims, really, like myself, of the devilish force.

Pasha tore me forcibly from the log. I threw my arms around it and didn't want to get up . . .

What's the matter, Citizen Gurov? Get up off the floor! Up! Stop your howling! And don't claim you've been stabbed by guilt towards me . . . I don't believe you . . . You're clutching desperately at a straw. If you hadn't lost your faculties, you'd realize you have no chance of salvation . . . And don't make me laugh with your muddled apologies. That's very funny. Beg pardon, mister, I froze your balls off! Very funny . . .

Well, all right. If you claim you've had 'a crisis and a change of heart', if it's true you've been 'stabbed by guilt', if you've 'put yourself in my shoes' and felt my humiliation and pain, then crack! Did you, personally, pulp Collectiva Lvovna Brutnikova? Again no! But I'm no rusty-guts sucker. Rat, you're looking for your chance, your mind is feverishly racing through your final options! A change of heart—hah! I ask you one last time: did you kill her? No. All right. Poxov! Let's have the material evidence of Gurov's foul iniquity. I'm fed up . . .

Your refusal to confess has such a desperate ring that I'm beginning to get curious. Still, I can't suppose that the crime has been purged from your memory like a worm from the belly . . . Don't say anything. I've decided to break you, and I will. As for why I should want to, that's not for you to know. If you're a gambler, try to guess my combination . . . You can't? Then keep your mouth shut.

Right now I'd give a lot for the chance to spend a couple of minutes in your shoes, in your hell, if I could come right back out of the stench. I can imagine the voluptuous sense of emancipation with which you passed that first night. You clutched the two lovely pearls in your fist and never shuddered at the dead woman's presence in the house . . . The next day an oak coffin was brought from the storehouse, from a supply dating back to the czar. You dressed Brutnikova in her service cap and Stalin-style tunic. The gun moll of the twenties and thirties lay in her coffin, drowning in flowers and the secret of her death. Next, you sent a telegram summoning Electra. Right? Right. Then the coffin with Brutnikova's body stood for twenty-four hours in the Security Police clubhouse. Then madame was buried—and now you'll have the moment that will repay you for the infinite happiness of success you experienced on the way back from the cemetery to the Party funeral feast, as you supported, with a true man's strong arm, the frail arm of the little orphan Elya.

Poxov! Drag it in here. Don't worry, it won't disintegrate . . . Look closely, Citizen Gurov. Look! I'm running a risk that you'll have a stroke—but look! Recognize the coffin? That's water-seasoned oak. In damp earth it doesn't rot for up to two hundred years, and in sand it can outlive our miraculous civilization.

You think this is a hoax? No. Open the lid, Poxov! Citizen Gurov, don't be stupid. Perceive reality. Maybe you'll extract some crumbs of benefit.

See how the gabardine of the tunic has lasted on the skeleton. The roses still have a faint colour. The service cap is ridiculous on the skull . . . Here's the autopsy report, and a photo of the back of the skull. Take a look. By now it's quite unimportant exactly which moment you walked up to your beloved momma and brained her with a metal object wrapped in something soft. Will you confess? No. All right. By now it would be stupid to crack, and unbecoming. Besides, it's not even necessary . . . When Collectiva lost consciousness and hit the floor, most likely you dunked her head in the bathtub and she quietly drowned. You summoned Vigelsky. Gave him the white pearl. Received the death certificate. Destroyed all clues. Dried Collectiva's hair and laid her in her hateful bed . . .

But to this day I can't imagine why you hid the murder weapon in the coffin. Get it from the coffin, Poxov! Here it is, your double-ended spanner. Take it in hand! Why, look—how interesting. Your hand involuntarily reached for it! Why the hell would you have put it in the coffin? Malicious joy? Cynicism? . . . No; I think you feared a search. At some moment just before the arrival of the Chekists, Collectiva's colleagues, you stuck it under the deceased's back—just in case.

Shake your head all you want. Examine the wrench as if you don't recognize it. Put it back . . . Yes! Yourself! Bend over the coffin. Keep your eyes on the empty eye-sockets. You may pick up the skull in your hands. Take a look at the crack in the back of it, and the dent. And tomorrow we'll admire a group portrait: the Gurov family in front of this coffin.

Plonking yourself at my feet again! Have you gone berserk? Well, suppose I did pass up the fascinating spectacle of perfect revenge: what could you give me in return? You don't possess that kind of treasure, you really don't. Let's eat dinner . . . You can't swallow a thing . . ? Will you try to convince Electra that all these events, present and past, are a frame-up job? Useless. You figured that one correctly. No, don't push me to hurry and end this unholy mess. All in good time.

But still, how you'd love to eat your fucking cake and have it too! How you'd love to go on living and not shit yourself in front of your wife and grandson. You'll be in deep trouble with your grandson. He'll spit in your ugly puss. Won't even come to your funeral. He's a serious young man . . .

But enough of that . . . Why have you shown no interest in your daddy's subsequent fate, Citizen Gurov? . . . It's odd to think you ever had a father? A bad feeling. But you did. You had a father.

I just dreamed about my own father again. In the daytime. I lay back for a nap, while you sat and stared glassy-eyed at the oak coffin—which you lowered into the grave forty years ago, on nice fresh towels confiscated from kulak huts—and Ivan Abramych appeared to me. This was in our vegetable garden.

'Have you been taking care of the garden, you sonofabitch? Look around, numskull!' my father said.

I looked, and my heart stood still. In all the gardens, and on past the wattle fences, almost down to the Odinka, the potatoes were flowering, white and violet. The wind flattened the dark greenery of their leaves, carrying the potato smell of noonday hotly to my nostrils, and our garden alone was black. Not a shoot. Black were our seedbeds, like graves for the dill, the carrots, the cucumbers. Black our potato field.

'I'm not going to thrash you,' Father said. 'It's too late for that. But sit yourself down here and think how this happened, that you planted the seeds and the potatoes and nothing came up. I told you: Leave them, Vasya, give up, stop, we need to be reunited, don't destroy your soul. But now sit here alone, where every little hole has an empty seed in it, nothing even for the birds of the air to eat, nothing to please a stray mouse. You're a fool, that's all I can say.'

He walked off, melted away in the heat haze. I was left alone on the black earth, with the horror of eternal doom and incomprehension in my soul. And—such a strange thing! The July sun seemed cold to me. It flooded my face with a blizzard of freezing light, pierced my shirt with the icicles of its rays. But the earth, on the contrary, seemed hot and alive, like a stove. It drew me to it, or rather, into it, without coercing my will, without pain, without my desiring it—simply drew me in. And I warmed up, though I had frozen to the very marrow under the round ice of the sun; but I didn't feel the earth pressing around me, any more than I had formerly felt the edges of airy space on a windless day. At my eye-level lay yellow, ungerminated cucumber seeds, tiny dill and carrot grains, and five whopping sunflower seeds each the size of a horse's tooth. These I had planted for myself. I had meant to water them, grow them so big that the sunflower heads, when they ripened, would snap their stalks . . . I saw potatoes all wrinkled and withered, last year's horseradish sticking down unpulled, little roots of some kind . . . Over there was a little gold coin. My mother had dropped it, in her youth, and she never could find it . . . Over there, poultry bones, straw, twigs, humus, and the gift of our cattle—dung—richly mixed into the composition of the soil. But dead was the seed in it, dead the root.

And now, even before grasping the knowledge that had been revealed to me, I began to submit to it, in the ground as I would above ground, in the air. I breathed on the seeds and roots, and they grew warm and ready for life, and were not dead, as I had thought. If they did not warm, I took them in my mouth, overcoming, in my dream, the remnants of a foolish earthly squeamishness; I kissed them, gave them the liquid of spittle to drink, put them back in the spot they had occupied, and felt the life begin in each. And I was surprised: never, when I lived above ground, had I felt or noticed such a quantity of life on it! Life pressed around me from all sides. It was not a concept but a creature, infinitely many-sided, whose weakness, fragility, and dependency were equal to its omnipotence and the mystery of its origin. I was afraid to stir, lest I bump the dill sprout that was pecking its way through, or the greedy little green tongue of life poking out of the split cucumber beak. I didn't turn the potatoes over so that the white and lilac spikelets could more conveniently shoot up towards where I had been cold but they would be warm. They themselves found their way to the sun, and I understood that when I lived on earth I had not known the rules for treating life solicitously, fostering its growth, ripeness, and expectancy of the hour of harvest . . . I sensed that the vegetable tops above me were already greening, catching up with the neighbouring gardens and fields, and I heard a voice, perhaps my father's, perhaps one of my prisoners': 'In your pride, you held the opinion that there were dead souls on earth. There are no dead souls! But there is, in souls, an appearance of lacking life, and a readiness to live when they are sanctified by the breath of Light. This above all, Thou shalt not kill! Foster life! As for the rest, judgement will be passed without your help!'

That was my dream, Citizen Gurov . . . I dozed for five minutes or so, you say? Odd. I feel refreshed, and I know just exactly what I must do now. This is my last chance to see Father . . . I'm no longer at a dead end . . . Listen to me carefully. Get a grip on yourself, suck a nitroglycerine, and don't dump in your pants.

I give you your life . . . Yes, your life! Survive this piece of news, and later we'll go over the conditions attached to my gift. I, too, need to do some thinking about what's happened: an unforeseen and unexpected moment—not in a game, but in life . . . Don't be in a rush to learn the conditions of your survival. You'll find them acceptable. More than that: extremely advantageous.

I had a premonition of this moment, I think. But this combination is not at all what I expected . . . I like it. Thank you, Lord!

Well, how about it? Experiencing agreeable emotions? I can imagine . . . I too am 'blossoming psychically', to use your silly expression. We're both blossoming. Now, here's my chief condition: tomorrow, on my birthday, we'll have a drop of cheer and a bite to eat, we'll talk a bit, maybe sing a song or listen to some foreign gypsies, we'll have another drink, and then, Citizen Gurov, you will put a bullet through my head with this 'tough luck'.

Don't drop your teeth. I'm giving you something to chew on . . . I'm not about to delve into the details of my internal affairs. Consider that I've gone off the deep end, think what you like, make inferences and so on, but such a death, for me, is my last and only chance of seeing Ivan Abramych and all my people. As for you: live. The hour will come when you too will be judged. Your life is preserved, though without the return of your principal valuables and a large sum of money. Where it all went should be of no interest to you . . .

Oh, is that so! You believe that all this is just another subtle and perhaps final torture. You've resolved to meet it face to face, with no fear of blackmail, no fear of anything at all . . . You believe that when you consent to pump a bullet into my head you'll go wild with hope and joy, but the cartridge will prove to be a blank—if the gun fires at all, of course—and I'll burst into fiendish gloating laughter. After which I'll knock you off, since there've been a hundred times when you deserved a torment more terrible than death.

You simply haven't understood me very well, Citizen Gurov . . . On the contrary: after all that's happened, after the conversations, tortures, and mockery, you don't think I'm idiot enough to give you your life, never mind let you zap the man who deprived you of everything you had and who dug away the blockages of your despicable memory . . . That kind of logic is almost impossible to cope with . . . Then you don't consent to fire the shot that would save you? You don't believe me? But you know, if you won't take advantage of this last chance, and won't let me take advantage of it, I'll arrange a little reunion for you and your family. I will! Right over the coffin, over the skeleton in the tunic, over the skull in the service cap, over the faded roses, over the murder weapon! You won't croak beforehand, you can be sure of that. Do you consent? . . . Then

I'll try another tack. You'll consent. What choice will you have?

Poxov! Bring in the 'cabbage stump on wheels'. Someone, Citizen Gurov—do you know who?—was given that nickname by the inmates of a retirement home for Old Bolsheviks. Don't tax your brains. You won't guess. They gave that nickname to your own dearest daddy! He's being brought in now. Because of my unexpected change of plan regarding myself and you, I've decided to show you your daddy before your relatives arrive. But it's still not too late to prevent them from arriving. Do you accept my offer? No . . . Come ahead, Poxov!

This is all that's left of your father, Citizen Gurov. Do you recognize him? Hard to recognize. I agree. Do you recall any identifying mark? Take a look at your father's neck, or else you'll say I dug up this stump of a man on the Moscow suburban railway. Does he have a scar, pocked with little blue powder marks? There you are! Don't forget, he can see, though poorly. And he hears pretty well. But he can't talk. Don't stare at me with horror. This isn't my doing. I haven't sunk this low . . . Why he should lack speech when he's got his hearing I don't know. After all he's been through, apparently, he has no words. The doctors say that shock can do this kind of thing.

Conceptiev! Conceptiev! You have your son in front of you—Vasily! Can you hear me? Do you recognize him? Come closer, Citizen Gurov. Daddy might like to spit quietly in your puss. Come closer, or I'll wheel him over to you myself . . . Daddy doesn't want to spit. Even so, try to realize that this is Daddy. Daddy! Your father! You've been reunited. I still haven't told him anything about what you did to your mama. But I'll tell if you're stubborn. Naturally, I'll present your loved ones with evidence of your treachery. My briefcase—there it is. I'll present them with the evidence, unless, I repeat, you let me take advantage of my last chance to be reunited with the late Ivan Abramych . . . Do you hear, Conceptiev? The man you zapped in '29! You still haven't forgotten? You won't forget me, either, even after I die . . . Why do I want precisely you, Citizen Gurov, to put a bullet through my head? You're the last of the men I wanted to kill on this earth. I don't count your father as a man. I sympathize with him, to some degree.

He got more than I wished him. You're the last of the men with whom I wanted to square accounts in the most exquisitely cruel way possible, and I believe I have almost succeeded. But I want to see my father! Do you understand? I want to! I want to! If I scrag you I won't get another chance. Is that clear? You're a horse's ass! It's *not* that I don't wish to live and would rather die! I want to see my father! You don't believe me . . . I myself, in our terrible game, have schooled you to disbelief? True enough! Do you enjoy the prospect of a reunion and explanation with your dear ones, in front of Brutnikova's coffin and your stump of a father? You don't . . .

In that case, we've almost no time left. Decide. I've thought over the details of our bargain. The criminal dossier will be burned before your eyes. You'll light the match yourself. This is your version: a major burglary at the dacha. Because of it, you're on the verge of an infarct. Poxov and the doctor will stay on with you, for the time being. Tomorrow I'll show you my death certificate: a stroke. You'll shoot me in the heart, not the head. I want to feel the pain. I'll be buried at Sukhumi. I already have a spot in the cemetery. What else? The coffin will be reburied. All clues covered up. Your father will be taken to his retirement home, to finish watching the news programme 'Time'. He loves it very much. Your relatives will take care of you. By consenting, all you risk is that I'll have one more laugh at your expense. But I'm so deathly sick of that—you could feel my weariness, shame, and grief, if your soul were just a little bit more alive.

I need your answer . . . Quit babbling. As for digging down to what you call the mystical underlying cause of my desire, you never will. And with every second it becomes clearer to me that I'm acting rightly. My path is short, just a very little remains, but it's the right one at last, and God grant it may lead to where Ivan Abramych waits for me . . .

A real rat, aren't you! To answer your legitimate queston: I don't wish to engage in suicide, for I have realized that we are not the masters of either our own or others' lives. Is that clear to you? Yes, but not quite . . . Think. Decide . . . Who'll do away with me if you refuse? Don't worry, some trustworthy person will turn up. Remember: for you, as for me, there's just one way out. You will live only if you shoot me in the heart with this Walther, my good old 'tough luck' . . .

Look how Conceptiev's watching us! He's trying to form a concept of this strange Party convention we're having here. I gather he's recognized Brutnikova, your sexy stepmother. She's well preserved. Conceptiev, your dear little son pulped her . . . He's not surprised. He might have expected even worse from you. And of course he's right, even though he himself is a villain beyond compare!

When I found your old man, after he ended up in Siberia—thanks once again to chance—instead of on death row, he recognized me and implored me to do away with him. The tears flowed from his faded eyes, and I understood their mute plea. But I said to him, 'No, Conceptiev! If you've miraculously escaped my clutches, it means you're fated to live as you are. Live.

'Answer me this,' I went on. 'If you could live your life again, how would you live it? The same, or differently?'

He clenched his teeth and flickered his jaw muscles, giving me to understand that not only would he live his life in exactly the same way, he'd rip my guts out if I ever crossed his path. Right, Conceptiev? You see: he's nodding. I don't know how many times he cursed the chance that snatched him from death row. Now, evidently, he no longer curses it. You don't curse it, do you? No. He's happy to have even this kind of life. A life is a life! Right, bandit? Right. And don't you forget it, Citizen Gurov, when you're making your decision . . .

Conceptiev! You're not being sly, are you? You're not seething inwardly, and just pretending to be content in hopes of provoking me to deprive you of happiness, thus freeing you from the punishment of fate?

No. He's not being sly. He'll show us all yet. He'll conquer Africa. He'll get his hands on the Near East oil. He'll wipe Israel off the face of the earth. He'll shape up that old whore Europe. He'll go to work on China. He'll divide spheres of influence with the USA, isolating the New World from the Old and establishing the Iron Curtain between them forever, while South America, of her own accord, will fall into the mitts of the Communists. She's a fool. Oh, and after the world is partitioned, we'll quietly put the finisher on the US and Canada, when they've been demoralized by the steady surrender of all their positions in Europe, Asia, and neighbouring South America.

Do I understand your preliminary plans correctly, Conceptiev? He's nodding. I do. His eyes invite us to the TV screen, so that we may be convinced of his geopolitical correctness by seeing and hearing speeches from representatives of the Communist Parties of the capitalist countries . . . He's nodding. Now he'll start to cry. Look! He caught sight of Corvalán. Citizen Gurov, dry the tears on your daddy's cheeks. Disgusting? I'll do it, then. I'm sorry for him. More precisely, not for him and his wooden thoughts, but rather for the flickering little spark of life in him . . . See there! He's giving me to understand that I'm a rabid obscurantist, a subjective idealist, and a petty religious mystic . . . Fine. Let him watch 'Time'. Then he'll get fed. Is the old boy vital? He is. Eighty-four years old, and sometimes he yells in the night: he wants a broad. But he's not to get one, by my order. No broads!

When I came back from an urgent mission and learned that Conceptiev had been sent to Siberia, I burst out laughing hysterically. I didn't worry about it, however, for I realized that there was some system to the chance events by which my principal enemies kept slipping away from me, and I acquiesced in it, although I didn't know what it meant.

An hour later I was on the plane to Kolyma.

I arrived at the Communard Mine and walked into the camp. The camp was surrounded by a battalion of guards. There was an uprising under way. The Old Bolsheviks had mutinied, demanding a meeting with Stalin, or at least with Molotov or Kalinin. They just couldn't understand what was going on. If there'd been a counter-revolution, let them be told about it directly, for the great tragedy, as they saw it, was that the counter-revolution had taken refuge in their sacred Bolshevik slogans. They wanted the truth. They would consent to penal servitude and death, but they must know the truth. Bring Stalin to the camp! Send Molotov to the punishment block! Put Yezhov and Beria up against the wall! Long live Marxism-Leninism! Long live Communism, the radiant future of all mankind!

These slogans were written on the sheets in blood.

But if this wasn't a counter-revolution, the Old Bolsheviks declared, what was it? Sabotage! And the guards, if they thought of themselves as true Soviets building Communism, must assist in clarifying the truth. The Communard Mine, said the Old Bolsheviks, must be temporarily renamed the Fascist.

The mutiny was bad enough. But the week before, there had been a daring escape, by three thugs, two doctors, and Conceptiev. They must have been trying to make it to India, the camp commandant assured me. Why India? Because it was warm.

'Fool!' I said. 'Incompetent jerk!'

'I may not be much good at geography,' he replied, 'but I've become very knowledgeable about the psychology of thieves. They like to keep warm and not do a fucking thing. And in India, our dear Bolsheviks say, people do just that—nothing—instead of implementing the prophecies of the leaders of the World International.'

'Don't give me this, you animal,' I said. 'Why did Conceptiev leave! I'll roll you up in barbed wire, piss on you, and let you freeze! Why did he leave?'

The fool of a commandant explained that Conceptiev would never have left of his own accord . . . See? Your daddy's nodding.

They had led him away by force, like a calf. The thugs and the once intellectual doctors had all been so brutalized in the hell of Kolyma that they resolved on a cannibalistic route for their escape. They burgled the medical unit. They got hold of surgical instruments, chloroform, all sorts of crap, and took Conceptiev with them. The way pirates took live tortoises on their voyages . . .

Why Conceptiev? He was a very obtuse and fanatical zek, and slightly unbalanced from our filming and all the traumas of the investigation. He grassed, openly and secretly, on those who, in his opinion, doubted the omnipotence and truth of the doctrine; on those who tried to establish a causal connection between our principles and the preliminary investigation, the unbridled degeneration of the secret police, and the emasculation of all that was human in the witnesses in a case; on those who cracked wide open the pseudohumanistic demagoguery of the press, radio, and literature. Conceptiev grassed, and people were chucked out of the punishment shack naked, to shrivel at forty below.

So they took him with them. The intellectual doctors thought they'd kill two birds with one stone: provide themselves with victuals, and instil in Conceptiev a disgust for the doctrine, teaching him a good lesson. He's shaking his head . . . They did not instil disgust, he says. And how do you feel about Eurocommunism, Conceptiev? He's spitting!

At the time, I was convinced that all the escapees would either perish or get caught. In those days, in those parts, no one pulled off an escape. It turned out otherwise. If your daddy could wag the old tongue, he'd tell what it was like . . . He's nodding . . . Lenin was a fool when he opined, out of a lack of culture, that Beethoven's music was not human. Music has to be human, unless you mean it comes from God, and of course Lenin couldn't have meant that. But tortures that aren't human do exist. And they exist in so far as the Lord hasn't one iota of responsibility for them, *vis-à-vis* either Himself or man. They are wrought by the mind and hand of man himself. The blame for them is man's. And Conceptiev experienced them to the full. We ought to wheel him on stage right now, in his cart, at the Palace of Congresses in the Kremlin. We ought to applaud him—yes, him—as an example of fidelity to the Idea, as its martyr and the key to its future successes on all fronts in the building of Communism. And announce therewith that there has long been nothing human about Comrade Conceptiev and he is therefore our number two saint . . .

The escapees had been brutalized to the bitter limit, and I think when their grub ran out they amputated Conceptiev's left . . . no, he's shaking his head . . . his right arm. Amputated it under anaesthesia. They continued to walk, detouring around the smoke of any hunters, working their way through the deepest forests so as not to be discovered, even from the air. I personally directed the search. It led nowhere. One month went by. Another. How long did it take you to reach the coast, Conceptiev? Two months? He's nodding. For a long time they were lost, wandering around, as I understand it . . . His other arm was removed. Both sleeves, I suppose, went for spare mittens? Yes. He's filling you in on the details, Citizen Gurov. But if you hope that your son is suffering, Conceptiev, you're wasting your time. He's the wrong man. You raised him the wrong way. Stuffed him with the wrong ideas . . .

At first he walked, like the rest of them. After one leg had been amputated they carried him on a sort of stretcher, fitted to skis. Then he became as you see him now.

When did you lose your speech? Were you still in the taiga? He's nodding. And notice: neither the monstrously unsanitary conditions, nor his insane, ceaseless pains, nor his hunger (the escapees had a small supply of flour and cod-liver oil to support life in their tortoise), nor the cold, nor the torment of his soul . . . Aha! Perhaps it was precisely his lack of a soul, or its almost complete necrosis, that helped your daddy survive! Yes. He's nodding, he's smiling: not even a neutron bomb could get him!

Bravo! I don't know whether he watched as the stews made with his own limbs gurgled in the kettle over the campfire. I don't know whether he thought about death. The border guards found him on the shore. They recognized him from the photo I had circulated. They rescued him and dispatched him to a camp for Kolyma prisoners who had mutilated themselves. There he waited, until his great friend Stalin died and he was rehabilitated.

The thugs, who escaped in a stolen motorboat, died in a skirmish with a border-guard cutter. The doctors were picked up just in time by an American destroyer. I don't imagine they told the public overseas about their cannibalism.

Is your decision ripening within you, Citizen Gurov? Think . . .

Suddenly, in May of '41, I got a call informing me that Conceptiev had been found. Balls of fire! I flew back out there, to Kolyma.

I reached the hospital camp.

'Would you care to take in a show, see our big attraction, as we call it?' asked the chief physician, who had a normal human face. 'You'll spot your Conceptiev there, too.'

Off we went. The hospital compounds, one for men and one for women, were divided by a fence. It was topped with barbed wire and sharp spikes. On either side of the fence were barracks, operating rooms, kitchens, walks, morgues. A women's morgue and a men's morgue. We were standing in the women's compound, at the guardhouse. From there we had a good view of the whole fence.

'Send the men out to exercise!' the chief physician ordered, adding, 'Watch, Comrade Colonel.'

And presently Comrade Colonel saw, creeping out through little holes in the fence—through one hole, three, ten, twenty—erect male members of various sizes. The physician and the guards started to laugh.

And now, from the open barracks, here came the women, poor things, racing towards the erect members—squealing, whooping, laughing, hastily hiking up their skirts and wretched slips. They thronged around the fence, some banging with their backsides, some with their fronts.

I stood dumbfounded. This 'provincial attraction', as the physician and guards called it, was unbearable.

After an instant I collected myself, but something restrained me from giving the order to halt this outrage. I turned away from the women, trying not to hear their voices or laughter or cries, and looked at the lewd faces of the guards. Fixing each with my gaze, I asked the men where they were from. Smolensk. Vyatka. The Urals. Peasants? Yes . . . Why had they left the land?

They had been summoned to their District Committees, it seemed, and told there was a shortage of guards. As the most industrious and politically aware kolkhoz workers, they must therefore shoulder their rifles and study to be prison guards.

'Well, but what you're watching, is it interesting?' I asked.

The chief physician answered for them all: 'It's interesting from the point of view of how low they can sink, these traitors, thieves, spies, and enemies of the people in general.'

'Let's go to the men's compound,' I said. 'Call a crew of carpenters. Take down the fence. Let them copulate like human beings. I'll report you to Beria! I'll have you all shot!'

We arrived in the men's compound. Remember that moment, Conceptiev? Yes. Unlike you, Citizen Gurov, he remembers all.

Two zeks were holding him in their arms, pressing him to

the fence. I didn't realize at first that this legless, armless stump with the absolutely naked skull was your daddy. The longest prick of all belonged to him.

When the two kind zeks tore the bellowing cabbage stump away from the fence and lowered him into his trousers, I caught on. This was Conceptiev!

My God, I thought. Conceptiev! He *has* been eaten! But he's alive! *Alive!* And not only alive—still pushing! Now, that's breeding! That's strength!

There was something revoltingly captivating about your daddy, Citizen Gurov. Surely your heart can't keep silent now? Even mine was softened. But when it dawned on me that he had lost his speech, from the shock, I understood he'd had enough. Recognizing me, his eyes implored: 'Kill me, Hand, kill me!'

But we've already talked about that. Live, Conceptiev. You have met your son. I won't disturb your reunion just now. Have a few minutes alone with him. Since I too—if I'm lucky, if I'm forgiven—am to have a reunion and render an accounting to Ivan Abramych, I'll go and give a few orders with regard to covering up all the clues. So that by the time your relatives arrive, Citizen Gurov, everything will be stowed away, taken out, neatened up, put in apple-pie order. All you'll have to do is pose as a rich man with a heart attack who has been burgled, and reassure the folks that you still have enough dough and antiques to last their lifetime.

If you say no, then after I exhibit you to your wife and grandson in the presence of your father and adoptive momma, I'll bump you off and burn the house down. I won't personally bump you off. I can't—this is my last chance . . . By the way, it seems that Trofim and Trilby are dying to come to see you. They've scented a change of fortune. They've scented that I'm the one who stinks of carrion now, not you. Poxov! Let the poor creatures in . . . Look at this, will you! Sniffing your daddy all over in surprise. Snuggle up, now. Heave a few sobs; you have reason to. And think. Think. In exactly ten minutes I'll come for your answer . . .

Listen closely, Poxov. He'll consent. I know it, I believe it—he will. He can't help consenting, at that price. But after he consents, and after I'm gone . . . who knows where to, most likely blue blazes, because even if God forgives me, my father may balk—he could be mulish sometimes, to the point of causing harm, and then he'd curse his own mulishness. But Mother would forgive him, and next thing I knew they'd be sitting out front cracking sunflower seeds, and Mother would be telling Father, 'You may be a brain, Vanya, but all the same you're a fool.' Father would laugh and say, 'So I am. A shithead. Who do I get it from?' So I don't know if he'll be mulish or not, but when I'm gone, you pay Gurov back for me. In full. It's unthinkable for that pigfucking bastard to get out of this unscathed. Dispatch my body to the proper quarter immediately, and have the relatives of these two characters flown in. Let them all sit there, let them stand and stare at each other. Let Brutnikova's skull grin at them, and Conceptiev bellow at his son. If Gurov survives that little visit—plug him full of lead. Take this sin upon your soul, and I'll be up there chortling at the artful way I shitted on the bastard in our game. Let Fedya find out that his mother's been a purulent grass for lo these many years. Let him find out everything about his grandfather and great-grandfather. He should. He should know all the ulcerous lesions of all the lupus in the world, for he is destined to cure it . . . So . . . What else? My mind's a jumble. My soul is much cleaner and simpler . . . Burn the tapes. I myself will throw the document case in the fire . . . All of you are provided for, and free to leave. Go about your business, heeding only the dictates of conscience and highest duty. You've learned something from my life. Don't anybody get drunk and blab about the mind-boggling, romantic operation you happened to take part in. You'd all be up the creek.

Yes! Before I forget: go to Odinka together, all of you, on the fortieth day after my death. Sit on that giant log, hoist a glass in memory of my soul, have a snack, look around you at the land. Look around, then pour yourselves another: 'Glory be to God!' And say a prayer, of course . . . Things haven't been easy for me. What lies ahead is still harder. But even so, it's the way. The right way . . . I haven't left a will. No point attracting attention to anyone. There may be something I've overlooked, something I've forgotten; I wouldn't be surprised. You'll think of it, though. No case has been initiated against Gurov at headquarters . . . So far as they're concerned, I'm on vacation. For a colonel like me, a stroke is an easy death, and honourable . . . Well, back to Gurov . . .

What, can't you see your father wants to go to the toilet? Pick him up—he's light—and carry him . . . Like this. Look after him . . . Here, I'll help . . .

Don't put him too near the TV: his eyes will get inflamed. Turn it on. There's about to be a programme on the battles between labour and capital in America. But I'm such an idiot—what am I thinking of, at a moment like this? Conceptiev, why have you fixed me with your little rat eyes? What are you so glad about? Why are you laughing? Do you think you've finally got me cornered? You're nodding . . .

Your decision, Citizen Gurov . . .

You've thought it all over, but, for a number of reasons, you don't consent . . . This I didn't expect. I really didn't . . . In reaching your decision, did you base it on your own interests, or did you manage to grab a word with your father in the toilet? Your own interests. I see . . . Is this your final answer, or shall we bargain?

Guarantees? I can't give you any. I have a chance, and you have a chance . . . take the risk. You've taken risks before . . . Do you like the idea of a reunion over the coffin? No . . . But neither do you want to kill me . . . You're pleading on bended knee that I, as a religious man, should allow a draw? Do I understand you correctly . . ? But that's ridiculous. Ridiculous! It won't work. Just look at your daddy! This time he's laughing at you, too. He's happy that we're *both* cornered! Happy, Conceptiev? Yes, and no bones about it. Do you realize he'll die of happiness if you and I gobble each other up right before his eyes? Not 'possibly'. Certainly! You're a fool, and he couldn't care less who gobbles whom first!

Once again, I'm offering you the best possible choice. For there can be no draw in our game—though neither can we grasp what it means to win or lose . . .

I simply believe in my chance, and in the image of my salvation. And you believe in yours, if I understand you correctly. You want to live; my time has come to die. As for your daddy, he's got it figured, the old snake: under no circumstances can I go on living, but in that case I'll take you with me, and he'll end his days in the Old Bolsheviks' home. Do you realize he hates you even more than he hates me? You suspected as much . . . Poxov! We've diddled around long enough. Phone the duty officer. Have him put the whole family on the plane. Tomorrow at ten hundred hours, at the moment when the holiday parade starts, have everyone here, right at this table! Seat Conceptiev in an armchair at the head of the table. That is all! Carry out the order! Just a minute.

Citizen Gurov is anxious to know what I'm going to do after he's exposed . . . For one thing, we'll render first aid to Madame Electra, if need be. For another, we'll ship everyone back to Moscow. And what happens next I frankly don't care. You can all sizzle in hell!

Is that everything, Citizen Gurov? What now? You want to speak to your wife and ask her to get plane tickets for the 9th of November? So you do consent, you garbage! What 'further condition'? Leave your father here, to live in your house? Ho! Hear that, Poxov? But why? You can't mean you've come to love him? Look at him: he hates you so badly he's turned blue! All right. If that's what you want, I agree. Live, scoundrels! What's that, Conceptiev? You want to go back to your brainless buddies? No, you've kicked around government institutions long enough. Live under your son's roof. Maybe your great-grandson will set your mind straight, if you've still got one.

But again, what am I thinking of? What am I thinking of? How strange! At the end of life you're as flustered as a kid. You don't know what to take up, you can't focus on anything, it's as if you had all the time in the world . . . Are you pleased with the turn of events, Citizen Gurov? Poxov will teach you how to use the pistol . . . Squeeze. Bang. *Finis* . . . I feel like clawing your face with my hand one more time. You've begun smoothing out, filling up again with pale, dull, dignified oedema . . . What should I be doing? There's nothing I really have to do . . . I'll just live till tomorrow. Just live. I'm going to bed. But you stay here, join in the holiday celebration on TV . . .

Citizen Gurov, I think you're beginning to grow insolent. You're blackmailing me. What's this 'one indispensable condition'? Ah, you can't help wondering about the cursed chance that betrayed you into my clutches. I understand. With pleasure . . .

It was Pasha, many years later, who happened to put me on your trail, Citizen Gurov. He didn't have to, but he made a trip to Moscow especially for the purpose. We went to the amusement park; I lived not far from there, and we would not be overheard. We sat nursing a beer, and he said, 'I'm sorry, Hand, but I think I was wrong. That scumbag you wanted to erase, back before the war? He's alive.'

'No,' I answered. 'I got them all.'

'One's alive, I tell you. I recognized him, at a conference. I couldn't be wrong. It wasn't him that drowned back then, in the truck with the two accordions.'

'But how could you recognize him?' I asked. 'It's been so many years. What's his name?'

'The name is Gurov,' Pasha said, 'but he's the one you were after. It wasn't his face I remembered—I'm not good at faces—it was the way he handled the carafe when he was standing on the rostrum. The first time I ever saw him, he was addressing an assembly at the institute. He was reading a repudiation of his father, an enemy of the people, and thanking a high-minded slut and stoolie, a woman named Brutnikova, for adopting him on social principles. I couldn't be wrong. A speaker's handling of the carafe—for me—works even better than fingerprinting.'

While I nursed my beer and curbed the quiver of my cruel instinct for the hunt, Pasha argued, in his amusing way, that no two men on earth take the same approach to a carafe of water when they are speaking on the rostrum. If he once spotted this kind of strictly individual mannerism in a speaker, that would be enough for Pasha to recognize him, even if the man forgot his head somewhere and gave his speech without it, which happened repeatedly at the Party conferences, meetings, and

Central Committee plenums where Pasha sat keeling over with boredom. For lack of anything to do at his colossal villa—even more colossal than yours—he had pecked out a whole frigging monograph on the subject. He told me many curious tales, and I ended up believing him.

You're pale, Citizen Gurov. You shouldn't have much reason to turn pale today . . .

Pasha came to Moscow again recently. We met, had dinner, strolled around Red Square, and he said, 'Time's up, Hand! I've farted away my last fear! I'm retiring. Nothing scares me now. The kids are set. They're all abroad. My grandsons will go into diplomacy too. War doesn't scare me, or even a coup. Either way, they'll be better off abroad. Some day we'll be sorry we didn't dig in like the squintface Chinks. Good and sorry! And what's going on here at home? It's awful, Hand, awful! Personally, my whole region has drunk itself under the table. Two doctors, psychiatrists, undertook to gather statistics. How much did I drink, etcetera, etcetera. I got them to sign a statement that they wouldn't divulge the findings. So one day they bring in their statistics. Motherfucking numbers—they made my eyes pop! But the problem isn't just that people drink, Hand. Russia's been drinking for a thousand years. Problem is, they drink raw shit, and it degenerates the brain cells. The bastards get demented, at home and at work. Panther piss they guzzle—jug wines, fusel-oil, coffin varnish. And the worst of it is, you can't stick this on the Yids or the CIA. That's the trouble with the anti-alcohol propaganda. I should order the industry to produce a purified poison, so that the slaves in my region at least don't get demented. But here again, it's a vicious circle! I'd have to expand capacity, but Kosygin won't fork out. You're on your own, he says. Improve the quality of our poison, at the expense of diminishing quantity? Impossible! There'd be a sharp jump in inflation.

'But that's not the half of it. We've got nothing to eat! That's the real issue! No meat. Fish salty and rotten. The canned fish gives you gastritis. Thousands of workers reporting sick. But don't bother phoning the Central Committee about grub. All you get is: It was worse during the war, and we won anyway. They let you know you're not to pester them about it.

'And another bad break: an unannounced field investigation

by that fucking stupid *Literary Gazette*. Their sociologists decided to find out how I was doing on divorces. Got up a questonnaire, the picky parasites. And here they are, back with the results already: seventy-five per cent of divorces are due to the total or partial impotence of the men. They cross-examined the men. Again, seventy-five per cent can't get it up because of alcoholism and a regular dietary deficiency of meat, fish, and other haematogens. The local KGB chief summed it up: loose talk, pessimism, grumbling that reached the point of outright attacks. All the makings of revolt. Let some Stenka Pugachev show up and we wouldn't escape without a strike, at the minimum.

'I took measures. I asked the District Commander to begin manoeuvres. I brought the dissident Bulkov to trial, on charges of keeping a den. I had the papers print satirical articles on the Yids in haberdashery and Regional Supply, I forbade the Georgians and Armenians to peddle their vegetables, fruit, and flowers at the market, I arranged for shows by our celebrated figure skaters, I called for musical help from Zykina, Nikulin, Orero, and the Pesnyary, I gagged my liberal Yids with comic routines by Raikin and songs by Kobzon—and defused the situation a little. Whew! Don't tell me I'm not going to make it to retirement, I thought. Don't tell me the guys up top can't shut down this quasi-spy ring sociology! Can't they see that 'relaxation', this damned détente, may be handy for us in foreign policy, but for me, here at home, it's a slow knife in the back?

'And now another unlucky break. We can't foresee everything, Hand. That's weakness numero uno for us Bolsheviks and Stalinists. My housemaid, one Taska Peksheva, gutter-slut, former executioner, lieutenant, a person of experience, a killer—she started home from the Regional Committee commissary *on foot*. On foot, the fat whore! Something was wrong with the car. I kicked the chauffeur out of the Party after this incident.

'So she started out on foot, the toad, with a full satchel and a string shopping bag. She's got this weakness, see, for string shopping bags. She's walking along and she doesn't notice these two sturgeon tails peeking out of the damned shopping bag. Three drunks come up—not Yids, as luck would have it, and not involved in samizdat. A philologist, a historian, and a physicist. Buddies. They come up to Taska and ask what's that fish and where'd she get it. Who has it for sale, they'd like to know. Taska kept her head; she told some story and gave them the wind. They caught up with her again, and the physicist grabs her by the lapels.

'"Kolya!" he howls. "I swear by Kurchatov, that's a sturgeon!"

'Taska pissed in her pants she was so scared. In plain sight of everyone, the three buddies upended my satchel and shopping bag. That was it: catastrophe. Damned liberals, they dumped it all out on the asphalt—sturgeon, sausage, jars of caviar, pineapples, steak, special frankfurters, export-grade butter, a *filet* of pork, frozen strawberries, the chewing gum for my wife. Half the town came running to gawk at Party eatables. You don't need me to tell you what was said there, do you, Hand—the exclamations you'd have heard, the innuendoes and analogies. They leaned on Taska, and she cracked, told where she got the groceries from. But that's not the half of it—we just think no one knows about us. They do. They yell bloody murder behind our backs. But the thing was, when the Kay-Gee-Beesties wrested her away from the mob, Taska went ape.

'"I shot you before and I'll shoot you again," she bawled. "With my own two hands, you bastards! I'll draw a bead on all of you! Glory to Stalin!"

'The town was in an uproar. Now I played my trumps. I rushed commodities to the shops from army supplies, I herded strategic hogs to the meat-packing plant, I borrowed evaporated milk from my neighbour in the next region, I ordered beer to be peddled on the streets, and I commanded local TV to run that spy movie *Seventeen Instants*. Whew! The pressure had let up.

'And immediately I played my ace. I announced over the radio that we'd identified a case of plague. Plague! I personally wrote the scenario. After each of the seventeen goddamn *Instants*, the announcer—I personally was screwing her—reported on the progress of anti-plague operations. The Kay-Gee-Beesties had to hustle with the staging. But as it was, they didn't need to do a fucking thing. That's one battle I won from the people. I won! I kicked a couple of kolkhoz chairmen out of the Party and took some people to court for failing to supply the population with essential commodities. The store counters were emptied again, but now President Podgorny got fired, a draft of the new constitution was published, and life returned to normal . . .

Good morning, Vasily Vasilievich. Wake your daddy up. Let him take a leak. Get him dressed. The servants are off today . . . It's nice you can cope with everything yourself. I'd have done the same. But my father, I think, would have died several deaths sooner than live one day in Conceptiev's life . . . It's not a question of his disability, as you are pleased to call it . . . Go and drag him in here. The parade's about to begin. We'll have a light breakfast now and sit down to dinner about three o'clock . . . The plane with my pickled cabbage has been held up by the weather, but other than that, we're all set. Something's in the works . . . Yes, that's a hint, but only at suckling pig with buckwheat kasha. You had already begun to tremble, I see. Relax, and don't spoil my mood. I'm the birthday boy. Sixty years! And I'm the one who should be trembling, not you. Keep this up and you'll miss at two paces . . . Go on. Hear that? He's already rocking the bed.

. . . Put him over here. I'll turn on the TV. Good morning, Conceptiev! How did you sleep? . . . What did you dream . . ?

Vasily Vasilievich, shovel a nice tomato salad into your daddy. Some sturgeon, an omelette. To the sixtieth anniversary of your revolution, Conceptiev! I congratulate you on your career!

Yes. I see you're impatient, Vasily Vasilievich. You're urging time onward, as the wind urges onward the water of the rivers, but that doesn't cause them to stop flowing any sooner. I'm urging time backwards, and there isn't getting to be any more of it. We don't have to be patient much longer . . . Come to think of it, I'm in no hurry to speak my last words . . . Aha, my pickled cabbage has arrived. They'll set the table now. We'll indulge in something of a feast today, indeed we will . . . My treat.

But just now I want to go for a swim. You come too. Your daddy's already out there . . .

Look at him, sticking up chest-deep in the water! Already sunburned. He's snorting, rejoicing in the element. I'll rejoice in it too. And it won't cast me out. Or him, or you, or anyone—the sea will receive us all, as it always has. That's remarkable. The elements are the most democratic phenomena on our native earth . . . A warm element. Quite warm . . . I'm scared to plunge in for the last time. Like the first time . . . Come on! You're afraid of a cramp? Then here I go!

Nice! The absolute lack of democracy in the Soviet regime, in my view, negates the claim that it's an 'elemental mass movement'. There's nothing elemental or natural about it. A sea of unnecessary Soviets—that's our regime . . . Toss me a towel! It's sickening that I must first abandon forever this element, and only then the leaden sea of Soviets, the garbage heap of imposed ideas. Sickening. Look! Your daddy's lying on the water. He floats like a buoy. We wouldn't want him to go under . . . And he could be carried off to Turkey by the wind. The Turks would gape in wonder: what on earth is this? Take your daddy on to the shore of his beloved sea. Time for dinner . . . Goodbye, free element. Goodbye. Thank you . . .

Poxov! Listen to me closely. Since I doubt you'll succeed in finding the spot where our house stood, bury me under the giant log. You can't put a proper grave there in any case. You can't set up a cross, either. So bury me under the log, why don't you . . . Your car's like the wind. You'll be putting me in the boot? Just lay me on my side, and wedge a tyre against me. Be careful. No accidents. God forbid! The fuzz. Inspection. A corpse in the boot: Colonel Vasily Vasilievich Bashov. Lights out for you and your boys. Be careful.

As for this joker, erase him with no excess commotion, and not in his father's sight. I don't want to give daddy the pleasure. But before Gurov dies, let him realize that this is the end. Let him stand for a minute or two helpless and pathetic, between light and darkness, between darkness and light, a stranger to both. Afterwards confide all to Father Alexander. He'll think what to say, on whose behalf, before God . . . Once again, I thank you for humbly acceding to my will.

Sometimes my soul is visited by a strange emotion, one that Frol Vlasych Goosev talked about. Roughly translated into thought, it goes something like this: If man were not, on occasion, so criminally, cravenly, comically, and poignantly weak, he would seem *less* perfect. A spiritual forgiveness of another's weakness, and a profound feeling (equivalent to all-understanding) that weakness is common to everyone: these are signs of kinship with, and participation in, the *More* Perfect, and they also enable a man who has forgiven to hope for forgiveness.

Oh—Frol Vlasych! You know what, Poxov? His address is in my briefcase. Forgive me this one last weakness. Take a trip to the stinking city of Tula, where they make guns and gingerbread for our new colonies in Europe and Africa. Find Frol Vlasych. I know he's alive, rejoicing as always, and thriving. Find him and say . . . but I don't know what to say to Frol Vlasych . . . I don't know, and this—don't go thinking it's anything else, Poxov—this makes me rather scared . . . I feel as if I do know what to say, clearly I have the knowledge in me, but I can't say it, I can't think how. Yes, yes! Not I don't know—I can't!

But look and see how he's getting along . . . Pull a line on him if you have to, but keep in mind: he's a plain man, so plain that if he begins to suspect anything unnatural in your help or concern, nothing you can do will make him budge an inch.

Be the subtle serpent: get a fix on whether or not he has any manuscripts stashed away. I didn't keep him under surveillance, I give you my word, but I have an idea he must have been writing novels, essays, whatever, just singing, without thought for the genre of his song . . . Under no circumstances should you seize the manuscripts, if they exist. But you mustn't let them perish or be forgotten . . .

Astonishing. A man happier than Frol Vlasych would be hard to find, I think. And no force on earth is capable of taking away this man's freedom . . .

Time to sit down at the table. I'm on a cast-iron schedule . . . Just in case, I've left only the one cartridge in my 'tough luck'.

One's enough. So have no anxiety on that score—Gurov won't play up.

Pour us a drink, Vasily Vasilievich. Offer one to your father. The man's smacking his lips . . . The parade will be over soon. Parades, parades, parades, the whole sixty years. Depressing. Deadly depressing! And a lousy lie. Incompetent leaders at the top . . . How do you like them, Conceptiev? You're disgruntled? They're not tough enough, in your opinion? You'd tighten the screws, that's for sure. You feel they've let the people get out of hand? In China, and under Stalin, there was more order? Don't bother to nod. I know what you're thinking. You're opposed to any relaxation, on principle. But your son here doesn't take such an extremist attitude. Not to mention your great-grandson . . . What to do? Think, drink, and eat . . . Here, I've fished out some mushrooms for you. Take a drink of vodka. Your health! Have a mushroom . . . A nice boletus. Such a joy and delight! You, too, Vasily Vasilievich—have a drink!

I slept today for the last time, slept sweetly, there's no other word for it, and in my sleep there was neither space nor time, I saw nothing. In this ineffable dream state there was just a single thought, which lasted till the instant I awoke, although I heard no voice or in any case don't remember any, my eyes read no letters, words, sentences, or formulas, and I don't know how I perceived the thought.

You're right, Vasily Vasilievich, that can't happen. Your daddy's nodding. He agrees; Stalin did a paper on the impossibility of a thought's existing without words. In all honesty, I don't know how I grasped the thought of my dream. Possibly it was revealed through some sort of sign, but afterwards, still asleep, I withdrew so far from it that I couldn't make out the sign either, although the thought filled the space of my dream and remained distinctly clear, despite being ineffable. This was the thought:

'Wait not, Man, for strangers from outer space. Wait not, and do

not try to pick up their cries. You will hear none, because, in order to create life on His chosen Earth, the Creator expended so much vital energy taken from galaxies near and far that there was none left for the other stars, visible or invisible. That is why we pine for different sectors of the sky; that is why our anciently determined bond with the native constellations we have left behind still directs the course of our fates, the glimmerings of Chance, the flowering and fruition of our talents, and the throb of our propensities.

'When you, Man, yearn for strange visitors from space, you are yearning for yourself. And sometimes you are terrified at how far you have withdrawn from yourself.

'You yourself are a star, you yourself are a stranger. Do not forget yourself, do not withdraw, do not wander in apathetic loneliness. Thank Him Who chose our heavenly field, who populated it with trees, and not less than a quarter or even half of a star went into each tree; Who populated it with creatures, and if no less than a sixth of the sky went into the animals, how much of beauty's starry strength must He have expended to create you, giving you, in addition to everything else, an inviolable supply of energy for your higher needs, but not for tempting yourself with nonexistence . . .

'The apple fell . . . The planet turned . . . The star burned up . . . The little boy tore the bird's head off . . . The comet flew past . . . Executions all over the world . . . Black dwarfs . . . Dead souls . . . Particles . . . Transience . . . Star speaks with star . . . Man betrays . . . The supernova blazes up . . . We are in love . . . The Spirit bent over sleeping Matter as she tossed in her dreams . . . In you, Man, the complementarity principle merged with the uncertainty principle, and the theory of relativity died . . . The weak reaction, bursting into tears, pitied the strong reaction . . . God's gift of Freedom has not been harvested from the general field, and we have been told: Live!

'You are Ploughmen, Water Bearers, Virgins, Scorpions, double-starred Twins, Lions, Crabs, Pegasuses, Helmsmen, Scales, Swans, you are living forget-me-nots on the black velvet of the night. Live! At your hour, more swiftly than the light that speeds after you, you shall return whence you came. But those who have grown to love Earth more than themselves shall remain in the ground of her being!'

Suddenly I woke up. The dream and its thought did not immediately leave me. The window was thick with stars. The black, pink, and white pearls swelled in the starlight. They were lying on the bedside table, close to my eyes. Remember those pearls, Conceptiev? His jaw dropped.

No, nothing is lost in this world, gentlemen!

The pearls sucked the light of the sky into themselves, as flowers suck the light of the sun; it revived their inner composition, which had been famished for light even while under the thickness of the waters, and this unslaked and unslakable thirst for light was what imparted to the infinite mystery of their attraction the torment of perfect beauty.

And I felt the remnants of my soul opening to the live seed of the unknown light. I felt the greed—black, pink, and white—with which my soul sucked in the light's sweet waves and salty particles.

And when sleep had almost completely left me, my soul began to whimper, miserably and resentfully, like an infant removed from the breast. I winced and eased myself up a little, as if trying, with my shoulders, to hold open the two valves of the shell of my life, which were closing on me from above and below. But I did not have the strength to withstand their incredible weight, and I fell asleep again.

Please do have something to eat, have a drink . . . Are you glad to be alive, Conceptiev? Yes. And you, Citizen Gurov? Yes and no. Just now you're like a little boy sitting over the mill pond, logey from the springtime sun, waiting for the pressure of the water to wash away the dike of stones, wood chips, last year's sod and mud. All will be washed away, carried to the drifting ice floes, into which, in a shrinking, packed-down mass, are frozen your hours, days, and years, your mother and father, Collectiva Brutnikova, Dr. Vigelsky, stacks of denunciations, the shit of falsehood, urine of greed, snakes of treachery, and straw dust of pleasures, the little sparrows of your infancy are frozen into the ice, never to fly away. Never . . .

And I fell asleep again, but in my dream I was roused from my sleep by a stewardess on the underground.

'Altitude: ten thousand metres. Outside air temperature: seventy-three degrees below zero,' she said, passing drinks to the passengers in the carriage. Wine glowed scarlet in the crystal goblets. Pieces of ice floated in it, black, pink, and white.

The faces of the passengers, who sat opposite each other on the soft seats as one does in the underground, were hidden by newspapers. My astonishing, suddenly discovered farsightedness enabled me to read the text of the articles and make out the photos of political leaders. Actually, the articles had no text. They all consisted of one single sentence, repeated a thousand times and set in various typefaces. It was the headline of the editorial, the editorial opened with it and then used it as the transition to local news, commentaries, columns of news items, a satirical piece, letters from workers, reports from abroad, sports news, special features, and finally, an event which for some reason was simply called by its name—an event—but which ended with the same old sentence: WE ARE LIVING IN THE FRAMEWORK OF THE FIRST PHASE OF THE COMMUNIST STAGE OF DEVELOPMENT! L.I. BREZHNEV.

The passengers, my neighbours and the people sitting opposite, greedily swallowed every sentence. First they sucked at the letters, then they spat the full stops and commas on the floor. They held the exclamation mark and capital letter W *in their cheeks for a long time, like gumdrops. The letters* L I B R E Z H N E V *they chewed assiduously but without pleasure, using toothpicks, matches, their fingernails, and the glazed corners of their Party cards to pick out the bits that got stuck in their teeth.*

The weight of boredom took my breath away and stopped up my ears. Outside the windows was an eerie, absolute darkness. The carriage now swayed, now vibrated, now dropped into air pockets, and I didn't doubt in the slightest that we were flying somewhere, because my doubts were forestalled by the stewardess, as a charming symbol of flight, with her short skirt stretched tight over her firm buttocks, and tiny professional sparks of risk glinting in her eyes. We flew in absolute darkness, no landing was anticipated, and hopelessness oozed through the pores of my body into my soul, dripped into my heart, liver, kidneys, and bladder, and, having made sure that my balls were already chock-full of it, mounted again to my throat . . . Heartache and gloom . . . Gloom and boredom . . . Chasms above, below, and on either side . . .

'Take off your shackles and handcuffs! Unbuckle your seatbelts!' the stewardess said. 'The plane is landing at Dzerzhinsky Station.'

I think I yelled in my sleep, from the pure childish horror of the descent. You must have heard that cry, Vasily Vasilievich . . . You not only heard it, you also covered me with the blanket I'd thrown off? I don't believe you and never will. You're sucking up to me. What do you want to do, drag some final concession out of me?

Anyway. I yelled from horror in my sleep, said goodbye to life, and waited, although the instant before landing I tried to counteract the fatal blow by jerking my body upwards, inwardly elevating myself, with absolute confidence that this way I'd be able to create a certain salvific space between the flesh of the bizarre plane—which the earth's implacable pull had doomed to disintegration and death—and myself, who fearfully craved a continuation of life and trembled in the clear knowledge of what was approaching, pulling, approaching, what would happen in ten seconds, amid shock, din, and forever-blinding flame, in nine seconds, eight . . . five . . . three, two, one . . .

At that second I was evidently unconscious, but, when I came to, there was veined grey stone, the marble of the Dzerzhinsky underground station, sliding past the train windows. I sensed nothing absurd in an underground flight.

The first off the train was you, Conceptiev. After you, your whole detachment. Vlachkov, Latsis, Gurevich, Akhmetov, and the other thugs whom I personally had killed with this hand of mine. As they got off the train they tossed their newspapers to the floor, having read them cover to cover. Getting off last, I happened to look through the glass into the next carriage, which I hadn't noticed before, and there I saw my father. I was shocked by his loneliness. He sat drowsily nodding, like a weary man returning from a hard day's work.

I was about to jump back from the doors, which were slowly, ever so slowly closing, like the corrugated doors closing over the abyss of a crematorium after a coffin has fallen in. But at the next moment, with a cruel and malicious shove with her sharp little fists, the stewardess pushed me out to the platform of the accursed Dzerzhinksy Station, out to the cold grey marbled stone . . .

The train began its ascent. I didn't even have time to run to the window of my father's car, time to wave my hand or shout a word. The last carriage was already flying past me, and on its platform, dangling his feet into the abyss like a freight-train conductor, sat Frol Vlasych Goosev. With a gay and festive curiosity he gaped at the concave walls of the station and the pale blue sources of artificial light. He didn't fall off the platform when the train raised its head carriage and started to climb rapidly, though by all the laws of physics he ought to have crashed right down on me, into my waiting arms. The loneliness and cold were more than I could bear. I woke up . . . Stop! Stop! Stop!

Where's my briefcase? Why didn't I remember this before? Here are two little pages, out of the many that Frol Vlasych wrote in my office. Here they are! Word for word! This is the same thought that was ineffably present in the structure of my last dream . . . Word for word: '*At your hour, more swiftly than the light that speeds after you, you shall return whence you came. But those who have grown to love Earth more than themselves shall remain in the ground of her being!*'

My God! My God!

Take your father down to the sea, Citizen Gurov, and then come back . . . Goodbye, Conceptiev! I almost wanted to remind you of what my father said before you shot him. But I won't, for his sake. I won't. Goodbye . . .

Poxov! I've had a revelation: it has suddenly come to me what to tell Frol Vlasych. First, tell him that not a single word of his is lost. I've given up the idea of burning my briefcase. Make a copy of his 'testimony' and return it. He'll rejoice like a child, I know. Second, tell him that he once saved me from the noose by sharing his own life with me, his executioner. I am returning that life to him. May he receive—I haven't strength to do more—may he receive the life of my enemy, Citizen Vasily Vasilievich Gurov, the life which I have blindly pursued for forty years, and which, up till a minute ago, I had meant to destroy by a cruel fraud and a vengeful bullet, not fired by my own hand. But this, I recognize, would have been an evil still greater than if I had fired the bullet myself. It was hard for me to give up vengeance. Very hard. But now it's easy. Tell him, in a general way. He'll understand what happened to me . . .

I wouldn't have thought I'd go hot with shame. I'm wringing wet, as if I'd come from the steam room . . . I keep remembering all the noble speeches that I had the good fortune of hearing, to my torment and possibly my salvation. Ultimately, I must live up to them not only in my understanding but also in my deeds. And I understand that when I spoke in other men's voices I was afraid, I was stubborn in my blindness, I didn't want to speak out myself, I was evading an act. God has saved me, with the help of Frol Vlasych and my father's memory, from a last unforgivable step into the abyss. I will use it to save myself . . .

Nothing in all my life has been more joyful than this step. I do not fear what awaits me. Never have I had a greater desire to live than at this moment. I want so much to live, Poxov, that my flesh may be on the point of reviving—honestly, I feel like the little boy I was an hour before Conceptiev arrived in my village—but I have wronged life, wronged her in return for my own desperate wrong, and I must not live: I am guilty . . . Guilty. Very guilty. And could I ever have supposed that I'd be shamed to the depths of my soul, before none other than my murderer—Citizen Gurov?

Tell Frol Vlasych everything: such testimony gladdens a wise man, no less than miracles a child. Keep the briefcase. Don't burn it. The only things I'll burn, I think, are the grandson's denunciations, and his notes on the intimate conversations of his grandfather and grandmother. Those are more terrible than cannibalism—let them die with me. Accordingly, erase the tape with that story on it. Oh, but see that Gurov's dear daughter is disavowed at work. Let the people know their secret informers!

Goodbye . . .

You asked me a question just now, Citizen Gurov, that I won't be able to answer. I don't know how you're to go on living, 'in view of the fact that all your frameworks and substructures have palpably vanished from under your feet'. I don't know. How should I? I can't advise you. But have you given no thought to the possibility that after I die my colleagues, on my behalf, will wreak a last treacherous vengeance on you! . . . Like what? What indeed! Call in Electra and the others, open the coffin with your murdered Brutnikova's remains and the golden wrench, trot your daddy out, and then put you up against the wall—shamed beyond imagining, alone, a nothing.

'I am inclined to suppose that, by virtue of the obligation you have assumed, you will not betray your original promise'—you have a problem choosing natural expressions, Vasily Vasilievich. Simply put, you trust me? . . . I see, I see . . .

Pardon my curiosity—you don't have to answer this question—but what prompted you to keep your father in the house? In the beginning I kept trying to find out whether you had a soul, in order to mock it the more cruelly if it existed, but now this . . . I don't know why I want to know this. I've lost the capacity to think things out, devise schemes, explain myself. Well, but what prompted you?

You don't know either . . . You came close to regretting your decision, but you won't betray him . . . Is that so!

What bastards we are, really. What swine! When we land in the shitpile we can always scam out, come up with some dodge to gain revenge or save our skins. But we can't find words or explanation for the simplest, most normal act of natural good will! Perhaps we're too shy, we don't have the nerve to speak? Or perhaps Reason casts down his eyes, like a kid standing before his sad teacher when he's been up to shenanigans and is tortured by guilt, regret, stubbornness, shame, and a passionate desire for atonement—a passion wrongly nourished by his refusal to repent in public. A promise trembles on the bitten lips swollen with weeping: never again will he put drawing pins under the poor teacher's behind, pour ink on her chair, glue the pages of her register together, or naughtily stink up the air, he doesn't hate her, he loves her—but the promise does not escape his lips, and the wise teacher turns away, lest she laugh through her tears, lest she harden the boy's heart by her tears or her laughter, because the kindness in them is beyond his understanding just now . . .

You don't have the words, then. No . . .

Yes? Come in, Poxov! A phone call for me? Very strange. Just the wrong moment! Bastards, they don't even give you a chance to die . . .

That was Pasha Vcherashkin calling. Pasha . . . He wished me a happy sixtieth . . . We gabbed awhile. He rattled along about his children's careers. Hinted that his region was short on 'bacilli'. That was our word for meat and butter, back at the Children's Home. He asked me to send him some good herring. Even at the Regional Committee feed trough, you don't get good herring . . . He rattled along. Not really thinking about anything, I stared vacantly at the candelabra. A ray of light from our sun, yours and mine, was beating through the slit in the *portière*, playing in the crystal leaves. The air in the foyer was motionless, there couldn't have been the slightest breath of wind, but the crystal pendants trembled, blazing up in rainbows and tossing the falling ray back and forth to each other. The sun moved on, the foyer was plunged into twilight, and my soul was seized with horror. But the candelabra, defying the laws of light diffusion, still kept alive the tiny ray, which had forever flown from its native star, until it decayed completely in one of the crystal leaves . . . Or perhaps I was just imagining things . . .

Pasha talked, his words dying in my ear. I followed them with faint attention and responded indifferently to this sudden invasion of my memory by countenances and images from my past life . . . You were probably surprised to hear me laugh?

On the eve of the sixtieth anniversary of the Great October Socialist Revolution, Pasha had been invited to the Gogol Academic Theatre of Opera and Ballet for a *première* of the tragicomic ballet *Dead Souls*. Rubletto by Lobert—sorry, I'm bollixed up—libretto by Hubert Rozhdestvenko.

Pasha didn't want to go to the ballet. For his whole long life as a Party boss, he's been expiring of boredom in his personal box. So this time he balked. He reported sick. 'I'll read Gogol himself instead,' he said. 'The samizdat boys should follow his example: burn their own illiterature defaming the state and its procedures.'

No, that wasn't a slip of the tongue, Vasily Vasilievich. Pasha knows all about the Soviet regime, just as you and I do, but he's not going to let anyone undermine it, as long as he's around . . . You can see this as cynicism if you want, or a lack of integrity, or the hoodlumism of an overbearing bureaucrat, call it whatever you want. At sixty he doesn't give a damn about anything any more, except peace of mind, his children's careers, a serene old age, and his sporting passions. Despite his hatred of the Devil's work, Pasha follows Soviet expansionism the way some people follow soccer.

When the Hungarians and Czechs had their little to-dos, Pasha didn't sleep. He stayed glued to the radio and kept phoning the Central Committee to hurry up and throw in the paratroops, send tanks against the bandits, otherwise he couldn't guarantee calm at his metallurgy complex, mines, factories, and farms. Pasha got a heart attack, he supported 'our team' so passionately and stressfully. The rupture with China reduced the boss of the region to eczema. He was covered with yellow-crusted red spots and scabs. It took acupuncture—also Chinese—to cure him. Indonesia gave him insomnia and auditory hallucinations. The Israeli victory in the Six-Day War stopped him up something awful. Enemas and irrigation didn't help. Stomach cancer, they thought, with metastases from the intestines to the anus.

When Allende came to power in Chile, Pasha arranged for a youth demonstration in front of the memorial to the unknown soldier. Fireworks, too. And he ordered liverwurst and butter to be released for sale at the downtown delicatessen. But then, after the putsch by the junta, he was hit by a slight stroke, with partial loss of speech.

I found it hard to recognize this powerful man in the tottering patient on a ward at the Kremlin infirmary, to which he had been delivered by supersonic fighter. He wept, tore his hair, incautiously reproached Castro for dragging his feet, and generally acted like a deadbeat who has laid his last ten on a beloved, incompetent Army team that lets an absurd goal get by them in the last second of the finals.

I asked, rather harshly, if he'd finally gone bananas working for the Party.

'It's stronger than I am, this passion,' he said. 'I can't help myself, Hand. I'd be glad to undergo treatment, but with whom? And what would I say? That I want to root for Pinochet, even though I think his methods in the struggle against Communism discredit anti-Communism? They'd drag me straight to the psych hospital, the way they did to a certain General! It's an obscene passion, Hand. Really obscene, this game.'

Poor Pasha. He hasn't escaped unpunished for his forty years of totally schizophrenic Party work, destroying the Devil's idea with his left hand and strengthening it with his right. I told him goodbye. He'll be very surprised tomorrow when he receives the telegram about my death. 'I never expected it,' he'll say. 'Never expected it.' He'll shed a few tears. To be perfectly frank, I didn't hurry him off the phone . . .

Don't try, Vasily Vasilievich, don't try! You won't persuade me to give up on my 'untimely departure from the continuation of my life'. I'm forsaking mature socialist society. You have been reunited with your father. Now I want to be reunited with mine, though I don't know whether I'll be allowed . . . Chances are I won't be. But I'm ready to accept, after I die, the torment of this separation. I earned it—I interrogated so many, put so many to death . . .

And now you will do what you didn't succeed in doing, almost half a century ago. A martyr's death would have borne more fruit for me than the executioner's life that I have lived . . . I'm throwing my Party card into the fireplace. Forty years it's been slimy cold against my chest . . .

The card is gone. Its black ashes have been carried away up the chimney. Now they'll fall in the garden, on the white, pink, and black flowers, on the daisies, marigolds, gladioli, morning glories, and dahlias . . . I guess that's . . . everything.

Take the pistol. It's already loaded. All you have to do is squeeze the trigger here with your index finger, when I say 'Fire!' or 'Shoot!' or something like that . . . I can't seem to pick an expression . . . Get a grip on yourself! Doddering idiot! I said, get a grip on yourself! Or I'll do it *for* you! What's the matter, never kill a guy before?

Draw a mental line from the muzzle to my heart . . . Courage! . . . Too bad no one ever got to the suckling pig . . .

I do not apologize, by the way, for my outbursts of anger, rudeness, and bitterness, for reviling and manhandling you . . . Those are small things, I'm sure . . . Trifles . . .

Damn it, don't shake! You miss, and I'll clobber you on the conk for old times' sake, I won't be able to stop myself! . . . Extend your arm. Brace your elbow on the table.

My heart is aching so, yearning so . . . if I were a kid of twenty, I'd say my heart was bursting to go somewhere, out of my chest . . . It's true, my heart is bursting . . .

Receive me, Father . . . Understand the darkness of the wanderings of my reason, and the fury of my ruinous passion . . . Understand, Father, and receive my poor, sinless soul . . . It bears no blame for my deeds, for my falsehood, dissembling, and executions. None!

As the unhappy Count in my childhood book is innocent of my embracing the temptation to vengeance, so my murdered soul is innocent, one more human soul, receive it, Father, if it still breathes in this body now ready for death, receive it!

Shoot, Gurov! . . . Fire! . . . Wait! Wait! I forgot . . . I forgot . . . Wait! I forgot to burn the lined notebook! I can't allow people to find out . . . wait . . . what the grandfather said . . . let me burn it . . . in an intimate moment . . . to the

grand . . .

mo . . .

ther . . .

Koktebel—Pitsunda—Vilnius—Moscow—Middletown.
1977–1980.

TRANSLATOR'S NOTE

I am grateful to Professor Edward Keenan of Harvard University for granting me access to the manuscript of the late Kirill Kostsynsky's *Slovar' russkoj nenormativnoj leksiki* (*Dictionary of Nonstandard Russian*). For consultations on a variety of idiomatic expressions, I sincerely thank my friends Rima Zolina and Boris Hoffman.

Throughout the preparation of this translation, I have deeply appreciated the kind assistance of the author and his wife, Yuz and Irina Aleshkovsky.

S. B.